KASEY MICHAELS

how to
Tempt a
Duke

HQN™

Recycling programs
for this product may
not exist in your area.

ISBN-13: 978-0-373-77371-8

HOW TO TEMPT A DUKE

www.HQNBooks.com

Printed in U.S.A.

Dear Reader,

Rafael Daughtry went off to war a poor, barely tolerated relation, and returned six years later as the Duke of Ashurst. He was no more prepared to take up the reins of a great estate than he was to reunite with his childhood friend and neighbor, the young beauty he'd once called Charlie as she tagged after him and his cousins.

Rafe had to learn how to be a duke, and Charlie helped him there. She offered her assistance with his two sisters—twins not yet ready for a Season, but definitely grown beyond the nursery and schoolroom.

What she didn't do was trust him with her secret sorrow—whatever had happened in his absence that caused her to keep him at arm's length and flinch at his touch.

Rafe and Charlie raise the questions: are we who we were born, or who life made us? Is the past also our destiny, or can the power of love overcome even the most difficult obstacles?

As an author, I create characters like Rafe and Charlie, give them problems to overcome and then toss them together and let them "have at it," all the time rooting for that happy ending I want so much for them. I think you'll root for them, too. Stay tuned for the further adventures of the Daughtry family in *How to Tame a Lady,* Nicole's story, on sale in October 2009. And don't forget to visit my Web site at www.kaseymichaels.com for more information about all my books!

All the best,

Kasey Michaels

To my new editor, the one and only
Margo Lipschultz,
a woman with the patience of a saint!

how to Tempt a Duke

PROLOGUE

PARIS HAD BEGUN to lose its much-touted appeal. How many years had they all spoken about the day they would vanquish Bonaparte and march, triumphant, into this city of cities? When the mud of Spain sucked off their boots and the provisions didn't arrive, when they were sure their empty bellies were stuck to their backbones—talk of the glories of Paris would lighten their spirits.

But after five straight days of cold, drenching rain, thoughts had turned to how soon Wellington would order the troops back home to England.

It would be raining there, too, but at least it would be good English rain.

Not that Captains Rafael Daughtry and Swain Fitzgerald would be among the troops piling onto ships and heading for Dover and other English ports. They'd learned just this afternoon that they were among those assigned to escort Bonaparte to his new empire on Elba in a few weeks.

Fitz had told Rafe they should be pleased, that they would be taking part in something historic, a quite singular adventure with which to one day regale their grandchildren while they bounced them on their knees.

Grandchildren? That's when Rafe had narrowed his intense brown eyes and demanded his friend find them a place where they could both, with any luck, soon render themselves grandly drunk.

Rafe shivered now in his damp uniform and shifted his chair closer to the mediocre fire burning in the hearth of the tavern Fitz had chosen for them. He ran a hand through his overlong, self-barbered black hair, feeling the grease and grit that he had begun to doubt he'd ever be able to wash out of it, and then rubbed at the stubble on his chin. He'd have to locate a new razor in order to shave before presenting himself at Headquarters the next morning, and a clean shirt, as well. Just a *dry* shirt would do.

"Well now, would you look at that," Fitz said with a grin. "Huddling by the fire like some old maid who's never known a warmed bed. Would you be wanting a blanket for around your shoulders, Mistress Daughtry?"

"Stubble it, Fitz," Rafe grumbled, suppressing another shiver. Sometimes he wondered if he'd ever be warm again. "Where's this fine ale you told me about?"

"So many complaints from a man more used to sleeping in ditches these past years. And the devil with the ale—where's the willing mam'zelles?" Fitz pushed himself out of his chair and grabbed on to the innkeeper as he passed by their table. "*Parle vous* the English, *mon-sewer?*"

The fat and rather greasy innkeeper rolled his eyes as he rattled off a quick string of French that had Rafe laughing into his fist, especially the part where the man compared Fitz to a hairy, overgrown cockroach.

"Two mugs of your finest brew, Innkeeper, if you

please, and whatever hot food you've got in the kitchens," Rafe interjected quickly in flawless French as he tossed the fellow a coin, and the man bowed his way back to the bar.

"Damned frogs. They don't seem to know we've beaten them, do they, Rafe?"

"Oh, they know, and they hate us for it. The only thing saving us right now, I'd say, is the fact that most Parisians blame Bonaparte for getting them into this fix in the first place. I heard we had to put more guards around his quarters again today to protect him from his own once-loyal subjects. A part of me thinks we ought to stand down, and simply let them have at him. A personal escort of one thousand of his own men, armed, and in uniform? Dubbing him bloody Emperor of Elba? This is what we fought for, Fitz?"

"Does seem like we're coddling the little fellow, I agree. How long are you and I supposed to be guarding him, anyway? Not that I'm in any great rush to head back to Dublin. Wet and cold it may be right now, but Paris has Dublin beat all hollow for willing females."

"That's only because all the females in Dublin already know you and make sure to stay away."

"True enough," Fitz said, scratching at his neatly trimmed beard, his green eyes sparkling. "I have cut myself a bit of a swath through the local ladies, handsome devil that I am. Now answer my question, if you please."

Rafe drank deep from his mug as the barmaid plunked down two bowls of steaming stew and then winked at him before walking away, her pretty, rounded rump issuing a provocative invitation he felt oddly disinclined to accept. Still, if he paid her well enough, she might launder his shirt for him while he took a nap.

"How long? Six months or more, according to our orders," he said as he lifted a stained wooden spoon and prodded at the thick stew, knowing he should just close his eyes as he ate, and not ask himself if he could identify the meat. "I hope I can find an opportunity to talk to the man."

Fitz looked at him, eyebrows raised. "Talk to Boney? Why would you be wanting to do any such thing?"

Rafe crossed his arms and tried to *hug* some warmth into his bones before tackling the stew. "I don't know why I'm telling you, since you'll do nothing but make jokes at my expense, but I've been toying with the idea of penning a book about the war. You do realize, don't you, Fitz, that for all our years with Wellington, we never once encountered Bonaparte himself across the battlefield."

"And we never want to, to my mind. So you're setting yourself up as another Byron, is it?"

"Hardly. That would mean casting myself in the role of hero. Just a simple history, Fitz, one that nobody will read, not even those grandchildren you're trying to foist onto me. At any rate, we'll be back in England by Christmas, if you're still of a mind to accept my invitation to visit for a few months."

"I am. I've heard enough about your home to think I already know it, but I still want to meet this grand family you say you have, not that I've seen a letter from any of them in all the years I've known you. Or you penning more than the occasional note to any of them, come to think of it. And what then for you, Rafe?" Fitz asked as they ate. "Will your uncle the duke let you take back the reins on your imaginary estate?"

Rafe put down his spoon, his only mediocre appetite now completely gone. "I've never held the reins, Fitz, and you know it. Mother's succession of husbands did that, each one a worse steward than the last. At least they listened to my mother and refused all of His Grace's offers to put one of his own men in charge."

"Why would they do that?"

"Because my uncle would have offered his hand, and then taken back twice as much with both hands. That, and my mother loathes the duke."

"But the estate is yours, correct? You left England a lad, but you return having gained your majority."

"In a perfect world that might be so," Rafe said, rubbing at his eyelids, which seemed to wish to close even as he struggled to keep them open. "But, thanks to Willowbrook not being part of any entail, everything is under the control of my mother until I reach the age of thirty." He reached for his mug of ale once more. "And my mother? Does she play the good steward of her son's eventual inheritance? No, she does not. She marries, Fitz. It's what she does."

"Maybe she'd like to marry a nice young Irishman, then," Fitz teased, giving Rafe a jab in the side. "I'd let you run the place to your heart's content, *sonny,* while your mother and I— What would we do, Rafe?"

"I wouldn't even want to contemplate such a question. Besides, she was barely out of her widow's weeds when I left, so there may be yet another new stepfather installed at Willowbrook for all I know, and my sisters tossed back to the duke for safekeeping while dear Lady Helen plays at blushing bride."

"Oh, come on now, it wasn't all so bad, as I recall you telling me you spent most of your years with the duke and his sons yourself, until he bought you your commission. There could be worse fates than a generous uncle."

"That's what Charlie used to tell me. Drove me halfway round the bend, that little monster did, but she, like you, did have a point."

Fitz looked into his mug. "No, I can't be drunk yet, there's still too much ale in here. Charlie? And then you said *she?*"

Rafe smiled at the memory of a girl several years his junior: tall, thin, all long legs and elbows, trailing after him as if he were some knight in shining armor. "Sorry. I should have said Charlotte. Charlotte Seavers. Her father's estate cuts into my uncle's, also, like a wedge of pie. Rose Cottage and the land that's still a part of it are probably more of a thorn in His Grace's side than Willowbrook."

"Roses, thorns, that makes sense."

For some unknown reason, a memory he didn't know he still possessed rose in Rafe's head. He was in the apple orchard, hiding from his lessons with his cousins, and Charlie had called down to him from her perch in the branches of one of the trees. He didn't know how she did it, but she'd always seemed to know where he would be, and made sure that she was there, as well.

Sometimes he was flattered by the young girl's attention, and sometimes he was annoyed. That day he was annoyed, and to show his annoyance he'd picked

up an apple that had fallen to the ground and halfheart-
edly tossed it in her direction.

It had been a stupid thing to do. He might have hit
her with the apple. He might have startled her so that
she fell from her perch and was injured.

Instead, the little monster had deftly snagged the
apple out of the air with one hand, and then winged it
back in his direction.

He'd had that black eye for three weeks.

"Rafe? You're woolgathering again. I think I said
something about there being worse fates than a generous
uncle."

Rafe shook off the memory of his childhood, a move
that, oddly, made his head ache even more. "True. But
the boy I was at nineteen is not the man I hope I am now,
at six and twenty. Grateful as I am, I'm past the point
of accepting any more of the man's cold charity, Fitz. I
can't do anything to help my sisters. I'm thankful for
what my uncle has done for them as well as for me, but
it's time I made my own way in the world."

"Meaning?" his friend asked around a mouthful of
stew.

"Meaning, Fitz, that my sisters will be well enough
off with my uncle, so I've decided to remain in the
army. When you get straight down to it, fighting is the
only thing I know."

"This may come as a shock to you, my friend," Fitz
said conspiratorially, taking hold of Rafe's forearm,
"but I very much think we've run out of enemies to
fight."

Rafe smiled, as he was sure he was meant to do, and
when the barmaid returned with two more mugs of ale,

he pulled her down onto his lap and whispered into her ear. She giggled, nodded and instantly began nibbling at the side of his neck while Fitz muttered under his breath that it was always Rafe who had all the luck.

Fitz would think that, and probably with good reason. Rafe knew he'd been fortunate in his uncle in some ways. But he'd be damned if he'd live on the man's sufferance ever again. Perhaps, when a man didn't have much to call his own, his pride became all-important.

He also had his sisters to consider, and their futures. The twins had been no more than giggling, pestering children when he'd left for the Peninsula, years younger than Charlie. But they must be all of sixteen by now, and if Rafe knew his mother—and he did—Lady Helen hadn't given a thought to their futures.

He didn't know how he'd approach his uncle about Nicole and Lydia, but he hoped that between himself and his aunt Emmaline, the duke could be convinced to add to the small dowries arranged for both of them by their father, and give them a Season in London.

As for what he was to do about his shallow, lovable, spendthrift and woefully flighty mother? Now there was a question fashioned to keep Rafe up nights.

But no matter what, he was done accepting favors for himself from his uncle. He'd spent too many years listening to his bullying cousin George, Earl Storrington, referring to his family as *the beggars come to call* each time they'd been deposited on the duke's doorstep, bag and baggage. He'd swallow hard and accept help for his sisters, but not another bent penny for himself. He'd made that vow long ago.

Perhaps playing nursemaid to Bonaparte for these next six or nine months would give him time to formulate a plan for the rest of his life. For so many years, he hadn't considered much beyond the next day, the next battle, the next search for food and dry lodgings for his men. By silent agreement, neither he nor Fitz had dared to speak of a future beyond that next day, that next battle, or else they might jinx themselves.

Now that the war was won, however, and he had surprisingly found himself still in one piece, he could no longer avoid thinking about that future.

His rambling thoughts made his head hurt. Something was making his head hurt like the very devil… making all of him hurt.

"Here now, friend," Fitz said grumpily. "This poor girl is working herself to the bone, trying to get a bit of a rise out of you, if you take my meaning, and you're just sitting there like some lump, arms hanging at your sides, staring into the fire. Pass her to me, why don't you. I know what to do with a willing female."

Rafe snapped himself out of his maudlin musings to realize that the barmaid was now looking at him in some disgust. "Many apologies, *ma chérie*," he told her in French as he eased her off his lap. "You are very lovely, but I am very weary." He hooked a thumb in Fitz's direction. "And that hairy one over there has many coins."

The barmaid's fickle affections switched immediately as she smiled at Fitz and climbed onto his lap. "Ah, that's more the thing. That's it, sweetheart, wiggle that plump bottom about on me some more. The blazes with their pretty statues and showy gardens—*this* is all the

Paris I want to see," he said as the buxom young woman shoved her ample assets close to his face. "Sorry, my friend, but you know how it is. The better man, and all of that."

"That you are, Fitz," Rafe said quietly. "But before you go upstairs, you might want to slip me your purse for safekeeping. Damn," he said then, blinking rapidly as he shook his head. "What's in that ale, anyway? The room seems to be spinning."

"You haven't drunk enough for rooms to spin," Fitz said, looking at his friend. "You know, Rafe, you don't look too good. Here, let me play at nursemaid and feel your forehead." With one arm securing the provocatively jiggling barmaid in position, he leaned toward Rafe and did so, and then pulled back his hand, dramatically shaking it. "Blast it, man, you're burning up, do you know that?"

"I can't be, Fitz. I'm bloody freezing. It's this wet uniform, that's what it is." Rafe clenched his jaw, for his teeth had begun to chatter as he shivered again, missing the warmth of the barmaid's lush body if not the barmaid herself.

"I don't think so. I think it's that fever you picked up at Albuera, isn't it? It's back again, damn me if it isn't. Come on, let's make our way back to our quarters before you go passing out on me and I have to carry you the way I did in Vitoria."

Rafe waved off Fitz's offer. "Go have your fun. If it's the fever again I'm already as sick as I'm going to get. Take her upstairs and ruin her for all other, lesser men with your Irish expertise. I'll...I'll just wait for you here by the fire." He laid his head on his bent arms. "Too tired to go back out in that rain and damp anyway."

"Your Grace? Excuse me, sir, for disturbing you, but if I might have a word? Your Grace?"

"Rafe," Fitz whispered in a suddenly strained voice, nudging him in the ribs. "There's a funny-looking little man standing on the other side of the table, and he's talking to you. I mean, I think he's talking to you, because he most certainly couldn't be talking to me. He said *Your Grace.* Better sit up, friend. Something's strange here."

Rafe forced his eyes open and squinted at the bemused expression on Fitz's face as his friend continued to look across the table. "Bloody hell," he said, pushing himself erect to see a rather rumpled little Englishman standing there, just as Fitz had said. Except there were several of him…perhaps a half-dozen rumpled little Englishmen weaving and waving in front of him. He tried to single out one from the herd. "Sorry? May we help you?"

"You are Rafael Daughtry, are you not?" the man said. "Please say you are, Your Grace, as I've been hunting you now for nearly a month, ever since the cessation of hostilities allowed safe travel across the Channel. Perhaps none of your hopeful aunt's letters reached you?"

"You hear that, Rafe? *Your Grace.* He said it again," Fitz pointed out, pushing the barmaid from his lap, at which time the woman launched into a torrent of gutter French that would have made even Rafe blush, if he'd been listening to her.

"Indeed, I did say just that," the man said, sighing. "If I might be allowed to sit, sir?"

Rafe and Fitz exchanged puzzled glances. "Yes, of course." Rafe indicated the empty chair in front of the man. He fought to keep his eyes open. "But I'm afraid I don't—"

"No, I can see clearly that you do not. My name is Phineas Coates, Your Grace, and it is my sad duty to inform you that your uncle, Charlton Daughtry, the thirteenth Duke of Ashurst, as well as his sons, the Earl of Storrington and the honorable Lord Harold Daughtry, all perished tragically when their yacht sank off the coast of Shoreham-By-Sea approximately six weeks ago. By the rules of inheritance, you, sir, as your father's son and the last remaining Daughtry, are now Rafael Daughtry, fourteenth Duke of Ashurst, as well as holding the lesser titles of Earl of Storrington and…and the Viscount of Something Else that sadly escapes me at the moment. Sir? I say, sir. Did you hear me?"

Rafe had slowly lowered his head onto his crossed arms once more, hearing the man's voice only through the ringing in his ears. Funny, he thought, grinning. Last time the fever came back to torment him, he'd thought he'd seen angels. Never odd little men in ill-fitting hacking jackets and filthy red waistcoats. He liked the angels better….

"Rafe, answer the man," Fitz said, shaking him. "Did you hear what he said?"

"Yes, yes. Go 'way. Something in the sea…"

"Shoreham-by-Sea, Your Grace, yes. The late duke's sister, the Lady Emmaline Daughtry, commissioned me to also deliver personally to you her letter requesting your return to Ashurst at your earliest convenience. My condolences, er, and my felicitations, Your Grace. Your Grace?"

Fitz pushed lank strands of damp hair away from Rafe's face. "I don't think His Grace heard you, Phineas. But why don't you tell me more about this dukedom thing, all right? There happen to be any money to go along with all those fancy titles?"

"I'd say the man has fallen into about the deepest gravy boat in all of England—er, that is, His Grace is quite the wealthy man."

Fitz slapped Rafe on the back. "Did you hear that, Rafe? You're a rich man, you lucky devil! Wake up and we'll toast your good fortune. On your coin, of course, since you now have so many of them."

Rafe didn't move, even when Fitz took hold of his shoulder and shook him.

"Ah, now would you look at that, Phineas? Poor bastard. All his problems solved, his worries blown to the four winds, and he doesn't even know it. His Grace is going to be asleep for a while. But he'll be fine by morning, he always is."

Phineas nodded knowingly. "Ah. Drunk, sir."

"No, unfortunately for him." Fitz winked. "But I'd like to be."

"Yes, sir, Captain, I quite understand," Phineas said, hungrily eyeing Rafe's nearly full bowl. "In that case, as I was told not to leave His Grace's side for any reason once I found him, would it be an imposition if I were to join you for dinner, Captain? I must say, that stew smells delicious."

Friendship is Love without his wings.
                                        —*Lord Byron*

CHAPTER ONE

CHARLOTTE SEAVERS was on the hunt. And she was in a mood to take no prisoners.

Only scant minutes earlier Charlotte had been comfortably ensconced in the drawing room of her parents' small manor house, happy in her ignorance, enjoying the sight of a mid-November frost glittering on the newly bare tree branches outside her window while she stayed warm and toasty inside.

But then the housekeeper had brought her one of the letters just arrived with the morning post.

After taking another sip of sweet tea, Charlotte had opened the missive from her good friend, read it in growing apprehension and disbelief until, with her newfound knowledge, her blissful ignorance turned to righteous anger.

"Unrepentant liars and tricksters! Wretched connivers!" she exclaimed, her teeth chattering in the cold, for she'd left the house without taking time to search out a warmer cloak than the rather shabby one she used while gardening that hung on the hook just outside the kitchens. "They'll be lucky if I don't choose to murder them!"

She stomped along the well-worn path that led

through the trees from the manor house, to end halfway up the drive to Ashurst Hall. "And worse fool me because I believed them!"

What Miss Charlotte Seavers was referring to was her discovery, after months of the aforementioned ignorant bliss, that Nicole and Lydia Daughtry—in retrospect, mostly Nicky, with Lydia only following along because she felt she had no choice—had been pulling the wool over her eyes. Over everyone's eyes.

All this time, since the spring, when they'd first had word from Rafael Daughtry that he was well and aware of the deaths of his uncle and cousins, Nicole and Lydia had been cleverly putting one over on Rafe, on their aunt Emmaline, on Charlotte.

Oh yes, and Mrs. Beasley. But then again, pulling the wool over Mrs. Beasley's eyes was no great accomplishment, and the twins had the benefit of years of practice when it came to hoodwinking their governess.

In her haste to confront the Daughtry sisters and verbally rip several strips off their hides, Charlotte stomped on some wet, slippery leaves littering the path, and went down with a startled *"Damn and blast!"*

She just as quickly scrambled back to her feet, hurriedly looking about to be certain no one had heard her unladylike exclamation, and then brushed at the back of her cloak, pulling off damp leaves and bits of moss.

She took several deep breaths, hoping to calm herself, steady herself. After all, she was supposed to be a well-bred, civilized female, and here she was, racing through the trees like some wild boar.

But then she thought again of how Nicky and Lydia had spent the summer and fall posting letters back and forth, impersonating their brother to their aunt, and impersonating their aunt to their brother. Correspondence Charlotte had seen, had been allowed to read—all while the twins were doubtless laughing behind their hands at her gullibility.

Worse, if Emmaline hadn't just now written to her privately, her words and her questions contradicting things she had already said in the letters Charlotte had been shown by the twins, she would still be none the wiser.

From the moment she'd begun reading the letter, Charlotte's suspicions had been raised, as the handwriting was so very different from Emmaline's letters supposedly posted to Ashurst Hall.

But those suspicions had turned to a cold certainty when she read the words, "Charlotte, I vow I sometimes think Rafe is Nicky in long pants. The girl never could get her mind around spelling any word longer than c-a-t."

And here Charlotte had thought Rafe, for all his on-again, off-again schooling alongside his cousins, was next door to a yahoo when it came to grammar and spelling.

"They'll pay for this," she promised out loud, wiping her hand across her cheek to push an errant chestnut-brown curl back beneath her hood and depositing a smudge of dirt on her otherwise flawless skin.

Poor Emmaline, happy in her newly wedded bliss as she continued her long honeymoon in the Lake District, comforted with the knowledge that Rafe had sailed for home immediately upon receiving the news of his change of fortune.

And poor Rafe, going about his duties on Elba, assured that Lady Emmaline had everything at Ashurst Hall firmly in hand until his mission was completed, including the care of his young sisters.

"And me, duped by two miscreant monsters not yet out of the schoolroom—except that they most certainly did escape the schoolroom with their little trick," Charlotte muttered, lifting up the hem of her gown even as she stepped up her pace along the path. "Commiserating with the girls about how much they missed their brother...joking with them about how Emmaline seemed to have thrown all sensibility to the four winds thanks to her newfound love. Running tame through the house all these months, leaving the nursery and their governess behind, because their brother wrote that he would be delighted—no! de-*litted*—to allow them more freedom. Their *brother* wrote? Ha! I'll have their heads on a *platter,* I swear I will!"

Her mind on contemplated acts of mayhem, she broke free of the trees, stepping onto the gravel drive that twisted and turned on its way through the well-landscaped park.

The horse and rider appeared out of nowhere, heading for her at a vigorous canter.

Charlotte slid to a halt on the stones even as she threw up her hands and gave a quick, faintly terrified cry.

The horse, either in response to her unexpected appearance, or in reaction to his rider's immediate sharp tug on the reins, gave a rather frightened cry of its own. It then reared onto its hind legs, pawing at the air as if attempting to climb an invisible ladder.

The hapless rider was immediately deposited on his back on the hard-packed gravel.

No fainthearted miss, Charlotte had already collected herself. She bravely grabbed at the horse's now-dangling reins to keep it from bolting off down the lane, which, she readily saw, it appeared to have no intention of doing. She then walked toward the man she had unhorsed, hoping he'd get to his feet without assistance, which he would most probably do if he hadn't cracked his skull, or worse.

"Are you all right, sir?" she asked rather cautiously, keeping her distance even as she leaned over the man, whose many-caped brown traveling cloak was twisted up and around his head. "I'm most terribly sorry. I am *entirely* at fault for your misfortune, I know, but I believe it would be extremely considerate and gentlemanly of you to pretend that you hadn't noticed."

The man mumbled something Charlotte couldn't quite make out, which was understandable, what with him still all but strangled by his extremely fashionable cloak. She was, however, fairly certain that his response to her hadn't been quite as forgiving as she might have hoped.

"Excuse me? Perhaps if you were to loose the fastenings of your cloak you'd be able to free yourself from its grasp?" She rolled her eyes, knowing that she was most probably only making things worse. "Shall I...shall I fetch help?"

"God's teeth, no," the man said, struggling to sit up while fighting his way out of the cloak. "I feel bloody well embarrassed enough, thank you. I've no need of an audience." At last his head emerged from the tangle of cloth, his healthy crop of nearly black hair falling over his eyes. "Where's my bloody hat?"

"I've got it," Charlotte said, holding it out to him. "It's barely dented, and I'm confident that it will clean up quite nicely once the mud is dry and can be brushed off."

He still hadn't looked at her, instead busying himself attempting to rearrange his many-caped collars so that they lay flat over his shoulders once more. She counted four capes, graduated in size—very impressive. More would have classified him as a dandy, and less wouldn't be half so fashionable. Upside-down and over a man's head, however, all that fine London fashion was probably little more than a nuisance.

"Next, madam, I suppose you'll say I should be delighted with that piece of information. How fortunate I am. My cloak is only torn—ah, in two places—and my new hat is *barely dented*. Lucky, lucky me. Perhaps you believe I should be thanking you."

"There's no need for rudeness, sir," Charlotte told him, knowing that there was probably every need. She'd unhorsed the man, for goodness' sakes, ruining his fine clothes, which were apparently very dear to him. She probably also shouldn't point out that if he hadn't sawed so on the reins, his mount, which seemed a placid sort, may not have reared at all. No, she probably shouldn't mention that, either. "I didn't mean to unhorse you, you know. It was an accident."

"An accident, of course. I believe the fool who touched off the Great London Fire attempted the same sorry excuse. You ran into the roadway, madam. Next you'll probably say it was all my fault for having been on the drive in the first place."

"Don't be ridiculous," Charlotte said tartly, beginning to lose patience with the man. "You had every right to be here." Then she frowned. "And why are you here?"

The hat was all but ripped from her hand as the man finally got to his feet. But when he slammed the thing back on his head he uttered a quick curse and quickly removed it once more; it dropped, unnoticed, onto the drive.

She went up on her tiptoes. Goodness, he was a large man. Quite imposing. "What is it? What's wrong? Is it your head? I don't see anything." But, then, how could she? He was very tall. Charlotte was rather impressed; she'd known few men who stood a full head and shoulders above her not inconsiderable height. He actually made her feel small.

"Damn," he said, touching the back of his head and then bringing his hand forward once more, looking at the blood on his fingers. "Six years of war all but unscathed, and I take a head wound not a mile from home. Inflicted by a woman, no less."

Home. He'd said that. She'd heard him. He'd said *home.* Charlotte's eyes went so wide she was amazed they didn't pop straight out of her head.

While he fished in his pocket for a handkerchief to press against his wound, Charlotte eyed Rafael Daughtry, whom she'd last seen in the flesh the day he rode off to war, and only in her foolish, maidenly dreams in the intervening years.

He didn't look at all as she remembered him.

This man seemed to be twice the Rafe she remembered, or perhaps that was only because he weighed a good three stone more than the gangly youth whose wide, unaffected smile had always had the ability to make her knees buckle. The hair? Yes, that was the same coal-dark hair she remembered, if longer than she remembered.

But his features seemed sharper, more mature, and his skin was tanned from the sun in the way that the farm laborers were tanned…years and years of exposure to the elements that toughened the skin, made for small crinkles around the edges of his eyes.

She looked at him again, examining him.

These weren't Rafe's eyes. They were the same color, a warm, rich brown, almost sherry. But they were hard eyes, centuries-old eyes, not the laughing eyes of the boy she'd known. These eyes had seen things she could never imagine.

Charlotte suppressed a small shiver, one born of vague nervousness coupled with a definite curiosity. Why had she never realized that he would be changed by war, changed by his six long years away from Ashurst Hall?

"Rafe?"

He still held the handkerchief pressed to the back of his head. "Pardon me?" he asked, looking at her. *Finally* looking at her. Was that interest in his eyes? "I'm afraid you have the advantage of me, madam."

"If I do, Your Grace, it would be the first time," Charlotte said, dropping into a fairly mocking curtsy. But she couldn't seem to curb her tongue. "Perhaps I should have thought to unhorse you six years ago. Perhaps on the day you and George and Harold saw nothing out of the ordinary in speaking freely around me about the charms of the new barmaid in the village, just as if I wasn't there at all."

"Again, madam, I don't believe I—" Rafe blinked and leaned closer, looking intensely into her face. "*Charlie?* By God, it is you. And still wreaking havoc all over Ashurst Hall, I see. I should have realized at once. Maybe you should have thrown another apple at my head. I would have remembered then. You always were a bit of a menace."

Charlotte fought down the urge to go up on tiptoe again and box the man's ears. "While you, Your Grace, always were a bit of an insensitive *beast*. And it's Charlotte. Not Charlie. I *detest* Charlie."

"Really?" His quick, unaffected smile caused her stomach to perform a small flip. It was still the smile Charlotte remembered, if not the Rafe she remembered. "I rather like it. *Charlie*. Why would anyone with the least sense wish to be called Charlotte?"

She silently acknowledged that he had a point. She hated her name, passed down to her from a great-aunt who'd been so kind as to establish a small dowry in exchange for the infant carrying on her name. Still…

"Everyone calls me Charlotte," she informed Rafe tersely. "But *you* may address me as Miss Seavers."

"The devil I will," he told her, checking the state of his handkerchief and then, seeming satisfied with what he saw, returning the thing to his pocket. He looked at her again. "You grew up pretty enough, didn't you? But then, you probably frightened all the men away. I know you frightened me. You must be all of what, two and twenty?"

"Not quite, Your Grace."

"Then close enough," Rafe said, taking the reins

from her and turning once more toward Ashurst Hall, leaving her to either pick up his hat and follow him or just stand here in the drive looking like the sorriest looby in Creation. "I imagine you'll be putting on your caps any day now, preparing to lead apes in Hell."

Charlotte looked down at his fine, fancy hat and then raised her skirts slightly to employ one half boot to send the thing sailing off into the bushes. "Indeed no, Your Grace," she said sweetly, catching up to him. "I've simply been waiting for you to return so that we could marry, for I have always loved you from afar. I would think that should be obvious."

Ah! Now she had his complete attention. And all she'd had to do was tell the truth, shameful though it was. After all, it was the one thing she was confident Rafe would never believe.

"Zounds, I'm sliced to the bone with that cutting retort. You always were a funny little thing, weren't you?" he said, smiling down at her. "But you've made your point, Charlie, and I apologize. It's none of my business whether you are married or not. So, now that we've settled things between us, and I'm fairly well assured my wound isn't fatal, why don't you tell me why you were in such a hurry?"

Charlotte opened her mouth to answer him and then just as quickly shut it. The man had worries enough without learning that his sisters had made a May game out of them all for the past many months. "I…I was hurrying to get inside. I hadn't realized how cold it is until after I'd left the house."

He seemed to accept her answer.

"Do they know I'm coming?" he asked as they navigated a turn in the drive and Ashurst Hall was at last visible in the distance. "I wrote Emmaline from London, but I may have beaten the post."

"Yes…about that," Charlotte said, twisting her gloved hands together in front of her. "Emmaline isn't here at the moment." She looked at Rafe, wondering how much he actually did know. "She and her husband have gone to tour the Lake District as part of their honeymoon."

Rafe nodded. "The Duke of Warrington, yes. I inquired about him in London. A good man, from all accounts. But then who is in charge of the twins?"

That's a very good question, Charlotte whispered inside her head. "Why, I am, of course."

"*You* are? But you're barely more than a girl yourself."

"A few moments ago you had me donning spinster caps and leading apes in Hell," she reminded him, mentally adding to her list of Reasons To Murder The Twins—an already lengthy list. Now they'd made a liar out of her.

"Then you're staying at Ashurst Hall, and not simply on your way there for a visit? You were merely out for a walk."

"All right…" Charlotte agreed slowly, wondering how deep a hole she could dig for herself in protecting Nicole and Lydia before the sides toppled down on her head. "That is, I mean, yes. Out for a walk. Visiting my parents. Mama…Mama has taken a putrid cold, you understand."

"Probably acquired after walking outside in the cold wearing an inadequate cloak," Rafe said, grinning at her. "There may be a lesson there for you, Charlie."

She ignored his teasing. "But I'm not the twins' only guardian," she said, improvising rapidly. "Their governess, Mrs. Beasley, is of course in residence, as well as a household staff numbering more than forty. Nicole and Lydia have hardly been left to their own devices." *Devices, machinations, mischiefs—oh, they would pay for this, the both of them!*

"And my mother?" Rafe asked, obviously believing her. After all, why would she lie to him? Emmaline was right; men truly were gullible. "Is she also in residence?"

Charlotte shook her head. "No, I'm afraid not. Your mother, now, as she reminds us quite often, the Dowager Duchess of Ashurst, traveled to London for the Small Season, and from there to a house party in Devon, I believe it is."

"Is she really the Dowager Duchess? God, I suppose she is. That must have tickled her straight down to the ground."

"Except for the *dowager* part, yes," Charlotte said, smiling as she remembered Helen Daughtry's struggle between clasping an exalted title to her bosom and being thought old enough to be mother to a duke. "I think she has settled for Lady Daughtry."

"My mother never settles for anything, Charlie," Rafe said as he stopped at the bottom of the circular drive that led to the enormous front doors of Ashurst Hall and looked at the building. "I still don't believe this. I still feel like one of the beggars come to town."

He turned to look at Charlotte with those soul-deep eyes of his, and her stomach did another of those small flips. Really, she should try harder to control herself. "Now you sound like your cousin George."

"I suppose I do. They're really dead? This hasn't all just been some long waking dream, and I'm about to be shown to my usual small room near the nursery?"

"The duke's suite of rooms has already been prepared for you, Your Grace," she told him rather kindly, for she could now at last see traces of the old Rafe, the less-sure-of-himself Rafe in those sherry eyes. "Your aunt Emmaline saw to it."

"It's still difficult to believe he's gone. And his sons…"

"May they rest in peace," Charlotte said, still looking at Ashurst Hall, all four floors, dozen massive chimneys and thirty bedrooms of it. Somewhere inside those massive fieldstone walls two unsuspecting tricksters were about to find themselves firmly under the control of one Miss Charlotte Seavers.

"Well, that sounded a tad perfunctory," Rafe said, and she could feel his eyes on her. "You didn't care for George or Harold?"

Charlotte averted her head as she answered, shivering slightly, and not from the cold. "I really didn't know them that well these last years, once they'd for the most part taken up residence in London."

"Yes, the mansion in Grosvenor Square. I stopped there for a week before heading here. I thought my wardrobe needed replenishing. Bought this cloak, that hat." He looked at her questioningly. "Where's my hat, Charlie?"

She really had to stop feeling sorry for the man. "It's Charlotte, and I'm in charge of your sisters, Your Grace, not your hat."

"And now I remember that tone of voice, as well. You

left my new hat lying back there in the middle of the drive, didn't you, to punish me for that remark about spinster caps?"

"In the middle of the drive? I most certainly did not!" she retorted quite honestly.

"No, I left it there, didn't I? I take full responsibility. You know, Charlie, I wouldn't tell anyone else, but it's rather daunting, knowing I am now the custodian of all of this," he said, indicating Ashurst Hall, the estate, all of his inheritance, with the sweep of his arm.

"I can well imagine, Your Grace," Charlotte said, sighing as she thought of the twins. "Having an unexpected responsibility suddenly thrust on your shoulders is rather disconcerting."

"Harris, my majordomo in London, grew rather weary of calling me *Your Grace,* just for me to not answer him. I know it has been some time, but it's only now that I'm back in England that I'm beginning to realize the full consequence of what has happened. I was comfortable as Captain Rafael Daughtry. I'm not sure I'm up to this, Charlie."

Her heart went out to him at his unexpected honesty and humility, and without thinking she placed her hand on his arm. "You'll be fine, Rafe. And everyone at Ashurst Hall will help you."

"That's better. You called me Rafe. Please always do that, Charlie—Charlotte." He sighed, nodded, and then seemed to remember that he was the Duke of Ashurst and should not be admitting fear or apprehension or anything else remotely human or vulnerable. "I've kept you outside in the cold long enough. Let's go inside."

Charlotte pictured the look on the twins' faces when

they were confronted not only with their brother—and if he looked huge and imposing to her, what would the twins see when they saw him?—as well as one Charlotte Seavers standing next to him, looking at them with a knowing glare in her eyes.

"Yes, let's do that. At the least, you should have that head of yours attended to."

"Funny, my friend Fitz says that a lot about my head, although he makes the suggestion not half so politely. You two will doubtless become fast friends."

"Pardon me?"

"Never mind. Fitz and my coach will be along soon enough, making explanations unnecessary."

The front doors opened even as they walked up the wide stone steps.

"Ah, I see my late uncle's footmen are still as curious as ever. We've been observed, Charlotte. A good thing I didn't attempt to seduce you as we stood here, casting your reputation to the four winds."

"You wouldn't do that," Charlotte said, suddenly sober again.

"No, I wouldn't. Should I?"

She collected her scattered thoughts. "You know, Rafe, you're not half so amusing as you seem to think you are."

"Yes, Fitz tells me that, as well." He took her arm and, together, they entered the imposing foyer of Ashurst Hall, the cold and damp of the day immediately closed off behind them by the shutting of the door.

"His Grace has returned from Elba," Charlotte informed the fairly dazzled young footman who, instead of jumping-to to help Rafe with his cloak, just stood there, his mouth at half-mast, goggling up at his new master.

"Billy," Charlotte prodded quietly. "His Grace's cloak?"

"A big 'un, isn't he, ma'am?" the wide-eyed Billy muttered before he was pushed aside by Grayson, the starchy, silver-haired majordomo of Ashurst Hall.

"Allow me, Your Grace," Grayson said, deftly sliding the cloak from Rafe's shoulders even as he executed a perfect bow, one caught somewhere between perfunctory and fawning. "And may I be so bold as to welcome you home. I have already sent someone to alert the Ladies Nicole and Lydia. They await you in the main saloon."

"Thank you, Grayson," Rafe said solemnly before turning to assist Charlotte with her own cloak. "It's good to be home. My traveling coach will be here shortly. Please see that my luggage is attended to, and that there will be ample assistance shown my good friend Captain Fitzgerald, who has sustained an injury and will needs must immediately be carried to a bedchamber."

"It would be my honor, Your Grace," Grayson said, bowing yet again.

"His honor? Poor fellow is probably near to bursting his spleen, having to bow to me. The man would much rather kick me down the stairs," Rafe whispered as he and Charlotte made their way across the wide black-and-white marble tiled expanse toward the pair of doors leading to the main saloon. "I once put a toad in his bed, you know."

"I know. And it was two toads, one under his pillow and one deep beneath the covers, so that he thought he was safe once he'd removed the more obvious one." He took her arm, and she didn't even bother to pretend she didn't feel a small frisson of awareness course through her body. "And one thing more, although I would have thought you'd know. There is something about the configuration of the ceilings of the entrance hall that allows even whispers to carry to every corner."

"The devil you say." Rafe and Charlotte both then looked over their shoulders at Grayson, the man a good twenty feet from them. A man whose rather large ears had turned a most alarming shade of puce.

"Carry on, Grayson, carry on," Rafe called brightly to the majordomo, and then, his hand tightening slightly on Charlotte's forearm, he hastened her the rest of the way as Billy scampered ahead to fling open the double doors. "I'm not making the best of starts, am I?" he whispered.

"Oh, I don't know," Charlotte said as she looked ahead into the enormous main saloon, anxious to locate Nicole and Lydia. "I thought falling at my feet a nice touch. Ah, there they are, your dear, sweet sisters, eager to welcome you home."

Charlotte watched as Nicole leaped to her feet and then signaled with an impatient twist of her hand that Lydia also should rise.

The two of them stood in front of one of the satin settees, not moving, as if the backs of their knees had somehow become glued to that piece of furniture.

The twins were sixteen now, hardly the awkward near-nursery infants Rafe had last seen before he departed for the war. Charlotte wondered if he even recognized them, or they him.

The pair was as alike in their looks as chalk and

cheese. In fact, all three Daughtry children bore little resemblance to each other.

Nicole did share Rafe's near-black hair, but her eyes were far from sherry brown. They were violet, a shade Charlotte had never seen in any other eyes, and Nicole's dramatically arched brows and long black lashes only made that violet more startling, almost mesmerizing. *Witchlike,* Charlotte's father had once commented, not completely in jest, warning that in an earlier century the girl would have doubtless ended burning at the stake.

Nicole had lovely pale skin, but because she refused to wear her bonnet and loved to run free, there was always a beguiling sprinkle of freckles across her nose and cheeks and a glow to her skin that, although most unladylike, was perfect for Nicole.

In short, Nicole looked as she was—fresh, unbridled, a child of nature and full of mischief.

The complete opposite of Lydia.

Nicole's twin, who favored their mother, had hair the color of corn silk and eyes as blue as a summer sky. Her skin was unmarked by freckles because she was always careful to wear a bonnet—not because she feared freckles, but because she'd been told to always wear her bonnet. Shy, quiet, studious, Lydia was rather like a just-budding blossom, her head dipped to avoid attention lest she be picked from her comfortable spot in the garden before she was ready to bloom.

Right now Lydia's chin was bent so near her chest that almost all Charlotte could see of her were those huge blue eyes swimming with guilt.

Nicole's small, pointed chin, however, was fully raised, almost defiant.

If a portrait artist could capture the twins as they posed now, no volume of ten thousand words could do more to make clear the character of the two sisters.

Or who was in charge.

"Girls, how wonderful," Charlotte said after only a heartbeat in time—one that had felt longer than an age. "Your brother is returned to you. I've already explained that your Aunt Emmaline has placed me in the role of chaperone while she is traveling, and what a lovely time we've all had with me residing here with you until her return. Now don't just stand there like sticks, come welcome your brother home."

Lydia looked up, goggling in confusion at this full budget of lies Charlotte had just loosed on them. But Nicole, her mind always alert for mischief, never so much as blinked as she said, "And quite the dragon of a chaperone she is, so that we'd never dare to be on anything save our very best behavior, as suits the sisters of a duke. A duke, Rafe! Isn't it above all things wonderful?"

As she spoke, she advanced across the seeming mile of carpets, her arms outstretched, so that by the time she finished speaking she was close enough to launch herself into her brother's arms.

Rafe glanced at Charlotte as he slowly put his arms around his sister, a look very much akin to panic in his eyes.

"You...you've grown," he said at last, when Nicole finally stepped back, grinning up in his face. "I...I didn't realize..." He coughed into his fist. "Which, er, which one are you?"

"I'm Nicole, of course. You called me Nicky, which

I hated, but now I think it a lovely name. Lydia, don't just stand there like a lump, come say hello to Rafe." She turned back to her brother. "You call her Lydia," she whispered conspiratorially. "Really, there's precious little else you could call her, not with a starchy name like that."

Charlotte wanted to poke Rafe with her elbow, nudge him into some sort of speech. He needed to say something, he needed to put Nicole in her place immediately or else risk never having control of the reins. But he said nothing. Nicole had flummoxed him completely, her own brother. This did not bode well for the day the girl was set loose in London!

"Welcome home, Your Grace," Lydia said in her quiet, reserved voice as she curtsied and then held out her hand to him, quickly drawing it back when, Charlotte supposed, she realized her brother might feel the need to kiss it.

"Thank you…Lydia," Rafe said, and then watched as she returned to the settee and sat down, settling her skirts around her. "Lyddie?" he asked Nicole quietly. "I didn't even call her Lyddie?"

Nicole bit her bottom lip as she shook her head. "You wouldn't have dared. Mama says thank God we're not of the Roman persuasion or else Lydia would have crawled into one of their nunneries years ago. But she's all right. It's all in knowing how to handle her."

Charlotte rolled her eyes. "Which you do, correct, and always to your advantage?"

"She's my twin. I *protect* her," Nicole stated, her violet eyes dancing in her head. "Would you like me to pour you a glass of wine, Your Grace? When we were informed that you were seen on the drive, I just had time to order Grayson to fetch one of Uncle Charlton's best from the cellars. I'll pour a glass for everyone. We should make a toast and celebrate your return."

Rafe turned a questioning eye on Charlotte. "You allow them wine?"

"I most certainly do not," Charlotte told him, glaring at Nicole. "You'll have lemonade, my girl, and like it."

Nicole's full bottom lip came out in a pretty pout, but then she smiled. "See, Rafe? Charlotte is a veritable *dragon* of propriety. Aren't you, Charlotte? Why, I don't know what we should have done without her these weeks, with Aunt Emmaline gone."

Rafe was beginning to look like a man outnumbered by hostiles, and without a weapon to protect himself. "Weeks? Emmaline's been gone for *weeks?* She said nothing about that in any of her letters."

"Duly chastised by my dragon chaperone, I'll just go ring for Grayson to pour you that wine, Rafe," Nicole said, and hurried away, sparing only a moment to shoot a desperate glance toward Charlotte, one that warned *we'll be fine, as long as you don't muck it up now.*

Charlotte swallowed hard and turned to Rafe. He looked much too inquisitive. So she went on the attack. "Is that your way of saying that you don't believe I make a suitable chaperone for your sisters?"

"I... No, no, of course not. Please forgive me. Clearly, if Emmaline considered you competent to be in charge of the twins, who am I to question her judgment? But they're...they're not little girls anymore, Charlie, are they?"

"Charlotte," she said without much hope of him

heeding her. "And, no, they're not. Nor are they young women, much as Nicole would like to believe otherwise. Last week I caught her in Emmaline's chamber, attempting to put up her hair and wearing a rather garish pair of gold and ruby earrings Emmaline must have regretted the moment she purchased them."

Rafe shot a glance toward the settee, where the girls were holding hands and whispering to each other. "I begin to miss the war," he said dully. "Too old for the nursery, too young for a Season. What in God's name am I supposed to *do* with them?"

"What else?" Charlotte said. "You leave them here in the country while you go cut a dash in London. You conveniently forget about them until it's time to dress them up like Christmas puddings and send them out to the marriage mart, praying nineteen to the dozen that at the end of the Season you don't have to haul either of them back to the country again. What else do families do with daughters?"

Rafe grinned. "Do I detect a hint of censure in your voice, Charlie? Were you one of those hauled back to the country? Well, of course you were. Are all the men in London blind? Or were you really waiting for me to return home?"

Charlotte felt a rush of color invade her cheeks at his words, even if she probably shouldn't take any of them seriously. "I only said that because you'd made me angry," she lied, and then nearly cheered as Grayson approached them to inform His Grace that his friend Captain Fitzgerald had arrived.

"A most…singular gentleman, Your Grace," Grayson said, his tone making it clear that he had not just complimented the captain. "He desires your presence at once, sir."

"He does, does he? I'd rather think my good friend Captain Fitzgerald *demands* my presence."

"Yes, Your Grace. I knew him for your friend the moment he opened his mouth."

"An insult wrapped in velvet. Very good, Grayson." Rafe took Charlotte's hand and turned her back toward the entrance hall. "Come on, Charlie. I want you to meet a fellow reprobate."

"I wouldn't wish to intrude—"

"Nonsense. With Emmaline doing her flit, I don't know what I would have done if I'd had to face those sisters of mine without you. I want my friend to meet my friend."

Charlotte smiled weakly. How wonderful. Just perfectly marvelous. Rafe considered her his friend. His childhood friend. *Charlie*. Feeling a bit apprehensive about his new station in life and all the attendant responsibilities, his aunt Emmaline not here, not even recognizing his sisters, he probably felt about Charlotte as he did his most comfortable old pair of socks.

While she—well, what did she feel about him, for him? She didn't know. She'd loved the Rafe he'd been; the child she'd been had loved the youth he'd been. What would she discover about the Rafe he was now?

He looked on her as his friend, held her hand as a friend. Would he ever want more? And what would she do if he did? Would she tell him the truth? How would he look at her with those dangerous eyes of his if she did?

Suppressing a shiver, she followed him into the entrance hall.

CHAPTER TWO

RAFE TUGGED CHARLOTTE along with him as he returned to the entrance hall to see Captain Swain Fitzgerald being supported between two footmen, his splinted leg looking awkward as he kept his foot from touching the marble floor.

"There you are," Fitz bellowed when he caught sight of Rafe. "Do none of these idiots bloody understand the King's English? I want my crutches. Nobody will fetch me my damned crutches. They keep telling me that His bloody Grace insists they carry me. Damn it, Rafe, I'll not be hauled about like some bleeding baby."

"Grayson, see to it, please," Rafe said, letting go of Charlotte's hand and going over to lend his support to his friend. "Act like a baby, be treated like a baby. Why does it bother you so much to be helped? Or do you plan to crawl upstairs to your bed?"

"Bed? Oh, no, Rafe Daughtry, I'm not going to be carted off to any sickbed, no matter what that fancy London surgeon of yours said. I'm fine, better than fine, and perfectly capable of doing for myself. Just get me my damned— Well, *hullo, young lady.*"

Rafe grinned at the sudden change in his friend's tone. *"Yes, Fitz,* a lady, as opposed to your usual sort of female. Behave yourself, and I'll introduce you, you great hairy Irish ape."

"Pretty little thing. One of those twin sisters of yours?" Fitz whispered close to Rafe's ear. "Or can I take a run at her?"

"That depends. Are your intentions honorable?"

"Six and twenty years on this earth and they haven't been honorable yet," Fitz said, still whispering.

"I can hear you, you know," Charlotte said from where she stood just in the doorway between the main saloon and the entrance hall. "Both of you."

Fitz looked at Rafe in panic. "She can't hear me. Tell me she can't hear me."

"I'm sorry, Fitz but, yes, she can," Rafe said, laughing at his friend's expression. He was only amazed that she would say so. Then again, he'd been fairly amazed by everything about Charlotte since he first set eyes on her. Her stunning good looks, her pert tongue, her refusal to be overly impressed by his title even as she paid mocking deference to it. She intrigued him mightily.

Charlotte walked forward, stopping only a few feet away from the grinning Fitz. She looked him up and down as if assessing his injury, and then smiled into his face. "I don't think you'll be *taking a run* anywhere for quite some time, Captain."

"Fitz, ma'am, if you please, and I most truly beg your pardon. It's just that it has been many a long year since I've been blessed to be in the company of a real lady, and never since I've been in the presence of any woman as lovely as you."

"How very flattering, Captain," Charlotte said, dropping into a small curtsy. "I can see I must be very careful, or else a silver-tongued rogue like you might just break my maidenly heart."

Now Rafe gave a shout of laughter, forgetting himself enough to give his friend a hearty slap on the back, which nearly sent Fitz to the floor. "Oops, sorry, Fitz. I shouldn't want to knock your one good leg out from under you. Especially as Miss Seavers has already done it for me. Miss Charlotte Seavers, allow me to belatedly introduce you to my friend and companion for too many years to contemplate, Captain Swain Fitzgerald. Fitz, make your bow to Charlie."

"Hello, Fitz," Charlotte said. "It's a pleasure to make your acquaintance." She shot a quick look at Rafe. "As we're very informal here in the country, please call me Charlotte."

"So this is your Charlie, is it? You must have been a very *slow* youth, Rafe, my friend, not to see what a lovely piece of perfection your Charlie is. How you could have left her, I'll never know."

Rafe glanced at Charlotte, who immediately avoided his eyes.

"Ha, now I've made him mad, and put you to the blush, haven't I, Miss Seavers? Charlotte. I beg pardon, and I'm honored to meet you." Fitz looked toward the doorway. "Ah, and here are my crutches. Pass them over, if you please."

"Don't," Rafe warned the approaching footman. "I wouldn't want them close enough for my friend here to use to beat me into flinders when I say what must be said. I only sent for your crutches, Fitz, so you'd stop shouting for them to be brought to you. Grayson, see that the crutches are well hidden and Captain Fitzgerald is carried upstairs to one of the bedchambers."

"Damn and blast you to the far corners of hell, Rafe Daughtry! I won't be carried!"

"Fine," Rafe said. "Then you'll be dragged. But, one way or another, you're going upstairs."

"The devil I will! I— Pardon me, Charlotte," Fitz said, quickly inclining his head in her direction.

"Oh, don't mind me, Fitz," Charlotte assured him, smiling with what Rafe believed was unholy glee. "It has been a while since I've heard a good argument."

Rafe hoped his friend would at last listen to reason. "Fitz, you know what the man said. I would have left you in London if you hadn't sworn on your mother's head that you'd follow his orders the moment we arrived."

"Then aren't you the fool for believing me. I won't do it, Rafe. Lie mouldering in a bed for two full months? A man could go mad."

Rafe signaled to the footmen, now numbering four, he noticed. "Take him, please."

"No! Rafe, I'm warning you! Let me go, you miserable—"

Rafe watched as the servants carried Fitz up the winding staircase, shaking his head as Fitz alternated between cursing him and cursing the footmen...and then going silent as the pain from his injured leg forced him to give in to the inevitable.

"Poor man," Charlotte said. "What happened to him?"

"I could let Fitz tell you, I suppose. He's been working on a fine story this past week. I believe the latest version has something to do with how he was injured saving a child—no, two children, and their nurse—from a runaway cart. Quite the hero, our fine captain."

"But that's not true?"

Rafe took her arm once more, thinking to return to the main saloon, but then he remembered that his sisters were there and steered her toward the back of the house instead. "He was in such a hurry to step foot on solid ground again after a fairly stormy voyage that he ran down the gangplank and lost his footing on something slick on the dock. Went hell over lampposts into a stack of sea chests."

"Oh, dear, how ignominious. Well, his secret is safe with me. Um, don't you want to return to the main saloon?"

"I'd prefer to return to Elba and relative boredom, actually," Rafe said honestly. "I feel like an interloper here. And my sisters, quite frankly, scare me spitless. I shouldn't admit this, but I'm rather nervous around females after so many years as distant from polite society as a person can be without traveling to the far side of the moon."

"Do I make you nervous, Rafe?" Charlotte asked as he pushed open a door and they entered his late uncle's private study. Now *his* private study. Although he'd had to fight down the feeling that he should first knock on that door and request entry.

"Do you make me nervous? Truthfully, I think everything and everyone here makes me want nothing more than to go find myself a good war."

"Sorry, there are no wars here. I'll give you a few

moments to yourself, to look around," Charlotte said quietly. "Nothing's really changed very much."

He followed her with his eyes as she pretended an interest in a row of books on one of the bookshelves, seeing the young girl who had chased after him and George and Harold sometimes, and gone out of her way to ignore them at others. She'd been such a funny creature, he remembered. Tall for a girl, and rack-thin, all arms and long legs and too much hair that he'd more than once had to untangle from a branch when she got caught up chasing after them as they cut through the woods to the village.

A pest. She'd been a pest. Eight years younger than George, half a dozen years younger than Harold, four years Rafe's junior. And female into the bargain. A child, really; fifteen to his nineteen the day he'd gone off to take up his commission.

He hadn't recognized her out there on the drive. She was still tall, still thin, he supposed, but also nicely rounded. Her unruly mop of sable-brown hair seemed at least fairly tamed, most of it ruthlessly pulled back from her face to hang in loose curls partway down her back. Her hair looked…touchable.

Her warm brown eyes hadn't changed, hadn't aged… unlike his, which sometimes startled him with their haunted intensity when he caught a glimpse of them in his shaving mirror. He liked her nose, straight and yet somehow pert, and her wide mouth was full-lipped, and slightly vulnerable.

It was, in point of fact, only when she opened that mouth that the Charlie he remembered actually appeared. Charlie said what was on her mind, always, and never dressed her comments up in fine linen. He'd liked that about her, he remembered, even when he was thinking up ways to avoid her.

He had no inclination to avoid her now. Quite the opposite.

She'd believed herself in love with him, half a dozen years ago. Did that embarrass her now? She'd joked about it, out there on the drive, but there was no way he could be sure. How did he appear to her now? He wasn't the raw youth he'd been then, and very much doubted he looked *lovable*.

What happened to the innocence of young love, and to youthful stupidity, once the persons involved had moved on through the years? Was he really the duke now, with the Rafe he'd been banished to the past? Was she really Charlotte now, all grown up, and Charlie left behind in her childhood?

They were strangers now. Strangers who once believed they knew each other very well....

"Rafe? I asked you a question," Charlotte said as he stood in the center of the large, darkly paneled room that had been the scene of many a dressing-down from his uncle, who'd worried that Rafe's character might be tainted by resembling that of his flighty mother.

"I'm sorry, Charlotte," he said, giving a slight shake of his head as he quickly improvised a reason for his silence. "I was remembering the day I'd knocked George down for calling my mother a well-dressed trollop. Uncle Charlton warned me that I might be taller than George or Harold, stronger—even smarter—but I would never be more than who I was, so I should remember my place. I'm half expecting Uncle Charlton to come blustering in here at any moment, ordering me out of his private sanctuary."

Charlotte settled herself into one of the large leather chairs flanking the fireplace. "But he's gone, Rafe, they're all gone, the three of them, and you're exactly where no one ever thought you would be. Do you feel vindicated at all, Rafe, or overwhelmed?"

Yes, that was his Charlie. No one else would dare to ask him that question, ask the fourteenth Duke of Ashurst if his title sat uncomfortably on his shoulders. Even Grayson, whose opinion of Rafe had never been one of unmitigated admiration, wouldn't have dared to broach such a question.

Rafe approached his uncle's desk and perched himself on one of its corners as he smiled at Charlotte. "How do I look to you, Charlie? Do I look at all ducal?"

She shook her head. "I can't tell. Sit in his chair behind the desk, Rafe. Sit in *your* chair. It is yours, you know. Yours, and someday your son's, and then his son's. You are the Duke of Ashurst."

"Uncle Charlton must have thought much the same thing about his sons," Rafe said as he circled the large desk and gingerly sat himself in the great leather chair. "George and Harold never went to war, never risked life and limb for our King. And yet I'm here, and they're gone. Is it fate, do you think, Charlie? Or am I simply the accidental duke?"

Charlotte leaned forward in her chair, clasping her hands together on her knees. "May I tell you something?" she asked quietly.

"Please," he said, daring to lean back in the chair, happy to believe he was not sharing it with his uncle's ghost.

"You're an ass, Rafe," Charlotte said, sitting back once more.

Rafe laughed in spite of himself. "Such language! I beg your pardon."

"And so you should. You're the duke. The title is yours, *all* the titles are yours. You've had several long months to become used to that unalterable fact. This room is yours, this great hulking house is yours, the lands and farms and forestry and mills and all the rest of it are yours. George's yacht would have been yours, as well, except it sank. Oh, and the wealth is yours. Considerable wealth, more than considerable wealth. So don't you think it's more than time you stopped playing at grateful pensioner or undeserving interloper—and began *behaving* as the duke?"

"Well, I—"

"You don't tease with Grayson, or else risk giving him the upper hand," she went on as if he hadn't tried to speak. "I know your arrival was unexpected, but you've been home above an hour now, and still Grayson has not assembled the staff in the entrance hall to welcome you."

"I don't need—"

"Yes, you do! The staff has been answering to Grayson for eight long months, and Grayson has been answering to no one. Begin as you plan to go on, Rafe. Take charge. You were a captain in the King's army, surely you know how to order men about, make them do your bidding. You sent them into battle, by God, to fight and perhaps die for you."

"Running a household is scarcely akin to—"

"You think that? Oh, you poor deluded man. Grayson has been all but browbeating Mrs. Piggle—your housekeeper, Rafe—and the servants have aligned themselves with either one or the other. Ashurst Hall has been an armed camp since your uncle's death, I swear it. You need to put your foot down, today, or else prepare for a mutiny."

"You're serious, aren't you? Emmaline was in charge, surely. I can't imagine Grayson or anyone else riding roughshod over her."

Charlotte's eyes, so steadily boring into his, shifted slightly, hidden behind her lowered eyelids. "She… Your aunt was in mourning."

"Yes, of course. And then she was married. I can see why she wouldn't have been paying too much attention to domestic matters."

"Exactly!" she exclaimed, almost as if she was pouncing on his words. "Uh…yes, that's exactly it. In any event, what should concern you is what steps you need to take to set things to rights. After all, Emmaline won't be returning here, not now that she's the Duchess of Warrington, and soon to present His Grace with an heir."

Rafe looked at her in surprise. "She is? She never said any such thing in her letters to me."

"No…ah…she wouldn't have, would she." Again Charlotte averted her gaze. "Perhaps she didn't wish to speak of anything so private with a man? I received a post from her just today, apprising me of the coming happy event. Not even the twins know." She lowered her chin slightly. "The twins most especially do not know."

"Yes, and we're back to the twins. My not quite grown, yet no longer quite children either sisters. You're going to tell me I handled that badly, as well?"

"It could have gone better," Charlotte said, shrugging. "I would have liked if Lydia could have been more animated. And Nicole a little less so. Lydia will give you no problems, Rafe."

"But Nicole will?"

Charlotte sighed audibly. "As long as you're aware, you should be able to handle her."

"Really? How do you handle her, seeing as how Emmaline put you in charge of them?"

"I simply try to think of everything Nicole shouldn't do, and then assume that she will. A plan not without its flaws, I'm afraid, as I find my mind is not half so devious as hers."

"Now that's unnerving, as I seem to recall that there was little you wouldn't attempt. You were always either in a scrape or escaping one by the skin of your teeth. There were times I thought you headed for complete disaster, as I remember."

"So I've been told," Charlotte said rather tightly as she got to her feet, clearly cutting off that line of conversation. "Shall I ring for Grayson? You do need to put the man back in his place, and delaying that moment only undermines you more."

"I'll do it," Rafe said, also rising. "Although I probably should change my clothes before I walk the length of the line, my hands clasped behind my back, solemnly accepting the bows and curtsies of my staff. God, Charlie, you know I'm going to laugh at some point, and make a total cake of myself."

"Hide a straight pin in those clasped hands, and when you feel an undukely giggle coming on, simply stick yourself with it," she suggested, already heading for the door.

"A straight pin. Of course. What would I do without you, Charlie?"

She hesitated as she got to the doorway, and then turned to face him for a moment, her smile finally back after what he'd been sure was an awkward moment, although he didn't know why it had been awkward. "Keep calling me Charlie, Your Grace, and you might just find out!"

Rafe laughed out loud, watching her leave after having landed the perfect parting shot, and then shook his head, wondering why he suddenly felt so alone again.

He waited a few moments before following after her, hoping Phineas had ordered a bath prepared and unpacked at least one change of clothes for him by now.

As he mounted the stairs he continued to visually inspect his new home, the one he had run tame in often over the years, but only as his father's son, the poor relation abandoned, yet again, by his flighty mother.

He'd be all right, he'd be fine in a few days. His new circumstances just needed some getting used to, that's all.

Thank God he'd had the luck to stumble over good old Charlie—no, *Charlotte*. With Fitz out of commission, she was the only friend he had.

CHAPTER THREE

CHARLOTTE'S PACE increased as she neared the top of the staircase and turned down the hallway to her right, heading for Nicole's bedchamber. Once again, firmly blocking thoughts of Rafe from her mind, she was a woman on a mission.

When she reached the door, she didn't knock, but simply threw it open, stepped inside, slammed the thing behind her and declared, *"You."*

Lady Nicole Daughtry smiled into the vanity mirror as she continued to comb her long dark hair. "Hello again, Charlotte. My congratulations."

Charlotte stomped across the large pink-and-white bedchamber, her footsteps maddeningly muffled by the succession of priceless Aubusson carpets. "Your congratulations for what, Nicole? Not strangling you earlier?"

"Of course. Oh, and about that," Nicole said, turning on her satin-topped bench. "How did you discover our small deception? I knew the moment I first saw you that you knew. I slipped up somewhere, didn't I? Was it something my brother said to you? I can't imagine how else you could have known."

"And *I* can't imagine how you got away with such a

dastardly deception all this time," Charlotte admitted, taking the silver-backed brush from Nicole's hand and dragging it none too gently through the girl's hair. "Not only fooling your aunt and brother, but me, as well."

"It's that last part that rankles, doesn't it?" Nicole said, wincing as the brush encountered a knot.

"Considering that I was the only one here, actually reading the letters, yes, it rankles. Why didn't you tell me what you were about? I would have helped you."

The moment Charlotte said the words she realized that, indeed, she would have aided Nicole and Lydia in their grand deception. After all, Emmaline deserved her happiness and peace of mind, and Rafe had clearly wished to continue on as he had been before his uncle's death, escorting Bonaparte into exile and being a part of his guard. It wasn't as if the twins had been left unchaperoned in a cave somewhere.

Nicole tipped back her head and grinned up at Charlotte. "Yes, I thought you would have, but Lydia couldn't be convinced."

Charlotte pushed Nicole's head forward once more. "Liar. Lydia, as we both know, can be convinced of anything when you're the one weaving fantastic stories. Admit it, Nicole, it was you who decided not to share this adventure with me. You must have spent hours and hours composing those bogus letters. I could have helped. And I most certainly could have improved upon your abysmal spelling."

"In that case, I apologize most profoundly. Lydia, stubborn as she can be sometimes, would only agree to the scheme if I didn't make her have anything to do with the actual composition of the letters. You're not going to tell Aunt Emmaline?"

"No, I can't. She wrote to me in this morning's post. She's increasing. She and the duke are already returned to his estate, and she won't be traveling again until the child is born. It would do no good to upset her."

"Emmy's going to have a baby?" Nicole jumped up and grabbed Charlotte in a fierce hug. "How above everything wonderful!" Then she pushed away from Charlotte and frowned. "No, wait. That isn't wonderful. Who will present Lydia and me next spring, when we go to London for the Season?"

"You're not going to London for the Season, you wretched girl. You're only sixteen."

"Seventeen next month," Nicole reminded her. "Louisa Madison went to London at seventeen for her first Season."

"Yes, and she came home again three weeks later, humiliated and ostracized because she was so foolish as to allow a half-pay officer to kiss her in Lady Castlereagh's gardens. Do *you* want to be quickly married off to the vicar's third-oldest son?"

"Louisa was always a fool," Nicole said, shrugging. "I'd never kiss a half-pay officer. Indeed, I shall not even deign to dance with any rank lower than earl."

Charlotte rolled her eyes. "I'm sure your brother will be much relieved to hear that. But you're not going. You're too young, and there is no one to chaperone you."

"There's you," Nicole said, grinning at Charlotte.

"There most certainly is *not* me. I'm much too young to be a chaperone, for one thing, and I'd rather be locked up in Bedlam before I'd entertain any thought of attempting to get you to behave for more than five minutes. I mean it, Nicole. No. Stop smiling. Stop looking at me that way. Wait—where are you going? What are you going to do?"

Nicole was already halfway to the door, her unbound hair trailing halfway down her back. "Why," she said, whirling about to face Charlotte, "I think it should be obvious. I've been sitting up here, my every nerve shredded, appalled at what I've done. Hoodwinking my own dearest aunt, my own dearest brother. There's nothing else for it. I must go to him at once, and make a clean breast of my sins."

"You miserable little— Don't you dare!"

"But, Charlotte, you must see that it isn't fair to keep poor Rafe in the dark like this, can't you? I mean, not that *you* weren't most thoroughly in the dark for all these long months. Completely fooled by two young girls scarcely out of the nursery." She frowned rather comically. "Oh, dear, what will Rafe think of you once he knows?"

"Perhaps I don't care what he thinks," Charlotte said, hoping she didn't sound defensive.

"And as Mrs. Beasley would say, *pshaw.* Of course you care. Everyone knows you've always been half in love with him. Why, you still wear that ratty old scarf of his sometimes. I've seen you. Just like something out of a penny press novel, that's what Mrs. Beasley says."

Charlotte opened her mouth to protest, but she knew she'd already lost. "Oh, very well. Yes, I might have thought myself in love with him. But that was a long time ago. Now I just don't want him to think me a complete idiot. What do you want me to do? Because I can't be your chaperone. Old maid I may be, but you will need someone with much more social consequence than I, and at least twice my knowledge of how you and Lydia should go on. You're sisters to the duke, remember. I was only one of hundreds of lesser lights, never given a voucher to Almack's, partaking in only the tamest of gatherings…oh, I can't believe I'm agreeing to any of this."

Nicole returned to her dressing table and opened the top middle drawer, extracting a folded paper. "Here. Here's a listing of all our female relatives. I wrote it out some weeks ago, as it is always wise to be prepared for a last-minute change of plans. Lydia taught me that. At any rate, that's all that's left, you know—females. Rafe is the only gentleman among them on our papa's side of the family. And heaven knows we can't apply to Mama's family. They're all either pockets-to-let or locked up for card sharping."

"They are not," Charlotte said, unfolding the paper. "Who told you that?"

"Mama," Nicole said brightly. "She should know, don't you think?"

"I suppose," Charlotte said, reading down the short list of names. "Where did you get this list?"

"I copied it down from the family Bible, in Uncle Charlton's—that is, Rafe's study."

"That may explain it. Margaret, your grandfather's only sister, lives in Scotland and is sickly by choice. She never travels. I remember Emmaline telling me that when she was preparing the list for the memorial to your uncle and cousins."

"She isn't the only name," Nicole said hopefully.

"As for this second name, Irene Murdoch? Do you by chance recall the embarrassingly rude creature who spent three days here, seated in the main saloon with a constantly refilled dish of sugar comfits in her ample lap, telling all who would listen that she had always favored your late aunt's garnet brooch and felt certain Emmaline would gift her with it as a remembrance?"

"That *sow?* That's Cousin Irene? Oh, no. She won't do at all." Nicole leaned closer to look at the list. "Who else is left?"

"Considering the fact that I'm almost certain I was told that your aunt Marion died more than thirty years ago, I would say that leaves—" Charlotte smiled evilly "—only your mama to bring you and Lydia out."

"Mama!" Nicole's astonishingly violet eyes all but popped out of her head. "I thought you said we needed someone respectable. As she's between husbands at the moment, *again,* she'd probably chase after anyone who looked at either Lydia or me. It would be a *disaster.*"

"I rather think you're right," Charlotte said with some humor. "But there is another answer. As the duke, Rafe now has the responsibility of setting up his own nursery, as the Duke of Warrington and Emmaline are doing. Give the man a year, and he'll have found himself a fine duchess more than willing to bring you both out, seeing as how any woman with a modicum of brains would be more than anxious to see you and Lydia—mostly you, I expect—gone from Ashurst Hall."

And then she tried to ignore a slight pang in her chest.

Nicole took the sheet of paper, tearing it nearly in half, and began to pace. "A duchess. Rafe needs a duchess. Yes, of course. And Lydia isn't quite as ready for her Come-Out as I would like," she continued, clearly speaking for her own benefit. "I'd marry and she'd be left on the shelf, like poor Charlotte. A good sister wouldn't allow that, and Lydia would be lost without me...."

Charlotte folded her arms beneath her bosom and tapped the tip of one half boot against the floor, glaring at Nicole. "As I seem to be saying a lot today—I hear you, Nicole."

"What?" Nicole grinned at her. "Sorry, Charlotte. Wait a moment. What about you? Would you consider marrying Rafe? He isn't ugly, and he's very rich. And he seems to like you. And, since you already know Lydia and me, and you've admitted you at least *used* to love him, we wouldn't have...well, we wouldn't have to *break you in* the way we would a stranger."

Charlotte lowered her gaze to her shoe tops. "You can't plan someone else's life like that, Nicole. Rafe will marry where he wants to marry."

"Why? You weren't going to. People marry for many reasons. Aunt Emmaline told us that your papa was the one who chose—"

"I've changed my mind, Nicole," Charlotte interrupted quickly, determinedly blinking back threatening tears. "Go tell him. Tell Rafe what you did, make a clean breast of things, even if I have to then tell him that I lied to him, that Emmaline has been gone these six months or more, that I haven't really taken up residence here as your chaperone, that you hoodwinked me most thoroughly. Tell him all of it."

Nicole pulled a face. "I said something to upset you, didn't I? I'm sorry, Charlotte. I'm rude, and selfish, and only ever think of myself. It's just that it seems you and Rafe would suit, since you already know each other so well. And it would be so simple, you know, since we're already friends and—and you told him you're living here with us. That's what you said downstairs, too, isn't it?"

Charlotte's stomach dropped to her toes. "Oh, Lord, I did, didn't I? How could I have forgotten that lie?"

Nicole shook her finger at Charlotte. "And I suppose you thought it was easy, juggling stories, remembering every innocent little fib? I happen to look upon lying as a talent, one you clearly haven't mastered. So now what, Charlotte? Do we ask Grayson to send someone to fetch clothing for you? Dinner's in an hour, and you can't possibly go down in that frowsy gown."

"What's wrong with my gown?" Charlotte asked, looking down at her plain gray round gown of several seasons past.

"Well, my good friend, if you don't know that, then I agree with you. You cannot be put even nominally in charge of Lydia's and my new wardrobes when we go to London."

"I still don't understand why you think your brother would even consider taking you to London with him."

"You don't? We'll forgo a Season for now, because I am capable of listening to reason. But we *must* at least travel to the city in the spring with Rafe. Surely you see that? We've been locked up here or at Willowbrook for all of our lives. We'll be seventeen in a few weeks, much too old to be consigned back to the nursery for another year now that we know what it's like to be set free these past six months or more. Imagine the mischief I will get into if left here to my own devices while Rafe goes to London in the spring."

Charlotte sighed. "I'd rather contemplate being run down by a speeding mail coach."

"Exactly! A compromise, Charlotte. You can come along as our friend and very nearly a member of our family. See? I'm more than willing to compromise."

"You're walking a very fine line, Nicole," Charlotte warned her, wearying of the game. "I still could go tell Rafe the truth, and you and Lydia would never get out of this bedchamber, let alone to London."

Nicole gave her a quick hug. "Please forgive me, I'm so sorry. We shouldn't argue, not when we're both determined not to be found out."

"You're right, sadly. Which means we have to bribe Grayson if he's to send someone along to Rose Cottage with me for my belongings so that we can pretend I've been living here with you these past weeks. How much do you have in the way of pin money?"

"Me? I spent it all in the village last week. Don't you remember seeing my new pelisse? But Lydia hoards her allowance like a miser. She must have at least eight pounds in the reticule she has stuffed in her bottom drawer. She had ten, but the pelisse wasn't the only thing I purchased. There were these lovely yellow kid slippers Mrs. Halbrook assured me came straight from London, and I just *had* to have them."

"You borrowed money from your sister? Or did you simply take it?"

"Oh, don't go all prudish on me." Nicole smiled. "I'll return it next quarter and she'll never know. She'd only waste it all on books anyway."

"You're impossible."

"I know," Nicole said, hanging her head. "Lydia would have loaned me the two pounds, but somehow it was more delicious to sneak into her room and—well, I'll never do that again to my own dear twin sister, I promise. I think I got all of the evil and Lydia all of the good. If I'm going to make my debut in Mayfair I must strive to improve myself."

"Yes, you must," Charlotte agreed, not holding out much hope for that eventuality. "Beginning bright and early first thing tomorrow morning, I'd say. After you bring me that eight pounds and I go have a quiet chat with Grayson."

She stepped into the hall five minutes later, the eight pounds in her pocket, and leaned back against the closed door. Was she out of her mind? Only a fool would think she could get away with this charade.

In fact, she had only one thing on her side: Grayson's disdainful certainty that Rafe was an unacceptable duke. If she approached the butler correctly, let him believe he was pulling one over on his new master? Yes, then Grayson might cooperate.

She'd feel terribly about not going to Rafe with the truth about what his sisters had done, but in aid of what? The man seemed truly out of his depth at the moment, although she was certain he'd grow into his new boots in time. There seemed no good reason to upset him; after all, the twins were fine, their reputations intact, and the house hadn't burned down around all their ears, or anything.

And telling Rafe meant telling Emmaline, which Charlotte completely refused to do, not with the woman newly married and now expecting a baby.

"Have you convinced yourself?" Charlotte muttered quietly. She decided that she had, and that her greatest motivation wasn't really the idea that Rafe wouldn't learn the truth and thereby think her not only a liar but also the biggest imbecile in nature not to have seen through Nicole and Lydia's lies. Intent on locating Grayson, she headed for the staircase.

She stopped at the head of the stairs, realizing that, below her, the entrance hall was clogged with maids and footmen and cooks and tweenies…and Rafe.

Sinking to her knees so as not to be easily seen, she watched through the balustrades as, accompanied by a starchy Grayson, the new duke—his hands held clasped behind his back, she noticed—walked along the curving line of Ashurst servants, nodding his acceptance of each introduction, each bow, every curtsy.

He looked wonderful in his fine London clothes. His dark hair glistened in the light from the large chandelier, still slightly damp, telling Charlotte that he'd bathed away his travel dust in the time she'd been closeted with Nicole.

She blinked back tears yet again as Rafe came to the end of the line, where the six children of the head cook stood in a descending row. He then accepted a pastry from the youngest, ruffling the lad's hair before Grayson clapped his hands three times in quick succession, dismissing everyone.

"Thank you, Grayson," she heard Rafe say once the entrance hall was clear except for two of the footmen who took up their posts at the front door once more, as if expecting the Prince Regent's coach to come roaring up the drive at any moment.

"Yes, Your Grace," Grayson said, holding out one white-gloved hand for the small silver plate. "I'll take that for you, sir."

"The devil you will. The lad gave it to me, the only person to offer me a morsel of food since I arrived. I've allowed you to exercise your spleen, Grayson, as I know how loyal you were to the late duke. But be warned. I will suffer no more insolence from you, or from anyone connected with Ashurst Hall. The staff follows your lead, Grayson, and you are not as irreplaceable as you might believe. I doubt any of them will wish to follow you out the door, if you take my meaning."

"Yes, Your Grace," Grayson said, bowing. Then he turned on his heel and fairly marched out of the entrance hall, his chin high, his back ramrod straight.

Rafe turned about and looked up at Charlotte, his young, unaffected smile dazzling her. He broke off a bit of the pastry as he said, "That went well, Charlie, don't you think? I didn't even need to use the pin."

Before she could get to her feet, or form an answer, he'd popped the bit of pastry into his mouth and headed for the main saloon.

Charlotte stayed where she was, not yet trusting her legs to hold her if she attempted to stand. What was it Nicole had said to her?

Oh, yes. *What about you? Would you consider marrying Rafe? He isn't ugly, and he's very rich. And he seems to like you.*

"I like him, too," Charlotte whispered as she cooled one hot cheek against the wrought iron of the staircase. "Very much."

CHAPTER FOUR

"I HOPE YOU HAD a restful night," Rafe said as he approached his friend's bed, smiling as Phineas employed a scissors, neatly trimming Fitz's light brown beard. "How's the leg?"

Phineas made one last snip-snip, carefully folded up the towel he'd laid on Fitz's chest, and stood clear. "He'll tell you it's fine, Your Grace, but the servant assigned to sleep in the dressing room told me he moaned in his sleep on and off all the night long."

"And did he ask you, Phineas?" Fitz said, throwing out his arm, which the small man easily evaded. "I'm fine, Rafe. So the leg got jostled a bit in the coach. The bones are nicely settled again. I want my crutches."

"You can want them all you wish, but you can't have them," Rafe told him, gingerly sitting down on the side of the wide bed. "And the fever, Phineas?"

"All but gone this morning, Your Grace. We removed the splint, as the surgeon ordered, thinking that should ease him some. Does it ease you some, Captain?"

"Go hang yourself," Fitz muttered without rancor, reaching down to rub at his left thigh. "If I was a horse you would have ordered me shot, and I begin to think you would have been doing me a favor. How long are you planning to keep me locked away up here?"

"Two months, I believe I was told," Rafe said, genuinely sorry for his friend. "We'll have to find something to amuse you."

"Good. I'll take that pretty little redheaded maid who came in this morning to replenish the fire, thank you."

Rafe smiled. "Down but not out, are you, Fitz?" He waited until Phineas had departed the room, and then said, "In truth, I wish you could be downstairs with me. I met my sisters yesterday."

"That all sounds ominous. Are they horse-faced?"

"Hardly. And I'm told chastity belts are no longer acceptable garb for young unmarried sisters, more's the pity. I can only thank God Charlie was here to steer me through my first encounter. I've faced the enemy with less trepidation."

"Ah, yes, the fetching Miss Charlotte," Fitz said, stroking his short beard. "She seemed sorry for me. Do you think that sympathy would extend to visiting with this poor soldier, perhaps reading poetry to him?"

Rafe frowned. "She is pretty, isn't she? It's strange. I don't remember Charlie as pretty. I remember her as a thorn in my side, a perpetual pest. And as my friend. Sometimes the only friend I had here at Ashurst Hall."

Fitz's grin split his beard. "Well then, your friend can come *pest* me any time she likes."

"Only here the one night, and already you have designs on the ladies?" Rafe hoped his voice sounded light, unconcerned.

He shouldn't have bothered to try to dissemble.

"Staked her out for yourself, have you?"

"No," Rafe said quickly. Too quickly? "You really can be an annoying bastard, do you know that?"

"I do, and pride myself on it," Fitz said rather smugly. "I also pride myself on being able to take a hint, so I'll stop teasing you now. Still, if you won't send Charlotte to me, how about you order one of your new servants to round up some books I can read to pass the time? Better yet, someone to read them to me? The sound of Charlotte's lovely voice washing over me as I lie on my sickbed, for instance, my eyes closed in bliss, her every word soothing my pain— Your late uncle did own books, didn't he?"

"Thousands of them, yes. I don't ever remember anyone in the household reading them, however. But I can't promise you that Charlie would be agreeable. Besides, you're strong enough to hold a book and read it yourself." Rafe got up from the bed, alarmed to see his friend wince at the movement of the mattress. "Although perhaps tomorrow would be soon enough?"

"Damn it, I suppose so," Fitz muttered, once again rubbing his thigh. "You didn't tell anyone how this happened, did you? Bad enough I did it, without you running through the halls like the town crier, telling everyone about your clumsy oaf of a friend."

"Only Charlie. Sorry, Fitz. But she won't tell anyone if I ask her not to. Feel free to make up whatever heroic, outlandish story you want."

"The runaway cart doesn't impress you?"

"Actually, I was thinking more of the Frenchmen we shooed away from Elba the week before we departed for home."

"Come to rescue their emperor," Fitz said, nodding.

"But it wasn't me who saw them at the tavern and got suspicious. I never saw more than their backs as we chased them to their longboat. No, that's your story, my friend, as it was you who was nearly shot and not me, although I thank you for offering it to me. I'll think of something else, something equally heroic. Now go away, if you please. This injured soldier needs his rest."

Rafe left the bedchamber reluctantly, knowing he'd delayed facing his first full day as duke in residence as long as possible.

It was November. What duties did a duke have in November? When he wasn't away in London or at some house party or other, his uncle had always been riding out somewhere or another with his chief steward... That was it, he'd find his chief steward, and ride *out* with him.

Having decided on a plan, Rafe returned to his massive chambers to find Phineas already laying out his riding clothes in the dressing room.

"Ah, good, I don't have to go calling through this large pile, chasing you down. Miss Seavers says for you to hurry and get changed, Your Grace. And I've sewn and brushed your riding cloak for you, not that I can find that lovely new beaver anywhere. Your Miss Seavers said she thought she might be able to locate it, as you'll need something on your head with the chill being so in the air, not that I know where you're off to. Your Miss Seavers said something about showing your pretty face somewhere?"

"Oh, she said all that, did she," Rafe said, feeling an unreasonable reluctance to continue doing as Charlie dictated. Even if she was right, damn it. "She's not my Miss Seavers, Phineas. And perhaps I don't want to show my— Ah, hell's bells, Phineas, help me out of this jacket."

"Men are always ruled by petticoats when you get right down to it, Your Grace," Phineas said, helping to ease the superbly tailored jacket from Rafe's broad shoulders. "That's what m'father warned me when I was just a little tyke. Be he beggar or king, m'father would say, a man is bound to find himself under some woman's thumb sooner or later."

"Thank you for sharing your father's insight with me, Phineas. But I am not under any woman's thumb. I'm merely going along with what Miss Seavers suggests because she is more familiar with— And why am I bothering to say any of this to you?"

"I'm sure I have no idea, Your Grace," Phineas said, not turning away quickly enough to hide his smile. "I'll just go hang up your jacket now, seeing as how you've only the three rigouts until that mess of fine clothes you ordered in London catches up with us."

Rafe stood in front of the cheval glass to adjust his hacking jacket more comfortably on his shoulders. His new wardrobe was a far cry from the uniforms he'd worn—lived in, slept in, shared with lice and other vermin more often than he'd like to remember. Broiled in during the hot summers, frozen in for several cold winters.

"Phineas? Where are my uniforms?"

"Burned, Your Grace," the Bow Street runner turned valet said as he brushed at the discarded jacket. "Couldn't go selling the King's uniform to no bow-wow shop, now could I? The dregs of London lording it about on Piccadilly as if they were real soldiers? Weren't any use to you anymore, Your Grace."

"Burned? So they're gone?" Rafe felt a sudden desire to see his uniforms one more time. Surely not a rational thought. They'd been a part of his life for so many years; he'd planned to remain in uniform until Phineas had showed up with his startling, life-changing news.

"Excepting the ribbons and the braid and the buttons and such, yes, Your Grace. Sir? Your Miss Seavers is most probably waiting on you downstairs."

"Right," Rafe said, checking his appearance one last time. He knew his brown-and-tan riding clothes to be fashionable as well as proper, but he did miss the scarlet. He knew who he was in the scarlet.

He didn't know who he was now at all.

His hand had just touched the banister when he looked over the railing to see Charlie standing in the entrance hall. She was dressed in a close-fitting navy hussar's jacket and divided riding skirt, a matching shako hat tipped to one side on her head. She was tapping one booted foot in time with each impatient strike of his hat against her thigh.

He still couldn't seem to wrap his mind around the idea that Charlie had grown up. And grown up so prettily, too. He didn't know where she planned to take him, but they really should have a groom riding along behind them, as a young woman so beautiful, so eligible, should not be with a man unless chaperoned in some way.

As if Rafe was planning to pounce on her in any way. Which he wasn't.

Even if the thought had occurred to him.

"My apologies, Charlie," he called out as he rapidly descended the staircase. "I had not received your *order* until a few minutes ago."

She looked up at him, frowning. "My order?"

"Yes," he said, crossing the entrance hall to take his hat from her. "Something about showing my pretty face somewhere?"

Charlotte winced rather comically. "I must remember that servants have an unnerving way of quoting back just what they should forget, and forgetting just what they should commit to memory. I'm sorry, Rafe. But I did think this is something best not put off for another day. I suggest we begin with the forestry operations, and then continue to the cottages of the farm laborers, and then the mill. Or perhaps you'd like to ride into the village?"

"We could have discussed this all last evening, if you had deigned to appear at dinner."

"I was otherwise detained," she said unapologetically, although her gaze slid away from his rather guiltily. "I had to visit my parents with my maid and collect a few items I needed. Forgive me for not realizing you'd be lost without my presence."

"Touché, Charlie, your point is well-taken. I did miss you, as it left me staring down that long table while my sisters pointedly ignored me, Nicole talking nineteen to the dozen about some new bonnet ribbons while Lydia reinforced my initial conclusion that she's frightened to death of me."

"Lydia will come around. She's rather bookish. Quiet. I think you should be grateful. They are twins, remember, and both of them could be like Nicole."

"Heaven forfend," Rafe said facetiously, throwing up his hands. "Lydia's bookish? That can't be good, not if she's smarter than the gentlemen around her. Is she really a budding bluestocking?"

"Not quite, but she is a very serious young woman. Girl. She's always got her nose in a book, and very nearly lives in the library most days, curled up on a window seat with her latest discovery."

Rafe considered this for a moment. "Then she might be the one to choose some reading material for Fitz. He only a few minutes ago begged that someone come read to him."

"Oh, I doubt Lydia would ever dare to enter the man's bedchamber. But I can ask her to select a few books she might think Fitz would enjoy and have a servant deliver them to him."

"Yes, I suppose you're right. I mean, not that Fitz would ever—that is, Lydia is only a child, and—oh, hell, Charlie, I don't know what I mean. Is it cowardly of me to admit that I don't have the faintest idea of how to take care of my own two sisters? There I sat last night, at the dinner table, wildly attempting to come up with something to say that might engage them in conversation somehow. But what do I know of what would interest a female of that age?"

Charlotte looked at him in real sympathy. "You're worried they won't like you, aren't you? Oh, Rafe, that's so sweet. I don't think most men would care a fig what two sixteen-year-old siblings thought of them."

"Somebody has to be responsible for them."

"Responsible, yes. But you actually *care*. That's so sweet."

"Charlie, tell me I'm being sweet one more time and I swear I'm going to leave you standing here and go drink down half my uncle's wine cellars."

"Very well, we'll get down to business. You've

greeted the staff here, but you've many more souls who depend on the duke's living for their bread and butter and the roofs over their heads. They need to see you. Mr. Cummings is a competent steward, but they've been too long without a real master."

"You do realize, Charlie, that I have no more idea of what I'm supposed to do, or say, to any of these people than I do about how to handle Nicole and Lydia? I'm only a soldier."

"And as your troops looked to you to lead them, looked to you for strength and resolve and direction, believing you would take care of them, not betray them or put them in unnecessary danger, so do the laborers on your estate. Care for them, show kindness to them even as you lead them, and they will give you their loyalty."

"You make it all sound so simple, Charlie. Even as we both know it isn't all quite that easy."

The footman he now knew as Billy handed him his gloves and riding crop, and he and Charlotte headed down the wide steps to where more servants held the reins of their mounts.

"I don't see a mount for one of the grooms."

Charlotte looked at him askance. "You believe we need a chaperone, Your Grace? It's broad daylight, and we're going to the sawmill. I doubt we could get into much mischief between here and there."

"Never mind," Rafe said tightly, feeling heat climbing the back of his neck. "Just go get on the damn horse."

Charlotte waited until she'd been boosted into the sidesaddle and they had turned the horses down the drive before saying, "I've just thought of something that might help you during this first meeting with your tenants. Do you remember what we were taught as children to do if confronted by a wildly barking dog, Rafe?"

"Yes, I remember. Stand your ground, never show fear." Rafe smiled. "So my people are to be compared with angry canines?"

She wrinkled her nose, looking rather adorable, not that he wanted to notice; he was still faintly angry with her about the way she'd teased him when he mentioned a chaperone. "I suppose that didn't come out quite right, did it? But the advice is sound. Really, Rafe, you have to face it sooner or later. You're the rightful Duke of Ashurst."

"And I only climbed over three bodies to get here," he said, privately shocked to hear himself say the words. Was that how he really felt? Like an interloper? A ghoul come to dance on the graves of his uncle and cousins?

They rode along in silence for a few minutes more before turning onto a rutted roadway lined by dense undergrowth and trees that began only a few yards from them on either side.

Rafe felt Charlotte's gaze on him every few moments, until she finally said, "You know, there are no bodies, Rafe. They were never recovered. Emmaline held a memorial service in the estate chapel once all hope was gone, but there was…there was nothing to inter in the mausoleum. There are only brass plaques in front of where their resting places should be. Emmaline did her best."

"The letter she had Phineas carry to me spoke of a

new yacht, and a storm. I should have realized there was a possibility no bodies were ever found."

"It was all an avoidable accident, I'm sad to tell you. The crew wished to turn about when the distant sky turned ominous, but either your cousins or your uncle overruled the captain. The single man to survive long enough to be plucked from the waters by a passing ship also mentioned large quantities of wine and a few women aboard. Not ladies, Rafe. Women. You'll pardon my frankness, but George was always a loose screw. I can only wonder why the duke agreed to the excursion."

"You probably have no further to look than the few loose women," Rafe said as he thought about his uncle, who had always had an appetite for female flesh, the less respectable the better. An appetite he already knew his cousins had shared. "That had to be embarrassing for Emmaline to hear. And for you to have to tell me."

Charlotte shrugged her shoulders, her air of unconcern clearly forced. She obviously was only telling him what she felt he needed to know. "I don't think about it, not really. Or of them. They're dead now, so what's the point?"

"True enough. We're probably lucky to have any information at all, good or bad. I didn't know one of the crew survived."

"Not a member of the crew, Rafe. One Mr. Hugh Hobart. It was he who wrote to Emmaline about the last moments before the yacht sank. According to Mr. Hobart, George and Harold were belowdecks with their…um, their companions, all of them quite seasick, when the rogue wave struck, overturning the vessel.

Your uncle and Mr. Hobart were still on deck, keeping an anxious eye on the coastline as the yacht belatedly raced toward the port."

"Good God. They must have been terrified. We encountered a Channel storm on our way here. Our ship was a captured Spanish galleon, a formidable thing, and it was tossed about like a cork. I can't imagine what an angry Channel could do to a small yacht."

"Hence your friend Fitz's haste to disembark. Yes, I remember. The last thing Mr. Hobart wrote he remembers before he came to himself in the small boat they were towing is feeling the lurch of the yacht, and seeing the boom swing around to catch your uncle full in the chest and head, dealing him what was certainly a mortal blow. I'm sorry, Rafe."

"Yes, so am I," he said as Charlotte turned her mount onto the even narrower roadway he knew led to the lumber mill. Ashurst Hall was situated near enough the Sussex Weald to make forestry a lucrative part of the estate activities, seedlings planted wherever mature trees were harvested. Rafe could remember hearing his uncle lecture to George that to cut once is greedy and shortsighted, that a penny sown back in the earth for every pound that is reaped is the way to true wealth. The late duke was a hard man, but he'd been a fine steward of his lands.

"Mr. Hobart was invited to attend the memorial, but he was forced to decline, as he'd yet to recover from his own injuries. Emmaline truly wished to meet him, and learn more about her family's last hours."

"I suppose I should speak to the gentleman myself," Rafe said, watching as men began running from seemingly everywhere to line up alongside the roadway. "He was, I'm assuming, a friend of George's?"

"I don't know, you'd have to ask him. I'd never heard the name until his letter arrived and Emmaline shared it with me. Emmaline was equally unaware of the man, but that meant nothing, as your cousins had a large acquaintance. Ah, and here is Mr. Cummings now," she said as a horse and rider approached along the lane. "You don't know him, as your uncle took him on after Mr. Willard left for Hampshire to spend his declining years with his grown daughter, so don't worry that you don't recognize him. Still, you will address him as John."

"Yes, ma'am," Rafe said facetiously. "Here, now, I've just had a thought. Wouldn't it simply be easier for me to turn him off and hire you to run both Ashurst Hall and the rest of my life?"

He thought he saw a quick flicker of something unreadable in Charlotte's soft brown eyes. Anger? No. And not quite hurt, either. Something else. But what? Guilt? No, it couldn't be.

"I'm only trying to help, Rafe," she said quietly.

"Yes, Charlie, I know. Please forgive me," he said, reaching out a hand to touch hers as they held the reins. "I'd be lost without you and I know it."

Her smile didn't seem to quite reach her lovely brown eyes. "Oh, you'll not need me for long. I have every confidence in your ability to be a fine duke. Remember, Rafe, that some are born to greatness, some achieve greatness, and some—"

"And some have greatness thrust upon them. Yes, Charlie, I remember my Shakespeare, having studied it along with George and Harold while living here on sufferance. But I was not born to greatness, have achieved nothing remotely great, and I have had a title thrust upon me through no effort of my own."

Charlotte rolled her eyes in exasperation. "You really have to stop that, Rafe. It's both tedious and annoying. Did George or Harold deserve to be born as they were? Is anyone born to what they *deserve?* It's how you behave that determines how the world sees you, and how you see yourself. Now turn your hat around a bit. The dent is showing, and lends nothing to your consequence."

Rafe threw back his head and laughed in real amusement. "You would have made a top-notch master sergeant," he said, and then dutifully readjusted his hat. "And my boots, master sergeant. Do they pass muster?"

Her answer to his spontaneous outburst was a lift of her chin and a definite *"Hruumph!"*

"Your Grace," Mr. Cummings said as he drew his mount to a halt some ten feet away and doffed his cap. "We were told to expect a visit this morning. Welcome home, sir."

"Thank you, John," he said, urging his own mount forward and extending his right hand. "May I be honest with you? I'm here to throw myself on your mercy. Is there anything you'd like me to see here today?"

"Well, uh, Miss Seavers could…" Cummings shot a quick glance toward Charlotte, who, Rafe noticed, quickly shook her head. "That is to say, it would be my pleasure, Your Grace, to show you our much-improved sawmill. We've…uh, I've instituted some changes since His Grace's sad death, and accidents have been reduced more than half. I'm happy to inform Your Grace that we haven't lost a finger or a hand in more than six months."

Rafe looked toward Charlotte, whose cheeks had gone faintly pink. What the devil was going on here? "Is that so, John. Very commendable on your part, I'm sure. I should very much like to see these improvements."

"I'll leave you two to get at it, then," Charlotte said, already turning her mount.

Rafe grabbed at the reins. He needed to find out what the devil was happening here. "Oh, no, please, Miss Seavers, I wouldn't dream of allowing you to return to Ashurst Hall unescorted. I fear I must insist that you accompany us."

She smiled with her mouth as she skewered him with those intelligent eyes. "I'd be honored, Your Grace."

They followed John Cummings to the sawmill, passing the long single line of workers who variously waved their caps in the air or tugged their forelocks, depending on their age and station in the pecking order, Rafe imagined. "Your Grace, welcome home." He heard that all along the way; polite greetings, if not enthusiastic.

He also heard the loud calls to Charlotte. "Bless you, Miss Seavers," and "Long life to Miss Seavers." A small female child ran out of a cottage, most probably that of the caretaker of the sawmill, to present Charlotte with a small, scraggly nosegay of half-dead flowers.

As Rafe tipped his hat to the workers, *his* workers, he said with a smile pasted to his own face, "Is there something I should know, *Miss Seavers?* Something *else* I should know about the months between my uncle's demise and my arrival at Ashurst Hall? Or would you rather I encounter these little surprises everywhere I go?"

"Oh, all right, Rafe," she said rather wearily. "Emmaline was first taken with her grief, and then with…well, then the Duke of Warrington. John Cummings is a good man, but even good men need direction. I was…I was available."

"And willing. You always did have a talent for putting your nose in wherever you could, didn't you? I have to say I'm not surprised to learn that you've been busily running Ashurst Hall in my absence, although I wish Emmaline would have informed me of that fact in any one of her letters."

"Would you have returned home sooner, eager to relieve me of the chore, or to toss me out on my ear?"

"One of the two, yes. What was Emmaline thinking?"

"I'm sure I couldn't speak for your aunt. But as the woman betrothed to your cousin Harold, I suppose it seemed natural to some that I—"

"Excuse us a moment," Rafe called to John Cummings, who had already dismounted in front of the sawmill. He then grabbed Charlotte's horse's reins and turned both horses so that they were cantering once more back the way they had come. He reined in once they were a good two hundred yards away, hopped down from his horse, and had Charlotte standing on the ground beside him before she could mount a protest.

"Say that again," he ordered tersely.

"Honestly, Rafe, I don't remember you being so dramatic," Charlotte said, her head bent as if inspecting the nosegay still clutched in her gloved hand. "I said, as your cousin Harold's betrothed—"

"I heard what you said, damn it." Rafe cut her off, more angry than he could understand. He could barely see her through the red glare in front of his eyes. Charlie, his Charlie, betrothed to that sadistic bastard Harold? He wanted to throw up, hit something, scream out curses to the sky. Somehow, he only said, "Now explain to me why you didn't tell me this yesterday."

She clutched her riding crop almost defensively. "I didn't think it was important."

"Not important? You were going to be my cousin's wife, and you didn't think it was *important?*"

"It…it had been a very recent development, Rafe. We weren't engaged much above a fortnight before Harold died."

"Drowning in a bunk on his brother's yacht while celebrating his engagement to the woman he loved, no doubt, by cavorting with a prostitute. You couldn't have been cheered when Mr. Hobart shared that bit of information with you and Emmaline."

Charlotte shrugged, finally tearing her gaze from the flowers. "It wasn't like that. It wasn't to be that sort of marriage. I had no illusions."

Rafe shook his head, trying to understand. "So why? Why did you accept his suit?"

"I don't have to answer that," Charlotte said, her eyes flashing a warning Rafe couldn't ignore. "But I will answer, because it's clear to me that you're thick as a plank. The duke wanted Rose Cottage, just as he's always done, as his father before him had done. Papa finally agreed. The marriage…the marriage was meant to seal the arrangement. A sort of dowry. Such arrangements aren't unheard of, and I was already past the age of being considered an eligible debutante. It…it seemed a reasonable compromise."

"And you also agreed? You were willing to be a part of the bargain?"

She didn't quite meet his eyes as she answered him. "A second son is never a prime prize, but the second son of a duke is not to be sneezed at. And, as you have already pointed out, I am nearly two and twenty now, and marriage to Harold, who wouldn't bother me for long at any rate before seeking out the joys of London, beats leading apes in Hell all to flinders. Yes, Rafe, much as it's obvious to me that you don't want to hear me say the words, I agreed. Now stop goggling at me as if you've never seen me before, and let us return to John Cummings. At the moment, you look ridiculous."

Rafe rubbed at his lower jaw as he continued to look down at Charlotte for long moments. "No. I don't believe this. I don't believe you'd agree to a marriage with Harold, no matter how sensible a compromise it might be to some eyes. There's something wrong here, Charlie."

"There's nothing wrong here, Rafe, except that another man would be thanking me for my help these past difficult months, and not treating me to a near Inquisition," Charlotte said, turning to grab hold of the pommel with both hands. "Now make a step for me, if you please, Your Grace."

"We're not done discussing this, Charlie. Not by a long chalk."

"I am," she said curtly. "Are you going to assist me or not?"

"I will, but only because John Cummings and half the people on this estate are probably staring down the road at us. I mean it, Charlie. This isn't over."

"*It*, as you call the thing, was over when your cousin died. And none of it concerns you."

"The hell it doesn't. Give me your damned foot."

He threaded his fingers together and bent down, allowing her to place one booted foot onto his joined hands as she boosted herself back up on the sidesaddle.

He looked up at her for another long moment before remounting his own horse, which danced in a full circle as if no longer sure where its master may wish to next proceed.

Which was when Rafe's curly-brimmed beaver suddenly flew off his head and onto the ground.

"Rafe!" Charlotte yelled, her own mount now dancing light-footedly as the crack of the rifle shot seemed to bounce back and forth against the trees on either side of the narrow roadway.

He was beside her in a moment, his swift reaction to the gunfire born of long years and many battlefields. He grabbed her at the waist and pulled her off her mount even as he kicked his feet free of the stirrups. Together, putting his body between hers and that of the hard ground, they crashed to the roadway.

Rafe rolled over, shielding her body with his, even as he looked first to the left side of the roadway, then to the right.

He counted to ten. Then twenty.

There was no second shot.

Beneath him, Charlotte was attempting to regain her breath, which had been knocked out of her by the force of their joint plunge to the ground. "What… what…"

Rafe reached out to pull his hat closer to them and saw the two holes in the thing, one an entry point, the other where the ball had passed through on its way out again. An inch lower, and his head would have stopped the ball from making that exit.

"Interesting," he said, pretty much to himself. "Not amusing, but interesting."

"Interesting?" Charlotte pushed at him with her fists. "Get off me, you great hulk. You were almost killed just now. *Interesting?*"

"Must I?" he asked, trying to divert her even as his gaze concentrated on her full mouth. "I find I rather like where I am."

By this time, though, John Cummings and some others had reacted and were fast approaching along the roadway, leaving Rafe no choice but to help Charlotte to her feet.

"It was a poacher, Charlie," he told her quickly as she brushed off her skirt and tried to adjust her hat. "A poacher, someone out hunting. Nothing more than an accident, an errant shot."

"You can't know that. Somebody may have tried to kill you."

"And you want to share that theory with John Cummings?"

She looked at him for a long moment, and then shook her head. "No. I suppose not. But we will talk about this, Rafe."

"We're going to talk about a lot of things, Charlie," he told her, and then stepped forward, raising his arms to indicate that he was all right.

CHAPTER FIVE

FITZ POKED HIS INDEX FINGER through one of the holes in Rafe's now thoroughly ruined hat.

"Tell me again," he said, looking at Rafe.

"I don't have to tell you again. The roadway is flanked by fairly deep woods on either side. And, since Boney was twirling around like some dervish at the time the shot was fired, I've no clear idea which side of the roadway the ball came from in any event."

"So you made no pursuit?"

"Pursuit of what, Fitz?" Rafe said, rubbing his glass of wine between his palms as he stood beside the mantel. "There are only two conclusions. A poacher with dreadful aim, or somebody was trying to kill me."

"Or Charlotte," Fitz said, and then shook his head. "No, not her. Had to be you. Are you certain there aren't any other male Daughtrys out there looking for a dukedom or whatever it's called? What did Charlotte say?"

"She hasn't said much of anything, because I've been avoiding her ever since it happened," Rafe told him. "I passed the whole thing off as an accident and then we went on to the sawmill to make complimentary noises about a saw blade as high as that bed you're lying in, and that was that."

"And do you think that was wise? Not rounding up several dozen men and sending them to flush through these woods to find whoever had taken that shot at you, I mean?"

"At me, at a rabbit."

"You don't look like a rabbit. You're taller. Although perhaps there is some slight resemblance around the ears…."

Rafe smiled. "Point taken, thank you. In any event, I'm not going to lose sleep thinking someone is out to murder me." He hesitated, and then decided to tell Fitz what was really bothering him. "I've got something far more serious pressing on my mind at the moment."

"Here now, that sounds ominous." Fitz tried to lever himself up against the mound of pillows, but then winced and gave it up as a bad idea. "Shall I pull the bed curtains between us and play Father Confessor?"

"This isn't a confession, Fitz. It's something I learned and wish now that I hadn't." Rafe pulled up a straight-back chair and turned it about to straddle it. He leaned his chin on his crossed arms and looked at his friend. "Charlie was betrothed to my cousin Harold at the time he died."

Fitz frowned and remained silent for a few moments, then shook his head. "No, I'm sorry. I don't understand. This news upsets you? Why?"

"If I knew the answer to that, my friend, you'd have been the first to know of it. Why didn't she tell me, Fitz? She had ample opportunity. When I questioned why Emmaline left her in charge when she went off with her new husband, for one. And not just then. She had any number of opportunities to say, here now, Rafe, did you know I was all set to be bracketed to your cousin before he turned into food for the fishes?"

"And she would have doubtless said it just that way, too," Fitz said, smiling. "Betrothed is more than half as good as being married itself. Do you suppose they—you know?"

Rafe pushed himself back on the chair and got to his feet. "No, Fitz, I do *not* know. At least I don't want to know, and you'll oblige me by not saying anything remotely like that again."

"Really now? You know what I think, Rafe? I think you sound…jealous."

"That's ridiculous," Rafe said quickly. "It's just that Harold was such a— No, I shouldn't speak ill of the dead."

"Even if the man was such a—what? Boor? Bubble-head? Bully? Brute? That's the *B*'s. What else could you mean? Give me a hint here, Rafe. Give me a letter."

"*L*," Rafe said quietly. "Licentious. Libertine. Loose-screwed. Immoral. Debauched. *Cruel.*"

"You can stop now, that's enough of the alphabet. The man was beneath contempt, correct?"

"I thought so. Actually, I'd thought he was a braggart, both he and George, always weaving fantastical tales of their vast sexual escapades for their gullible younger cousin. But then I caught Harold out in the stables, in-dulging his…appetites."

"That sounds like something *I* don't want to hear. Still, I think you'd better tell me, if I'm to understand why his betrothal to Charlotte has upset you so much."

"All right, but it isn't pretty. One night as I returned late from a trip to the village, I heard someone whimpering in one of the stalls and investigated. I discovered Harold riding one of the kitchen maids like a damned horse even as he whipped at her bare backside with his riding crop. Christ, he'd draped a bridle over her and forced the bit between her teeth."

"Not a pretty picture you're drawing for me, my friend."

"No, it wasn't." Rafe rubbed at his temples, rubbing away the mental image his words had brought back to the surface. "Harold was a big man, but with his breeches caught around his knees it wasn't even a fair fight. I damn near killed him, Fitz, beating him unconscious with his own riding crop. It took three grooms to pull me off him."

"I'd have held them back for you even while I cheered you on."

Rafe smiled weakly. "I know you would have, and we could have been hanged together. In any event, that's when the duke bought me my commission. I left Ashurst Hall two mornings later at dawn, and never saw Harold or George or my uncle again."

"You know what I'm thinking, Rafe? I'm thinking I finally understand why I've heard so little about your family these past years. But let me see if I understand this. The duke *rewarded* you for horsewhipping his son?"

Rafe looked at his friend. "No, not quite. I was young, Fitz, and a hothead. When I found out that the stables were often Harold's *playing* ground, I warned the duke that if I ever caught out Harold mistreating a woman again, I'd make sure I killed him. I think my uncle both believed me and believed that Harold would continue to indulge himself with any woman he fancied, willing or otherwise. Which, by the way, the duke assured me was nothing out of the ordinary for healthy young gentlemen, and that the maid probably enjoyed the exercise. *Go die or grow up,* that's what the duke told me to do. To my uncle, you understand, *I* was the one who'd been in the wrong. Harold was simply doing what men do."

"What soulless bastards do, you mean. Animals. Would Charlotte have known about her fiancé's proclivities, do you think?"

Shrugging his shoulders, Rafe sighed and said, "I can't know what she knew, can I, Fitz. But it certainly was an open secret that both George and Harold were every inch their father's sons. You said bastards? Do you know how many bastard Daughtrys there are around Ashurst Hall? I knew of at least eleven. My mother pointed them out to me, warning me not to accidentally marry one of them and give her grandchildren with donkey's ears or some such thing."

"Well, now, friend," Fitz said as he held out his wineglass to be refilled, "I really don't know what to say to you, or what you might want to hear. But what I'm thinking is that your childhood friend has somehow disappointed you. Am I wrong?"

"No, I think you're right. She admitted that it would have been a marriage in exchange for her father's land and her security and position. It wasn't to be a love match. I... Maybe I'm simply *surprised.* Shocked to think that Charlie has grown up to be the sort of person who would... Never mind."

"Trade her body for the off chance of one day being

a duchess? After all, only George stood in the way. That smacks of ambition, not an uncommon trait in females."

Rafe pointed a finger at Fitz. "That's not it," he said, cudgeling his brain for something close to the surface, but still hidden from him. And then he thought he had it. "Ashurst Hall. She did it for Ashurst Hall. Not the title, not this building we're standing in. The people, Fitz. She did it for a saw blade, and a—a new layer of thatch on the laborers' cottages, and a— *Was she out of her mind?*"

"I couldn't venture a guess on the state of Charlotte's brain box," Fitz said, smiling, "but I think you may have just dropped a few slates off your own roof, my friend. No woman marries for the chance to play at estate manager."

"You're right. She wouldn't have had to marry Harold to do that. She would have had more luck marrying my uncle. He would have had the land he so coveted, she would have had Ashurst Hall to play with...."

"You need to drink more, Rafe, or less. Either way, the state you're in right now is not conducive to clear thinking, I'd say. I'd further say that if you want to know why Charlotte allowed herself to be betrothed to your unlovely cousin, you need to *ask* her."

"She's told me she refuses to discuss the matter anymore."

"Oh, did she now. And you're going to agree to that? Captain Rafael Daughtry, who once hung a thieving quartermaster up by his ankles until he told him the whereabouts of the provisions his men were dying without? Captain Rafael Daughtry, stopped by a mere female in petticoats? I should have perished on the docks, rather than live to see this sad day. For shame, Rafe Daughtry, for shame!"

Listening to his friend's joking banter, Rafe at last realized what he'd seen in Charlotte's eyes earlier. Shame. Shame, and not a little fear. That's what he'd seen when she'd told him that she'd barely known George or Harold these last years. Any time George's or Harold's name was mentioned, that same look had crept into her eyes. Shame, mixed with fear. But why? Why? "Cut line, Fitz, I'm not afraid of her."

"No? Then what are you afraid of, my old friend, if you're not afraid to ask her?" Fitz asked in all seriousness.

Rafe's response was so low Fitz had to strain to hear him. "Perhaps I'm afraid she'll answer me...."

WITH THE DUKE IN RESIDENCE, Charlotte had informed the twins that they would once again be considered amply chaperoned and she was going to return to Rose Cottage and her parents. The same parents she'd sworn to secrecy the night before, when she'd raced home to have her maid, Marie, pack up her clothes and move them and herself to Ashurst Hall.

She knew she couldn't remain at Ashurst Hall. There was no good reason for her to stay, for one thing, no need for further deception on that head.

But that wasn't why she'd left the morning following the visit to the sawmill. She'd gone, fled, because she needed to breathe. She couldn't do so when Rafe was in the same room with her, looking at her, willing her to tell him things she didn't want to think about, let alone tell him.

Charlotte's mother, whose world consisted of her roses and her greenhouse, still barely realized her daughter was back, or that she'd left in the first place. But her father knew, and nervously avoided her, as he'd done ever since the night the Duke of Ashurst had ridden up to Rose Cottage to explain why the modest estate that had been in the Seavers family for six generations was about to become a part of Ashurst Hall. Why Charlotte was to become Harold's wife.

For five days, Charlotte endured her mother's vagueness and her father's shame, before confronting them both at the breakfast table. "The new duke has been in residence for nearly a week. It's more than time that we pay them a call, offer our condolences on the loss of his uncle and cousins."

Edward Seavers mumbled something into his cravat. Something that sounded very like, "Not while I have breath in my body."

Charlotte looked at her father, the man who had aged overnight, who had taken a blow from which, even all these months later, he had not recovered. She had once believed him her rock, her refuge. Now, even as he tried to hide his feelings, he had become her accuser.

"Papa, please, it's over. Lady Emmaline helped me locate the marriage contract. We burned it in the duke's fireplace and scattered the ashes. Rose Cottage is still yours. The new duke coming home can't change that."

"I'd given my word and my hand," her father said. "I'd given my daughter, such as she was. And I will never forgive myself. Rose Cottage means nothing to me now."

Charlotte looked toward her mother, who sat at the

bottom of the table, and saw that, once again, the woman wasn't listening. Georgianna Seavers had always been a gentle soul, prone to forgetfulness and vague fears. She, too, had changed in these past months. She'd begun talking to herself, for one thing, and sometimes when Charlotte looked in the woman's faded blue eyes, she saw a blankness that terrified her.

"Papa, Rafe won't take Rose Cottage. I know him, and he'd never do that. Mama will be safe here, I promise. We must go on as if we've nothing to hide, nothing to fear. Please, at least you can come with me to pay a morning call on the new duke. Mama seems more herself today, and well enough to come to the table. It's the perfect time."

"He's a Daughtry. How can we trust him?"

"I can trust him, Papa, because he is no more like George or Harold than you are. Rafe is a good man."

"Then it is even more imperative that I tell him, make a clean breast of things," her father said, sighing. "I once believed myself to be a man of honor, if nothing else."

Charlotte felt her body go cold with panic. "No, Papa, you can't tell him! I destroyed the marriage contract. We could all be sent to prison if anyone learned that I did that."

Edward Seavers pointed one long finger at his daughter. "You said he's a good man. A good man wouldn't have us clapped into prison. Either he's a good man or he's not, Charlotte. You've seen him. I only remember an impatient young lad chafing at his circumstances."

"You can't tell him, Papa. Please, I know you mean well, but think of me."

That's when she saw the disappointment in his eyes. It was only a flash, there and just as quickly gone, but she'd seen it. She'd seen it often in these past months.

"You still blame me, don't you, Papa?"

"No, no, my dear. Of course not. But if you hadn't gone out alone that night…" He looked toward his wife, who was admiring the way the morning sun filtered through the lace curtains, to make a design on the tablecloth. She was tracing bits of that pattern with a fingertip, smiling vaguely. "Let's not talk about this anymore, Charlotte. It's all too upsetting."

"Yes, of course," Charlotte said dully, realizing that her father had used her embarrassment to get his own way. Rose Cottage hadn't always been like this, a place of shame and secrets. She'd had a happy, even carefree childhood. Now her father looked at her almost as if he didn't wish to acknowledge her. And her mother? Ah. How many times had she wanted to go to her mother and be held in her comforting arms? "And you would rather not pay a morning call to the duke, is that correct, Papa?"

"Give him our sympathies if you should chance to see him, dear, and explain that your mama is not well."

"Yes, Papa," Charlotte said, pushing back her chair. "May I be excused?"

Edward looked to his wife, who was still intent on tracing the lacy pattern of sunlight on the tablecloth. "Yes, dear, you may. Will you be returning to Ashurst Hall today, then?"

"No, Papa. There's really no need. I thought I'd help Mama in her greenhouse."

"She'd like that. Georgianna? Did you hear that? Charlotte is going to help you with your plants."

Georgianna finally looked up, passing her gaze from her husband to her daughter. "Oh, hello. What a terrible hostess I am, not paying attention to my guest. Would you like to see my pretty flowers?"

Charlotte blinked back tears. "Why, yes, ma'am, thank you. I should like that very much." She helped her mother rise and, taking her thin, cool hand, she led Georgianna out of the breakfast room.

An hour later, after one of the maids came to fetch Georgianna for her midmorning medicine and a small nap, Charlotte used a stiff brush to ruthlessly scrub the potting soil from beneath her fingertips and changed into her riding habit, intent on taking her mare for a bruising, mind-clearing run.

She refused the company of the groom, promising she would only be riding their property and Ashurst Hall fields, and not venturing into the village or onto any of the roadways bordering the estates. As the groom knew he could not keep up with Phaedra in any case, he only nodded his head as he led the mare toward the mounting block.

Charlotte kept Phaedra to a walk until she was clear of the stable yard, and then only allowed the too-fresh mare a canter until they were out of sight of both the stable and the house.

"Now, Phaedra," she urged as she leaned forward, whispering into the mare's ear. "Now!"

The horse's ears flicked, and Charlotte could actually feel its strong muscles tensing as it gathered itself to explode into an instant gallop.

Her heart pounding along with the rhythm of Phaedra's shod hooves flying over a harvested field,

Charlotte kept her head low, urging the mare on, welcoming the sharp bite of the late-November air, willing all her jumbled, unhappy thoughts out of her head as the wind dried her tear-wet cheeks.

The low hedgerow separating Rose Cottage land from Ashurst Hall grew closer, but Phaedra didn't hesitate, didn't slow. Instead, the mare seemed to push herself even faster, and only at the last moment launched herself into the air as horse and rider flew smoothly over the obstacle, landing neatly far on the other side.

"Good girl!" Charlotte shouted against the wind rushing at her. "You want to fly, don't you? Oh yes, Phaedra. Let's fly away. Let's fly far, far away!"

Another hedgerow loomed and then was behind them, and then another, before Charlotte reluctantly slowed Phaedra to a canter, and then into an easy walk. She looked around her, at last orienting herself to her surroundings, and realized that she'd gone farther than she had planned, and was too close to Ashurst Hall itself to feel comfortable.

"Come on, girl," she said, turning the mare. "Time to go home." This time there would be no mad gallop, no exhilarating jumps over the hedgerows. Her mind was clearer now, yes, but now that it was clear, she needed to fill it again with some sort of plan as to what she would do next. She couldn't just run away from her troubles, appealing as that notion might be.

She approached the first low gate and urged Phaedra close to it so that she could reach down and lift the rope latch holding it shut. She hesitated as she heard the sound of hoofbeats, and looked up to see Rafe cantering toward her on his bay gelding.

She felt momentarily sick to her stomach—why, she didn't know. Was she upset because she didn't want to see him, or had she deliberately ridden this way in the hope that she would? She could no longer trust herself to know the answer to such questions.

He looked so handsome, sitting tall and straight in the saddle, the brim of his hat shading his eyes, hiding their expression from her. Was he happy to see her? Or was he still full of questions and ready to take this opportunity, out here, isolated from anyone at Ashurst Hall, to insist that she answer them?

She wasn't ready for that. She would never be ready for that. Giving in to impulse, she quickly lifted the rope latch, ready to flee. She'd learned to live with the look of disappointment in her father's eyes. But she didn't think she could survive that same disappointment directed toward her by Rafe.

"Hold up, Charlie," he called to her. "I was just on my way to pay a visit to you and your family. We can ride together."

Charlotte sighed and latched the gate once more, realizing she couldn't run from him forever. She waited until he'd drawn his mount up next to hers before she spoke. "I would ask that you postpone any such visit, Rafe. My mother is not feeling well."

"Still with that putrid cold?" he asked, leaning down to lift the rope lock before his mount pushed the gate open with its broad chest.

"What? Oh. Oh, yes," Charlotte said, easing Phaedra through the opening and then waiting as Rafe shut the gate once more. "But I'll be sure to tell her that you inquired about her, thank you."

"Do that, yes. I'd hoped to deliver an invitation to dine at Ashurst Hall. My very first guests, Charlie. I know I should be hosting dinner parties for my neighbors. The earl, the squire, the vicar. But I thought I'd start with you and your parents. After all, they've known me since I was in short pants."

"You want to *practice* on us, Rafe?" Charlotte asked, charmed into smiling at him. "How honored we are, I'm sure."

His wry expression delighted her. "Damn, you caught me out. Yes, I wanted to practice on you and your parents. But, mostly, I wanted to see you, talk to you, and offering a dinner invitation to your parents seemed one way through the door. You've been avoiding me for nearly a week, Charlie. Why?"

She gazed off into the distance, not really seeing anything, but unwilling to look at him. At least she had what seemed like a reasonable explanation ready for him.

"That's nonsense, Rafe. There was no reason for me to remain at Ashurst Hall once you were in residence. The girls are more than adequately chaperoned by Mrs. Beasley. I'm afraid I've been such a...such a fixture at Ashurst Hall since Emmaline married that the servants might look to me rather than you, and that's not right. You needed to establish yourself as the master of the household."

"Is that what I was supposed to have been doing these last days, rather than admiring millstones and tsk-tsking at poorly draining fields while pretending to know what I was about? Blast, Charlie, you should have left me a note. I had no idea. Obviously I'm lost without you."

Now she did look at him. His unaffected grin dazzled her, so that she was forced to frown at him and look away once more. Did he have to be so appealing to every sense she possessed? So delightfully full of foolishness? "You have Grayson, and Mrs. Piggle."

"Yes, about Mrs. Piggle…"

"Oh, dear. That sounds ominous. The woman can be overset at times. Did Grayson try to usurp her position with the kitchens again? Is she all right?"

"Overset, you say? Now, you know, Charlie, a man could be forgiven for thinking that you mean that Mrs. Piggle, when *overset,* would take to her bed and refuse to come out."

Charlotte bit her bottom lip for a moment, to suppress a smile. "One could think that, yes. If one didn't know Mrs. Piggle. Was it very awful?"

Rafe reached over and took hold of Phaedra's reins. "Let's stop here awhile, all right? Let me help you down and we can walk and talk."

He dismounted first and walked both mounts to a nearby tree, looping their reins over two low-hanging branches, and then approached Charlotte, his arms held up to her encouragingly.

She allowed him to put his hands on either side of her waist and she braced her hands on his shoulders. She raised her leg over the pommel and, Rafe still holding her, slowly slid along his body until her boots touched the ground.

He was looking at her rather oddly now, as if he might be able to see inside her mind if he only concentrated hard enough. She hadn't the heart to tell him that, if such a thing were possible, he wouldn't like what he saw.

"Thank you," she said, quickly removing her hands from his shoulders and stepping back a pace. Her boot heel chose that moment to land on a wobbly stone, and she would have fallen if Rafe hadn't grabbed her waist once more, pulling her toward him.

"Steady," he said, looking down into her face. "Fitz warned me I'd have beautiful ladies throwing themselves at my feet now that I'm the duke, but I never supposed you'd be one of them."

"Very amusing, Rafe," Charlotte said as she put her hands over his and attempted to pull them away from her waist. "And no different from the way you fell at *my* feet not so long ago. Now I suppose we're even."

"Only if I take that fetching hat from your head, toss it onto the ground, and do a jig on it," he told her, losing his smile. "Charlie…Charlotte. I really have missed you these past days."

She was very aware of his hands at her waist, the sweetness of his breath as they stood so close together. "I…I'm sorry…"

"Ah, you're apologizing. Then you have been avoiding me. Why, Charlotte? What did I do wrong?"

She looked up at him in some amazement. "You? You didn't do anything wrong."

His grin was back. "Oh, good. Then it's all your fault?"

She knew he was teasing her, but still she nearly burst into tears. She put her hands on his forearms as he held on to her, not knowing what else to do with them, frankly. "You want to know about Harold, and I don't want to tell you about Harold. So, yes, I suppose it is all my fault that I won't indulge your idle curiosity."

"Ouch, that was a flush hit." Rafe tipped his head to one side, looking at her assessingly, and then nodded. "All right, Charlotte—and notice I'm calling you Charlotte now, just as you asked. There are things in my life, events, things I've done I would rather you never learned about. It only seems fair that I offer you the same consideration."

Charlotte nearly collapsed, her knees had gone so weak in her relief. "Really, Rafe? You'll agree that we won't discuss my engagement to your cousin."

"I'd rather forget there had ever been an engagement, yes."

"Thank you, Rafe," she said quietly. "Really. Thank you for understanding."

Now he shook his head. "No, Charlotte, you're wrong there. I don't understand. I just know that if pushing you to explain means that you keep avoiding me, then I'll find a way to never bring up the subject again."

"Oh, Rafe, I'm so sorry…"

"No, no more *I'm sorry,* either. Here's an idea. I think we've been arguing, fighting, although clearly from a distance. Now we've cleared the air, so to speak, and we should seal our friendship again."

"You're insane," Charlotte said, relaxing her guard. "Because if you think I'm going to be talked into pricking my finger and mixing blood with you again, the way you had me do when I was ten, then I have to tell you, Rafe Daughtry, I am no longer quite so—"

His kiss took her totally by surprise, the smiling warmth of his mouth coming down on hers, cutting off her protests and setting small fires of awareness everywhere their bodies touched.

His hands left her waist to encircle her, pull her closer to him, and she grabbed his upper arms; needing to hold on, to anchor herself, because she thought she might otherwise fly off into the skies, she felt so light, so suddenly free.

And then he attempted to insinuate his tongue into her mouth, and Charlotte froze in panic, her entire body stiffening as she tried to pull back, push him away from her.

"Charlotte?" Rafe asked her as she lowered her head, hiding her eyes from him, her breathing fast, almost painful. "What's wrong, sweetheart? Surely Harold—"

At his words, his clear assumption that she had been kissed many times, kissed and probably so much more, Charlotte covered her face with her hands and turned her back on him.

"Jesus, I'm an idiot," Rafe said, putting his hands on her shoulders, and then removing them just as quickly as she flinched from him. "I should go see Fitz and have him kick me down the stairs with his good leg. Charlotte—Charlie—I promised we wouldn't talk about Harold, and the first thing I did after making that promise was to break it. Clearly you…you cared for him. Can you please forgive me?"

Charlotte dropped her hands and turned to look at Rafe in real astonishment. "Cared for him? Is that what you think? You couldn't be more wrong. I *loathed* him. Damn it, Rafe, can we please just not speak of this again? He's dead, he means nothing."

"He means something, Charlotte," Rafe told her quietly. "He'll mean nothing only after you decide to trust me enough to let me help you forget him. But for now, for as long as you want, we'll pretend whatever you want to pretend. So—let me tell you about Grayson and Mrs. Piggle."

She thanked him with her eyes, took a deep, steadying breath, and asked him to tell her what Mrs. Piggle had done.

"Ah, so you know that she would have *done* something, don't you, Charlie? And yet you never warned me."

"I warned you that you had to settle Grayson or else there would be a problem," she offered as they left the horses to graze and walked along the hedgerow. She actually had begun to relax. How did Rafe manage to so easily put them back on their once-easy, friendly footing? She didn't know. But if he was trying, then she would try, as well.

"A problem, yes. *Hell to pay* would have been more exact. She set fire to his bed early this morning."

Charlotte stopped, goggled at Rafe. "She did *what?* The entire house might have gone up in flames, for God's sake. What's *wrong* with that woman?"

"In her defense, I will tell you that she didn't *mean* to burn down the house. According to Nicole, whom I cravenly sent to Mrs. Piggle's quarters to elicit her side of the story, Grayson supposedly undercut Mrs. Piggle's authority by going straight to the cook for the week's menus."

"Not the first time he's done that, either," Charlotte said, sighing.

"So I've been made to understand. In any event, Mrs. Piggle burst into his rooms to confront him. Grayson objected—I can imagine he would, seeing as how she caught him changing his drawers. I shouldn't say drawers to you, should I? Sorry, I've been a soldier much longer than I've been a duke."

Charlotte tried to hold back a grin, but lost the battle. "Never mind that. Tell me what happened next."

"All right. The indignant Grayson threw said drawers at her head. She responded by picking up the small candelabra that was close at hand and tossing it at *his* head. Grayson used his drawers to smother the resultant small fire, and I'm caught between turning the both of them off or insisting they marry at once, as I believe seeing a man without his drawers compromises a woman. What's your opinion?"

Charlotte had been slowly shaking her head throughout Rafe's explanation. Now his question caused her to inwardly cringe at a memory of her own. "I would think that seeing Grayson without his drawers is punishment enough for the woman," she said in all honesty. "But, to be serious here, Rafe, you do have to do something. This feud obviously could turn deadly if it isn't settled."

"I know. If they were under my command, I could have them court-martialed, I suppose. As it is, and with both Nicole and Lydia very much taking Mrs. Piggle's side in the matter, I'm without a single notion as to how to go on. And Grayson has been at Ashurst Hall for as long as I can remember. They couldn't have been fighting like this when my uncle was aboveground. He wouldn't have allowed it."

"Everyone was rather afraid of your uncle, which made Ashurst Hall run smoothly, if not happily," Charlotte told him, stopping to look at him. "When he died, it was as if they'd all been handed their freedom in many ways. Everyone adores Emmaline, as you know, and they kept at least a semblance of peace while she was still in residence. But it has been, as you said, hell to pay ever since. I think you may have to let one of them go. Or both of them. Clearly this feud will never be settled."

"Yes, I thought you'd say that," Rafe said as they turned and headed back toward the horses. "Fitz said much the same thing. Will you help me, Charlie?"

"You want *me* to turn them off?" she asked, incredulous.

"No, of course not. But, with Emmaline gone, and with me having not a single idea as to what is required of a housekeeper for such a large house, I could end up hiring someone even less well suited than Mrs. Piggle."

"You know, on second thought, I'd hate to see her turned off. She is highly competent," Charlotte said, having a natural sympathy for the housekeeper. "And really not at fault. After all, Grayson goaded her into what she did by insisting that Cook is under his jurisdiction rather than hers. The rest, what happened after that, was merely…well, bad luck."

"The hierarchy of servants, I'm beginning to believe, is more strict than that of society in general. There is a definite pecking order—that's clear to me now. But she did start the fire."

"Not intentionally," Charlotte countered almost angrily. She took a breath, reminded herself that she and Rafe were speaking about Mrs. Piggle, and not her. Or at least Rafe was. "Grayson is equally at fault. Although I know it is always easier to blame a woman for every wrong thing in this world."

Rafe took hold of her arm and turned her toward him. "Really? Is that how you see the world, Charlotte?"

"It's how I see the world seeing it, Rafe. Isn't that why you men keep us from holding property or having a say in politics or earning our bread in anything but the most servile ways, or—"

"Or choosing whom you wish to marry?"

It was as if she were having two conversations at once, one with Rafe, and one with herself. "Yes, all right, if you must. Or choosing whom we wish to marry. We must be very dangerous creatures, us women, that you men feel this need to keep us so firmly under your thumbs."

"You need to speak with my valet. He says just the opposite. But we'll leave that for another time. Will you help me?"

"I…I can speak to Mrs. Piggle for you, I suppose."

"I'd rather you moved back in to Ashurst Hall. No beds were set on fire when you resided there to chaperone the twins. Just until I can sort this out?"

She should have known. Rafe never gave up easily, and never had. He would push at her and push at her, and because she cared what he thought of her, she would eventually give in, do what he wanted.

But not without a fight.

"There's no need to be that extreme. I can most certainly ride over every day. Besides, you are the one who must deal with Grayson."

"No, that won't do. I need you to *be* there until I can work something else out somehow. Please? As a friend? If I agree to deal with Grayson, will you return to Ashurst Hall? Mrs. Piggle is there for appearances—at least for now. Besides, I haven't been in female company in six years, or at a civilized dinner table, come to think of it. I don't think I can take another meal with Nicole and Lydia without having someone else there to speak of something other than how I am most certainly taking the two of them to London with me in the spring—which I most certainly am not, by the way."

"Ah, so that explains why you'd hoped to invite my parents to dine. You planned to use them to protect yourself from two girls barely out of the nursery."

"I know. I'm so ashamed of myself," Rafe said, grinning, clearly confident he was winning their battle. "I'm a deplorable duke, a coward, a white feather man, deserving of all your scorn. Will you do it? Please? I mean this, truly—I'd rather be back on the battlefield. At least then I know who the enemy is, and she's not wearing skirts."

"Oh, all right," Charlotte said on a deliberately melo-dramatic sigh. "I shouldn't, but I will. But only because you should be attending to more important matters con-cerning the estate, rather than domestic problems within your household staff."

"No, you're doing it only because you know I'll drive you to distraction until you agree. Again, I'm so ashamed."

"No, you're not. You're never ashamed. And, somehow, you always get your own way."

"Not always, Charlie," he said quietly, making a mounting step for her with his clasped hands. "But I also never give up."

CHAPTER SIX

NOW, INSTEAD OF RIDING over from Rose Cottage several times a week to check on the twins and meet with John Cummings on estate matters, as had been her practice since Emmaline married, Charlotte made use of the path through the woods to visit her parents, and then escape back to Ashurst Hall.

She hated that word: *escape.* But she was honest enough to acknowledge that she was behaving very unlike a loving, dutiful daughter.

Was she shallow, selfish, or both? An unnatural child? She knew she might very well be all of those things.

At the same time, she was also avoiding Rafe except for those times they all gathered for meals, or in the main saloon in the evening. Not that he often returned to the main saloon, choosing instead to keep his friend Fitz company.

Anyone would think the man was avoiding her.

Which, Charlotte thought as she bustled along the path she'd traveled the day she'd quite unexpectedly *run into* Rafe, made it easier for her to avoid him.

She knew what he was doing. He was giving her time before he came at her again with his questions. She was aware of what she was doing. She was taking that time, gratefully.

Since he was almost always on horseback, she kept to the path when she visited her parents.

Since he rose early to breakfast in the morning room before heading out with John Cummings, she took her morning chocolate in her bedchamber.

Since she knew he still longed to ask her about Harold, she chattered about inanities with Nicole and Lydia whenever there was a lull in dinnertime conversation, knowing listening to "female talk" made him uncomfortable and anxious to leave the table.

Even as one of the girls was saying something, Charlotte was searching her brain for the next topic of conversation, and the next. Which was why only last evening she'd ended up giving her permission for the twins to begin planning their London wardrobes.

Charlotte frowned as she made her way along the path, remembering the near bellow that had come from the head of the table when Nicole had clapped her hands in delight and crowed, "*See,* Rafe, Charlotte agrees we should accompany you to London when you and Captain Fitzgerald travel there in March. She agrees that we can't be left here to *moulder.*"

"I didn't say that!" Charlotte had protested, and then realized she probably had. "You have to go to London in the spring, Rafe," she told him, knowing he was trying, in his inept, male way, to find a way to be closer to his sisters. "The twins have never been off the estate as far as I know. It seems rather cruel to deny them a short trip to the city."

"Yes, Rafe," Nicole had said gleefully. "Cruel, that's

what it would be. Not to mention how dangerous it would be to leave us here to our own devices. You have no idea the trouble Lydia can get herself embroiled in when she's of a mind to do mischief."

"Nicole!" the always quiet, well-behaved Lydia exclaimed in embarrassment.

Charlotte smiled into her serviette. Nicole certainly knew how to toss the cat in with the pigeons when she wished to get her own way. Rather like her brother.

"Please, Rafe?" Nicole implored, pressing her palms together as if in prayer as she looked up the table at him. "It's just as Charlette said. We've never been *anywhere*."

Charlotte had expected Rafe to put his foot down, firmly, but after his initial outburst, he had mostly been looking at her, his eyelids narrowed as if he was deep in thought. And then he'd smiled, quite evilly, she thought.

"Only if Charlotte agrees to accompany the pair of you and keep you out of trouble. Charlotte?"

"That wouldn't be proper," Charlotte had said quickly. "Not to mention most probably impossible, at least for the latter part."

"Ah, but there you'd be wrong, Charlie, because it would be possible. Even probable. I've had a note from my mother, you know, in which she informed me that she will be joining me in residence in Grosvenor Square for the Season, so having you there won't be considered improper. Besides, it's the only way I'll agree to any of this."

So now Charlotte was going to return to London, this time to reside in the Grosvenor Square mansion of a duke, not a narrow rented house in Half Moon Street, which had been all her parents could afford for the single Season she'd had four years ago.

Although the twins would not officially be out, Rafe would be inundated with invitations to balls and routs, the duke's private box at the theater, perhaps a voucher to Almack's. Not that she expected to be included in those invitations, but it was possible. After all, she would be in the residence with the duke, and for all outward indications a guest of his mother; it would be difficult to ignore her.

And she'd be miles and miles from Rose Cottage and all the unhappiness there that she so longed to escape.

Mostly, there would be Rafe. Rafe would be in London.

"Clearly I'm out of my mind, believing anything will come of that, not once he realizes just how important he is now, as the duke," she muttered as she stepped over an exposed tree root, only to have the hood of her cloak catch on a low-hanging branch she knew was there and always took care to avoid.

She stood still as she attempted to reach behind her and free the hood from the branch, and realized that the woods were almost unnaturally quiet. She heard no birdsong, no soft rustlings of small creatures scampering through the undergrowth. "Drat, everyone's gone to roost. It's going to rain, and with me stuck to this stupid tree," she grumbled to herself as she tugged at the hood with more urgency.

The sun, usually reaching the ground more fully at this time of year with many of the leaves already fallen free of their branches, had slipped behind a sky that had somehow become one huge, dark cloud when she wasn't noticing, so that it seemed more like dusk than noon.

And then, as if obeying some silent command, the wind began to blow from the southwest. Not a breeze that would make the leaves skitter along the ground at her feet, but a real wind. The sort that howled through the treetops, bending them low even as it picked up fallen leaves and even loose dirt and small stones, whipping everything into the air and dancing it all about to some discordant melody.

The temperature seemed to drop all at once, as if Nature had thrown open a window on winter, and Charlotte shivered, her fingers trembling as she struggled to free her hood from the branch that seemed to pull away from her now, until she was forced to untie her cloak or risk choking on the strings.

Her heart was pounding as she fought to wrest the cloak free, even as her mind sought a reason for this sudden violence. She'd seen many late-November storms in her nearly two and twenty years, but she was certain there had never before been one like this, a storm so abrupt, with so little warning.

She'd read about just such a storm, however. She imagined everyone had either heard the stories or, as she had done, read Daniel Defoe's *The Storm,* which chronicled the devastation of more than a century ago that had swept across England. Over seven hundred ships had been sunk in the Channel, an equal number in the Thames. From Bournemouth to London, and beyond, the destruction had been terrible, with fields flooded, houses destroyed, trees downed and thousands of people dead.

How many of those unlucky thousands had been caught out-of-doors in the first blasts of the storm?

That storm had come suddenly, too, without warning, and by the time it had blown itself out two days later, much of lower England had been changed forever.

"Stop that! It's just a storm!" she warned herself, her warning swept away by the wind.

Wrenching her hood free at last, Charlotte fought to wrap herself in the cloak once more. She drew the hood close around her head, covering her face as dust threatened her mouth and eyes. She turned about, putting her back to the wind, and nearly pitched forward onto the path from the force of it.

She was in danger here, with trees all around her, any of which could snap at any moment and come crashing down on her. She had to get to shelter, and quickly.

Considerably closer to Ashurst Hall than Rose Cottage, Charlotte debated no more than a split second before turning into the wind once more and heading toward Rose Cottage.

Ashurst Hall was huge, made of stone, and could probably withstand any storm. But Rose Cottage was half-brick, its upper floor constructed with stucco and timber, its roof thatch, and completely in the open on all sides.

And then there was her mama's beloved greenhouse, with all its glass panes everywhere: its sides, its entire roof.

When she'd left Rose Cottage, it was knowing that her papa had just an hour earlier taken the pony cart to the village to replenish her mother's medicine at the apothecary's…and her mother had been in the greenhouse, repotting some plants. Her mother, who was blessedly oblivious to the majority of what occurred around her.

"Oh, God, please…" Charlotte prayed fervently as she made progress slowly, fighting the wind, moving from tree trunk to tree trunk, her cloak billowing behind her, catching the wind and slowing her progress.

She untied the strings and the cloak immediately soared up over her head and was gone into the treetops, leaving her clad in only her thin muslin morning gown.

The rain came then, a near wall of water that began all at once, hitting Charlotte full in the face as it fell almost sideways. She was instantly drenched to the skin, barely able to keep her eyes open against the sharp sting of rain turned to small daggers by the force of the wind, even finding it difficult to breathe.

Behind her, she heard a terrible ripping sound, and turned about to see the dead tree she'd just taken refuge behind a few moments earlier seemingly being wrested from the ground by its roots. It fell halfway across the path, its uppermost branches tangled in the branches of other trees.

She wanted to weep in her very reasonable terror. She wanted to find the sturdiest tree she could find and hide herself behind it, out of the dangerous gale. She wanted to curl herself into a little ball and cover her ears to keep out the sound of the wind.

Charlotte kept moving. With blowing rain nearly blinding her, with smaller trees down everywhere now, disguising the path she knew so well, she was afraid she might wander off it, get lost in the woods. But she kept moving. To remain where she was couldn't be considered an option.

And then, in front of her, she saw Rafe charging toward her along the path. She squeezed her eyes shut, disbelieving what she'd seen, and then opened them again, certain he'd be gone.

But he wasn't.

His head bare, his dark hair plastered against it, and dressed only in his hacking jacket and buckskins, his fine riding boots sinking into the muddy swamp that the path had become, he half ran, half stumbled toward her, was blown toward her by the wind.

His arms closed around her and she sobbed his name against his chest.

"Thank God!" he shouted against the top of her head, raining kisses down her hair and cheek. "Thank God." He grabbed her at the shoulders and pushed her slightly away from him. "Are you all right? Can you walk?" he asked, still shouting, but even this close to him she was having trouble hearing his words.

She nodded, and then shivered uncontrollably as she looked up at him, her savior.

He kissed her full on the mouth, and she clung to him, giving her terror to him, taking his strength in return. She had much to fear from such intimacy, but the storm had at least for the moment robbed her of those particular nightmares.

"Jesus!" Rafe put his arm around her shoulders, drawing her close against his side as he headed them both back the way he'd come, this time moving into the wind. Turned half-sideways, he tried to shelter her body as best he could, but Charlotte knew they were both still at the mercy of the storm.

As if nature didn't believe she had sufficiently gotten the point, the ground shook as a streak of lightning struck close enough to burn its brightness into her eyes. Somewhere close by a tree exploded halfway down its trunk, and she could smell burning wood.

"Rafe! What…what's happening?" she shouted to him. "Is it the end of the world?"

"Don't talk," he yelled into her ear. "Don't open your mouth—you'll drown." And then, his wet hair slapping across his cheeks and forehead, his face running with rain, the man smiled at her. *Grinned* at her. "Buck up, Charlie! This is no time to be a *girl!*"

Which, stupidly, caused Charlotte to begin crying in earnest. Just like a female.

Her face burrowed into his armpit, she gave up thinking, gave up worrying that a tree might come crashing down on them at any instant, and concentrated on the enormous effort of putting one foot in front of the other.

She'd lost one of her half boots already to the sucking mud, and the other slipped off her foot as they neared the end of the path. Charlotte didn't notice.

Free of the trees, the wind and rain were even worse, and Rafe staggered slightly before steadying the two of them and pushing on up the slight incline toward the rear prospect of Rose Cottage.

"Jesus-God." Rafe stopped pushing forward, if anything, his arm tightening even more around her.

With a real effort of will, Charlotte raised her head and looked toward her home.

Rose Cottage had several brick chimneys, two of

them at either end of the house, rising above the roof by a good fifteen feet. At least there had been two of them this morning. Now there was one still standing over the partially destroyed thatched roof, the second having toppled in the wind, to crash through the glass-paned roof of the greenhouse.

What was left of the greenhouse. There could not possibly be a single pane of glass left unbroken, and the entire structure, bereft of much of its support with the loss of the glass panes, looked less like a building and more like a jumble of twisted sticks that had been blown almost sideways by the wind.

"Mama!" Charlotte struggled to break free of Rafe's tight grip, but he held on, redirecting her to the front of the house and the main entrance. He pulled her up the slippery marble steps and pushed her into the deep embrasure even as he grabbed the brass knocker and beat on the door with all of his might.

It was no use. The servants had to be hiding in the cellars by now, and the sound of the storm would have muffled the banging of the knocker in any case.

"Stay…here!" Rafe ordered.

Charlotte could only nod before, with her back to the door, she slowly slid down it onto her haunches, too exhausted to lodge a protest. It was so good to be out of the wind, the rain. She could stay here forever and ever, and never know what horror might lay behind that door.

She watched almost disinterestedly as Rafe pushed his wet hair out of his face with both hands and looked out into the storm from the relative respite offered by the door embrasure. He gazed left and right, and then plunged into the storm once more, coming back to her a few moments later, carrying the cast-iron boot scraper in the shape of a hunting hound.

How on earth had he freed it from the foot-long spike holding it into the ground? One look at his face gave her the answer. Rafael Daughtry was clearly a man determined to find a way inside Rose Cottage, no matter what it took.

"Charlie! Cover your head with your skirts!" he shouted to her even as he raised the cast-iron piece like a weapon. Charlotte struggled with her clinging wet skirts to do what he said, turning her body away from the door constructed of thick dark oak pierced by a half-dozen leaded stained-glass windowpanes.

It took several tries, but at last one of the panes broke under Rafe's assault, and then the others quickly followed.

Charlotte got to her feet to watch as the spike on the bottom of the boot scraper was then used to break out the framework, once more marveling at Rafe's strength as he brought the heavy cast iron against the obstacle again and again and again. He must have been a fierce soldier.

At last he tossed the scraper to the ground and reached an arm inside the broken door, searching for the heavy brass latch.

She heard his low curse.

"It doesn't open? Someone must have used the key to lock it against the storm! Now what do we do? Rafe, I have to get inside! Mama— *Rafe!* What are you doing? Rafe, *stop it!*"

He'd reached down and grabbed the sodden hem of her gown and petticoats and was pulling all of it up around her.

"Don't fight me, Charlie. I'm too big to get through, so you have to do it. Raise your arms above your head. That's a good girl. Get inside, fetch the key. This is just in case you rub up against any of the remaining glass in the opening. Wouldn't want to scratch that pretty face, now would we?" he said just before he pulled the gown completely over her head, shrouding her in it.

Then, before she could protest, he picked her up by wrapping his strong arms around her cotton-pantaloon-clad thighs, and shoved her headfirst through the opening in the door. Rather like a human battering ram laying siege to a castle, she thought wildly. At least he'd been gentlemanly enough to break the glass first; she probably should be grateful.

She screamed as she felt herself bending at the waist in midair, her scream muffled by the material now hanging down over her head and arms, blindly waving those arms as she searched for, prayed for the flagstone floor of the foyer to come up and meet her.

Then she was rolling head over heels, landing on her back in a thud, all her breath knocked out of her and small shiny silver stars swimming in front of her eyes as she struggled to gulp down air.

"You going to rest there all day?"

Charlotte dragged the heavy wet skirt and petticoats off her face. She tipped back her head and saw Rafe's face leaning half-inside the opening, and realized that if her skirts were still all above her waist, then below her waist there was nothing but her wet and clinging cotton pantaloons that ended above her knees, and her bare legs and feet.

Rafe seemed to realize that, as well, and she watched as he openly raked her with his laughing brown eyes. "Yes, I'd noticed. Very nice, Charlie," he yelled above the sounds of the storm. "Almost as fetching as your round bottom as it passed by me a moment ago. And yet, much as I'd enjoy standing here with the wrath of Nature at my back, admiring the view—*go find the damned key!*"

She scrambled to her feet, slapping down her skirts as best she could, and raced to the small table just inside the doorway, pulling open the drawer with enough force to separate it from the table. If not for her grip on the handle, it would have fallen on her bare toes. As it was, the contents of the drawer clattered to the flagstone floor and scattered everywhere.

"Send a woman to do a man's job—"

"Shut up!" Charlotte shouted at him, dropping to her knees to pick up the large metal key. A moment later the lock was undone and Rafe had stepped inside, slamming the door behind him.

"For all the good that does us if the wind changes," he said as he turned away from the door. "Come on, Charlie, let's go find your parents."

"My mother," she said, steadied slightly by the feel of his strong hand clasping hers as they headed deeper into the cottage. "My father drove in to the village before I left to return to Ashurst Hall. Please God, he's still there, and safe. But Mama was in the greenhouse when I said goodbye to her. The storm came up so quickly, Rafe. If she was still out there when the chimney fell—"

"I'm sure she wasn't," Rafe assured her as they hastened down the hallway that led to the kitchens, slowing only to glance quickly into the rooms they passed along the way. By the time they'd turned into the short hallway that led to the kitchens, Charlotte was calling for her mother's maid, the cook, anyone who might answer her.

The kitchens were empty, the fire in the grate smothered by the tumble of bricks and soot that had come racing down the chimney as it toppled.

"We have to check the greenhouse."

"No, not yet, sweetheart. It's too dangerous out there, and no one will be upstairs, not with the roof about to come off. The cellars first," Rafe said as Charlotte tugged on his hand, intent on heading for the morning room, and the entrance to the greenhouse. "They're bound to have taken shelter in the cellars. Especially after that chimney came down. They wouldn't have stayed upstairs."

But the only person they found crouching in a corner of the cellars was young Bettyann, the Seaverses' maid of all work, her knees knocking together as she rocked back and forth, her eyes wide and wild and staring at nothing.

Rafe stepped forward to question the girl, but Charlotte had already turned and run back up the stairs, leaving him no choice but to follow her. "Charlie! You can't go out there!" He grabbed her by the arm and pushed her into a chair in the morning room. "Damn it, Charlie, I mean it! Stay here, or I'll tie you to the chair!"

She nodded, agreeing with him because it was easier. "Find her, Rafe. Please."

He squeezed her hand. "I'll find her."

She could see the wreckage of the greenhouse

through the French doors that, miraculously, had not yet shattered. Waiting just until Rafe had pulled them open and disappeared from sight, she tiptoed after him, stopping only when she remembered that her feet were bare. The broken glass would cut them to ribbons.

She raced back to the kitchens, to the rack of cloaks and the boots lined up on the floor below them. She stepped quickly into a pair of her father's heavy-soled boots and clumped back to the morning room.

Rafe was standing there, waiting for her. His eyes were unreadable, but she saw his jaw muscles working as he kept his mouth firmly shut, his lips a tight line.

"She's not out there?"

"I need something to—" He cast his gaze around the room, definitely searching for something. Then he walked to one of the tall windows and, with a mighty pull, tore down the heavy brocade drapes.

"Rafe? What are you doing? Whatever it is, I'm doing it with you. She's out there, isn't she? Mama's out there, and she's hurt. You can't stop me from going to her, Rafe, you can't."

He hesitated, looking down at her feet, and then nodded. "She's alive, Charlie," he said, stepping close enough to touch her arm. "She's alive, but…" He took a breath, let it out in a rush. "Look, I don't want you to see this, all right? I'll bring her to you, but you have to stay here. Promise?"

Again, she agreed. She'd agree to anything, if he'd just bring her mother to her.

Bunching up the draperies, he headed back out into the storm, the horrific sound of the wind and rain intensifying as he opened the French doors again, and then closed them firmly behind him.

Charlotte counted to six, unable to wait until she'd reached ten, and followed after him.

She could barely push the door open against the wind, and only managed to squeeze through the narrow opening before the wind, swirling madly inside the ruined greenhouse, shifted again. The door was ripped from her hands, the topmost hinge twisting loose so that she had no choice but to abandon any effort to close it again.

Still, with the greenhouse being on the leeward side of the storm, the wind was only half as fierce as it had been as they'd approached the cottage.

It took some moments for Charlotte to get her bearings, as overturned tables that had held her mother's precious plants and flowers prevented her from moving straight ahead inside the long, narrow structure. There were bricks everywhere, as if the chimney had hit the roof of the greenhouse and then exploded through it, showering the interior—and anyone inside the structure—with deadly debris.

Charlotte continued to pick her way forward.

"Charlie, get back! Damn it, don't come any— Oh, Christ!"

She'd nearly stepped on her.

Martha Grimsley's body lay half-hidden under a fallen tower of redbrick, only her lower torso visible. What had the cook been doing out here, in the greenhouse? There could be only one reason: when the storm had struck, Georgianna Seavers had refused to leave her precious flowers. And Martha, who had been the Seaverses' cook for thirty years, would never leave her mistress.

Charlotte stared at the lifeless body, unable to tear her gaze away until Rafe staggered toward her. She saw her mother cradled in his arms, one of the brocade draperies wrapped about her protectively.

"Mama!"

"She's alive, Charlie," Rafe shouted. "We have to get back to the— Christ! Charlie, *move!*"

She looked up, as Rafe had done, and saw that the twisted framework of the ruined building had begun to lean even more ominously. She stepped slightly to Rafe's right and peered deeper into the greenhouse. If Martha had been out here, then her mother's maid wouldn't have been anywhere else. "Ruth? Where's Ruth?"

Rafe shook his head. "We can't help either of them. And we need to get your mother inside. Now, Charlie— the sky is falling!"

She hurried ahead of Rafe, not stopping until she was back inside the morning room. He ran past her, as the morning room was now open to the elements and no place for her injured mother.

"The cellars, Charlie. We have to get her to the cellars."

Charlotte followed, stopping in the doorway to look back one more time, stupidly reluctant to leave the bodies of the two loyal servants to the storm, only to slap her hands to her ears as a horrible, unidentifiable sound seemed to shake the entire house.

The greenhouse, its metal and wood solidly bolted to the far wall of the morning room, gave up its fight against the storm and collapsed, taking most of the wall of French doors with it as Charlotte watched in disbelieving horror. Was the entire house about to come down on their heads? Rose Cottage had stood for more than one hundred years. It didn't seem possible. Nothing that had happened in the past hour seemed possible....

"*Charlie!*"

Not knowing what else to do, Charlotte pulled the heavy oaken pocket doors shut, leaving that terrible vision of hell on earth behind her as she rushed to Rafe and her mother.

CHAPTER SEVEN

RAFE WALKED INTO FITZ'S bedchamber, carrying two of
the late duke's crystal snifters in his uninjured hand.
He'd also tucked a decanter of the man's best brandy
into the crook of his arm. He said hello to his friend
before depositing everything on one of the dressers.

"A man shouldn't drink alone," he told Fitz as he
poured them each a measure of the amber liquid and
carried one of the snifters over to the bed. "Reading
again? You're becoming quite the bluestocking, aren't
you?"

"I will admit to learning a few things I didn't know.
Shall I bore you with my newfound knowledge?" Fitz
motioned with his head for Rafe to deposit the snifter
on the bedside table, and then closed the book, using
his finger as a marker, and held its cover toward Rafe.
"Your sister Lady Lydia was kind enough to bring this
to me yesterday, while we were all wondering when
we'd be hearing the hoofbeats of the four horsemen of
the Apocalypse thundering down on our heads."

Rafe looked at the book, frowning. "Lydia visited
you, gave you this? Really? What is it?"

"A retelling of the storm that all but blew this fair
island away more than one hundred years ago. Imagine

this, Rafe, if you will." He released his saved page and turned to the front of the slim book. "Now where is that? Ah, yes, here. This is how the man tells it.

No pen could describe it, nor tongue express it, nor thought conceive it unless by one in the extremity of it. No storm since the Universal Deluge was like this, either in its violence or its duration."

Rafe took the volume from Fitz and read the author's name on the frontpiece before tossing the book down on the bed. "Daniel Defoe. Well, Daniel, I can't agree with you. I couldn't describe what happened here, and I was in the middle of it.

"You weren't out there, Fitz. We faced some violent storms on the Peninsula, but never anything like we experienced yesterday. The entire episode seems like a nightmare now that the sun is shining so brightly. Except that two of our barns and several outbuildings have been all but flattened, all the haystacks were scattered to the four winds, I've got a half-dozen injured foresters, and John Cummings told me several dozen sheep are dead. It would seem that sheep, Fitz, instinctively gather themselves together in a low spot in order to shelter from a storm and won't move from it, even when common sense says to get yourself the hell somewhere else. So they drowned."

Rafe pushed his spread fingers through his hair. "Christ, Fitz, what a mess I've inherited. Give me a good war anytime."

"Yes, I see your point. It's a bleeding pity, that's what it is, you being the duke, and being saddled with this great estate and all that terrible money. I could weep for you, truly I could."

Rafe toasted his friend with his brandy snifter. "Point taken. At least this house is still in one piece, which is more than can be said for Rose Cottage. John and I rode over this afternoon to supervise the removal of the bodies. Rose Cottage looks like it took a direct hit from one of Bonaparte's cannon. I can't believe we got Charlie's mother out of that wreck of a greenhouse alive."

"How is the lady today?"

"Other than the very large bump on the back of her head and some fairly nasty cuts from the falling glass, I'd say she's much recovered, if still somewhat dazed. I don't know if she took refuge under that table on her own or if her servants put her there as the chimney came tumbling down, but even though she was pinned in place by it, that table probably saved her life."

"*You* saved the lady's life, my friend. That was a brave thing you did."

"I only happened to be there, Fitz, that's all. There were five fatalities that I've heard about so far. The two Seavers servants, and three others in the village who were mortally injured when their entire house collapsed around them. I can only wonder how large this storm was, how widespread the devastation. I think we've been spared a reenactment of Defoe's storm, thank God, but not by much."

Rafe got to his feet when a timid knock on the door was followed by his sister Lydia's entrance, followed by that of Mrs. Beasley, a gray mouse of a woman who might be forty or eighty, it was difficult to tell. The only thing he felt certain of was that being governess to Nicole and Lydia had the ability to age a person past her years.

"Ah, Lady Lydia," Fitz said in greeting. "Once again forgive me for not rising. You've more books for me?"

Lydia nodded, staying a good distance from the bed, several heavy volumes clasped to her breast. "I had thought, if you enjoyed Mr. Defoe, you might like to read one of his most wonderful works, *Robinson Crusoe.*"

Mrs. Beasley waited just behind Lydia until Fitz agreed that he would very much like to read the book, but would enjoy even more listening to Lady Lydia read it to him. Then she scooted past Lydia and took up a seat in one corner of the room before pulling an embroidery hoop from the knitted bag she carried with her and settling down as if she planned to remain where she was until Lydia quit the room.

"I have your permission, Rafael?" Lydia asked quietly, turning those huge blue eyes on him. What was she so damned nervous about? It wasn't as if Fitz was going to leap from the bed and compromise the child. The man was old enough to be her…well, no, he wasn't.

Still, he'd never heard that particular soft tone in Fitz's voice, not in all the years he'd known the man. And the smile he'd offered Lydia, the one she had returned so shyly?

Was he, Rafe, reading too much into a simple show of friendship?

Because Fitz would never consider Lydia in that way. Even though Lydia was definitely beautiful, almost frighteningly beautiful. Especially if you were her brother, and you knew you were responsible for her. Responsible for her, and equally responsible for Nicole. Responsible for Ashurst Hall and every person who lived there. Responsible for the ruined barns and the scattered haystacks and the laborers' cottages all needing new layers of thatch on their roofs. Responsible for every fallen tree and every stupid drowned sheep and...

"I see no problem, no," Rafe said quickly when he realized everyone was looking to him to answer Lydia's question, gesturing that she should take the seat he'd just vacated. "I'll just take this with me," he said, reaching for the decanter with his injured hand before remembering the cut on his palm, which led his thoughts straight back to Charlotte and how he'd felt when he'd realized she might be out in the storm and could be lost to him. "No, you keep it here. I'll be back later."

"Planning to tuck me in like some infant? Rafe?" Fitz asked as Rafe headed for the hallway. "Are you all right, friend? You're looking a little queer."

"I'm fine," Rafe said, trying not to look at his sister again. "I just remembered something I've forgotten to do. I must write to my mother and invite her to join us in London for the Season."

"But...but, Rafael," Lydia said, proving that, although she didn't talk much, she certainly did listen. "You told us the other night at dinner that Mama had already written to *you* about coming to Grosvenor Square for the Season. And that makes it all right that Charlotte comes with us, correct? Because Mama will be there, too, to lend us respectability?"

"Yes, Lydia, but now I must write to Mama with the particulars of her visit. I misspoke, that's all. I mean, of course she wrote to me, just as I said she did." He decided he'd better make his escape before he talked himself into even more lies. "Fitz, enjoy your story."

Rafe abandoned his snifter on one of the hall tables, the part of him that felt a clear head was necessary to him overruling the part of him that would like nothing more than to drink until he couldn't think anymore. He couldn't even keep his lies straight, not when Charlotte was involved. She was invading nearly his every waking moment, coloring his every thought.

He headed for the duke's—no, for *his* private study, and heavily plunked himself down behind the large desk. He sat forward, his elbows on the desktop, and lowered his head into his hands.

When had he last slept?

He'd been inspecting a fouled well with John Cummings and doing his damnedest to think of something to say about the thing that wouldn't brand him as brick stupid, when the world had seemed to go silent and the estate manager lifted his head like a hound and sniffed at the air.

"A bad one coming, Your Grace, and will soon be upon us. You'd best return to Ashurst Hall."

"And you?" Rafe remembered asking as the sky turned darker and the wind began blowing across the open field as if summoned to prove the estate manager's point.

"My cottage is just beyond this field, Your Grace." Even as John Cummings spoke, the wind intensified, so that both men were forced to clamp their hands to their heads to keep their hats from blowing away. "And you are closer to Rose Cottage, Your Grace. You might wish to shelter there, although you are of course welcome to come with me."

"No, thank you, John, but I think I will ride to Rose Cottage. It seems a good excuse."

"Pardon, Your Grace?"

Rafe hadn't bothered to explain that he'd been hoping to find a way to see Charlotte again.

And then the wall of water that could not be called anything as mundane as rain had hit them, and the two men mounted their skittish mounts and went their separate ways.

Rafe was drenched through to his skin by the time he rode Boney straight into the small stables at Rose Cottage, and then raced to the house, banging on the knocker for a full minute before anyone inside could hear his knock above the howling of the wind.

"Your Grace!" the maid who'd opened the door exclaimed even as she dropped into a low curtsy. The same maid whose body he'd seen in the wreckage of the greenhouse not an hour later. "Is Miss Charlotte with you, please? We're all that worried, what with her taking the path back to Ashurst Hall and all, and her papa gone to the village. We're just us wimmen here, and can't go fetching her, Your Grace."

Rafe didn't want to remember what had happened after that, when he'd learned that Charlotte had left Rose Cottage not fifteen minutes before he arrived, definitely not enough time for her to have walked to Ashurst Hall.

His panicked dash across the lawns, and plunging into the darkness of the wildly blowing trees.

His first sight of Charlotte frantic minutes later, looking so vulnerable as she fought against the power of the storm.

The way the wind molded her sodden muslins against her body so that they clung to her high, full breasts, outlined her long straight legs, all but defined her sex…

No. He wouldn't think of that. He would banish that image from his mind now and forever. Only a bastard bankrupt of any last shred of morality would look at a woman in such duress and see anything beyond her fear and the need to rescue her.

She'd held on to him with all of her strength, her shivering body pressed hard against him. He'd looked down into her frightened eyes, her pale skin drawn tightly over her high cheekbones, her full bottom lip trembling in terror and cold. He'd kissed her, in his fear, in his concern for her, and she'd kissed him back.

Rafe flung himself back in the leather chair, as if to distance himself from his thoughts. Damn, what was wrong with him? He wanted to tell himself that his reaction had been no more than one of relief, having found her safe and unharmed. But fool that he was, he wasn't idiot enough to believe that clanker.

And she'd been so brave. Through the worst of it, she'd never wavered, never dissolved into hysterics, even when she'd disobeyed him and entered the greenhouse, to see the cook's body crushed beneath the toppled chimney.

It had only been after he'd had Charlotte and her mother safe in the cellars, and had chanced several forays upstairs to fetch blankets and bandages, bread and cheese from the kitchens, that she broke down once more.

How long had he held her in the darkness of those damp, dirt-floored cellars as the sounds of the storm raged above them? Three hours? Six? More? How many wretchedly impure thoughts had he fought down during those long hours? More than he cared to think about, even as now, at this very moment, he swore he could still feel Charlotte's warm body pressed intimately against his.

Rafe abruptly got up from the desk and walked to the window to look out at the east prospect of the lawns surrounding Ashurst Hall. Two laborers wearing baggy brown trousers and gray smocks were busy picking up small branches and other debris and loading them into wheelbarrows. Otherwise, there was no imprint left by the storm on this, the leeward side of Ashurst Hall.

Rose Cottage hadn't fared half so well. Rose Cottage land, being nearly surrounded by the Ashurst Hall estate, perhaps once had been better protected from the elements, but one of the late duke's ideas of *persuasion* so Edward Seavers would consider selling to him had been the ruthless harvesting of all the trees on the western prospect of the house. Leaving Rose Cottage completely exposed to the worst winter storms.

When Rafe had at last dared to leave the cellars one more time, he found that nearly all the windows had been broken on the west side of the structure, and the furniture in those rooms was jumbled about, tipped over, the draperies torn by the sheer force of the wind.

But the morning room had suffered the most damage. When Charlotte had joined him, she told him that the room hadn't been a part of the original structure, but a single storey added by her father with the express purpose of serving as a retreat for her mother as well as an entrance into the greenhouse so that she didn't have to go out into the weather to tend to her flowers. Clearly the construction had not been on a par with that of the rest of Rose Cottage.

So now the Seaveres were in residence in Ashurst Hall, and would be for some time to come, while Rose Cottage was repaired.

Rafe raised his gaze to the ceiling. If he figured correctly, and he was confident he did, Charlotte's assigned bedchamber was directly above his head. He didn't know which chambers had been assigned to her mother and father, and didn't much care, now that he thought about the thing.

He shouldn't care where Charlotte's bedchamber was, either, but he did. He didn't want to imagine her in that bedchamber, sleeping, bathing, dressing. Undressing. But, again, he did.

"Damn. Blast and confound it, man," he muttered, bringing his fist down hard on the windowsill. He took several deep breaths, hoping to steady himself. "What's wrong with you? It's only Charlie."

"Well, yes, it is," Charlotte said, her voice coming to him from the doorway, the door he'd forgotten to close. "Shall I go away again?"

Rafe turned around so quickly he nearly lost his balance. "Charlie! I… That is— Oh, hell. What do you want? Is something wrong?"

She walked into the study and sat down in the same chair she always occupied when in this room, her hands tightly clasped in her lap.

"Wrong, Rafe? I suppose that would depend. If you're asking about Rose Cottage, I hear that it may be months before it is once again fit to be occupied, which you might consider unfortunate news for you, as you've volunteered to house us Seavers for the duration. If you're asking about my mother, I'm happy to say that she's taking nourishment and…and is much again as she was the last time I saw her before the storm."

Rafe attempted to put her at her ease. "I think Ashurst Hall is up to the challenge of housing three more people. And how is Miss Charlotte Seavers?"

She looked him full in the face in that disconcerting way of hers that meant that, no matter how hard he tried, he would not be able to discern her true feelings. "Miss Charlotte Seavers is feeling quite sad at the moment, yet extremely grateful to the Duke of Ashurst. In point of fact, Miss Charlotte Seavers cannot imagine her fate, or that of her mother, if it had not been for the extreme and even foolhardy bravery demonstrated by the Duke of Ashurst. Miss Charlotte Seavers, in short, is eternally in the debt of the Duke of Ashurst."

Rafe bowed, mocking her formality. "The Duke of Ashurst was only happy to have been of service to Miss Charlotte Seavers. In point of fact, the Duke of Ashurst believes his debt to Miss Charlotte Seavers for all her contributions to Ashurst Hall and the Daughtry family is still far from paid, and if there is anything else he may be able to do to assist Miss Charlotte Seavers, she has only to ask."

"Really?" Charlotte asked, looking up at him from beneath, he noticed, her very long, thick lashes.

He tipped his head to one side, immediately on his

guard. She hadn't just happened to have dropped in to see him, or even to thank him. She'd come here with another purpose in mind. And that purpose had upset her, drawn a white line around her mouth, put a shadow in her eyes. "Yes. Really. Why? What do you want, Charlie?"

"Well, I'd begin by asking that you never again call me Charlie, but why doom myself to disappointment. Instead, Rafe, I'd like to ask you to never, never ever tell anyone how we gained access to Rose Cottage during the storm."

"Oh, that." Rafe smiled as he sat down in the facing chair. "It was necessary, Charlie."

"It may have seemed so at the time. But was it necessary to pull my skirts up over my head?"

He pretended to think about the answer. "You mean *exposing* you that way? Is that what you mean, Charlie?"

She rolled her eyes. "You didn't *expose* me, Rafe. I was still…covered. I mean, if my father should ask you how we— I wasn't exposed, Rafe."

The thin cotton pantaloons had been wet through, plastered to her body, and made nearly transparent. He should know, because her rounded bottom had been mere inches from his eyes as he'd boosted her into the opening. He should know, because he could still see her as she'd looked then, and as she'd looked moments later as she lay, winded, her legs splayed out on the flagstone, her nipples, taut from the cold, easily discernible beneath the wet muslin of her bodice.

Hell may have been crashing down all around them, but a glimpse of heaven had been there, too. Oh yes, he'd noticed….

"Rafe?" she prompted nervously when he didn't answer. "I said, I wasn't…exposed. Now you say it."

He rested one elbow on the arm of the chair and slowly rubbed at his mouth and lower jaw as he looked at her. She was frightened. He didn't know why, but he knew fear when he saw it. What in hell did she think he might say to her father? Rafe also felt sure that no matter how he tried to reassure her that he'd say nothing to anyone, she wouldn't believe him.

Defeated, she frightened him. He didn't like that she so obviously felt vulnerable. It was probably time to make her angry.

"Rafe—say it. Please."

He dropped his hand and deliberately smiled at her as he got to his feet—for a soldier survived by knowing when to attack and when to beat a hasty retreat. Once he'd said what he was going to say, retreat would be the only sane option.

"You know what, Charlie? Now that you've brought the matter to my attention, I think I may have compromised you. In fact, when we take into consideration the possible damage to your maidenly reputation, and my responsibility as a gentleman to protect the gentler of the species, I think we should probably be married. See to it, will you, as you're so good at organizing things? There's a good girl."

He hadn't made it more than ten feet before one of Charlotte's black kid slippers missed his ear by at least a yard before serving a glancing blow to a brass bust of Zeus and falling to the floor.

That was another thing—Charlie had atrocious aim. The apple she'd once hit him in the eye with had been aimed, she'd told him later, at his feet. She'd once shot an arrow toward a paper target he and his cousins had nailed to the side of one of the barns. And missed the barn.

He bent and picked up the slipper, carried it back to her. "Are you done feeling sorry for yourself now?" he asked her. "We did what we had to do yesterday, Charlie, what was necessary. And what we did was between us. But I wonder—why would you think I'd tell your father?"

"I...because..." She took the slipper from him and bent to slip it back on her foot. "I don't know. I'm not thinking clearly, I suppose. The world is upside-down right now, isn't it?"

He looked down at the top of her head, something in his chest twisting almost painfully. "Yes, I suppose it is. But we're still friends, Charlie, aren't we?"

She lifted her face to him and he saw the brightness of unshed tears sparkling in her eyes. "Yes, Rafe. We're still friends."

CHAPTER EIGHT

CHARLOTTE CARRIED the tea tray carefully on her way up the back staircase from the kitchens in order to spare her maid the trip. Marie had steadfastly stayed at Georgianna Seavers's bedside those first few days, and now it was just accepted that she would take Ruth's place as both maid and, in many ways, keeper of the woman, who was prone to wandering off by herself.

She ascended slowly, as the skirts of her merino gown were fairly full and the steps were not only steep, but narrow and twisting. She could barely see her shoe tips as she attempted to keep the tray balanced.

Perhaps that explained why Charlotte didn't realize she wasn't alone on the staircase until Nicole appeared as if out of nowhere, colliding with her and sending the tea tray and its contents clattering to the stairs.

"Oh, for the love of heaven, Nicky—what are you doing, barreling down the stairs like that?" Charlotte said, watching as the silver teapot rolled down the stairs, spewing hot water everywhere. "Are you all right?"

Nicole shook out the folds of her dark cloak and grimaced. "I've cream all over me, Charlotte. Couldn't you have been more careful?"

Charlotte spared only another moment lamenting

the shattered china that had probably been in the Daughtry family for countless generations before she lifted her head and glared at Nicole.

Because Nicole was wearing a cloak.

"Careful? Is that what I should have been? Yes, I believe you're right. I should have been careful to tie you to your bedpost whenever you'd have to be out of my sight. Where did you think you were off to this time, hmm? Have you learned nothing since—never mind that now. Help me pick up what's left of my mother's evening tea."

"I'll get that, miss," someone said from behind her. "Heard the ruckus all the way down in the kitchens, all of us. Thought the storm was back, Cook did. She's still hidin' under the table. Crikey, such a mess."

Charlotte turned on the narrow landing to see one of the kitchen staff balanced on the stairs below her, holding the silver sugar server in one hand. "Thank you, no, Dara. If you'd be so kind as to fetch her a broom, Lady Nicole will clean up her own mess."

"Me? But, Charlotte—" Nicole began, and then quickly shut her mouth.

Charlotte had turned to glare up at Nicole. "After all, she has nowhere else to go and nothing else to do. Isn't that right, Lady Nicole? Here, let me hand your cloak down to Dara so that it isn't ruined any further."

Nicole's eyes went wide. "But then she'd see that I— That is, no thank you, I'd rather keep it on. It's…it's rather chilly here in the stairwell."

So, it was just as Charlotte had thought. She told Dara to fetch the brush and dustpan, waiting only until the sound of the maid's footsteps faded before saying quietly, "I should tell your brother, Nicole. That would put paid to any notions of traveling to London, wouldn't it?"

"Oh, Charlotte, no, don't do that," Nicole pleaded as she squatted to begin picking up some of the broken china. "I know I'm horrid and deserve any punishment, but Lydia is so counting on visiting some enormous book emporium while we're there. She'd be heart— *Ow!*"

Charlotte grabbed the girl's hand as Nicole dropped the shard of china, to see blood welling up in a fairly long cut on her palm.

"Come along with me," she said as the maid rejoined them. "Dara, I have to see to Lady Nicole's injury. But I'm convinced that she will be happy to mend those sheets I told you about, once her hand is bandaged. Bring them to her rooms tomorrow morning, won't you? Lady Nicole will be there all day."

"Mend sheets?" Nicole stomped back up the stairs ahead of Charlotte. "I'd rather scrub pots in the scullery. At least, thanks to you, I already know how to do that."

"Yes, you do," Charlotte said as she followed Nicole down the hallway to her bedchamber. "By the time you learn your lesson, you may also know how to pare mountains of potatoes and clean out fireplace grates. No wonder Emmaline married her duke in such haste. She had a choice of him, or staying here and allowing you to drive her into an early grave."

"I wasn't doing anything all that wrong," Nicole said as Charlotte closed the door and locked it behind her. "And my cut isn't all so bad, either. You can leave me to it."

Charlotte jammed her fists onto her hips. "Take… off…the cloak."

"Oh, all right." Nicole grumbled, and a moment later she was standing in front of Charlotte, clad in riding boots, an ancient pair of buckskin breeches and an equally aged shirt that had probably belonged to either George or Harold decades earlier. The clothing fit her like a second skin, proving that, although she was only sixteen, she was more woman than child.

The girl's near-black hair was scraped ruthlessly from her face and tied at the nape, the severity of the style actually drawing attention to Nicole's startling violet eyes and the rare, sculpted beauty of her features. There wasn't any man in the country fool enough to believe she was anything but female, and if any of those men chanced to see her like this…

"Oh, you dangerous idiot," Charlotte said on a sigh, feeling decidedly sick to her stomach. "Where were you headed this time?"

"Nowhere terrible." Nicole crossed to her dressing room and splashed some water into the washbasin before wincing as she lowered her hand into it. "No one would let me go see the damage. Rafe told us about it, but I wanted to see it for myself, most especially Rose Cottage, where those poor women died. I was only going to ride out on Juliet for an hour or so. The moon is nearly completely full, and—"

"Why would you want to see where Ruth and Martha died?" Charlotte asked, picking up the soap and grabbing Nicole's hand to wash at the wound. She may have rubbed harder than she should, but Nicole didn't protest.

"I don't know, Charlotte. It was stupid of me, wasn't it? But there's simply no excitement at Ashurst Hall. It's just one day turning into the next day, and Lydia isn't even paying me any attention, choosing to spend all her time reading to Captain Fitzgerald and listening to his outlandish stories. I'm bored to flinders, Charlotte, I really am. And you know what happens when I'm bored to flinders."

"Yes," Charlotte agreed, turning her back on Nicole, her heart heavy. "I know exactly what can happen. Let me find something to bind that hand with, and then you can get out of those clothes you'll never see again."

"Don't bother, Charlotte. I'd only have to sneak back up to the attics for more, so we'd both just be wasting our time, wouldn't we?"

"If your brother knew—"

"But he doesn't have to know, does he?" Nicole stood still while Charlotte tied a strip of clean white linen around her hand, and then began unashamedly peeling herself out of her inappropriate clothing right in front of her.

Charlotte knew she should tell Rafe. After all, Nicole was his sister, and he was her guardian. But then, if he confronted Nicole, she might have one of her rare flashes of conscience and tell him that there had been other times she'd donned men's clothing and slipped out of Ashurst Hall. She might, to get some of her own back, even tell him that her friend Charlotte knew she'd ridden out at night before because she'd caught her at it months earlier, just weeks before the duke and their cousins had drowned.

And then Rafe would look at her and ask her... No,

Charlotte wouldn't tell him that Nicole had tried to slip out of the house tonight.

"I have to ride out in the moonlight, Charlotte, when nobody can see me," Nicole said as she slipped a night rail over her head and fought her arms and head through it. She emerged with her eyes shining. "You can't know how *freeing* it is to forgo a sidesaddle and ride astride. Juliet feels it, too, I swear it, and when we take the gate into the west meadow it's as if we can fly. There is no other feeling like it, not in this world."

Charlotte held up her hand, cutting Nicole off. "You take Juliet over that gate? That's a five-barred gate. Nobody is foolish enough to test their mounts with that gate. Do you know what could happen to you if Juliet shied at the last moment, or caught a hoof and you both went down? You'd be out there, in the dark, nobody even knowing you weren't in your bed. Good God, Nicole, have you no sense at all?"

"Apparently not," Nicole said, grinning at Charlotte wickedly as she brushed past her and back into her bed-chamber. "Oh, stop scowling at me like some scolding old maid who doesn't understand what fun is because she never dared to have any of her own."

"Yes, that's me. The country bumpkin who has no idea of adventure or fun. Go to bed please, Nicole," Charlotte said tiredly. "Just go to bed."

"No!" The girl rushed over to Charlotte and grabbed her arm just below the elbow. "You're going to tell him, aren't you? I said something mean to you just now, and now you're going to tattle on me. I'm so sorry, Charlotte. I shouldn't have said that you never have any fun." She threw herself at Charlotte, hugging her tightly.

"Please, Charlotte. Please don't tell. He might take Juliet away from me."

"I don't think Rafe would do that," Charlotte said, and then sighed. Yes, he might do that. It seemed a fitting punishment, after all, and possibly the only way to keep Nicole safe.

Her face buried in Charlotte's neck, Nicole began to cry, hard, gulping sobs that would melt a sterner heart than Charlotte's.

"I have Lydia, Charlotte, and I have Juliet. They're all I've got. Please…"

Charlotte put the girl from her, looking at the eyes that reminded her of drowning violets. "We leave for London the end of March. Will you promise me you won't ride out on Juliet at night anymore between now and then? That you'll ride out only in daylight hours, taking a groom with you if you plan to ride anywhere other than the estate, and only using your sidesaddle? Because unless I have your solemn promise—"

"I promise! I promise with all my heart," Nicole said earnestly. "Oh, you're the best of good friends! I hope Rafe marries you, so we can be sisters. Wouldn't that be wonderful!"

THEY CARRIED HIM HOME on a gate six days before Christmas, John Cummings and four of the laborers who saw what happened and came rushing to the rescue.

Halfway there, Rafe decided he'd been coddled long enough and ordered the men to stop so he could get off.

"But, Your Grace, you struck your head," John Cummings protested as Rafe clamored to his feet, feeling only slightly woozy.

"Yes, John, I know," Rafe said, gingerly touching the lump on his forehead. "Believe me, I know that better than any of you. What I don't understand is what in bloody hell happened. Boney's never behaved like that before. No, that's not true. I remember another time not that long ago that I was forced to make a close acquaintance with the roadway. But I know how that happened."

He watched as John Cummings and one of the laborers exchanged quick, worried glances.

"Gentlemen?" he prodded, raising one eyebrow, which hurt the lump on his forehead, so he dropped the pose with a low curse. "John? Speak up."

"It was something with the saddle, Your Grace."

"And?" Rafe asked as the estate manager and the laborer looked to each other again.

"Not the saddle, Your Grace, not precisely. Somehow a nail got between the blanket and your mount's back, and when you climbed into the saddle… I've seen nails like it at the smithy, for shoeing the horses."

Rafe looked to his mount, the gelding being led by another farm laborer. "Is Boney all right?"

"Yes, Your Grace. I, uh, when we caught up with him I managed to pull it out."

Rafe winced at the thought. "So the nail was there ever since I rode out this morning, and finally turned somehow, to injure Boney when I mounted after checking on the progress at the mill?"

The laborer—Joseph was his name, Rafe remembered—scratched at the side of his head as he pulled a face. "Joseph? You want to say something?"

"Yes, Your Grace. I don't think wot happened is wot you think happened, begging Your Grace's pardon. I think wot happened is somebody put that nail there, just so, whilst we were all in the mill. Ain't no way you coulda ridden all the way out ta the mill without that thing stickin' the great beast that way. Ain't no way, Your Grace."

"That will be enough, Joseph, thank you," John Cummings said tersely. "Since His Grace no longer needs assistance, please head back to the mill, all of you. I'll escort His Grace back to Ashurst Hall."

Rafe thanked the men, taking back Boney's reins, and lifted the saddle slightly to see the wound left by the nail.

"Nothing really to see, Your Grace. The nail went straight in and came straight out again."

"And do you think it was put there deliberately, John?" Rafe asked as they walked side by side back to the main drive leading to Ashurst Hall.

"I think it's possible, Your Grace. Your mount was unattended while we were inside the mill. Not much of a prank, was it? Somebody's head will roll for this one, Your Grace, I promise you."

"I don't know that we can put this down to a prank, John," Rafe said after some moments of thought. "Not when I consider that I may have been shot at a few weeks ago."

"But…but you said that shot must have come from a poacher. Your Grace!"

"Yes, I am, aren't I? And in less danger on the Peninsula, it might seem, for at least there I could see the enemy advancing on me from the front. Have I made someone angry, John, do you think?"

"I…I really couldn't say, Your Grace."

"Of course you could. Tell me what you've heard. Forewarned is forearmed, you know."

John was silent for several minutes before he spoke again. "There were a few who thought it somewhat queer that all three of your relatives were killed at the same time, and in a storm that wasn't all so terrible as you'd think it would be to sink a brand-new yacht with its good crew."

"Really?" Rafe stopped at the juncture of the smaller path and the main gravel drive, out of sight of Ashurst Hall. "I think I need to hear more about this accident that took my uncle and cousins. What do you know, John?"

The older man shrugged his shoulders. "I don't know very much, Your Grace. Only what I heard all those months ago, when it all first happened. Your uncle's valet, who traveled to Shoreham-by-Sea with His Grace but remained at the inn that day? He came back to gather his belongings and move on, saying as how it seemed queer to him."

"He said that, did he? What else did he say, John?"

"It was only him, talking wild in his grief, you understand," John Cummings said nervously. "Nobody paid any real attention, seeing as how he'd stopped by the Bull and Grapes in the village while he waited for the mail coach to London, and was pretty much in his cups the whole time and all...."

"John," Rafe repeated. "What did the man say? If it was Richards, my uncle's valet for as long as I can remember, I know it wasn't anything complimentary to me. Let me hear it."

The estate manager sighed deeply. "He said you

were the poor relation, Your Grace, and that you'd always been jealous of your cousins, and even tried to kill the younger one, so that His Grace was forced to buy you a commission in order to save his sons from your unfounded hatred. He said the war was all but over—it was, sir, you know—and that it wouldn't have surprised him—Richards, that is—if you'd sneaked back to England and found a way to make that yacht sink the way it did. Or…or mayhap hired someone to do the deed for you."

"He said all of that, did he? Richards always did have a tongue that ran on wheels, and an imagination that raced right along with it. So now I'm a murderer, John, three times over?"

"There might be some who believed the man, Your Grace. Jumping over three dead men to a dukedom couldn't be easy, and yet it happened all at once, yes, Your Grace. And someone might be trying to give you some of your own back, as it were, Your Grace, yes, that could be it. His Grace, rest his soul, was not an easy man, and his sons less than useless—God grant them mercy—but they had friends here they ran with when they were in residence. Strange friends, Your Grace, rough and tumble and enjoying the carouse, you might say."

"I remember them," Rafe said, nodding his head as he ran names through his mind; George and Harold had been in many scrapes in their youth, some of them almost too much for their father to save them from the guardhouse. "So I'm to be punished, is that it? Frightened by a shot that misses when it might have hit, dumped from my horse on my pride, or even to snap my neck. It's one theory, John, thank you. And, since I have nothing more sensible to suggest, I suppose I'll have to make a visit to the Bull and Grapes one evening soon."

"May I have the honor of accompanying you, Your Grace?" John Cummings said, pulling himself up to his unimpressive height and trying without much success to suck in his ample stomach.

"Thank you, John. And thank you for the gallant rescue, although the gate may have been a trifle overdone. I'll see you tomorrow morning at nine, and we can continue our inspection of the repairs on the oasthouses."

"Yes, sir, Your Grace," John Cummings agreed, bowing even as he kept concerned eyes turned to Rafe's face. "No one from Ashurst Hall would think to harm a hair on your head, Your Grace. It has to be one of those hotheads from the village. Please, sir, take care, in any event."

"I'll do that, John. After all, we wouldn't want the third time to be the charm. Oh, and one more thing. Not a word of this to anyone. The nail could have been stuck within the blanket and then somehow turned, and everyone seemed satisfied that the shot came from a poacher. This will be our secret, John."

The estate manager nodded his head knowingly. "I understand, sir. I won't breathe a word of it to Miss Seavers, Your Grace. On my honor."

Rafe grinned. "You're afraid of her, too?"

"Afraid? Why, not at all, Your Grace. What would there be in Miss Seavers to be afraid of, sir?"

Rafe lost his smile. "Never mind, John, it was a poor attempt at a joke at best. I'll see you tomorrow at nine."

He walked Boney as far as the circular drive, at which

point a groom came running to relieve him of the horse, mumbling something about the head groom having already prepared a healing poultice for the gelding's injury.

"They know, then?" Rafe asked, pointing toward the house with his chin.

The groom nodded furiously and then turned Boney toward the stables.

"Wonderful," Rafe said, touching two fingers to the now-throbbing lump on his forehead. "Knowing Charlie, she'll have set up a cot for me next to Fitz, so as to make a more efficient sickroom."

He made it as far as the third step of the portico before the door was flung open and Charlotte was standing there, one hand on her hip.

"Look at that horrid bump! What did you do this time, Rafe?" she asked.

"You know, Charlie," he said, brushing past her, "if my dear mother had ever been even remotely maternal, I imagine she would have said something very much like that to me. But you're not my mother."

"I'm not your keeper, either, but you certainly seem to require one. One can only marvel that you made it through six years of war unscathed."

Grayson, just then passing through the entrance hall, snickered audibly before quickly clearing his throat and ordering one of the footmen to take His Grace's gloves and riding cloak.

Rafe hesitated between heading straight up the stairs to his rooms and ordering a tub and wanting to talk privately with Charlotte.

The tub lost.

"If you'd please accompany me to my study, Miss Seavers, where I'm sure you'll be delighted to berate me even more in private," he said, bowing to her in, he knew, a fairly insolent manner.

Without so much as a blink to indicate the verbal hit he had thought he would score, she ordered a basin of cold water and some towels be brought to the study and then followed him down the wide hallway.

"Fitz wants to see you at your earliest convenience," she said as they entered the study. "I think he wants to laugh at you for being thrown from your horse a second time. Poor man. An invalid, with so little to enliven his existence. He sends his thanks."

"I live only to amuse you all."

"Then I'm sorry to say that as far as I'm concerned, you're failing miserably in the attempt. What happened, for pity's sake? How did you manage to fall off your horse again?"

Rafe poured himself a glass of wine, having made his decision; it was time to tell Charlotte what he had concluded. If she hadn't fainted in the greenhouse, she wasn't going to turn missish on him now.

"I didn't fall off Boney. I was bucked off even as I was mounting, and with only one boot yet in the saddle. What happened wasn't an accident, or a result of my clumsiness. A shoeing nail was shoved up and under Boney's saddle. Still so happy, Charlie?"

He turned to face her, the glass in his hand. "What? You've lost your smile? I'm not as amusing as Fitz? What a pity."

"I...I don't understand. Wait." She instructed the maid who'd entered the study to put the basin and towels on a nearby table. She then followed the servant to the door and closed it, turning the key in the lock before leaning back against the wood. "Are you saying that someone tried to injure you?"

"Or kill me, yes," Rafe told her, taking the wrung-out cloth and putting its blessed coolness to the aching bump on his head. "I'll take care of this myself. Not that your touch isn't as gentle as the spring rain, of course."

"I'll ignore that, as you're clearly injured. Sit down, Rafe. No, not behind the desk. On this couch. And…and put your feet up. You should be lying down. And give me back that cloth so I can position it correctly on the bump."

"Charlie, stop fussing," he told her as she made to lift a soft velvet throw from the back of the couch, obviously planning to tuck him up to his chin like some puling infant. "I'm fine. I'm angry, but I'm fine."

She stopped fussing—which amazed him—to thread her hands together, clasping and unclasping her fingers several times as she looked at him. "I…I don't know what to say, Rafe. Why would anyone want to hurt you?"

"John Cummings has a theory," he said, removing the cloth to turn it, and then pressing it against his forehead once more. "I somehow arranged the deaths of my uncle and cousins, in order to step into their shoes."

Charlotte sighed. "Oh…that."

Rafe, who had been just about to lie down as Charlotte had suggested, remained seated, his spine going very straight. "What do you mean, *oh, that?*"

She pulled over an embroidered footstool and sat

herself down on it. "I mean, the late duke's valet, Richards, made a fuss about that, but I rather believe it was knowing that you wouldn't wish to keep him on as your valet that prompted his outburst. Nobody paid him any attention."

"John said Richards might have found an audience at the Bull and Grapes. I can think of a few who might have listened."

Charlotte frowned for a moment, and then shook her head. "No. You're thinking about the Martin brothers, aren't you? Joshua and Jacob, and their friend Samuel? They're gone, Rafe, all three of them, dead on the Peninsula. And Samuel's cousin Henry, who made up the remainder of George and Harold's horrid friends? He lost a leg at sea when a cannon broke loose in a storm. I doubt highly that Henry has sworn some oath to avenge their deaths."

"Then he would also make a poor candidate for hiding out in the trees in order to take a shot at me."

She raised one eyebrow. "Oh? You mean you're no longer going to insist that was an accident? Some poacher?"

"Perhaps not entirely. It still could have been a poacher. Someone aiming at a rabbit."

"A very *tall* rabbit," Charlotte said with some scorn.

"Yes, Fitz already pointed that out, thank you. But it wasn't until John told me about the nail that the shot began to take on a more ominous explanation. In fact, the day of the shot Fitz and I entertained, only for a moment, that the miscreant might have been targeting you."

"Me?" Charlotte rolled her eyes…those huge brown

eyes. "Why on earth would anyone want to hurt *me*, Rafe? People *like* me."

Now he grinned. "And they don't like me? Is that what you're saying? That it's entirely plausible that someone doesn't like me, doesn't like me enough to attempt to put a period to my existence? Well, thank you very much, Miss Seavers."

"Oh, be quiet," she said, getting to her feet even as he, being a gentleman, also rose.

She was caught between him and the footstool, a circumstance she realized at once, so that she stepped back, and nearly fell.

"Steady," Rafe said, grabbing at her elbows and pulling her toward him.

She looked up at him, blinked a time or two, and Rafe felt the atmosphere in the study changing, warming by at least five degrees. She lifted her fingers to his forehead and gingerly touched his injury.

"That's a horrid bump. Are you sure you're all right?"

"I'm fine," he said, slanting his head slightly, his attention drawn to her full, wide mouth. "The incident… both of them…could still be put down to accident, coincidence."

"Yes, I suppose so.…" Charlotte said, and then he watched as she compressed those lips, and seemed to have some difficulty swallowing. "Although it probably would be prudent to…to be prudent. Take, um, precautions."

"Probably. Ashurst Hall can't keep stacking dukes in the family mausoleum. We've rather run out of replacements."

"That's not funny." Charlotte attempted to tug her arms free and turn away from him.

He could let her go. He should let her go. He should stop teasing her. Stop trying to ferret out her secrets.

"Charlie?"

She sighed impatiently. "What, Rafe? I feel silly, standing here like this."

"I'll let you go in a moment," he assured her. "Just answer this one question, all right? Would it have upset you if something had happened to me?"

She looked up at him, obviously startled by the question. "Would I…? Oh, for pity's sake, Rafe, what sort of question is that? Of course I'd be upset. In fact, I'd be…I'd be— Is that all? I should go check on Mama now that I know you aren't badly hurt…."

"You'd be what, Charlie?" he persisted, his voice dropping to a near whisper, suddenly desperate to know what she hadn't said. "Sad? Devastated? Would you weep for poor dead Rafe? Would you wish we had… wish we had gotten to know each other better when we had the chance?"

She slowly shook her head. "You're impossible, do you know that? I never know when you're joking with me and when you're serious. If you're ever serious, which I very much doubt. We aren't children anymore, Rafe. You're not the poor relation and I'm not the pesty, probably quite obnoxious girl who chased after you like some moonstruck— Oh, let me go!"

"No," he said, lowering his head toward hers. "I don't think so. Not just yet…"

Her lips were cool, dry, and instantly pursed, as if his kiss put her in mind of sucking a lemon. But then, as he pulled her closer, she began to respond, her mouth softening, a sigh escaping her lips as she lifted her arms up and around his neck.

He wasn't going to make the same mistake twice. He didn't attempt to deepen their kiss. But it was damned hard to hold her like this and not want more. So much more.

Rafe raised his head, looked down at her questioningly. "There. That wasn't so bad, was it?"

"I don't think it's polite of you to ask me that."

He slid his hands down to rest his palms against the flare of her hips. "When have you ever known me to be polite?"

"I see your point," she said, and her smile decided his next move for him.

He pressed his lips to her temple, and then her cheek, moving slowly, cupping her face in his hands, careful to keep their bodies separated.

He took his time, advancing and retreating. He kissed her forehead, her ear. He lightly rubbed his thumbs along her jawline, watching as her eyes closed, and then he kissed those eyelids.

Her lips parted at last. He could feel her body begin to relax as she slowly granted him her trust.

This time, when he took her mouth she didn't instinctively stiffen her lips as if he might attempt to invade her in some way. There would be time to teach her the finer points of kissing, time to correct the mistakes his blundering cousin Harold must have made.

For now, he'd concentrate on easing her nervousness. His kiss remained chaste, unthreatening, and he broke it before he could forget that the purpose of the exercise was to calm Charlotte's fears, not stoke his own already-stoked fires.

"We're making progress, aren't we?" he said, a whisper away from her mouth as she opened her eyes, seemingly surprised to see he'd only moved a heartbeat away from her.

"I think so, yes," she said, and then, God love her, she smiled at him again. "You're a very nice man, Rafe."

"Only nice? Then clearly I wasn't doing it right. Do you think we should practice some more?"

"I think we should stop talking nonsense, and that you should go up to your chamber and lie down." She turned away from him, and then turned back to add, "And I wasn't afraid when you kissed me, you know. Not the first time, and not now, either. I was…I was merely…startled."

"Yes, of course. And now I suppose you're going to tell me that we'll never talk about this?"

She nodded, tight-lipped again. "Please."

"Then I'll take my knowledge of this strange inter-lude with me to the grave. Which, if whoever dislikes me gets his wish, may be sooner than I'm planning on, come to think of it."

"Rafe…" Charlotte began tentatively, and then shook her head. "No, never mind."

"Say what you have to say, Charlie, just as you always do."

"All right, even though I know I'll make you angry," she said. "I was only going to say that you may joke as much as you wish, but I want you to promise me you'll also be careful."

"Agreed. Now, how do you propose I do that,

Charlie? Hiding in my chambers doesn't hold much appeal."

She shook her head, sighing. "I know. But you were a soldier, Rafe. You should know how to proceed when the enemy is about, yes?"

"I do, yes. I proceed with a full regiment at my back, something I sadly lack at the moment. And before you volunteer, remember that you won't be allowed a pistol. You'd probably aim at the enemy, and shoot me. I still remember the apple, you know."

"If you refuse to be serious—"

"And there you're wrong, Charlie. I am serious, deadly serious. And I'll take ample precautions, I promise you. What I won't do is spend my days and nights constantly looking over my shoulder for bogeymen. The two incidents still could be explained away as accidents, you know."

"And I could be Her Royal Highness Princess Charlotte," Charlotte countered hotly. "But I'm not. Just as you aren't invincible. Remember that, Rafe Daughtry!"

She turned with a swish of her skirts and headed for the door, her dramatic exit impeded slightly when she depressed the latch and realized the door was locked.

At any other time, Rafe might have laughed at her comical look of exasperation, quickly followed by the opening and then slamming of the door.

But not this time.

He picked up the cloth and wet it in the cool water again before taking it with him as he went to sit behind the desk.

A large family portrait hung over the fireplace directly in his sight across the large room. His uncle stood on the bank of a picturesque bend in the stream that ran through the estate, a fishing pole in his hands, two hounds at his feet. George, all of sixteen or seventeen, lounged on a fallen log, an open book balanced on his knee.

"Probably the only book he ever read," Rafe said quietly before lastly looking at his cousin Harold, painted as he sat cross-legged on the grassy bank, his elbow propped on his knee, his chin in his hand. The picture of youth and innocence. But Rafe knew better, knew what his cousins had become.

Rafe got up and walked over to the fireplace to stare up at the portrait. "What did you do to her, Harold? You did something. *What did you do?*"

CHAPTER NINE

CHARLOTTE WAS MORE than aware that, while she was once more taking pains to avoid being alone with Rafe, he was obviously once more doing the same with her.

What a pair of fools they were, but maybe it was for the best. At least for now. He knew she needed time, and he was willing to give it to her. She'd thank him for that, but he wouldn't expect it, and she didn't think she could form the right words.

He seemed to know when she had ridden over to see the progress on the work being done on Rose Cottage, just as she knew it was safe to sit with the twins in the main saloon for tea each afternoon because Rafe no longer made an appearance.

They'd run into each other in the upstairs hallway one morning, and although they smiled and said hello, the moment was so awkward, so tense, that she'd had to redirect her steps to her bedchamber and collect herself before she could continue on to check on her mother.

The sheer enormity of Ashurst Hall made it possible for the two of them to continue avoiding each other. And all accomplished without anyone else realizing that their lack of contact was maintained only by silent, mutual agreement—unless one was foolish enough as to count Lady Nicole in that number.

Then again, at least Nicole only saw events as to how they pertained to her. That was one of the benefits of youth and innocence, Charlotte supposed.

"You know, Charlotte," Nicole commented with studied casualness the day before Christmas as the three young women worked together in the morning room, stringing bits of holly meant for a garland over the mantel in the main saloon, "if you were more accustomed to fibbing, you wouldn't have to avoid Rafe as if he might be carrying the plague."

"Excuse me?" Charlotte said, and then quickly sucked at her index finger, as she had jammed the needle into it. "I'm not avoiding your brother."

"Of course you are," Nicole said brightly, winking at Lydia, who only rolled her eyes and sighed. "And I appreciate very much that you didn't go tattling to him about…well, you know. And I've been very good. Bored to flinders I must tell you, but extraordinarily good. So you can probably talk to him again. After all, it's not as if you'd tell him *now,* because then he'd wonder why you didn't tell him *then.* See? We're perfectly safe."

"We are not perfectly anything, young lady. Misbehave again and I will go to Rafe so quickly your eyes will spin in your head like pinwheels, and damn the consequences to myself. Is that understood?"

"You shouldn't swear," Lydia said quietly, and then blushed to the roots of her blond hair. "I'm sorry, Charlotte. But you shouldn't."

Nicole frowned. "But…but then, why are you avoiding Rafe? Did he do something terrible?" She leaned across the table, grinning. "Did he try to kiss you? Lydia, look at her—she's blushing as badly as you. He *did,* didn't he?" She clapped her hands in glee. "Tell us. Tell us *everything.* We'll be fending off suitors in London in a few months, you know. Please tell us. Was it horrid?"

"Captain Fitzgerald swears," Lydia said, clearly not paying too much attention to her twin, which was probably safer for her. "He always apologizes very nicely, but he will slip now and then. Especially when we're talking about the war, you understand. That damned Bonaparte! Well, that's what Captain Fitzgerald says."

"Lydia, be quiet," Nicole warned, still looking at Charlotte. "Oh, he did, didn't he? He *kissed* you. But now you're angry with each other. Why?"

"We're not angry with each other, Nicole. Lydia, you were right before, you shouldn't swear, not even if you're only repeating what Captain Fitzgerald said."

"Sorry," Lydia mumbled, and then put down her needle. "I really must go now. We're reading Shakespeare again today, you know. Captain Fitzgerald is so funny when he speaks the lines of the three witches." She lowered her voice even as she put her hands in front of her, wiggling her fingers. "'Double, double toil and trouble; fire burn and cauldron bubble!'"

Nicole watched as her twin exited the morning room. "She imagines herself in love with him, you know," she said matter-of-factly. "Silly little twit, I do worry about her. She's bound to have her heart broken. That will never happen to me. Love is only for those who don't mind having their heart broken time and again. If any heart breaks once I am the toast of London society, it won't be mine."

Charlotte bit her cheeks to keep from laughing at this silliness. "You plan to be a breaker of hearts, Nicky? Really?"

"Oh, yes," Nicole said very seriously. "I've watched Mama, you understand. She marries because she fancies herself in love, and then her heart is broken when her husbands leave her."

"They *died,* Nicole. That isn't leaving her, not in the sense you mean. People do die, you know, and it's rarely their idea."

"When it comes to my father and his successors, I think I beg to differ. All three probably felt they were making a happy escape."

"Ouch!" Charlotte stuck her finger yet again at the sound of Rafe's voice behind her. She turned to glare at him, her finger in her mouth. "Don't *do* that!"

"My apologies," he said, bowing. "Perhaps I should employ a herald of trumpets in future? I didn't wish to interrupt, Charlotte, but your mother's maid is dashing up and down the stairs and peeking in corners as if she lost something, and I thought I would come fetch you and— Whoa, be careful, jumping up like that."

Charlotte, instantly thrown into a panic, shook off his steadying hands. "It must be Mama. Marie can't find Mama."

"And that's a catastrophe?" Rafe asked, frowning in confusion. "Yes, from the look on your face, I'd say it is. Very well then, let's go look for her. Nicole? You look upstairs, and we'll search down here."

"I have to speak to Marie," Charlotte said as Rafe followed her out of the morning room. "I have to know how long Mama's been gone."

"She's not *gone*, Charlie. Where would she go?"

"I don't know, Rafe," she answered dully as they headed for the main staircase. "Papa drove to the village to arrange for more thatch to repair the roof. Perhaps he took her with him, and Marie forgot. Marie! Hold there a moment. When did you last see Mama?"

The maid halted on the stairs and turned her tear-wet face to Charlotte. "I'm that sorry, Miss Charlotte," she said, wiping at her eyes with the hem of her apron. "I only closed my eyes for a moment, but I must have fell asleep somehow."

"How long?" Charlotte repeated, her heart pounding in her chest.

"Stop, Charlie," Rafe interrupted. "Can't you see you're frightening the poor woman?"

"Yes, yes, I'm sorry, Marie. It isn't your fault. But I need to know how long it has been since you saw her. Concentrate, Marie, please."

The maid looked toward Rafe. "I've been looking for her for a while, Your Grace, but she's…"

"Yoo-hoo! You can call off the hounds, or whatever. I've found her!"

Charlotte and Rafe turned to look at Nicole, who was walking toward them, leading Georgianna Seavers by the hand. The woman looked calm, unruffled, and Charlotte felt an insane urge to burst into tears.

"Mama! Where have you been? Marie was calling for you," Charlotte said, her knees nearly buckling in relief. The previous week they hadn't found her until they checked the grounds. Georgianna had been outside without a cloak, looking for her flowers. If she'd gotten as far as the trees, the results could have been disastrous.

"Hello," Georgianna said to Rafe, dropping into a small curtsy as she smiled at him with her lovely, vacant blue eyes. "Welcome to our home."

Charlotte felt Rafe's gaze shift momentarily to her, and she involuntarily winced, wanting nothing more than to melt into the tile floor. She wasn't embarrassed by or for her mother; she was ashamed that she hadn't told Rafe about her mother's condition. They were living under his roof; she should have told him.

But then he would have asked her questions, questions she didn't want to answer.

"I'm so gratified that you have invited me, Mrs. Seavers," Rafe said smoothly, lifting the woman from her curtsy and bowing over her offered hand. "'Tis a pleasure, ma'am."

"And you, as well, young lady," Georgianna said to Charlotte. "I'll have to be sure that Martha knows there will be two more places needing to be set for dinner. We're having roast chicken."

"Yes, Mama, that's very nice," Charlotte said as Marie rushed forward to slip Georgianna's arm through hers. "You just go upstairs and rest for a while. Martha will see to everything."

No one spoke as the maid led Mrs. Seavers up the stairs, but once they were out of sight, Nicole said, "I found her in the kitchens, Charlotte. Ordering the evening menu. She's right, we are having roasted chickens. Cook had sat her down at the table and given her a scone and cup of tea. Charlotte? She said *young lady* when she looked at you. Why did she say that? She didn't know you, did she? And she called Cook Martha. Isn't Martha the name of the cook at Rose Cottage? You know, the one who died in the storm?"

"Later, Nicky," Rafe said, taking Charlotte's arm. "Thank you for finding Mrs. Seavers for us. Come with me, Charlie. I think you need to sit down."

"No, I'm fine," Charlotte said, but she didn't fight him as he led her to his study and sat her down on her usual chair. "Really. I'm fine, Rafe."

"Here," Rafe said moments later, handing her a glass of wine. When she didn't take it, he lifted her hand and actually wrapped her fingers around the stem. She felt so numb, she allowed it. "Sip it slowly if you aren't used to it."

She did as he said, shivering slightly as the liquid hit the back of her throat. "Why would anyone want to drink anything so bitter?"

"For any number of reasons, I suppose," Rafe said, taking the chair opposite hers. "What just happened, Charlie? Nicky was right, your mother didn't recognize you."

Charlotte took another sip of the wine, as the first had seemed to soothe her stomach and make her feel comfortably warm inside.

"Charlie?"

She blinked back sudden tears. "I don't want to talk about Mama, Rafe. She is how she is, that's all."

"Then what I saw has nothing to do with her injuries at Rose Cottage?"

"No." Charlotte shook her head. "It happened before that. She...she's never been strong, you know, her mind, that is… Papa and I always took care of her, kept her from upsets. But she's been much worse since— Oh, Rafe, sometimes it hurts so much…."

Rafe put down his wineglass and went to his knees in front of Charlotte's chair, taking her glass from her and pulling her forward, into his arms.

His sympathy undid her.

She wrapped her arms about him tightly and cried into his shoulder, huge, racking sobs she'd not allowed herself in the long months since that night, the night her mother had collapsed.

"Sometimes…sometimes I want to go to her. I…I want to tell her that my mother is ill, so she'll hold me in her arms, so she'll comfort me and tell me everything is going to be fine, just fine. I miss her so much…."

"Ah, sweetheart," Rafe said, rubbing her back as he pressed kisses against her hair. "Why didn't you tell me she's ill? Why did you think you had to hide this from me?"

Charlotte pushed herself away from Rafe reluctantly, and dug in the pocket of her gown. She looked at him and sniffed. "I don't seem to have a handkerchief."

"At least I can help you there," he said, handing her his own large white linen square. "Go on, Charlie, give it a good blow."

She smiled in spite of herself. "Yes, Your Grace," she said, and then did as he'd instructed. "I don't suppose you want this back."

"There's my girl," Rafe told her, giving her one last hug before getting to his feet. "And you don't have to explain anything to me. I've seen that look before, you know, the one your mother turned on me. When the view outside your head is too much, some people decide it's safer to only see *inside*."

Charlotte took one last unladylike swipe at her tear-damp cheeks with the backs of her hands. "See only happy things, you mean?"

"Something like that. I've held my share of dying soldiers who thought I was their mother come to tuck them in bed, and a few who didn't look injured anywhere, but just took their minds and hid them in some place where they felt safe, where the ugliness and the horror of war couldn't reach them. I don't know, I can't explain the why or the how of it, Charlie, but we protect ourselves. We each find our own way."

Charlotte bit her lips together to hold back another sob. "I think you explained it very well, Rafe. Mama's mind took her somewhere safe. I…I just wish she'd let me visit."

He handed her the wineglass once more. "Here, drink up. You'll tell me more when you want to, if ever."

She shook her head, refusing the wine. "If I tell you one thing, I suppose I must tell you it all. Everything's… connected. And I do want to tell you, Rafe. A part of me does."

His smile was gentle. "And which part of you is in the room with me right now?"

"The part that knows you deserve some answers, I suppose."

"Then the part of me that wants to hear those answers is ready to listen." He sat down once more, holding his wineglass in both hands. "What happened to your mother, Charlie? Why is she hiding?"

Clutching his balled-up handkerchief in her fist,

Charlotte lowered her head and began to speak, slowly at first, and then almost quickly, as if once begun, she wanted the telling over as rapidly as possible....

It had been a lovely early spring day, and she'd ridden over to Ashurst Hall to visit with Emmaline, who had just received some new gowns ordered from London and wanted her opinion on them. She hadn't bothered to change into her riding outfit, but wore only one of her older morning gowns and a short pelisse.

She'd stayed for dinner, not really taking notice of the time, so that it was almost completely dark by the time she called for her horse.

Not that she thought anything of it, for her mare knew the way back to Rose Cottage on her own, and the moon was full. As she told the groom who brought Phaedra to her, she'd be back at Rose Cottage in the time it would take the lad to saddle a horse and accompany her.

That was her first mistake.

Charlotte had just leaned down to close the gate on the second field when Phaedra lifted her head and sniffed the air, sensing another horse in the area.

Almost before Charlotte could register that fact, a horse and rider appeared out of the dark, sailing over the just-closed gate and galloping off across the field, toward Ashurst Hall.

But not before the moonlight caught the rider full in the face. Charlotte recognized Nicole Daughtry.

"If Emmaline could find a way to do it, she ought to tie a heavy red brick to that girl's ankle," Charlotte muttered as she turned Phaedra around and followed after Nicole. She caught up with her as they entered the stable yard, now deserted, as the groom had most probably gone to bed in the low building behind the stables immediately after Charlotte left.

And with a few coins jingling in his pocket, she imagined, because he'd had to know that Nicole's Juliet was not in her stall.

"You're not going to cry rope on me, are you, Charlotte?" Nicole asked as she gracefully dismounted—and Charlotte saw that the girl had been riding astride, wearing man's trousers.

"I'd *like* to turn you over my knee and give you a good spanking," Charlotte told her, grabbing Juliet's reins. "You could have broken your neck out there, taking fences in the dark. So give me one good reason why I shouldn't tell your uncle what you've been doing."

Nicole immediately burst into tears. "No, please, don't tell him. He'll beat me."

Charlotte rolled her eyes at this typically Nicole melodramatic statement. "Don't be ridiculous. His Grace would do no such thing." But then she considered the man, and the situation. How well did she really know him?

Emmaline really didn't speak much about her brother, who was so very much older than her, a man who spent the majority of his time in London or visiting with friends. And, for all the times over the years that Charlotte had run tame at Ashurst Hall, she herself had instinctively stayed away whenever she knew the duke was in residence.

More important, Rafe didn't like the duke. He didn't like his cousins. They'd been friendlier when everyone was younger, but for at least three or four years before

Rafe had gone away, he'd stopped seeking their company when he and the twins were plunked down at Ashurst Hall by their flighty mother.

She'd once asked him why, and he'd told her she was too young to understand. Only on the day before he left to take up his commission in the army did he take her to one side, warning her to steer clear of Ashurst Hall whenever the cousins were at home, which, thankfully, wasn't often.

Then he'd given her the scarf he'd had hanging around his neck, kissed her on the forehead, said, "Behave, Charlie," and that was the last she'd seen or heard of him in nearly six years.

She still occasionally wore that scarf, and for the rest of the time it hung tied to her bedpost.

"Charlotte? You won't do it, will you? You won't tell my uncle?"

Charlotte shook her head, coming back to the moment. "No, I won't do it. Not if you promise me that you'll never do this again. Nicole?"

The girl nodded frantically. "I won't, I won't. I promise."

"All right," Charlotte told her, not believing her, but knowing that it was only getting later, and that soon her parents would wonder where she was. "How did you get out of the house without anyone noticing?"

"I…um…I left through the kitchens. Why?"

"Because that's how I want you to get back inside, that's why. Don't let anyone see you, especially not in that ridiculous rigout you're wearing. Go, Nicole. You've already been out here where anyone can see you for much too long. I'll take care of Juliet for you."

Nicole grabbed on to Charlotte, giving her a fierce hug. "You're the best of good friends, Charlotte. Thank you!"

Mumbling something about probably being out of her mind to have given in so easily, Charlotte tied Phaedra's reins to a post and took up Juliet's reins, leading her into the stable. She'd have to remove that ridiculous saddle, brush the mare down, locate her stall, fetch her some fresh water and feed—

"Well, hello there. I thought I heard voices. Come for a visit, have you? How…opportune."

Charlotte stopped in her tracks as she looked up into the startlingly blue, rather close-set eyes of the Duke of Ashurst's oldest son.

"Good…er…good evening, my lord," she said, dropping into a quick curtsy. "I, um, I'm looking for the groom, to have Nicole's horse taken care of, you understand. He…he said he would meet me here and…"

As she spoke, she began backing away from the man, who was so very tall and muscular in his London clothes, and who was looking at her so strangely.

With each step she took backward, he advanced a step. "Now, now, Charlotte, don't tell fibs. There's no groom coming, and we both know that. The servants know when to make themselves scarce."

As Juliet backed up with her, Charlotte felt herself awkwardly trapped against the mare's flank, so that there was no way to avoid George Daughtry's hand as he cupped her chin tightly in his fingers.

He turned her head one way, then the other. "My, you have grown up, haven't you? Had yourself a Season, as I remember, too. Didn't take, did you? Or are you still pining for my reprobate cousin Rafe? Too bad. He won't ever come back here, you know. Not after our sire tossed him out on his ear. But no matter. I'm here, Charlotte. Harold and me both. And, as they say, any port in a storm, hmm?"

Charlotte could smell the strong spirits on George's breath and, even though she didn't really understand what he was saying, what he meant, she did know that she needed to get herself out of the stable.

George must have read her thoughts in her expression, because just as she dropped Juliet's lead and turned to flee, his arm snaked out and he grabbed her elbow tight in his fist. "Now, now, now, Charlotte. You don't want to leave just yet. You haven't seen Harold. You really do need to see Harold. He's playing a game of sorts, you understand. You might want to play, too. Yes, I think that a splendid idea. Simply splendid."

"No, I—"

George roughly pulled on her arm, and Charlotte stumbled, pitched forward so that it was impossible to dig in her heels as he dragged her down the length of the large stables and shoved her onto the floor of the last stall.

Charlotte struggled to rise, but by then George had placed his booted foot on her back, pressing her down into the straw again with ease.

She braced her hands against the floor and was able to raise her head enough to see her surroundings, as there were at least three lanterns placed around the large birthing stall.

That's when she saw Harold.

He was not five feet away from her, naked as the day

he was born. Huge, fleshy, the skin that hadn't been touched by the sun gleaming a pasty white. Rolls of fat hung at his waist. And, almost worse, on his spittle-dotted face he wore an expression caught between a sort of animalistic ecstasy and unadulterated *meanness.*

He knelt tight behind an equally unclothed female who was on all fours in the straw, her face hidden by her long hair. He had one hand gripped tight on the woman's waist while he slapped at her back with a riding crop. As Charlotte watched in horror, unable to look away, he laughed and yelled, "Yoicks, my pretty bitch! Yoicks and away!"

And then he saw Charlotte. His eyes widened, his jaw went slack, and he began pumping into the poor, captured creature like a man possessed. In moments, he let out a guttural scream of triumph and collapsed on top of the female, pushing her onto the floor.

"Very prettily done, Harold, if a bit noisy. But now you've got nothing left, brother," George said from above Charlotte. "I suppose I'll have to do the honors." He ground his boot heel more firmly into her lower back.

"The devil you will!" Harold exclaimed breathlessly, pushing himself back on his haunches. "It's my birthday, not yours. Give her over to me."

"Very well, you may have her first. Then I'll show her what a real man can offer."

Charlotte screamed as George took hold of her hair and dragged her up onto her knees. She couldn't control her terror, couldn't think, wasn't physically strong enough to fight either one of them. They were going to rape her. They were going to do to her what Harold had just done to that poor, sobbing female who was now curled into a ball in a corner of the stall, attempting to cover herself.

"No!" she managed, twisting in George's grasp. But it was no use.

His fist still wrapped in her hair, George pushed Charlotte at his brother. "Kiss him! Come on, Charlotte—kiss him! Do it. Do it now, or I'm going to have to hurt you." He leaned down, close beside her ear. "I'm going to hurt you anyway, my dear, in ways your maiden mind cannot begin to fathom. I'm going to hurt you until you cry out with delight at each new sweet pain. Isn't that exciting?"

"Always the braggart," Harold said, going up on his knees to face Charlotte. And then he seemed to hesitate. "George? Are you sure we should do this? She's not just some trollop."

"No, you shouldn't do this," Charlotte said quickly, her eyes stinging with tears as George pulled hard on her hair. "Just…just let me go, Harold. I won't tell anybody. I swear it. I won't ever tell."

Harold looked up at his brother. "George?"

"She's a virgin, Harold. We've come this far. When was the last time you had yourself a virgin, hmm?"

Harold wet his lips. "You know the answer to that. Never." His eyes were concentrated on Charlotte again. "They're really better?"

"You'll never know that, brother mine, until you've had one, now will you? Oh, for God's sake, Harold. Let her go now and she'll tell everyone. Papa told us not to soil our nest, remember? What happens to our allowance if he finds out? But once we're done with her, she won't breathe a word, if only to save herself. We have to do this."

"No, please no," Charlotte cried, reduced to a pleading whisper now. "I won't tell anyone. It…it's my fault. Rafe warned me that—"

She cried out as George pulled on her hair once more.

"Did you hear that, Harold? Rafe warned her. *Rafe.* Our dear cousin, who beat you with your own riding crop. He *told* her, Harold. She knows. *Now* do you want to let her go?"

Charlotte stiffened when, as if he meant it to be his answer, Harold put both his hands on her breasts, squeezing them painfully as he brought his vile mouth down on hers. He forced his tongue into her mouth, nearly choking her.

Charlotte did the only thing she could do.

She bit him.

She bit down hard on his tongue, until she tasted his blood in her mouth.

Harold pulled back, yelping in pain, and George let go of her hair, only to bring the flats of his hands hard against her ears.

Charlotte collapsed, unconscious, onto the straw.

She didn't know how long she lay there, but when she at last dared to open her eyes, it was to see a pair of shiny black boots not two feet in front of her face.

"Idiots. I planted my seed in a worthless vessel, and she bore me a pair of idiots."

"Papa, that's not fair. She bit him. What else was I supposed to do? But she's not dead. You said she's not dead."

"Easier if she were." The duke's voice was cold and matter-of-fact. "No marks on her. We could have put her out in the fields somewhere, next to a fence, and everyone would assume she died falling from her horse. As it is…"

Charlotte closed her eyes again, hoping the Duke of Ashurst had not noticed that she was awake. She was alive. They hadn't raped her. But now would they kill her, on His Grace's orders?

"All right. Here's what we do," the duke said, beginning to pace the straw floor in front of Charlotte's body. "George, we'll need my coach. Put my team in the traces."

"Me? But, Papa, I don't know how to—"

The sound of a slap was followed by that of George's feet as he hastened to do his father's bidding.

"Good one, Papa," Harold said, giggling. "It's all his fault anyway. He's the one who brought her here in the—"

"I don't know which of you disgusts me more," the duke said. "But I'll deal with the both of you later. For now, let's use this disaster to our advantage."

"Yes, Papa," Harold said quietly. "May I…may I ask what you plan to do?"

The duke's low laugh sent a shiver down Charlotte's spine. "Open your eyes, Miss Seavers, for I know you're awake. There you go. Now sit up, and pay attention. We're about to solve the age-old problem of that thorn in my side, the ownership of Rose Cottage. Harold, meet your betrothed. Miss Seavers, my felicitations, and welcome to the family."

"Be-betrothed? But, Papa—"

"Shut up, you imbecile. And for God's sake, put on your drawers. You're enough to turn my stomach. When George gets back, rip her clothes. *Handle* her a bit, make her look as if she's just done what you and that idiot brother of yours planned to do with her. I'll be waiting in the coach."

"I woke the groom," George said, coming back into the stall. "Don't worry, I paid him enough to keep his mouth— What ho? Why's she looking at us that way? Are we going to kill her anyway?"

"I should disown the both of you," the duke said, shaking his head. "God only knows what will happen to this place once I'm dead and gone." He turned on his heel, preparing to leave the stable, but hesitated long enough to add, "Do as I said, Harold. Now."

Charlotte had been looking around the stall, desperate for a weapon, and finally saw one in the far corner. A pitchfork. She looked toward it, looked at the brothers, and then toward the pitchfork once more.

George saw what she was doing, and she'd barely scrambled to her feet before he'd pushed her back down by lifting his foot against her chest and straightening his leg.

"Do what, Harold? Come on, tell me. He's mad enough as it is."

Rather than tell him, Harold reached down and grabbed Charlotte's bodice in both hands, ripping it and the chemise beneath it down to her waist, exposing her breasts.

Instinctively, Charlotte moved to cover herself, which left her defenseless as Harold fell on her, kissing her roughly, pushing himself against her until her lip bled.

"There," he said at last, rolling off her. "That should be enough even to satisfy him, don't you think?"

"I don't know what you're talking about," George said. "Just get dressed, for the love of God. I'll take her out to Papa."

Once curled into the corner of the coach, praying they were done with her, Charlotte felt her head being tipped backward as someone pushed the mouth of a flask halfway down her throat, its contents nearly drowning her. She summoned the strength to push the flask away, and then promptly vomited all over herself on the way back to Rose Cottage.

To be presented to her parents.

Rafe rubbed at his temples. "My God…oh, my God. Charlie…"

But Charlotte hadn't finished. She hadn't wanted to tell Rafe what had happened to her, but once she'd begun it was as if she couldn't stop. She'd kept some things from him in the telling, things she still wasn't ready to face, but he had to know the worst of it. Only then would he understand.

"The duke told my parents that he'd discovered his sons in the stables, cavorting with their drunken slut of a daughter. He'd never seen such wanton perversion, God's truth, he hadn't! But no matter how I'd tempted them, he said, his sons weren't blameless in the matter, and there would be punishment enough to go around."

"The bastard!" Rafe was pacing the carpet, had been pacing it since she'd begun speaking about that horrible night. Halfway through, he'd thrown his wineglass into the fireplace. He looked as if he wanted to throw something else now.

"I might whelp in the fall, he told my parents, only God knowing which of his sons was the father, but that didn't matter because George certainly couldn't be wasted on a nobody like me, no matter how good my family or the long-standing *friendship* between the Seaveres and the Daughtrys. He sounded so smooth, so in control, and all Papa could do was hold on to my mother as she wept."

Rafe stopped his pacing. "All right, enough, Charlie. I understand now. The duke, cognizant of the fact that his sons had compromised you, even if you were willing—and how could your father have believed any of this?—would give you his younger son. In exchange, of course, for Rose Cottage and the land he'd coveted for years. Never let it be said that my late uncle ever failed to see an opportunity dropped into his lap."

"Yes," Charlotte said, sighing. It was almost over. "I had no choice, not with Papa refusing to listen to me, believing everything the duke told him."

"Because it was my uncle telling him, I'm sure. It's difficult to call a duke a liar."

"Harold told me later that George worried that he'd killed me, so that's when he went to fetch his father. The idea was all the duke's, yes, although he may have saved me from worse treatment at the hands of his sons. But that didn't save my mother, Rafe. She collapsed the moment the duke left the house, and she's been… Well, you see what she's like. And I'll never be able to tell her the truth."

"And your father?"

"He says he believes me, but I know that he blames me for what happened to Mama. Only a few weeks later the duke and his sons were dead. But the damage had all been done."

"And can't be undone, not all of it," Rafe said, getting to his feet. "I want no part of Rose Cottage, Charlie. I'll inform your father of that fact, unless you'd rather do it."

"Thank you. Emmaline and I burned the marriage contract, you know. Papa says we could be put in prison for that."

He turned to her, smiling weakly. "Good for Emmaline. So she knew the truth?"

Charlotte nodded, and even found a small reason to smile. "I had to tell someone. When she heard of the betrothal, she thought I'd gone mad."

"And now you've told me. I can only apologize for my uncle, my cousins, and be glad they're dead. You should hate all Daughtrys, Charlie, and I wouldn't blame you."

"You're not like them, Rafe, and never were. That's probably why I get so angry with you when you act as though you're some sort of interloper, or think that you don't deserve the title. It was your uncle and his sons who didn't deserve the title."

Rafe walked over to her, but then stopped a few feet away, ran his hands through his hair. "I want to hold you, Charlie. I want to take all the pain away. But that would only ease my pain, wouldn't it? The last…the last thing you want now is a man's touch. Any man's touch."

"I'm being foolish, Rafe. You aren't them, I know you're not, but…"

"But not right now," he said quietly. "I understand. And I won't press you anymore, I promise."

She nodded, blinking back tears, and slowly got to her feet, like an old woman for whom simply living was often a painful burden. "I need to go upstairs now, to see to my mother."

She was halfway to the door before Rafe's question stopped her.

"Would you have gone through with it, Charlie? Would you have married him?"

"I don't know. I've asked myself that question a thousand times, both before and after Harold died. Would I dare to run away, even kill myself, in order to avoid the marriage? Could I do that to my parents, with Mama so ill and Papa having given his word? And even now I really, truly don't know. I shouldn't have been in the stables that night, Rafe. I shouldn't have ridden out without a groom in attendance. I'm not blameless in this."

"But then Nicole would have taken Juliet into the stables, wouldn't she? Nicole would have seen…"

"I know. For a long time, that was my only solace."

He nodded, and then looked to the portrait again. She would never want Rafe Daughtry to look at her the way he was looking at that portrait.

She slipped out of the room, unnoticed.

RAFE DIDN'T KNOW EXACTLY why he was feeling more comfortable both in his skin and within his changed circumstances, but he was.

Perhaps he had taken his first steps toward confidence the day he had ordered the portrait of his uncle and cousins removed to the attics.

Perhaps it was because Charlotte had goaded him, insisting that he was not his uncle or his cousins. That he was so much better than they had been, and he should no longer feel guilty about having stepped into their dead boots.

Perhaps it was because, while he'd been off fighting his war, Charlotte had fought one of her own, and somehow come out of the horror just as frank and open and honest as he remembered her to be.

Or perhaps it was because he'd gone upstairs to Fitz the evening Charlotte had told him what had happened to her, bared his soul, and the two of them had made great inroads on the late duke's store of brandy before Rafe finally passed out lying sprawled at the bottom of his friend's bed.

Whatever the reason, and even if it was a combination of all of those things, Rafe now rode the fields of Ashurst Hall with new confidence. He sat at the head of the table in the formal dining room without once glancing at the chair near the bottom of the table, where he'd once sat, welcomed on sufferance.

John Cummings had noticed the difference in his employer. The estate manager now asked, then did, rather than doing and then informing Rafe of what he'd done. Rafe spent long evenings studying years' worth of estate books. He took copious notes on planting dates and field yields and market prices, just as he had once managed guard duty schedules, battlefield maneuvers and the rationing of supplies when the provisions wagons had not kept up with his advances in the field.

As Fitz had told him—as he'd thrown a volume of *Hamlet* at his head—Captain Rafael Daughtry was not a stupid man. He was a capable man, perhaps even brilliant when he put his mind to a thing, and it was about damn time he showed the world what a duke should be.

Charlie wasn't a coward. Rafe couldn't be a coward.

He and Charlotte hadn't spoken of the past again, not since that day. They rather danced around each other for nearly a fortnight, but slowly, carefully, they began slipping back into their former easy relationship.

Now, near the end of January, they were somehow once again the best of friends; laughing, joking, teasing. With no secrets between them, they could actually enjoy each other again.

Even if he sometimes caught out Charlie looking at him from across a room or down the length of the dinner table, a question in her eyes, her mouth slightly opened as if poised to say something to him, something that might change both their worlds.

Even if that meant that Rafe had to sometimes isolate himself from her, when the urge to hold her, to kiss her, to soothe her and teach her became almost overpowering.

But he'd wait. He'd bide his time.

He had no other choice, did he?

Edward and Georgianna Seavers began to join them at the dinner table, and if Georgianna considered herself the hostess, what did it matter?

Yes, there had been one potentially embarrassing incident on Twelfth Night. Georgianna had been quiet throughout the meal, but when a servant had placed bowls of custard and berries in front of everyone, she had roused to ask, "And what is this?" even as she seemed to misjudge her movement and dipped her fingers into the golden-yellow confection.

"Georgianna!" Edward Seavers had admonished in horror, getting to his feet to attend to his wife, who was now looking at her custard-coated fingers in some astonishment.

"But that's how we *all* eat custard on Twelfth Night, isn't it, Nicole?" Lydia said quickly, dipping her own fingertips into her bowl. "Yum!" she exclaimed as she stuck her fingers into her mouth. "A real Daughtry family tradition!"

Nicky hadn't hesitated more than a moment before dipping her own fingers into her custard, and as the servant watched, his jaw at half-mast, they all dipped their fingers into their bowls.

Georgianna's expression had gone from confused to astonished to pleased, her faded blue eyes actually twinkling as she exclaimed, "Aren't we silly!"

Rafe had looked quickly to Charlotte, to see her blinking rapidly, obviously near to tears. But then she'd leaned over and kissed Lydia on the cheek. "You have the kindest, most loving heart I know," she'd told her, and then she looked up the table and smiled at Rafe.

Now Georgianna left her rooms to have afternoon tea with Charlotte and the twins. She'd also begun to occupy herself in the Ashurst Hall conservatory, happy to be back with her pretty flowers, some of which they'd managed to save from the greenhouse at Rose Cottage.

And there had been one thing else....

Edward Seavers had come to Rafe two evenings ago after dinner, to declare that he was a man of honor and therefore needed to confess that he had all but deeded Rose Cottage to the late duke and felt he must honor that agreement with Rafe.

Rafe had remained seated behind his desk as he listened, a quill pen in his hand, the estate books open in front of him, his vision suddenly turned red with barely controlled rage. He forced himself to tamp down the need to curse the man who'd spoken of his *honor.* When he finally raised his head and spoke, his voice was deceptively soft, like velvet over stone. "I understand, Mr. Seavers, that the deed was not the only possession of yours that your honorable self had been about to hand over to my uncle."

The older man's complexion had blanched and he'd grabbed on to the back of a chair as if afraid he might collapse. "She *told* you? Oh, the shame of it! We…we shall leave at once, Your Grace."

Yes, that was it. *That* was the moment Rafe had become the duke in more than name.

He'd put down his pen, slowly, carefully, and gotten to his feet. "You believed him, Mr. Seavers? You took the word of my uncle over that of your own daughter?"

"But…but I *saw* her. My God, I still see her standing there, staring at me. Just staring at me, her eyes condemning me as I agreed to the duke's plan. It… it was a magnanimous gesture on His Grace's part, considering what Charlotte had done. To give his son…"

"To take Rose Cottage and the land he'd coveted for years, you mean. Charlie told you that the man was lying, that his sons were lying. She's your daughter. Why didn't you believe her?"

"I did believe her…I do believe her. I…I suppose I believe her." Edward Seavers walked around the chair to collapse in it, his body slumped as if he were feeling his defeat all over again. "But what choice did I have?

The sons would have talked, spread the story of Charlotte's sin everywhere. She'd have been ruined."

"And her parents along with her," Rafe had pointed out. "Surely you considered the consequences to your wife and yourself?"

Charlotte's father ran a shaking hand over his thinning hair. "Yes, yes, all right. I had to consider my wife. And myself." He had looked at Rafe as if for understanding. "But Charlotte shouldn't have been there. She is not entirely blameless."

"You blame her for the actions of my cousins? If they had raped her, would that have been her fault as well?" Rafe had looked at Edward Seavers then and seen not simply a man grown too soon old, but a weak man who had probably always been a weak man. Why had he never seen it all those years ago? Charlie had always been strong because she'd always had to be strong. Parent to her own parents.

"You don't understand," Seavers had all but blurted.

"Oh, sir, but I do," Rafe answered coldly. "I understand completely. You don't deserve her."

He sat down once more, his hands drawn up into fists as he rested them on the desktop. He was Captain Rafael Daughtry at that moment, a man used to quick decisions, accustomed to giving orders.

"This is the way it will be, Mr. Seavers. You and your wife shall remain here as my guests until the repairs to Rose Cottage are concluded, and then you will please me very much by leaving my home. I will be civil to you while you are here, indeed, for as long as you live. But you, you alone, will know how much it sickens me just to look at you."

"Your Grace…"

Rafe shot him a look that had quelled many a sergeant major. "Don't interrupt me, sir. Never interrupt me. You and your wife will return to Rose Cottage, but as my tenants, as I will have the deed to your estate and manor house in my possession by the end of the week or know the reason why."

"But…but…"

"I don't want the damn place. Not for me. I will collect no rents. You will continue to manage your estate and your finances as if nothing has changed, but Rose Cottage is mine, to dispose of as I wish, when I wish. Displease me again the way you have displeased me tonight, sir, tell anyone of this change in ownership, and that will be sooner rather than later. Is that understood?"

"This is about Charlotte, isn't it?" Edward Seavers sighed heavily. "You want me to forgive her."

"No, Mr. Seavers. I believe it is time you went to her, and begged *her* to forgive *you*. In any event, Charlie will remain here when you and your wife return to Rose Cottage. She will travel to London with my sisters and me in late February as we join our mother there, she will have a Season as she deserves, some happiness and gaiety she more than deserves. And, Mr. Seavers, if I am very lucky, very, *very* lucky, at the end of that Season she will have put this past terrible year behind her, the damage that you and the duke and my cousins did to her, and she will agree to marry me."

Edward Seavers blinked several times, the corners of his thin mouth twitching as he seemed caught between a smile and sheer astonishment. "Marry…marry her?"

"Yes, Mr. Seavers. The wrong we Daughtys have

done her must be mended. Please notice yet again that I'm not asking you. I'm informing you. Breathe a word of this conversation to anyone, however, and you and your invalid wife will be removed from Rose Cottage immediately. You are done making decisions for Charlie in what you feel is in her best interests, and I'm not about to repeat that sort of mistake."

Edward Seavers got up slowly and walked toward the door. He turned back just as his fingers curled around the latch, to ask quietly, "You love her, then?"

"You gave up your right to ask that question a long time ago. Good night, Mr. Seavers," Rafe answered before turning his back on the man.

Once the man had gone, Rafe refilled his wineglass, not entirely surprised to see a slight tremor in his hands as he poured. For halfway through his meeting with her father, Rafe had realized something.

He did love Charlie. But that was nothing new, for he'd always loved Charlie. She'd always been a part of his life, he'd simply accepted that, even when she'd driven him nearly to distraction, following him about like some loyal puppy.

Did he *owe* her something for the harsh treatment she'd endured at the hands of his uncle and cousins? Yes, of course. As the duke, as her friend, he knew he had an obligation to her. To the child she had been, to the woman she'd become. Marriage was the obvious answer, a logical payment for the debt of honor the Daughtrys owed her.

But this was more. So much more. This…this *feeling,* this strange, exhilarating, frightening, unexpected *feeling*—this was more than loving her as his comfortable friend, as his helpful companion.

He'd fight for her. If she asked him, he would unhesitatingly die for her. He'd sell his soul to Hell for her.

How? How did this happen? When did it happen?

Rafe drank down his wine in one long swallow and then collapsed into the chair behind the desk. "So this is what it's like to be in love?" he mused quietly. And then he frowned. "Damn. Now what do I do?"

PART TWO
London, March 1815

Love conquers all things;
Let us too surrender to Love.

—Virgil

CHAPTER TEN

THE MANSION in Grosvenor Square had been taken out of Holland covers and apparently dusted, waxed and scrubbed from cellar to attic by a staff that had done nothing but eat their heads off for over a year while the Daughtry family was, at least outwardly, in mourning for the late duke and his sons.

Charlotte spent nearly a full day inspecting all of the magnificently appointed rooms, complimenting the staff while giving silent thanks to the late duchess for her excellent, refined tastes. Indeed, there was only one truly ugly elephant's foot table to be found on all of the four floors of the mansion, and that tucked into a small sitting room on the ground floor, reserved for callers not deemed important enough to be ushered upstairs to the main drawing room.

Chinese wallpapers abounded on the first floor, and all the dozen bedchambers had been appointed with the most modern conveniences, including four water closets. Nicole, giggling as she joined Charlotte for that part of the tour, had declared them "positively decadent!"

Charlotte, if she had been prone to employ such terms, would have reserved that particular description for Lady Daughtry, who had descended on the mansion within an hour of her family's arrival in Mayfair. Helen Daughtry (Carstairs-Higgenbottom) had arrived in a magnificent cream-colored coach driven by four matched bays with, good Lord, pink plumes strapped to their heads.

She had floated into the mansion and up the staircase in a cloud of scent and a pink, velvet-trimmed traveling ensemble that scarcely covered her slim, shapely ankles. Her masses of blond hair were piled high on her head, with fetching ringlets tumbling down over her left ear and onto her artfully rouged cheek.

She kissed the twins, warning them not to crush her gown, smiled vaguely at Charlotte, and demanded that her son, the duke, present himself to his beloved mama at once.

Oh, and she'd like a glass of wine, please, chilled. This she directed at Charlotte, who could only suppose that Lady Daughtry had taken her for a servant or lady's companion.

Charlotte had been of a mind to refuse Rafe's insistence that, while in Bond Street to shop for the twins, she also avail herself of a dressmaker before they were all engaged with other patrons come to town for the Season. Looking down at her simple morning gown that was in its third—no, its fourth—Season, she'd decided to give in gracefully and order a few gowns for herself.

When Lady Daughtry pleaded a total disinterest in a trip to Bond Street—she had her own modiste, who came to *her,* you understand—it was left to Charlotte to shepherd the twins on their first foray into the world outside Ashurst Hall.

To her surprise and amusement, Captain Fitzgerald had begged to be allowed to be a part of their company. He didn't look the sort of man who would enjoy an outing that included shopping for bonnets and gowns and ribbons and gloves, but he was adamant that he wished to go along.

This worried Charlotte a little. She knew that he and Lydia had become very good friends, close companions, but surely their relationship couldn't be any more than that. She'd have to speak to Rafe about her suspicions at some point, wouldn't she?

Three hours later, with Nicole having a spirited debate with herself over which of two bonnets suited her best, Charlotte joined the captain as he stood leaning against a wall, looking rather as though he might bolt for the street at any moment.

"Fitz? Why are you here?" she asked him quietly.

He straightened, nodding to Lydia, who had held up a straw bonnet decorated with bunches of bright red cherries. "Yes, very nice, Lyddie. But the one with the blue ribbon better accentuates your lovely eyes."

Charlotte opened her mouth to comment on that bit of flattery, but then closed it again, shaking her head. She was still amazed that the man addressed Lydia as Lyddie, and that Lydia seemed to be just fine with that.

"Never mind, Fitz, as I think I know the answer. Lydia asked you to accompany us, didn't she? And you couldn't conjure up some way to refuse her because she asked so prettily. She has you wrapped right around her thumb, doesn't she?"

Fitz leaned close to Charlotte's ear. "Can you keep a secret, Charlotte?"

"I've been known to keep my own counsel, yes."

"I lost the bet."

"Pardon me? You and Lydia have been *gambling?* You taught her to play whist or some such thing? Oh, Fitz, she's only a—"

"No, no, no, not that sort of bet. I wagered that Lyddie couldn't remember the names of all the capitals of Europe, and she wagered that not only could she remember the names quite well, but she would also wager that I could not name all the counties in England. If I won, she would polish my boots for the first day I was allowed to get about without my crutches. And if she won, I would take her shopping on Bond Street when we came to London. I forgot Lincolnshire, by the way. Had all the other *shires,* but not that one."

Charlotte covered her mouth with her hand as she tried not to laugh at him. "You're so good to her, Fitz. You know, Nicole and I believe she fancies herself as half in love with you. You'd best be careful."

Fitz shot a quick look at Lydia—looking more than simply fetching in her bonnet with the blue ribbon—and shook his head. "She's only a child, Charlotte. Barely out of the nursery. Oh, she'll break a dozen hearts, that's for certain, but not for a few years, by which time she'll have forgotten all about me."

Charlotte lowered her head. "Don't count on that, Fitz."

He grinned. "I'm not. Mostly, to tell the truth, I'm counting on me. But it helps to be modest, don't you think?"

"You're impossible," she told him. "But I mean it, Fitz. Women aren't all so fickle in their affections."

"Ah, yes. Like you with Rafe."

"Fitz!"

"Oh, and his affections for you, as well. And, no matter what the obstacles, I'm counting on the two of you to overcome them all," Fitz whispered as Nicole approached them, a bonnet in each hand, her smile triumphant.

"I don't know why it didn't occur to me sooner, Charlotte. I've decided to take them both." She raised her left hand. "This one for riding in the Park, and *this* one for walking in the Square. Oh, and the first one I chose? That will be reserved only for Sundays. What say you, Captain Fitzgerald, since Lydia has somehow set you up as our arbiter of fashion?"

But Fitz was looking out through the large window onto Bond Street, his brow furrowed. "Stap me if that isn't Lieutenant General Hill out there. Looks a little queer without his uniform. More like everyone else, you know? And running to fat, as well, which is what being at peace will do to a soldier. Ah, and look who he's got with him! God's teeth, I haven't seen him since our last night in Paris, and I don't think I saw him much once the ladies arri— Ah, never mind that. I wonder what he and Daddy Hill are talking about so earnestly."

"Why don't you go outside and see for yourself, Fitz?" Charlotte said, wondering what Rafe would say when he received the milliner's bill for *seven* bonnets. "Nicole, don't you think you could make do with two?"

Nicole smiled in that way she had, as if she knew she was terrible, and delighted in that fact. "No, Charlotte, I really don't think I can survive without all three. When we have our Come-Out next year, I do not think I shall settle for less than a dozen, so I'm really being quite good. Besides, Rafe should be prepared for what will happen to his pocketbook in another year. It seems only fair."

Charlotte gave up the fight, only remarking that if they didn't all soon show some prudence, poor Captain Fitzgerald would have to find his own way home, for the coach would be overflowing with their purchases.

Lydia joined them, her eyes on the front window of the shop. "Who is the captain speaking with, Charlotte?"

"Why, I don't know. He said he saw some people he knew on the flagway, but I don't think I see the one gentleman anymore. Oh, here he comes, and he's bringing the younger man with him. Nicole, behave."

Nicole rolled her eyes in frustration. "Why is it never *Nicole and Lydia, behave?* Why is it always just me?"

"Do I really have to answer that?" Charlotte said quietly, her heart sinking when she saw the serious look on Fitz's face. "Fitz?"

He smiled at her, a warning in his eyes, and then introduced the gentleman with him as Tanner Blake, Earl of—" What is it you're the earl of, Blake?"

"Duke now, I'm afraid. My father passed on to his heavenly reward—at least that's our hope, although I have my doubts as to his ultimate destination. He died last spring, while I was still in Paris with you and Rafe. I'm the Duke of Malvern now, Fitz. Are you impressed? Lord knows I am. Ladies, it is indeed my extreme pleasure," he then said, sweeping them all an elegant leg, his eyes resting a little longer on Lydia's serenely beautiful face.

Charlotte and the twins dropped into curtsies, Lydia's gratifyingly demure, and Nicole executing hers with her head held high, examining the Duke of Malvern quite openly.

Charlotte could understand Nicole's interest, for the Duke of Malvern was an extraordinarily handsome young man, with twinkling green eyes and a fine crop of dark blond hair worn in the latest style, she supposed. He was tall, at least as tall as Rafe, and much of the same age, if she was any judge. He wore his fashionable clothes as if born to them…a man raised to be what he had become, and comfortable in his own skin.

"Our most sincere condolences on your loss, Your Grace," Charlotte said, and the girls, bless them, only nodded their agreement, remaining quiet as they should…because Charlotte had delivered several lectures on the behavior expected of young girls not yet out if they expected to step foot outside the mansion while they were in Town.

"Charlotte, I'm loath to do this, but I must beg your pardon so that I may go off with Blake here for a bit. You know, to split a few bottles and weave each other fanciful stories of how the war couldn't have been won without either of us. Would you mind returning to Grosvenor Square without me?"

Charlotte looked to the twins, who had already evinced a suggestion that they visit the ribbon shop they'd passed on their way to the milliner's shop.

"I think we can manage, Fitz, yes. The coach is just outside, so we'll be quite safe if we linger here for a while. Your Grace," she then said, dropping into another curtsy, the girls quickly following suit.

She shot one more quick look at Fitz, who only shook his head slightly, warned Lydia that he'd be heartbroken if she didn't choose the bonnet with the blue ribbons, and quit the shop, his arm around the duke's shoulders.

"I should like one like him when I'm choosing partners in the dance. Him, or a dozen like him. Isn't he the most handsome man you ever saw, Lydia?"

"I didn't notice," Lydia told her sister. "The captain looked upset, didn't he, Charlotte? Do you suppose we've tired him out? I think he still favors his injured leg when he's fatigued."

"Oh, cut line, Lydia," Nicole teased. "He's not a baby, and you're not his nursemaid. They're probably off to some club where they will attempt to drink each other under the table," Nicole said. "Oh, to be a man and have such freedom."

Lydia and Charlotte exchanged glances, the younger girl saying, "But then who would wear those lovely bonnets, Nicole?"

"Yes, Lydia, I see your point," Nicole said, still balancing the bonnets in each hand. "It's a difficult choice. I know I will adore dancing at balls and being admired as I ride in the Park. But I do think gentlemen *laugh* more, don't you, Charlotte?"

"Perhaps," Charlotte said, knowing that for all their smiles of a moment ago, neither Fitz nor the Duke of Malvern had seemed at all amused. "Let's finish our shopping, shall we?"

"YOU'RE LOOKING RATHER pleased with yourself," Fitz commented, slipping into a chair in the private study at the rear of the mansion.

"I suppose I am, Fitz," Rafe said, putting down the paper he'd been reading. "I've just received notice that I'm expected in Parliament tomorrow, to take up my uncle's seat in the House of Lords. God's teeth, I'll probably have a fit of the giggles and damn myself for all time."

Fitz rose from the chair, as if unable to sit still, and went over to the drinks table. "Some wine?" he asked, already pouring out two measures. "My congratulations, by the way. You'll be a good man to have in Parliament right now. I've got news."

Rafe accepted the wineglass, watching as his friend began to pace the study. "Clearly. And are you going to share that news with me?"

"It's Bonaparte," Fitz said, turning to look at Rafe. "I've just come from meeting with Tanner Blake, who I saw speaking with Daddy Hill on Bond Street. God, that man was magnificent at Almaraz, wasn't he?"

"Yes, he was, both of them, actually. What in hell were you doing on Bond— No, never mind. Continue."

"Yes, I will, and I'll make this short, because I don't like saying any of it. Bonaparte has quit Elba, clearly not enamored of being emperor there. He's already landed near Cannes with his one thousand soldiers, and is reportedly marching to Paris."

"My God…" Rafe said slowly, easing back in his chair. "We said it, Fitz, you and I. We knew he'd never be content to live out his years in exile. Now what?"

"Now, my friend, Major Tanner Blake and I—he's a duke now, you know. You dukes are getting fairly thick on the ground these days. In any event, Blake and I have already presented our shining faces for whatever duty is required of us, and will be departing for the continent just as soon as Old Hooky decides where he wants to go. He's still in Vienna, it would appear."

"And I'm going with you. You say Napoleon is on his way to Paris? Perhaps his reception won't be what he supposes, and the French will save us the trouble of having to round him up again."

Fitz shook his head. "Dispatches are coming in from Paris and elsewhere, Blake told me. King Louis is dithering, gathering up all his fine clothes and jewels and such, but it would seem he's about ready to quit the city, abandoning his subjects, and the throne we propped him up in. Bloody stupid fat coward. That will land all of France right back in Boney's lap. Blake thinks we'll all be gathering in Brussels."

"Good enough." Rafe got to his feet. "When do we leave?"

"Blake and I leave tomorrow. He's got his own yacht, and we've been commissioned to get ourselves to Brussels and begin riding the countryside, mapping it for the Iron Duke. You, my friend, go nowhere. You're the duke now, remember?"

Rafe nearly said, "So what, so is Blake, and he gets to go." But that would be childish in the extreme. "Let you go off by yourself, Fitz? Without me you'd be lost in five minutes in the wilds of Belgium, and probably never be heard from again."

"I knew you'd say something like that. It will be hard without you, no question, my friend, but you have responsibilities here now. You're about to take up your seat in the House of Lords, remember? And think of the good you could do us if you worked with the War Office here in London. Maybe you could explain to them that soldiers need food, and munitions, and the occasional new pair of socks, hmm?"

"I can't, Fitz. I can't stay here, not with Bonaparte on the loose again. I'd go mad."

Fitz lost his smile. "Don't be selfish, Rafe, because that's what leaving here would be, you know. What would Lydia and Nicole do without you? Ashurst Hall can't stand to lose another duke, its *last* duke at that. Blake's got three younger brothers—yes, we already discussed this, knowing you'd be all hot to go with us. But you're the last of your line until you get some sense in your head and marry Charlotte and produce a few heirs."

"Leave Charlie out of this, if you please." Still, Rafe sat down once more, picking up his wineglass. "But you're right, Fitz, damn it all. I can't risk it, not with the twins to consider. It's clear my mother's useless, and I care too much for the twins to leave them in her care. So Blake really feels there'll be a battle?"

Fitz finally sat down, his energy of a few moments ago dissipated, and rubbed at his thigh. "Well, I doubt he'll surrender and get sent back to Elba just because we ask him nicely, and we can't let him run around loose, now can we? Christ, Rafe. All these years of war, all the good men who died—for this? How can one man's ambition cause so much trouble?"

"I imagine soldiers asked the same of Julius Caesar, Alexander and so many others. Perhaps the better question is to ask why there are so many blockheaded politicians mucking about in what should be a soldier's war. We'd have executed the man, Fitz, you know we would have, or else handed him a loaded pistol and given him some privacy. I suppose the fellow deserved at least that much." He shook his head. "We saw him, Fitz, all those months. Was that a man who wished to die in his bed? How many more will die now, do you suppose, in order to give him his glorious death?"

"You're still scribbling in that journal of yours, aren't you? Do you really believe you understand the man now?"

"I don't know. There were times, watching him walk out alone at twilight, that I thought he might be mellowing, realizing his mistakes. Clearly I was mistaken. What else did you learn?"

"In Vienna, the Congress is meeting to have Boney labeled an outlaw. They're only waiting on his wife to condemn him. Then we'll gather the Allies, Blücher and the rest. One battle, Rafe, one decisive battle. They tell me that's how the Iron Duke sees the thing. He'll be in charge, too, so we're sure to win it."

"Even though he and Bonaparte never faced each other in the field. Damn, I wish I could be there." He looked toward the door at the sound of a knock, and called out for whoever it was to enter. "Charlie," he said, slicing a warning look at Fitz. "Back from Bond Street so soon? Did my sisters run you ragged?"

"I don't think so," she said. "Do I look ragged? No, don't answer that. Oh, sit down, Fitz. You don't have to jump to your feet every time I enter a room. Rest your leg. Answer this instead, if you please, both of you. You don't really think you two are going back to the continent, do you? Haven't you had enough of war?"

Fitz pushed himself out of the chair he'd just sunk

back into, saying, "And I think I shall leave the two of you to your discussion while I go round up Phineas and ask him to pack my bags. Thank the Lord I stopped him before he could make a bonfire of *my* uniforms."

"Rafe?" Charlotte prodded when he remained silent once Fitz had quit the room.

He motioned her to a chair near the fireplace, much like the pair at Ashurst Hall. "Sit down, Charlie. And stop glaring at me. I'm not going. And how did you find out about Bonaparte?"

She took up her seat, slipping out of her shoes and quickly tucking her feet up beneath the skirts of her gown. "I think we walked all of Bond Street, twice," she said, rubbing at her toes through the material, clearly at ease with him here in his private study. "But to answer your question, if it's gossip you're after, Rafe, head first for the shops. They're filling with fashionable ladies picking out bolts of material suitable for Brussels in the spring. One excited lady in particular was demanding a rigout complete with gold epaulettes. Your mother, Rafe."

"Lord save us." He rubbed at his forehead. "Bonaparte is on the loose, and she's worried about her wardrobe? Where does she think she's going?"

"I told you, Rafe. Brussels. A woman the modiste identified for me as Lady Uxbridge was telling someone about a letter she'd had just this morning from her daughter who is visiting in Paris. The news is that, as Lady Uxbridge tells it, the *tiger* has broken loose, but she is to be assured that everyone is safe, with many planning to remain in Paris until June, or else adjourn to Brussels if the news turns dangerous, as the army is to amass there and the balls may be more well-attended."

Rafe gave a short, exasperated laugh. "So much for cloaking any of our movements in secrecy. And you're telling me that my mother is planning to remove to Brussels?"

"The very moment all those epaulettes are sewn to her redingotes, yes, I believe so. You're truly not going, Rafe? Because—"

"Because I owe it to my sisters and Ashurst Hall not to have my bloody head blown off. Yes, Charlie, I know."

"Well, that's very gratifying, Rafe, but that wasn't what I was about to say. I was about to say that I'd worry for you…and miss you very much."

"And now I'll say it's very gratifying to hear that. Thank you, Charlotte."

She lowered her eyelids, avoiding his gaze. "Yes, you're…you're welcome." Then she looked at him again. "I shouldn't know what I would do without you, you know. You're my dearest friend in the whole world."

He smiled at her, unable to think of a thing to say to her in return.

If there was ever a reason to load one of the dueling pistols he'd found in a case in a drawer in his desk and put it to his head, being called Charlotte's dearest friend in the whole world was probably it.

"I should go upstairs and check on Lydia," Charlotte said as she slipped her feet back into her patent slippers and stood up. "The moment she realizes that Fitz is leaving us she'll go off into a tizzy."

Rafe also stood. "Does Lydia go into tizzies? I've

often thought that she is almost worrisomely level-headed."

Charlotte smiled. "That's only because Nicole is so often animated, making her sister seem too quiet. Rafe?"

"Yes, Charlie?" he prodded when she didn't say anything else, but only remained where she was, looking up into his face.

"I was…that is, when I overheard Lady Uxbridge, my heart clenched in such terrible fear for you that I couldn't rush back here quickly enough, all the way trying out arguments meant to keep you from leaving… leaving your sisters…."

He lifted her hand, noticing that it was ice-cold, and pressed his lips to her wrist. "Believe me, I'm not going anywhere," he told her quietly. "I made a promise to myself the night I learned what my uncle and cousins had done to you. I will never leave you, Charlie, and you will always be safe with me."

She withdrew her hand, her expression suddenly tight. "How…how very condescending of you, Your Grace. That…that you should have thought to set yourself up as my protector. Am I to be your ward now, and you my guardian? I do have parents, you know, Rafe. I'm no orphan you've taken in from the storm. Well, not an orphan, at any rate. The storm is rather a given, isn't it?"

Rafe winced at his verbal clumsiness, after they'd made such great strides the past few months. But then he blundered on, fairly certain he was only digging himself a deeper hole, yet unable to see a way out now that he'd begun. "I said that wrong, didn't I? I only meant that you should never be afraid of me. That I would never even think to… No, that's not quite right, either, is it? What I mean is that, not now, of course, perhaps not for a long time…but if you ever decide that you feel safe enough with me, then I—"

"Then you what, Rafe?" she asked, tipping her head to one side as if attempting to see inside his head, which would surely shock her. Slowly her eyes narrowed, and her mouth set in a thin line. "You think there's something wrong with me. That's why you've been so…so *gentle* with me, as if I should be wrapped in cotton wool. You think I'm damaged in some way, don't you, Rafe? Somewhere in my mind."

"Christ, no!" he told her earnestly. "You've got a better mind, are more sane, than anyone I've ever known."

"Then what is it, Rafe? Is your concern more particular? Do you think what your family did to me haunts me day and night, that I may put a brave face on it, but I'm now frightened of the entire world, and you most particularly?"

"I am a Daughtry, Charlie," he said, wondering if it might be prudent for him to back up a few paces. "And I have kissed you, you know, and I'm not quite sure I asked your permission first."

He watched as she blinked back tears; he was sure they were tears. But of what? Anger? Shame? Had he just ruined everything again, after so many months spent attempting to make amends for his family, take away the fear he'd felt shiver through her body when he'd dared to hold her, kiss her?

She took his hands in hers and stepped closer to him.

"Rafe, I'm sorry. I've been thinking only of myself. I can see now that I put you in an untenable position from the moment I told you about Harold and…and that night. You're the best of good men. I've told you that and told you that. I'm not afraid of you. I…I loved you at one time. The way Lydia considers herself in love with Fitz, I believe. I loved you, but the child I was loved the boy you were then. Now I'm learning to know the man you are now. I, um, I very much like the man you have become, Rafe."

He began to lower his head toward hers, but when she squeezed his hands, he stopped.

"I'm sorry, Rafe. Because you are right about some things. I don't think I'm ready yet for all that goes with…with caring for someone the way females are supposed to do, no matter what my feelings for you. What I saw that night in the stables at Ashurst Hall was so violent, so ugly. What they did to me was so degrading…."

"You need to banish those memories from your mind, Charlie. George and Harold were not normal men. They cared only for their own twisted desires. Don't measure all men by their yardsticks. Don't measure me that way, please."

"And I've told you that I don't," she said, sighing. "I know you're not like them. But I'm like *me,* and I can't seem to change who I am, who they made me. At least not yet. And we're good friends, Rafe, aren't we? Do we need more than that for now? Do you need more than that right now? Because if you do…"

"I need whatever you can give me," he told her as she trailed off, and before she might say something like *because if you do, I can't give it to you.* "I'll take whatever you can give me."

Now a tear did spill down her cheek.

God, how he longed to hold her, to kiss her, to prove that she had nothing to fear from what should be the most natural and normal physical exchange of affection given to mankind.

But he couldn't do it. Not now, not yet. She'd seen his cousin Harold in the throes, had been rightly repulsed by what she'd seen. Banishing that sort of horrific vision and remembered pain was not a miracle accomplished with a few clumsy assurances, a few tentative kisses.

"And now, before we both tie our tongues in knots, go away, Charlie," Rafe told her, dropping a quick kiss on her nose before she could resist him. "I've got to get myself over to the War Office and volunteer my services. Fitz gave me strict instructions as to how I could best help him by remaining here in London."

Charlotte looked up at him gratefully. "And I should go find Lydia and try to calm her fears about the man's safety. Fitz is a good soldier, isn't he, Rafe? He isn't foolhardy?"

"Fitz?" He had a quick memory flash into his mind; the one where Fitz, mad as all hell because he'd just had his second horse shot out from under him, had waded into a small troop of the enemy on foot, waving his sword and cursing them all to Perdition. The enemy had fallen back, probably convinced their attacker was some sort of invincible Irish devil. "No, Charlie. Fitz isn't foolhardy. And Bonaparte may not raise another army willing to die for him. This still may all come to nothing, and my mother's epaulettes will all have been wasted."

"I dearly hope you're right. I'll tell Lydia that we aren't certain there will even be a battle. Not that I can hope such a possibility will calm her."

Rafe watched her leave the room, and then released a long sigh. He'd never been a patient man, but Charlotte was teaching him patience. Indeed, he could even be said to be acting in a virtuous manner when it came to putting Charlotte and her fears above his admittedly baser desires.

As he poured himself another measure of wine, he thought of something about virtue that he'd learned as a child in his cousins' schoolroom. Was it a quote from Diogenes, or perhaps Prior? Something about virtue being enough in itself?

"Not that it matters," he mused as he threw back the contents of the glass before heading out to the foyer to call for his horse. "Because if virtue is in fact its own reward, it's no great wonder to me that vice has so many friends."

CHAPTER ELEVEN

THE LONDON SEASON of 1815 was to be absent many of its hostesses and even its debutantes, as the scene of many of its festivities had relocated to Brussels, where even the Duke of Wellington hosted several balls for the amusement of the populace.

"According to Fitz," Rafe remarked at the breakfast table the last week of April, "you would think they're all awaiting invitations to the battle itself when it comes, and vying for the best seats to watch some damned— some dashed frolic."

"How very naughty of him, and you. Your friend makes us all sound like ghouls, Rafael," Lady Daughtry complained as she poked her fork at the scant food she allowed on her plate. "Indeed, we go to Brussels to lend our support and succor to our brave soldiers."

"By attending balls and otherwise parading about in all your finery," Rafe said, winking at Charlotte. "Yes, I see the sense to that. Please forgive me."

Charlotte bit back a smile. Listening to Rafe and Lady Daughtry go back and forth at each other was better than any play she might have seen at Covent Garden.

Nicole giggled into her hand while Lydia ignored

them all, choosing instead to read for at least the twentieth time the letter from Fitz that she held on her lap beneath the table.

Rafe had worried at first that the idea of Lydia and Fitz exchanging letters might put ideas in his sister's head she was too young to harbor—or understand, for that matter. But as time passed he'd changed his mind, telling Charlotte that he was glad Lydia was writing to Fitz, as he scarcely had time himself to scribble more than the occasional note to his friend. Fitz needed to know that there was someone here who worried about him. As long as the letters were the sort that passed between friends, of course.

Charlotte could have told him not to worry. Because she was concerned for Lydia, and because she was, at least nominally, acting on Rafe's behalf, Charlotte had peeked at one of the letters before it went with the post. Lydia had written to Fitz about the fine turbot they'd had for supper the previous evening, and that the tweeney had taken a tumble down the stairs and twisted her ankle. Oh, and that the weather continued fine, and she hoped the weather was likewise fair in Brussels.

Not exactly a torrid love letter of the sort Lady Caroline Lamb supposedly penned to Lord Byron. Still, it was obvious to everyone that Lydia believed herself firmly and irrevocably in love with Captain Swain Fitzgerald.

"And another thing," Lady Daughtry piped up, recapturing Charlotte's wavering attention. "I won't forgive you for forcing me to miss the ball held to honor the King and Queen at the Hôtel de Ville because you withheld your permission for me to travel to Brussels.

You're not at all like your father. He was more than happy to give me anything I wanted."

"Yes, I remember. But as you say, Mother, I am not at all like him. You overspent your allowance and I refused your milliner's bill. Now that you've received your allowance for this quarter, and paid that bill, you and your epaulettes are free to fly wherever you wish."

"You are cruel and heartless," Lady Daughtry declared with some feeling.

"True. I'm also solvent, and intend to remain that way—unlike my father. And *you* will live within your allowance. Do you really wish to bring this all out for another airing, Mother?"

"No, I most assuredly do not, and you're vile for doing so, especially in front of delicate female ears… and Charlotte, of course."

Well, that put me in my place, didn't it? Charlotte thought, amused, and not insulted one bit. After all, you'd have to respect someone's opinion before you could be cheered or hurt by hearing it expressed.

Lady Daughtry, after that dramatic pause for effect, continued her litany of complaint. "Now, where was I? Oh, of course. My friend Lady Capel wrote to me to say the reception for the King and Queen was all one could wish. She said that to be mean, you know, just as if she hasn't been hiding away in Brussels for the past year to escape her husband's many debtors."

"You're doing it again, Mother. Still, so nice of you to come back to finances," Rafe said, once more looking to Charlotte, who didn't bother to shoot him a warning glance; the man was enjoying himself. "There is, having arrived with the morning post, Mama, a new stack of tradesmens' bills on my desk that threaten to collapse it. Would you happen to know anything about them?"

Lady Daughtry gave a dismissive wave of her hand. The one, Charlotte noticed, with the new ruby ring on her index finger. "Pish tosh, Rafael. A few necessary last-minute trifles, no more. Or would you have your mother the laughingstock of Brussels, clad in her rags and tatters? Heaven forfend, Rafael! You do have your reputation to consider, you know. I am only doing my part, lending you the consequence that befits the Duke of Ashurst."

"Yes, Rafe," Nicole said, her violet eyes dancing, her elbows propped most inelegantly on the table as she popped a bit of toast into her mouth. "Pish tosh! And shame on you."

Charlotte looked to Lydia, to see if there was anything to be heard from that quarter, not surprised that the girl didn't seem to notice that there was anyone else in the room. Poor thing. Penning long letters to Fitz every day, and then tearing them up, only to write him a few lines concerning only the most mundane details of her stay in Mayfair. How terrible it was to be in love and yet afraid to express it.

Choking slightly on a bite of ham as the words *and you know that better than most* skittered across her brain, Charlotte took a drink of juice and said, "What time will you depart for Dover, Lady Daughtry?" Oh dear, did she sound concerned, merely polite, or as if she couldn't wait for the dratted woman to stop chattering and take herself off? Probably the latter, considering the quick, hard look the woman sliced her.

"I still don't think I should go," Lady Daughtry said,

sighing theatrically. "To leave my dear innocent daughters this way is one thing, but to depart knowing that a young woman barely old enough to be called anyone's chaperone will be residing under my son's roof? Rafael, once again I implore you, consider appearances. For Miss Seavers's sake, send her home to her parents where she belongs." She smiled at Charlotte. "After all, my dear, it isn't as if anything will come of this, you know."

"I beg your pardon," Charlotte said, bridling at last, although careful to keep her smile intact. The woman did dig, and dig some more, until she finally managed to find something that could cause upset.

"No, no, my dear," Lady Daughtry said, reaching over to pat Charlotte's hand, "it is I who should beg yours, speaking so plainly. You're not children anymore, you and Rafael, gamboling about the fields of Ashurst Hall with Rafael's poor deceased cousins, Lord bless their departed souls, like the young scamps you once were. Innocent, you understand. You have your reputation as a responsible spinster to consider now, and Rafael has his duty. After all, just because you are firmly on the shelf, even if you steadfastly refuse my very sensible suggestions that you put on your caps, doesn't mean that people won't gossip."

Really, that was just too much. The woman couldn't spread on her meaning any thicker if she'd used a trowel. Charlotte's flash of anger subsided, and she laughed out loud.

But Rafe, it would seem, had not been similarly amused.

"Mama, that will be enough, thank you," he said

tersely, getting to his feet. "I'll have the coach brought round. You don't want to be on the road after dark in order to reach your posting inn."

Lady Daughtry sighed the sigh of the misunderstood and folded her serviette as one of the footmen scurried over to pull back her chair for her.

"Very well, Rafael, I've said what I've said and I'll say no more," she said, taking Rafe's arm. Yet as they walked, together, from the morning room, Charlotte could hear her still bending her son's ear. "I believe I am not above taking a hint. Let this be on your own head. However, I have taken the liberty of placing a list of names on your desk, young ladies of quality and breeding who are remaining in London for the Season. I particularly wish to direct your attention to Lady Katharine Musgrave. Lovely girl, twenty thousand a year, I hear, and sure to lose her baby fat before too long. And then there's Miss Amelia Whitehead. Only ten thousand a year from that quarter, alas, but she's one of six, so the family is known for its sterling breeding qualities. Oh, and Miss Susan…"

Nicole, who had stuffed part of her serviette into her mouth as her mother gave courting instructions to her brother, tossed the serviette onto the table and brought her fist down on the tabletop as she howled with laughter. "Did you hear her, Charlotte? She's made a *list!* Oh, poor Rafe. Is it bad form to feel sorry for a duke, do you suppose? Gad, I'm glad she's leaving. She keeps telling me I won't *take* in Society because my hair is too dark, and then she tells Lydia that *she* won't take in Society because she is too intelligent."

"We can suppose she knows, Nicole," Lydia said, at

last folding Fitz's letter and placing it on the table. "After all, she has been married three times."

"We only can pray she'll find a fourth husband while she's in Brussels, and that he then doesn't have a period put to his existence by Boney's troops within a week of the ceremony. Although that has been Mama's luck, hasn't it? Still, as she is so fond of saying, she makes a lovely widow. Now what's wrong with her?" she asked as Lydia fled the room.

"You mentioned the battle," Charlotte said, sighing. "I pray there is no need to confront Bonaparte, but if we must, let it be soon, and over quickly. Your sister is being worn to a frazzle with her worrying. Are you finished here, Nicole? I think the servants would like to clear the table."

The two adjourned to the hallway, Nicole still munching on a piece of toast, to meet Rafe coming toward them.

"She's gone!" he exclaimed as he flung his arms wide, looking as young and naughty as Nicole. "Oh, and, Charlie? Mrs. Buttram has arrived, bag and baggage, and is even now being shown to her rooms. Your reputation is saved."

"Yes, it is, although I doubt it was in danger. Why didn't you tell your mother about Mrs. Buttram, Rafe? She's convinced we're all going to run wild here, disgracing the family name."

"Yes, that was probably mean of me, wasn't it? I'm just happy that I heard of the woman. Lord Peters swears by her." He looked at Nicole. "You won't put anything past Mrs. Buttram, pet, to hear Lord Peters tell it. She's been playing companion and chaperone for more Seasons than you've been alive."

Nicole smiled sweetly. "It's not *me* she's chaperoning, Rafe, remember? Me or Lydia. She's here to protect Charlotte from *you*. Now, if you'll excuse me, I have to see to my sister, who is probably curled up on her window seat, sighing and mooning again. Honestly, love is so exhausting."

"I'll join you shortly," Charlotte said, but Rafe quickly said that he had other plans for her this morning. "Oh? I thought you'd be leaving for the War Office again. You seem to live there."

"And you miss me terribly, don't you?" He smiled at her as they walked toward the stairs leading down to the foyer. "I've asked your maid to fetch your bonnet and all that sort of thing. I thought we should celebrate my mother's departure by taking a drive through the Park, but then I realized that the Park is for nannies and infants in the morning, so we'll take a stroll instead. All right?"

"Yes, I think I'd like that. Thank you."

"You know," he said as he held out his arm to her when they got to the flagway, "I didn't realize how much I wanted my mother gone until she left. I may find it possible to spend more time in Grosvenor Square now that I won't pass that time attempting to avoid her."

"Am I supposed to respond to that, Rafe?" Charlotte asked facetiously.

"Yes, of course," he said, turning them to the left, placing Charlotte away from the roadway. "You are to say how very delighted you are that I will be gracing you with my esteemed presence."

"Oh my, I'm to say all of that?" she teased him. "You begin to sound like your mother. How wearisome it must be, carrying around all that *consequence*."

"The woman could take the joy out of anything, couldn't she? All, of course, while *she* is enjoying herself mightily. Tell me you don't suppose Nicole is like her."

"As your mother would say, *heaven forfend!* No, Rafe, Nicole is young, and she harbors some rather strange ideas—no thanks to her mama. But she'll be fine, she and Lydia both. They're only children."

"For another year," he reminded her. "Next spring they make their debuts in Society. Do you think we ought to warn them? Society, that is." He then nodded at a gentleman approaching them on the flagway, only stopping when the man placed himself squarely in front of them.

"Your Grace," the man said, sweeping off his curly brimmed beaver and bowing with a flourish. "Forgive me for accosting you in this ramshackle manner, but I was just on the way to leave my card at your domicile when you and the young lady appeared."

"Really," Rafe said as Charlotte looked at the man and his rather outlandish fashion that had his shirtpoints so high they must keep him from turning his head more than a fraction.

"Yes, Your Grace," the man continued. "I could not assure myself you should wish to see me, so I'd planned to take the coward's way out and merely, well, leave my card, and hope that you might be willing to receive me. But now here you are, you and this young lady." He bowed to Charlotte, who dropped into a slight curtsy, not knowing if she was honoring an earl or a tradesman come to dun Rafe for his mother's bills.

"Well, sir," Rafe said matter-of-factly, "until I know who you are, I really cannot answer you, can I?"

"Lord! See how clumsy I am, having met you this way? A thousand pardons, Your Grace. The name is Hobart, Your Grace. Hugh Hobart. I...I was on the yacht with your uncle and cousins that fateful day."

"Were you now," Rafe said as Charlotte tightened her grip on his arm.

There was a moment of silence that threatened to become most uncomfortable. Charlotte stepped into the breach. "How terrible for you, Mr. Hobart, to have been a part of such an unfortunate tragedy. It is only to be praised that you survived. Isn't it, Your Grace?"

Thus prodded, Rafe replied, "Indeed, yes, Mr. Hobart. Very nearly a miracle."

Hugh Hobart nodded furiously. "Yes, Your Grace, it is that, it is very much so that. Not that I escaped injuries, both to my person and to the quietness of my mind. That I, unworthy as I am, should live, and your family perish, and their lovely companions with them. We'd all been so enjoying ourselves." He sighed and shook his head. "Pray God theirs was a quick and merciful death, and may their souls rest at peace in heaven and suchlike."

Charlotte had only a rather slight acquaintance outside her own family and the bits of Society she had seen during her single Season, but she was beginning to believe she and Rafe were standing here confronted by what some would call an *encroaching cit.*

He was a young man, not more than five years Rafe's senior, she would suppose, his features too sharp for true handsomeness, his nose needle-thin and too long, his eyes rather close-set. Indeed, he had the look of a hungry ferret, all in all, a marginally upsetting man who had missed being a gentleman by a whisker, casting him forever in the realm of the nearly-ran.

The man's manner seemed well enough, but definitely strained, a mixture of stilted manners and conversation not fit for a lady's sensitive ears.

Rafe seemed to think the same, as his tone definitely turned cooler as he said, "Yes, then, very good, Mr. Hobart. Was there anything else? Miss Seavers and I wish to continue our stroll."

Mr. Hobart, rather than bowing and taking himself off, stepped more firmly in front of them, blocking their progress. "There…there is the one thing, Your Grace, reluctant as I am to bring it up in the company of your companion."

"Very well, have out with it," Rafe said as Charlotte looked up at him, her eyes telling him she agreed, and that he might as well get this over with now, rather than to have the man ever appear in front of them again. "This would be about money, would it not?"

"Ah, Your Grace, I hadn't planned to be quite so straightforward as that. But yes, if we're to talk with the gloves off, so to speak, it is about money that I have dared to confront you in this ramshackle manner. In point of fact, it is about a considerable amount of money, owed to me by your late cousin."

At last Charlotte understood. My goodness, she was standing on the flagway, conversing with a cardsharp, a gamester. Why, it was very nearly delicious. And to think she could have remained in the country, and missed all of this!

"Which one?" Rafe asked, stepping forward, putting Charlotte slightly behind him, just as if she hadn't already heard and seen everything.

"Why, Harold, Your Grace. I'd be branded as a fool to sit across the table from his brother, who had the devil's own luck—not at the end, of course, what with him drowning and all. But Harold fancied himself his brother's equal in all things, you understand, very much to the benefit of myself and others like me. I am not proud of what I do, Your Grace, but a good man fallen on hard times must live by whatever wits he has."

"And your wits led you to the card table, where you fleece young idiots with more hair than wit. You were correct in your initial assumption, Mr. Hobart. You should have passed us by and simply left your card. As it is now, you owe Miss Seavers an apology I shall not allow you to render, as you've already passed beyond the bounds of the decent. Good day to you, Mr. Hobart."

Charlotte watched as Hugh Hobart's close-set brown eyes narrowed. "Gambling debts are a matter of honor, Your Grace," he declared in a cold tone that sent a shiver down her spine. "I have your cousin's IOUs. The debt outlives him, Your Grace, as you well know."

Mr. Hobart reached inside his waistcoat and withdrew at least a dozen scraps of paper, holding them up to Rafe. "Five thousand pounds, Your Grace, that's the sum of it, give or take a farthing, and no more to be said on the matter, if you take my meaning."

"You suppose I care about my dead cousin's reputation, Mr. Hobart? Did your injuries in the *tragedy* extend to a hard knock on your head that has rattled your brains?"

Charlotte bit her bottom lip, caught between a smile and concern that Rafe might be making a mistake. She wasn't a woman of the world, far from it, but she did know that gambling debts were to be satisfied even before one paid for such mundane things as food and clothing.

But Mr. Hobart seemed defeated. He looked up at the sky, as if seeking heavenly advice, then down toward his boots, for if one quarter didn't answer him, perhaps he should be seeking assistance from a lower realm.

"If you'll step aside, Mr. Hobart, and allow us to pass?"

The man nodded, and then took one last look at the sky before shouting something unintelligible and rudely pushing Rafe and Charlotte into the gutter.

A moment later, a large chunk of masonry smashed on the flagway precisely where she and Rafe had been standing only that one moment earlier.

"Charlie! Are you all right?" Rafe asked her, gathering her close even as he looked up at the topmost story of the tall, thin house attached to his own mansion.

"Yes, Rafe, I'm fine," Charlotte assured him, although she was certain he could feel her entire body shivering in shock and fear. "Look up there, Rafe. It was a piece of the facade. If it wasn't for Mr. Hobart—"

"Yes, sweetheart, I know," he told her quietly. "It's either that or heavenly intervention, and I prefer to believe the former." He took her hand and led her back onto the flagway as Hugh Hobart kicked at a few bits of the facade that had landed near his shiny Hessians. "Mr. Hobart, you put yourself in danger in order to save us. We owe you our thanks."

"You do that," Mr. Hobart said smoothly, suddenly appearing like a man who'd looked inspiration in the face and was more than eager to seize this unexpected opportunity, turn a profit on it. "I'd say you owe me exactly five thousand pounds of thanks."

By this time, others walking in the Square had gathered around them, drawn by the commotion and pointing up at the house. More than a few were bemoaning the terrible state of affairs that had led to the house being abandoned by its owner and allowed to fall into such disrepair.

"And who might be that owner?" Rafe asked a red-faced woman frantically fanning herself with her handkerchief.

"Why…why *you* are, Your Grace," she said even as she curtsied to him. "That is to say, your uncle took the house from the former owner after the man had a bad run of luck at the tables last year. Poor Sir Richard. Hanged himself in his study, you understand, more fool him for wagering against the duke, a man without conscience or heart."

The woman seemed to belatedly remember that she was speaking ill of the dead, and to the new duke at that. She melted back into the small crowd just as a very large gentleman was calling out for everyone to step aside, and moved those along who didn't react as swiftly as he wished by prodding them with his cane.

"You there—yes, you, standing there thinking you've had a lucky escape. Not that you didn't, but I saw everything from my carriage as I was driving into the Square. There was a man up there on the roof, I saw him plain as the nose on your face. Tossed that stone straight down at your heads." He turned to Mr. Hobart and tipped his hat to him. "Good thing you were here, lad, to save the day!"

"Why, thank you, kind sir," Hugh Hobart drawled, bowing. "I believe the duke was just thinking much the same thing."

CHAPTER TWELVE

RAFE WISHED FITZ were here with him. Together they could talk out the events of the morning, and perhaps come to a conclusion. He also could have introduced his friend to Mr. Hugh Hobart, who had left Grosvenor Square with a bank draft for five thousand pounds tucked up in his waistcoat, the IOUs burned in the grate.

Fitz would have known what to make of the man. He also would have accompanied Rafe as he had taken the key his majordomo provided and inspected the property from whence the masonry had fallen. *His* property.

That he hadn't immediately inspected the house was because he was otherwise occupied with Charlotte, who had flatly refused to return to the mansion without him and order the key sent to him with one of the footmen.

No, not Charlotte; she was having none of it. Whoever had been on the roof was probably already long gone, she reasoned, and if he happened to still be inside, what good would it do anyone for Rafe to be shot by the man.

Knowing she was right, and because there were still so many people milling about—many of them looking at him as if the falling masonry was *his* fault—he'd only taken her arm and asked Hugh Hobart to accompany them back to the mansion.

His later inspection of the house, accompanied by two brawny servants and with a loaded pistol in his hand—it was either that, or Charlotte would have followed after him with a brace of the things—proved to be another shock.

He'd known his uncle and cousins, among their other vices, gambled deep at the clubs; indeed, his uncle had often boasted that it was his hand at the table that filled the Daughtry family coffers much more than any income from his estates.

But to take a man's house, his home? To strip it to the walls, as this town house was, leaving only a paltry few sticks of furniture? Or perhaps Sir Richard had sold off his furniture, bit by bit, in order to pay his gaming debts, and his uncle had taken possession of nothing more than the run-down shell that had clearly once been a magnificent domicile.

No matter what, the house was now his, a house where the former owner had hanged himself.

As he'd inspected every floor, every room, a thought took hold in his brain and began to grow.

What a perfect residence for his mother when she returned from Brussels. If she agreed, he'd put Charlotte to work on the project immediately.

It wasn't a perfect solution, but as he knew he didn't possess the means to somehow transport Helen Daughtry to the far side of the moon, it remained an intriguing possibility.

Charlotte, however, when he brought up the subject after dinner that evening in his study, where the two of them had taken to retiring to discuss matters of the day, was not quite so enamored of his brilliance.

She was much more interested in impressing on Rafe that someone clearly was attempting to *murder* him, and that—and only that—was her concern. Did he really believe she'd prefer to occupy herself choosing fabrics and furnishings, all of which, by the way, his mother would probably loathe unless they were gilt, and pink, and horribly overdone.

"Don't frown at me and behave as if I'm supposed to pretend I didn't notice what went on this morning, Rafe. I know I'm only a female, but—"

"Oh, you're so much more than *only a female,*" he interrupted, toasting her with his wineglass. "Any other woman would have had a case of strong hysterics when that chunk of masonry came down at us. I'm extremely proud of you. I mean it, Charlie."

"Well, thank you, I suppose. But are you sure you wouldn't prefer a lovely creature with twenty thousand a year and only a few extraneous pounds to shed?"

"Oh, Christ. You heard that?"

"Of course I heard that. Your mama made certain that I did, just as I heard all her other barely veiled remarks meant to put me in my place—which, according to her, is back at Rose Cottage. Except, of course— as I shouldn't have given you a chance to change the subject—that I can't leave you here alone now to ignore what are very obvious attempts to murder you."

"I'm not aware that I have any enemies," he said quietly. Charlotte wasn't Fitz, wasn't a soldier, but she was intelligent, and Rafe valued her opinion. "If we can rule out what happened at Ashurst Hall, that is, because I believe we can. My cousin's friends, any of them who are still aboveground, wouldn't have followed me to London."

"I know, I've already concluded that. Somebody came to Ashurst Hall and made the attempts," Charlotte said matter-of-factly, rolling up the ribbons that hung from the bodice of her very fetching new gown, making a knotted mess of them. "What do you think of our Mr. Hugh Hobart?"

"I was just about to ask you the same thing. I think, first of all, that he's not *our* Mr. Hugh Hobart. With any luck, he's gone now, happy with Harold's satisfied gambling debt." He looked at her from beneath his lowered eyelids. "Unless you're thinking something else?"

"I am. I'm thinking that Mr. Hobart was very lucky this morning, to have been where he was, when he was."

Rafe frowned. "Go on."

"Consider this, Rafe. Hugh Hobart couldn't have positioned us more neatly to have our heads crushed by that falling masonry," she offered, tipping her head as she looked at him, gauging his reaction.

"True. But it was a chance meeting."

She nodded, saw what she was doing to her ribbons, and frowned in consternation at the mess she had made. "Unless he was watching for us, stationed out there in the Square, hoping you would walk out one day. You do walk out fairly often, after all."

"And he likewise stationed a cohort on the roof of my new home while he lurked in the entrance of some alleyway, days and nights on end, through wind and rain and damp, just waiting for me to step outside? And, to top the thing, he pushed us out of the way, saving us both. Does all that seem logical, Charlie?"

She sighed, shook her head. "It all seemed so, yes,

when I was telling myself what I thought, upstairs. But no, I'm afraid it doesn't. In fact, it seems a dreadful waste of time and effort."

"So where does that leave us?"

"I don't know. We don't like Mr. Hobart. We agree on that?"

"Most definitely," Rafe told her. "Putting aside everything else that happened this morning, I wouldn't like the man simply because he was friends with my late cousins. It shows a lack of character on his part, don't you agree?"

"I doubt friendship is what attracted them to each other. Now think about this, if you please. Mr. Hobart was there when your uncle and cousin drowned. He was here today when we were almost killed. Either the man is a jinx of the first water, or he needs looking into, Rafe."

Rafe nodded his agreement. "You've got a clever mind, Charlie. I say that because it's true, and because you seem to be agreeing with me on all counts. No, I doubt mutual respect and admiration was the attraction."

"Definitely not. Which begs the question again, the one you just asked. Where does that leave us?"

Rafe thought about this for some moments, pacing the carpet. "I imagine we'd have to ask ourselves why Hugh Hobart would want me dead."

"If he'd wanted you dead, Rafe, you'd be dead. He pushed you out of the way, remember?"

"So the man's now a hero?"

Charlotte just looked at him, and then shrugged. "Or he wants something else. Since we're getting nowhere discussing the ubiquitous Mr. Hobart, let's get back to you. Are you certain you haven't offended anyone?"

"No, Charlie, I'm not certain. But if I have, certainly not enough to have anyone dogging me for these past months, attempting to kill me."

"Do you know what I think, Rafe?"

"I can't say that I do, although I doubt you'll allow me to remain in happy ignorance. Go on, Charlie. What do you think?"

"Wretch. I *think,* having thought about this all of the day, that you could have been shot at any time. Lord knows you rode out at Ashurst Hall every day, and move about the city now without incident."

"I was shot at, remember? I still regret the loss of that hat."

"Ah, yes, but that actually could have been an accident. A poacher, remember? Even you thought so. And the shoeing nail caught up in Boney's saddle? Also an unfortunate accident."

"The masonry. Again, not unheard of in the city, I understand. I mentioned something this afternoon at the War Office and was told two people were badly injured just last week on Brook Street in an episode similar to ours. Sans the presence of Mr. Hobart, that is."

"Our incident, Rafe, as you call it, was also accompanied by a man on the roof *pushing* the masonry down on us."

"Yes, he was seen. But, in keeping with your theory, he might not have been seen, and the whole thing put down to an accident. Clearly, if I am to die, someone does not wish that death to be termed a murder."

"And think of the time and energy expended, Rafe," she pointed out, again amazing him. "Three attacks over the course of nearly five months. The man is determined, and quite patient. Unless there were other incidents you did not realize were actually attempts on your life?"

Rafe thought for a moment, and then shook his head. "Nothing that I can recall. The last time anyone shot at me was on Elba, and that was the enemy doing the firing. I doubt I was the only target."

"On Elba? But I thought you were only there to make sure Bonaparte didn't decide to leave. Why would there be any reason for violence?"

"I saw some strangers in the tap at one of the inns and questioned why they'd landed on Elba," Rafe said, thinking back over the incident. "Frenchmen, you understand, at least the one who spoke to me was French. I didn't see the other man except from the back as they left the inn. Fitz and I followed, called for them to halt—I wished to ask them a few more questions—and one of them turned and fired at us. I wonder now what would have happened had I been able to capture and question them. After all, it wasn't three months later that Bonaparte did his flit."

"Why had the two men come to Elba? Did the man you asked say?"

"For repairs to their ship," Rafe said, rubbing at his chin. "After the shot was fired, Fitz ran to summon the troops while I followed the men, but I lost them in the dark. They must have had a longboat pulled up somewhere, and disappeared with it."

He shrugged his shoulders. "No, that incident had

nothing to do with what's happening now. Unless," he said, not above teasing Charlotte, "the second man I saw but really didn't see had hired the Frenchman to murder me, making the incident appear as if I was killed while fending off an attempt to free Bonaparte. There is that. Having failed, the man has returned to England to continue his quest to see me belowground, and brought his French hireling with him. Think back, Charlie. When the masonry missed us, did you perhaps hear someone above us cry *Mon Dieu, foiled again?*"

"There are times, Rafael Daughtry, when I could cheerfully choke you. Besides, it would be much easier to concentrate on Mr. Hobart, since at least we know who he is. I can't like him, no matter that he may have saved our lives. And now he is not only five thousand pounds richer, but he believes we feel in charity with him for his good deed. His smile was insufferably smug when you asked him to accompany us back to the mansion, in case you hadn't noticed. I suggest you hire someone to have him followed."

Again, she had come to the same conclusion as he had, and he'd already planned to hire a Bow Street Runner for just that purpose. It wasn't all that jolly, surviving six years of war, just to come home and have part of a building tossed down at one's head.

"Agreed." He sat down beside her on the leather couch. "Now, having truly talked the subject of Hugh Hobart to death, is there anything else we need to discuss this evening? How is Mrs. Buttram settling in?"

"Ah, yes, Mrs. Buttram. At the moment, she is most concerned with placing me in the pecking order, as she seems to believe there must be a clearly explained reason why I'm here. I believe she is caught between wondering if I am an upper servant, a governess, or your ward, and I'm afraid I won't be able to fend her off for long without giving her some sort of answer. Nicole says she's a dragon, not that I noticed any fire shooting from her rather prodigious snout."

"You are here for a reason," Rafe told her, daring to lift a hand to her hair, wrap one of her curls around his finger. "You're here to serve as a supporting prop to me in my hour of need."

"If you refuse to be serious…"

"I'm always serious, Charlie, when we talk about how I feel about you."

Charlotte twisted her hands together in her lap, the air in the study suddenly filled with tension. "Sometimes…sometimes I think you simply feel responsible for me, as if you owe me something because of what happened with your uncle and cousins. There, I've said it. I don't like sympathy, Rafe."

"And that's what you think? That I feel *sorry* for you?"

She lowered her head, once more occupying her hands in her attempt to ruin her ribbons. "Why shouldn't you? *I* certainly feel sorry for me. It was terrible, Rafe, what they did to me."

He cupped her cheek in his hand. "I know. They took something from you that you never really had."

She looked up into his face, and his heart squeezed painfully in his chest. How he longed to hold her…and so much more.

"I…I don't understand."

"No, I'm sure you don't. And I'm not sure I know

how to explain what I mean," Rafe said, pleased that she hadn't pushed his hand aside, that she was remaining on the couch beside him, not preparing to make some excuse to escape his proximity because it was just the two of them, alone together in the small circle of light cast by the fire and a few candles; man, and woman.

"Charlie, I feel your fear when I kiss you. When I try to put my arms around you. That's what they took from you, sweetheart. They took something that should be beautiful and turned it into something evil, ugly and painful, and unbelievably crude."

"What he was doing to that woman...what he tried to do to me..."

"Shh, I know," Rafe said, stroking her smooth cheek. "It doesn't have to be like that."

Now she did try to push herself away from him. "I'm not entirely stupid. I know that. I mean, in my mind, I know that. And I know, in my heart, that you would never hurt me, not ever. And...and I know we're not children anymore, and that what you think you want from me is what we should both want...and I do, I do! But then you're so understanding, and so...so damn *gentle,* as if I might shatter into a million pieces, and I feel like such a fool because you look at me as this poor mistreated *victim,* and I'm not, Rafe. I'm not! I know how it should be between us. When I think you could be in danger I just want to come to you, and hold on to you and—"

This time he didn't gently cup her face between his palms. This time he placed his hands on the back of her neck, and held her fast as he silenced her protests with his mouth.

He felt the initial softening toward him, perhaps even the beginnings of passion, but he knew it wouldn't last. She would draw back from him in a moment, and he would have lost her again.

Rafe spoke against her mouth. "Smile, sweetheart," he crooned to her. "Smile as I kiss you, as you kiss me back."

She put her palms against his chest and pushed away from him, but not in fear. "Smile? Why on earth would you say such a thing?"

"I don't know. The words just popped into my head. We're supposed to be happy, damn it, remember? Try it, Charlie. We'll both try it."

"You're insane," she said. But she smiled for him.

Before she could stop, he curled up the corners of his own mouth and kissed her again.

And damn, but the feeling was different; immediate and extremely pleasant. Her mouth was soft, and she wasn't holding back from him, didn't seem ready to jump up and flee from the room.

He kissed the corners of her mouth, slanting his first one way, then the other. Not attempting to introduce more intimacy, but just exploring her full, wide mouth that haunted his dreams. She sighed, began to melt into him.

And then she giggled.

He tried to remain solemn, the teacher giving a lesson, but the sound of her delight exploded that dream, and he began to laugh as well.

Mouth to mouth, their hands on each other's shoulders, they shared something that might be as singular, and as rare, as genuine passion—they shared joy.

When he ended the kiss, it was to see Charlotte's

lovely brown eyes dancing with glee, and not a single fading shadow of fear or unease.

"Charlie?"

"Rafe?" she responded sing-song.

"Are we insane?" he asked her.

"Why, yes, Your Grace, I do think that is a distinct possibility."

"Well, at least we're insane together. There is that."

"I need to go check on the twins before they come looking for me." Charlotte stood up. "I…thank you, Rafe. I can't imagine what I was afraid of," she told him, smoothing down her skirts. "In fact, I…I rather look forward to your next lesson."

"Things are growing warm at the War Office, but I'll see if I can fit another lesson into my schedule," he said, also getting to his feet. "Or we could simply continue with the current lesson. We started with smiles. We could now advance to outright grinning?"

As he put out his arms she danced away from him, looking happier and more carefree than he could remember seeing her since he'd returned home from the war. Something had happened between them here this evening. He didn't know quite what, but something had happened. Something good.

"I have to go," she told him after a short hesitation, and quickly headed for the door.

"Charlie…?" he called after her. "You were about to say something, weren't you? What was it?"

She turned and looked at him from beneath her lowered lashes. "I was…I was about to tell you that, frightened as I was that night, I couldn't help but notice something about your cousin Harold."

Harold, the bastard who had been coupling with that poor unknown woman, rutting like a low animal. Did Rafe really want to know what Charlotte had noticed? "And what was that?"

"Well," she said slowly, and then finished in a rush, "he wasn't wearing so much as a stitch of clothing, you know. And, horrified as I was, I thought—well, I thought he looked exceedingly silly."

Of all the disclosures he could have thought she'd make, what she actually said was the last thing Rafe could have expected to hear. He laughed and shook his head. "Poor Harold. He always was rather...fleshy."

"And pink," Charlotte, seemingly encouraged, added. "Like a pig. And that has...has bothered me all this time. I mean, I don't...I don't think men are very pretty, I guess I should say."

"No, I suppose not," Rafe said, sorry he'd pushed her to share her thoughts with him. Damn Harold!

"Yes, but...but I also think..." She lowered her voice, but he could still hear her. "I don't think you would look silly at all. I...I think—not that I dwell on such things!— but I imagine you are probably quite beautiful."

"Charlie..." He took two quick steps toward her, but she'd already turned and fled the room.

CHAPTER THIRTEEN

Brussels
28 May 1815

My dearest friend and compatriot,

How much, do you think, can a man march on Parade before that man considers death at the hands of the enemy a blessed release? I feel badly for the troops I drill daily, as we all cool our heels and wait on that damned Boney. You joked when you named your gelding after the man. Would that he had been similarly castrated, eh?

And yet, with Blücher and his army still an uncomfortable distance from Brussels, I suppose we should be glad that Boney is dragging his heels. Leave it to the French to always be late, yes?

Wellington is a cagey one. Outwardly, he is all parties and balls and graciousness, while behind the scenes he has us all scouring the countryside for sight of the enemy, and charting possible battlefields and the various strategies he might employ.

There is no denying it, old friend, a momentous battle is coming, and soon. I'm sure you read the dispatches, and they all say the same thing. One fight, one tumultuous day in the field, one victory, and the nightmare is over.

And then, I fear, you and I may enter into our own battle, for I will say something now that will probably infuriate you.

I love your sister, Rafe…Your Grace. I know, I know. She's only a child, just seventeen, while I am suddenly ancient at six and twenty. Which is why I give you my solemn vow that I will do nothing to influence Lydia in any way, not until she's had her Season next year.

It's only because I'm far removed from Grosvenor Square and you can't call me out or knock me down, that I'm brave enough to confess what's in my heart…who is in my heart.

I'm nothing but a soldier, Rafe, with little to offer a duke's beloved sister save a run-down Irish estate and my complete and utter devotion. But if you will at least consider my suit, and my heart, I will pray that I might be allowed to harbor the hope of one day gaining your blessing.

For now all I can ask is the obvious, that you keep my dearest Lyddie safe. I miss her so terribly, her smile, her sweet ways, her gentle humor and her fine mind. For the first time, Rafe, I fear battle, now that I have so much to lose…
Your Devoted Servant and Humble Petitioner,
Captain Swain McNulty Fitzgerald
P.S. For God's sake, Rafe, burn this letter! I sound like a silly, superstitious old woman!

WITHOUT A WORD, Rafe handed Fitz's letter to Charlotte, who had been sitting quietly in his study, working her embroidery hoop, and then returned to his seat behind his desk.

He steepled his hands in front of his face and lightly tapped the sides of his fingers against his mouth, watching her as she read.

Her eyes scanned the pages, once, and then again, before she laid the letter in her lap and looked across the room to Rafe, her eyes swimming with tears.

"Oh, Rafe," she said quietly, her voice breaking slightly. "This is both beautiful and sad. And so very frightening."

"I know." He brought a fist down on the desktop. "Damn him!"

"Rafe!" Charlotte got to her feet and walked over to the desk, confronting him across its surface. "Fitz may be seen by some to be reaching above himself, above his station, but we know his heart is pure and—"

"That's not it, Charlie. Christ, I couldn't ask for better for Lydia," Rafe interrupted her, slamming back his chair and heading for the drinks table to pour himself a measure of strong spirits.

"No, of course not. Because he's your friend, and we know what a fine, exemplary man Fitz is…."

Rafe drank the two fingers of brandy in one swallow, and then poured another measure before returning to his chair. "He's maudlin, Charlie. He's feeling sorry for himself, and thinking like a man more worried for his own survival than defeating the enemy."

"Wouldn't any rational person feel that way?"

Rafe shook his head. "No, not a soldier. A soldier

thinks only of the battle, only of the men under his command. To think about yourself, about the chance you might not survive the day? That's worse than cursing yourself. That brings you to cautions that often end with your destruction. Fitz knows that. This isn't to be his first battle, the first time he's faced the enemy. He *knows* that!"

"But what can we do?"

"I don't know. I can't go to Brussels. He'd know I'd come to nursemaid him, and that would only make things worse. He's a grown man. He's a fine soldier, better than a fine soldier. Brave. Fearless. He's saved my life more than once. Damn it, why did he have to fall in love *now?*"

"I doubt many people plan falling in love, Rafe." Charlotte retrieved the letter and put it down in front of him. "He's said what he felt he needed to say. And it would seem he knows he's being dramatic. When the time comes, when Bonaparte finally appears, he'll be fine. He's just spending too many days and nights waiting, that's all. There's been too much time to think about the battle."

. Rafe picked up the pages, scanned them again. "You're probably right. No, you *are* right. His first words were of his men, of Wellington and the battle. I can see him now, sitting alone, his candle and the level in the bottle at his elbow both lowering as he wrote, until he finally said some things he almost immediately wished he hadn't."

"He wants you to know he loves Lydia. I think that's wonderful."

He looked up at Charlotte. "Thank you, Charlie. As

always, you're the sensible one. Besides, if I wrote to him to tell him not to be maudlin, what good would it do? Better to write that he should not be a horse's ass, and get himself home safe so he can court Lydia." He opened the top drawer of the desk and pulled out a sheaf of paper with his ducal crest on it.

Charlotte handed him his pen and pushed the ink pot closer to him. "That's what he wants, Rafe. Your blessing."

He was already scratching out his salutation. "Well, then he's a bloody fool to think he wouldn't get it. My God, he's my friend, and I love the idiot. I don't know what I'd do without either one of you, damn it."

"Either one of us idiots," Charlotte said cheerfully, turning to leave the study. "Ah, Your Grace, you do have a silken tongue."

"Charlie, wait—" he said, looking up at her. "No, never mind. You know what I meant, what I mean." And then he smiled, seeing her enjoyment. "I'm a soldier still, and as smooth around the edges as I was the day I left Ashurst Hall a raw youth of nineteen."

"Yes, you really do have to work on acquiring some consequence, Rafe," she told him, clearly holding back a laugh. "Perhaps you should take up pinching snuff, or carrying a quizzing glass? Think how that would please your mother."

"The devil with pleasing my mother. She'd have me trumped out like some mummer, whirling about uselessly in Society, and bracketed to a pudgy heiress who is as brainless and shallow as she is. I much prefer you, Charlie."

"Again, Your Grace, your compliments fair bid to

overwhelm me," Charlotte said, gathering up her embroidery hoop. "Now, tear up whatever it is you wrote, and pen Fitz a cheerful note that gives him your blessing and says nothing else save that you're looking forward to his return so the two of you can get yourselves shamelessly drunk while he tells you tales about Bonaparte."

Rafe looked up at her, realizing what she'd just done. "You have just tried to tease *me* out of being maudlin. Haven't you, Charlie?"

"Perhaps. Did it work?"

"It did. Thank you."

"You're welcome," she said quietly, looking at him in a way that, once again, gave him hope that everything would end happily for them both, together.

He'd been at the War Office nearly day and night, sometimes even sleeping on the couch in the office he'd been provided. Marshal Ney, changing allegiances as often as most men changed their linen, had gone over to Bonaparte again, as had many others. Rafe and the others working with him had been considering strategies from every angle for weeks now, and just when they thought they knew what Bonaparte would do next, something like Ney's defection would rear its ugly head.

But the inevitable battle would come, Bonaparte would be defeated once and for all time, and he and Charlotte would return to Ashurst Hall, where they could devote themselves entirely to themselves. How he longed for that day.

"Charlie..." he ventured, and then hesitated, not knowing what to say.

She seemed to know that, too, and said, "You have to hurry, you know, as you already told me you're needed for something at the War Office, and you'll want to catch the afternoon post with that letter. We'll see you at dinner?"

He nodded, and then turned back to his letter.

THE FOYER CLOCK HAD JUST struck midnight when Charlotte decided that she was being silly remaining in the drawing room, one ear cocked toward the hallway, waiting to hear that Rafe had returned from the War Office or wherever he'd been since their time together that afternoon.

She knew he'd been genuinely upset by Fitz's most recent letter. She also worried about Fitz, who was a good, kind man, but Rafe's concern must be ten times hers. Especially since they'd been soldiers together for so many years. There had to be a special bond between soldiers that she, a mere woman, could not hope to understand, never having risked her life on a battle-field.

Rafe hadn't returned for dinner, but had only sent a note round explaining that matters would keep him at the War Office until at least nine o'clock, and they should simply dine without him.

Charlotte understood that, too, that nine o'clock had been a possibility, but that she could not hold him to that hour, and he would remain where he was as long as he was needed.

Still, she'd hesitated about going upstairs to bed until she saw him again, hoping that he was no longer so worried about Fitz.

And then there were those attempts on his life. He knew someone had tried to kill him at least three times, maybe more. He knew that *she* knew it. That was why he'd taken the time to send a note earlier, why he always notified her if he was not going to be back in Grosvenor Square when he said he would be there.

Because she'd worry, even though there had been no further attempts or problems since the day Hugh Hobart had saved them from the falling masonry. And, as Rafe reminded her when she spoke of that incident, he also had not seen Mr. Hobart peeking out from any alleys since then. It was as if the entire incident hadn't happened.

Still, she worried. She worried while attempting to appear as if she didn't worry.

But now that Lydia and Nicole had gone upstairs, and even "The Buzzing Bees," as Nicole called Mrs. Beasley and Mrs. Buttram, had given up their incessant chattering and taken themselves off to bed, Charlotte felt rather uncomfortable sitting here alone, and so obviously waiting for Rafe.

She put down the embroidery she hadn't been paying attention to anyway and walked into the foyer, picking up one of the small braces of candles left there to light the mansion's inhabitants to bed. She gave a look to the remaining brace of candles, those reserved for Rafe, and sighed. Really, he was a grown man, and she was being ridiculous, worrying about him.

But he'd been so upset by Fitz's letter...

Lifting her skirts with her free hand, Charlotte nodded a good-night to the lone footman waiting for the return of the duke, and made her way up the winding staircase, pausing near the top when she thought she heard voices below her.

Rafe. He was back.

Should she hurry to her room so he didn't see her and realize she'd been waiting for him? Should she stand her ground and ask him if he really believed it was nine o'clock? Should she ask him if he'd eaten, or if he'd like her to ring for something from the kitchens?

Should she stop behaving like a hysterical ninny?

"Rafe," she said as nonchalantly as possible when she heard his footsteps behind her on the stairs. "I was just now going up to bed and—"

As she spoke, she'd slowly turned around, and one look at his face was enough to make her forget whatever else it was she had been about to say.

"Rafe? Rafe, what's wrong?"

He put a hand to his forehead, pale beneath dark hair that was damp and curling on that forehead. His other hand gripped the railing as if he might fall if he let go.

"Nothing…nothing's wrong. Just…I think I fell asleep at my desk at some point. Stupid…"

She hurried up the few remaining steps to the landing and then stood aside as he joined her. Even in the flickering light of the candles she held and those burning in wall brackets along the hallway, she could see that he wasn't well. His eyes were too bright, his cheeks unnaturally flushed.

She put the back of her hand against one of those flushed cheeks, and quickly drew it away. "My God, Rafe, your face is on fire! You're ill!"

"No…no, I'm not," he said, pushing past her, fairly

lurching down the hallway toward his bedchamber. "It's just this…this damn fever that plagues me sometimes. It comes, it goes. I'll be fine by morning. Don't…don't worry about me, Charlie. Go to bed."

Charlotte watched as he struggled to depress the latch and enter his bedchamber. Go to bed, would she? The devil she would! The man was ready to fall down!

"Stop that," she said tersely, slapping his hand away from the latch so that she could open the door for him. "Now go inside and let me ring for Phineas. Oh, drat! Phineas isn't here, is he? It's his free day, and he's with his mates, gossiping and drinking themselves cock-eyed." She took Rafe's hand—his hot, dry hand—and pulled him into the chamber, quickly setting down her candle on a nearby table. "Come on, you need to get into bed."

"I think so, too," Rafe muttered, already attempting to strip off his neckcloth. "Hot in here…"

"Yes, yes, of course. Hot in here," Charlotte said, still maneuvering him across the large room and toward the high, four-poster bed. Once there, she turned him about and began pulling off his jacket, which wasn't easy, as his tailor had done a fine job of molding it to Rafe's tall, well-muscled body.

"Why didn't you tell me about this fever? I've heard that some of our soldiers who served on the Peninsula contracted fevers. Why didn't you say anything?"

He dipped his head down, touching his forehead to hers. "Nosy little Charlie, has to know everything," he said almost boozily, as if he could be deep in his cups. His breath was hot on her face. "Want to know something else? Want to know what I think about, Charlie?

How I want to lay you down in soft grass and take the pins from your hair and the clothes from your body. And then touch you, everywhere, all over…and kiss you, and then sink deep inside you…"

Charlotte fought the quick, panicked urge to leave him where he stood and run from the room.

But he didn't know what he was saying. It was the fever, that's all. He wasn't like Harold or George. He wasn't! What he wanted from her wasn't ugly; it couldn't be ugly, not with Rafe.

"Yes, yes," she steeled herself to say brightly, "that all sounds simply wonderful, Rafe. Now give me your arm, because your sleeves are so tight that—ah, there's a good soldier. Now the other one."

The jacket joined the neckcloth on the floor and she quickly unbuttoned his waistcoat and urged him to shrug it off his shoulders, leaving him clad only in shirt-sleeves and buckskins.

She began unbuttoning his shirt.

She shouldn't feel attracted to him at this moment. But she did. Was it because he seemed so vulnerable? She certainly couldn't be afraid of him, not right now. Not that she had ever been afraid of him. She ran her fingertips down his bared chest, marveling at his hard muscles, and she shuddered inside. He was so very male, every inch of him.

Then he swayed where he stood, and she shook off her foolish thoughts.

"Your shoes. Rafe, your shoes." She went down on her knees in front of him. "Lift your foot, Rafe. Yes, that's good," she praised him, slipping the evening shoe from his foot. "Now the other one. Ah, perfect."

She got to her feet, catching him as he began to weave from side to side.

"Cold. So cold in here," he said, his eyes closed. "Damn this godforsaken place, Fitz. We either freeze or burn…"

Barely able to support his weight, Charlotte prayed quietly, "Sweet Jesus, help me, please. I have to get him into bed." To Rafe she ordered, "Stop that, Captain Daughtry! Stand still, soldier! *Good.* Now stay like that until I can turn down the covers."

She roughly pulled at the satin coverlet, sending pillows flying everywhere, her one hand gripping Rafe's upper arm to keep him steady on his feet.

"There! Now help me, Rafe. You have to help me. Rafe? Rafe, do you hear me?"

"Yes, Fitz, I hear you. Don't want to bed her, but at least she's warm. She could wash my shirt…" he said, and then tried to swallow. "Thirsty. Many apologies, *ma chérie.* You are very lovely, but I am very weary."

Charlotte didn't know what he meant about the woman, and at the moment she didn't much care. She just wanted Rafe to lie down before he fell down, probably toppling her to the floor with him.

"Sit down on the bed and I'll get you something to drink. I promise."

She gave him a little push and he obeyed her, half slumping on the side of the mattress. Gracious, why had she never before realized just how big Rafe was, how much stronger than she, even dreadfully sick and half out of his head?

"Good," she said, and then she put both her hands against his chest and gave him a mighty push, sending him backward onto the bed. She then picked up his feet, and by dint of perseverance, some shoving that brought her hands into extremely personal contact with his body—she'd think about that later, while she was making up excuses for not ringing for some servants to help her—managed to get his legs up on the bed and beneath the covers.

Nearly exhausted by her efforts, Charlotte looked about the dim chamber, at last spying a pitcher and a tooth glass on a high chest in his dressing room. With shaking hands, she poured a measure of cool water into the glass and ran it back to the bed.

"Here, Rafe," she said, holding out the glass, "drink this. Rafe, open your eyes! You need to drink this."

He tried to lift his head from the pillow, but his body didn't seem to want to obey him. With another muffled prayer that was probably more of a curse, Charlotte yanked up her skirts and climbed onto the mattress. She knelt there, doing her best to raise his head from the pillows and not spill the water as she brought the glass to his lips.

He drank thirstily, but his teeth began to chatter so violently that she was forced to pull the glass away, fearful he'd bite straight through it.

"Cold, Fitz…" he whispered, his body shaking all over. "So bloody cold. Can't get warm…"

Rafe's rambling words repeated themselves in Charlotte's head as she watched him react to the fever. She felt so powerless.

He was already under the covers. There was a fire in the grate, but his was a large room, and even in May, large rooms like this could be very cool at night.

Poor darling. He was burning up, yet he was cold. Shivering. And out of his head. Talking about some unknown woman. Talking to Fitz as if the man was in the room with him. His teeth chattering.

Don't want to bed her, but at least she's warm.

Charlotte understood now.

The woman wasn't here. Fitz wasn't here. But she was here. *She* was warm....

Charlotte slid off the bed, slipped out of her shoes, took a deep breath and then lifted the covers, crawling in beneath them until her body was up against Rafe's.

He didn't seem to notice. He was still shivering, still burning up with fever.

She wasn't helping him. Yet she'd come this far, dared this much.

She lifted his arm away from his body and moved closer, pulling his arm around her as she snuggled tight against his side.

She smelled the maleness of him, felt the outline of his body pressed against hers, was amazed at the blazing heat coming from him.

There was a moment of panic, one so swift and frightening that she nearly bolted from the bed. But this wasn't Harold. This was Rafe. Who needed her. Who'd never hurt her.

Closing her eyes, she slid her hand across his chest, half hugging him, willing him to feel the heat she was giving him, to take from her, to heal himself. She levered her left knee up and across his thigh, until she was completely wrapped around him, as if protecting him from some unseen enemy.

His body moved against hers, turning slightly onto

his side as if seeking even more heat, and he slid his arm toward her beneath the covers. His hand somehow found and closed around her left breast.

Oh God...

His sigh was deep, audible, and his body seemed to at last relax. His breathing became more measured, less rasping.

Charlotte waited. For days, years, aeons, she waited, her body melded to his, his hand still cupping her breast. She felt strange, as if something delicious was curling somewhere in her stomach—warm, welcome. She felt a need to *give,* to *share.*

Which was ridiculous.

"Rafe?" she said at last. "Rafe, are you all right?"

His only answer was a soft snore and another sigh as he at last moved his hand from her breast—only to slide his arm around her back and pull her even closer. His sigh had been one of pure contentment.

She'd done that? She'd brought him contentment?

Then why didn't she feel content herself? Why did she feel that there should be so much more than that?

Why did she *want* so much more than that?

Stop it! Stop it!

He'd told her he'd be fine by morning. She imagined he should know the truth of that.

But there were a lot of hours between now and morning, and she didn't like where her mind was going. Or perhaps she did like it, but also knew she shouldn't....

She tried to move, slip out of his grasp, but he only tightened his grip on her in his deep sleep.

His body was so hot, yet she wasn't really uncomfortable. And she was helping him. She'd just stay a while longer, until he was a little bit better, and then she'd leave him, go to her own chamber and try to forget any of this had happened.

Yes, that's what she'd do. With her cheek pressed hard against his chest, with the length of his body so intimately clinging to hers, with his arm around her as he sought her warmth, Charlotte made her decision.

CHAPTER FOURTEEN

RAFE AWOKE with a pounding headache and his mouth so dry his tongue was cleaved to the roof of it, while he seemed to be lying on sheets drenched in sweat.

Slowly, he remembered. The fever. Damn. He hadn't had a recurrence since that day in Paris when he'd found out he was now the Duke of Ashurst. He'd thought he'd never have to suffer its effects again.

He tried to open his eyes, but his lids were so heavy he gave that up as a bad job. But he knew that if he just lay here for a few minutes, slowly his strength would return, at least enough of it to leave the bed and go find a basin in which to soak his aching head.

He moved to stretch out his legs, but then stopped, realizing that it wasn't the sheets that were tangled around him, but something much more intriguing.

Forcing his eyes open, he looked down at the mass of tousled hair just below his chin. "Well, I'll be… Charlie?" He raised his, he realized, rather numb arm, and rubbed at her shoulder. "Charlie, wake up."

She mumbled something low in her throat and snuggled closer into his side.

Well, wasn't this interesting? Although it would be nice if he could remember how she got here.

Remaining quite still, because if he woke her up she'd leave him—that much he could be sure of at least—Rafe tried to remember the events of the previous evening.

He got as far as half climbing, half falling into his town coach outside the War Office. But he remembered nothing after that. This didn't frighten or surprise him, because Fitz had more than once told him he'd said things or done things in the midst of the fever that he couldn't remember.

As long as he hadn't frightened Charlie. As long as he hadn't said or done anything that destroyed all the slow progress he'd made over the months, gaining her trust, allaying her fears, banishing her nightmares.

But she was here, wasn't she?

God, yes, she was. And it felt so good to have her here. She felt so good.

He shifted slightly on the bed, careful not to disturb her, until he could move her more comfortably against his shoulder. That move brought his hand intriguingly close to her waist, and he gave in to temptation... running his hand along her side, glorying in her soft curves, the intriguing swell of her hip.

Rafe closed his eyes, allowed his fantasies of so many long, lonely weeks to invade his brain...

In his mind, he felt his hand stray to Charlotte's soft breast, to cup it, to gently awaken her body to what his touch could do for her...for them both.

She'd melt into him, her body reacting to what her waking mind still feared. He'd take her mouth, and she'd sigh into his, wordlessly inviting him to educate her in the glories of physical union when love, true love, is the teacher.

To touch her...to possess her...to slay all her demons

and send her soaring into the heavens…the two of them, together, sealing their love even as they bonded their bodies.

She didn't know. She couldn't know.

How he longed to teach her…

Rafe felt his own body stirring with desire. Did he dare? Would he frighten her?

God. How he wanted. How he needed…

And he was a sweat-soaked, probably stinking mess. Not even he liked waking up with him after one of his fevers. So much for early-morning fantasies. Passion departed, to make way for common sense.

"Charlie?" He shook her shoulder again. "Come on, sweetheart, time to wake up. It's morning."

She roused slowly, stretching out her legs, arching her back like a kitten waking from a nap…and then sat up in the bed quickly, her hand pushing so sharply into his lower belly that he nearly lost his breath.

"Rafe!"

God, she was beautiful. Slightly muzzy, her features still softened by sleep, her hair a tangle of dark honey around her face and shoulders.

"Sleep well?" he asked her in what he knew was a stupid attempt to keep the atmosphere light.

"I…uh…oh, my God, it's morning!"

"I think I already said that," he mumbled, rubbing at his abused stomach.

She blinked rapidly. "This is all my fault. I should have left you once you were sleeping but…but I wanted to stay." And then her eyes widened. "The twins…the servants! People will be up and about at any moment. Really, Rafe, I have to go. I have to go now."

Rafe lifted his hand and ran his fingertips down the side of her cheek. He wanted to concentrate on one bit of information she'd let slip in her agitation—that she'd wanted to stay with him. "But we'll talk later? We have a lot to say to each other."

Biting her lips between her teeth, she nodded her head in agreement and then slipped from the bed.

He fought the urge to call her back as she picked up her shoes and padded across the floor to the door. Once there, her hand on the latch, she turned to look at him. "After breakfast?"

"Yes, after breakfast. The War Office will have to get along without me today. We'll go for a drive, the two of us."

Charlotte smiled, the idea clearly pleasing her, and depressed the latch, stepping into the hallway.

"Miss Seavers? Oh, the shame, the shame!"

Charlotte slammed the door shut and leaned her back against it, as if an enraged army was about to break down the door.

"You probably should have peeked your head out first," Rafe said, trying not to smile at the look on her face.

"Shut up," she gritted out between clenched teeth, and any notion of a loverlike drive into the countryside vanished from his mind. "Just you shut up, Rafael Daughtry. I have to think."

"Is that so? All right. But, while you're thinking and I'm shutting up—who is out there in the hall, screeching at you?"

Charlotte closed her eyes and sighed. "Mrs. Buttram." She pushed herself away from the door and walked over to the fireplace to sit down on one of the chairs and slip her feet into her shoes. "How could I know the dratted woman would be up and prowling the hallways this early?" She glared at him. "Stop laughing—this isn't funny!"

"Are you sure? I'm fairly well amused. How *amused* did we get, by the way, as my memory is a little foggy."

"Stop doing that. There's nothing to remember. You were sick. I put you to bed."

"I'm half-undressed. Did you take unfair advantage of me in my debilitated state, Miss Seavers?" he asked her, and then grinned again as she picked up an ivory statuette from the table beside her and made as if to launch it at his head. But at least she didn't look frightened anymore.

There was a loud knock on the door, followed by Mrs. Buttram saying, "I will meet with the pair of you downstairs in one hour. Duke or no, it is *my* reputation as a competent chaperone that concerns me. This insult will not stand, Your Grace, do you hear me! *This will not stand!*"

"Yes, yes, thank you, Mrs. Buttram. Now go away," Rafe shouted as he threw back the covers and got out of bed, and then winced as his headache reminded him that raised voices were not in order at the moment. "This will not stand? God's teeth, what a dragon. For a moment I thought Wellington himself was on the other side of that door."

"Oh, God. This is all my fault," Charlotte said, lowering her head into her hands. "Now what do we do? Nicole and Lydia will have been awakened by now. What do I say? What do I tell them? What do I tell

Emmaline? What sort of example am I setting for two young, impressionable girls entrusted into my care?"

Rafe padded over to her in his stockinged feet. He couldn't remember ever seeing Charlie so flustered. "That sounds ominous. Maybe you should begin again, and tell me everything that went on here last night so that we can sort it out between us."

"Nothing!" She hopped to her feet. "Absolutely *nothing* happened here last night. I told you. You were ill. You were cold. Your teeth were chattering, for pity's sake, and you were half out of your head. I think you thought I was Fitz."

"Sweetheart, I would never think you were Fitz. He's taller, for one thing, and has that ridiculous beard."

"Oh, stop trying to make this all seem less ominous than it is, Rafe. I'm trying to explain. You looked pathetic. So, yes, I lay on the bed next to you to try to keep you warm, that's all. And…and I fell asleep. That's *all* that happened."

Rafe lost his teasing smile. "You did that? After all that's happened, after my damned cousins…and how you feel about being touched, and—you did that for me? I'm humbled, Charlie. I truly am. Thank you."

She lowered her gaze to the floor. "Yes, well, it…it wasn't so terrible. And you were very sick." She looked up at him. "You look much better this morning. I think your fever broke."

"I think so, too. Really, I'm fine, and I apologize if I frightened you. Fitz has told me I look like death on a mopstick when the fever hits me. But it's gone nearly as quickly as it arrives. Did I, that is—did I behave myself?"

She bit her bottom lip between her teeth for a moment, and then nodded. "I already told you. Everything that happened was entirely my fault."

He looked at her inquiringly. "So something did happen? Why, Charlotte Seavers—is my virtue still intact?"

"Once again, Rafe, it would please me greatly if you would stop trying to divert me and simply shut…up. What are we going to do now? Mrs. Buttram is about to have an apoplexy that something so sordid happened while she was on the premises, and in truth, I can't blame her. But you just know she won't allow us to simply sweep what she saw under the rug and pretend it didn't happen."

"True. The woman makes her way in the world shepherding debutantes, chaperoning them, making brilliant matches for them—or at least that is her reputation. That, and, according to Lord Peters, we should all rub along just fine, as long as I remember that the woman never stops talking and couldn't keep a secret in a locked chest. We'll have to announce our engagement. I'm serious, Charlie."

"Compromised. You're saying I've been compromised. No, I won't allow that. This might sound ridiculous, considering the fact that I am the one responsible for this mess, but I completely and utterly refuse to be seen as having been compromised by a Daughtry *twice!*"

And with that rather damning parting shot, Charlotte stomped out of the room.

"NOT TO BE CRASS," Mrs. Buttram said an hour later in the drawing room, once Charlotte had pleaded her case.

The chaperone lifted her right foot from the floor. "But why don't you, as the lower classes say, pull this one—it has bells on it."

Charlotte looked to Rafe in obvious confusion.

"Please, allow me," he said. "She thinks you're lying to her, pulling her leg, so she's suggested you pull her *other* leg, because it has bells on it."

"But what do bells have to do with anything—and I'm *not* lying. You were sick. Tell her, Rafe. Tell her how sick you were."

He leaned closer, to whisper beside her ear. "I can't, sorry. I don't really remember much of anything that happened last night."

"Rafe, you aren't being in the least amusing. You *promised...*"

"I was under duress. You were clearly hysterical, and threatening me with that statuette, remember? Not that I was ever in any danger of you hitting me, even if you did throw it."

"Seduced you, did she? While you were drinking deep, I imagine, as you don't look quite the thing this morning, Your Grace, if I might be so bold," Mrs. Buttram said, nodding her understanding. "People will try to tell you differently, that men are always the aggressor, but I know that it's almost always the female, especially when there is a title and fortune involved."

"Mrs. Buttram, please excuse us, but Miss Seavers and I were having a private conversation," Rafe said, actually hoping she'd continue. Charlie had to be made to see reason.

The woman obliged him by going on as if he'd never spoken. "Oh, the stories I could tell you, Your Grace.

You have to watch these quiet ones. They're sneaky. And the mamas aren't much better. I remember the time a certain ladyship who shall remain nameless—I am nothing if not discreet—actually took her own daughter by the hand and *sneaked* her into a certain lordship's chamber during a house party, and then personally tucked that poor child up in bed with him while he slept. She'd earlier drugged his wine with laudanum, as it turned out."

"Rafe," Charlotte whispered, "make her stop."

Mrs. Buttram patted her hair with one gloved hand. "The banns were called within a fortnight, they were. I made sure of that, let me tell you! As I said, it is my reputation that concerns me, a lone woman trying to earn her daily bread. I don't really care what all of you do or why you do it. Just so that you don't allow such sordidness to rub off on me. You do understand that, don't you, Your Grace?"

"I do, yes, Mrs. Buttram," Rafe told her, bowing slightly in her direction. Really, the woman was being most helpful. "Lord Peters was quite emphatic in his recommendation of you as the premier chaperone in all of Mayfair. To ease your mind, madam, let me be so honored as to tell you that Miss Seavers and I are, of this moment, betrothed."

"Rafe! You *promised!*"

Nicole, whom it would seem had been hiding just out of sight in the hallway, gave out a loud whoop and came running into the drawing room to clasp Charlotte close and wish her happy.

"But…but…" Charlotte looked to Rafe, partly in anger, partly in a plea for help.

Lydia, always one to hang back and allow her twin the spotlight first, came up to Charlotte and smiled at her. "This is the most *wonderful* news, Charlotte. Aunt Emmaline will be so pleased. I know she was appalled when you were to marry Cousin Harold. I'll go immediately upstairs and write to her."

"But…but…" Other than that feeble mumble, Charlotte couldn't seem to say much of anything.

Nicole finally let her go, only to rush over to Rafe and give him a hug, as well. "Now my Come-Out will be perfect. Just *perfect!*" She wheeled about to grin at Mrs. Buttram. "And *you,* you horrid old biddy, will have *nothing* to do with it!"

"Nicky! Apologize."

"Yes, Rafe," Nicole said, not sounding at all penitent as she gave a quick apology and then raced from the room, probably to add her own note to her aunt Emmaline.

"Oh, don't worry about that, Your Grace," Mrs. Buttram said with a small wave of her hand. "I'm used to spoiled children. She's going to be a rare handful, you know. Now, if you'll excuse me, I'll leave the two of you alone, as you must have much to discuss, and it's a bit too late to worry about the proprieties in any event, isn't it?"

Charlotte waited until Mrs. Buttram was gone before closing and locking the drawing room doors behind her and turning on Rafe. "How could you do this, Rafe? Upstairs, you promised that you wouldn't…."

"I know," he said, shoving his fingers through his hair. How could he explain himself? "Upstairs, your arguments seemed reasonable—that it would feel, to you, as if you'd been compromised twice by the same family.

I agreed there would be no pressure, that we'd continue on as we have been, taking our time, doing what we've been— Oh hell, my head was aching enough that I probably would have agreed to anything. But did you see her, Charlie? My God, the woman was close to *drooling.* If I hadn't said what I said, she would have resigned her position and gone charging around Mayfair to tell everyone about the den of iniquity that is the Ashurst household."

"Nicole and Lydia," Charlotte said, her shoulders slumping as the realization struck her. "You couldn't have any such gossip attending to them, could you? Not if they're to make their debut next Season."

Rafe frowned. "The twins? Oh, all right, I see your point. Yes, it could have made things difficult for them, certainly. But I wasn't thinking about Nicole and Lydia, Charlie, when I said what I said to Mrs. Butttram. I was thinking about *you.*"

"Me? For pity's sake, Rafe, I'm *nobody.* I was nobody when I had my Season, and I'm nobody now. Besides, I didn't ask you to protect me. I most certainly didn't ask you to sacrifice yourself for me."

And here it was. Time to be honest. Although he probably wasn't doing himself any favors, not the way Charlotte was reacting to what he'd done so far.

"There's no sacrifice involved. I know I couldn't pick a worse time to say this—but I love you, Charlie. I do. I love you."

Charlotte seemed caught between tears and anger. Anger, for good or ill, clearly won. "No, Rafe, you don't. You *care* for me. And I thank you for that. I helped you find your bearings when you first came into the title. You want to thank me for that. You want to make up for what your family did to me. And I appreciate that. I may even intrigue you because… well, because I'm the way I am. You might see me as a challenge to your manhood and your powers of… of…"

"Persuasion? Seduction?" Rafe said helpfully. "Oh, I don't think so, Charlie. I think it goes way beyond that. Why can't you believe I might love you?"

"Aha!" She pointed a finger at him in triumph. "There, you said it yourself. *Might.* You don't know, do you? No, don't answer that. Because you *don't* know. You know what's wrong with you, Rafael Daughtry? You're *good.* You're just too good. But that doesn't mean you have to make up for how terrible your uncle and cousins were. And I…and I am not some poor, tragic victim you seem to feel this great need to protect or rescue. I'm me, I'm Charlotte Seavers, a grown woman, and I had to learn to take care of myself long before that horrible night in the stables. You don't even *know* me, not really. All you know is Charlie, your childhood friend. There are limits to friendship, Rafe, and I will not allow you to sacrifice yourself to that friendship in order to save a reputation your family stripped from me long ago."

Rafe didn't know what to say. She may as well have slapped him. Or, just perhaps, she'd finally gotten through to him, because finally—finally—yes, he understood what was wrong, what had been wrong between them from the beginning.

"Nobody likes to be put up with on sufferance, do they, Charlie—Charlotte. Not the poor relation choking on the charity offered him by his uncle, or a woman who sees herself as strong enough, brave enough, to take care of herself. You're a rare woman, a rare person. Do you really believe that I pity you? That everything that's happened between us since I came back has been out of pity?"

She bit her bottom lip for a moment, tears standing in her eyes. "I... No, I don't think you pity me, Rafe. I think you like me. And I'm glad about that, because I will always treasure our friendship. I value your honesty, your earnest, responsible nature. I've always loved you, when we were younger, when I was a child. I...I trust you."

He needed to push at her, have her say it all, now, so that maybe they could begin again. "But you don't trust me to know my own mind, my own heart?"

"If...if that night had never happened? If you'd simply come home from the war and seen me again, and begun to court me the way I'd dreamed about all the years you were gone? I'd be the happiest woman in all of England, Rafe, I really would. I won't lie to you, because that aids nobody, and the truth means nothing for two people in our situation. But that's not what happened, and we can't pretend it has. You kiss me, and I have to fight the fear that flashes inside of me, even as all I want to do is kiss you back."

He walked toward her, holding out his hand. "But we've been making progress, Charlie—Charlotte. Haven't we?"

One of her tears escaped, to run down her cheek. "Yes, Rafe. We're making progress. But that doesn't mean you're in love with me, or even that I'm in love with you."

"Then what does it mean?"

"I…I don't know. I just know that I will not be a party to a betrothal that could in any way be construed as being thrust upon you. I know what it's like, Rafe, to have a betrothal forced on you."

"You really mean that, don't you?" he asked her quietly. "Even now, you're thinking about me, and not yourself. Charlotte, for the love of Heaven, could you just for this one time think about yourself?"

"I *am* thinking about myself, Rafe, even selfishly," she told him just as quietly. "If…if we are ever to be more than we are now, I need to know that we have come to that decision together, and in our own time." She lifted her chin in defiance. "And the devil with the drooling Mrs. Buttram!"

So much was clear to him now. So much he hadn't realized, perhaps hadn't wanted to see. He'd been protecting her, she'd been protecting him. They were both idiots. Not that it would probably be a good thing to tell her that right now.

"All right," he said at last. "We're agreed on this much at least. The devil with Mrs. Buttram. Tell me, as you've been more in her company than I, do you think she's amenable to bribery?"

She looked at him in such obvious relief that he knew he'd said just the right thing. Finally. "I wouldn't rule it out without making the attempt, no."

"Then that's decided," he said, holding out his hand as if he wanted to seal some sort of bargain with her.

But when she put her hand in his he drew her closer, so that they were only inches apart.

"Rafe?"

"You said we would come to our own decision, in our own time. I'll do my best to be happy with that, to take heart from that. But I want to make one thing perfectly clear, Miss Charlotte Seavers, even as we, as you say, agree to start over. I…love…you."

"Oh, Rafe…"

He bent and kissed her tear-wet cheek, and then let go of her hand.

"Oh, Rafe, the woman says, just as if she hasn't yet figured out that if I'm to tackle Mrs. Buttram, that leaves her to bring Nicole and Lydia down from the treetops by informing them that she isn't betrothed to their brother."

"Wretch," Charlotte said with some feeling, wiping at her eyes.

"Ah, but suddenly a hopeful wretch. Now run away, *Charlotte,* before I remember that I'm a duke, and should insist upon all my orders being obeyed."

"You would never *order* me to marry you, Rafe."

"You'd be surprised what I might do, if you test my supposed *goodness* too far, Miss Seavers. Now scoot!"

Charlotte scooted.

THEY STARTED OVER. Which made perfect sense to them, even if no one else understood. Not that they cared what anyone else understood.

Rafe made it a point to be home for dinner each evening, even if he then had to return to the War Office immediately afterward.

He brought Charlotte flowers he'd purchased on a street corner from a cheeky little mite who'd called him *guv'nor.*

He gifted her with a copy of Lord Byron's *Childe Harold's Pilgrimage: A Romaunt,* along with the gossip that the great man's marriage to Miss Annabella Milbanke only a few short months ago looked to be an unhappy one for the Romantic poet.

He took her hand and they stole moments alone in the Square, walking arm in arm as they discussed the matters of the day or, very often, said nothing at all, but simply enjoyed each other's company.

"Rafe is courting you, isn't he?" Nicole asked one afternoon in the Drawing Room as Charlotte held a ribbon over the basket containing the black-and-white kitten Rafe had given her two days earlier. "He compromised you, and now he's courting you, which certainly seems a strange reversal. Lydia says she understands, but then she would say that, as she adores pretending she's smarter than I am. I, however, am not so proud that I refuse to say that I don't understand. I don't understand at all."

Charlotte kept her eyes cast downward, watching as the kitten went up on its hind legs, trying to catch the swinging ribbon. "Is it really necessary that you understand, Nicole?"

"Necessary?" The girl wrinkled her delightfully pert nose. "No, I suppose not. But a good friend would understand why I'm curious."

"Or a good friend would refrain from allowing her curiosity to show, and wait patiently for the moment the other person felt comfortable speaking about such a delicate matter."

"Oh, nonsense. Not that I'm insulted, because we both know I've never been patient. So you couldn't possibly mean me," Nicole said, causing Charlotte to laugh despite herself. "Now tell me why he's calling you Charlotte now."

Charlotte allowed the ribbon to drop into the basket, as the kitten was beginning to seem frantic to have it, and sat back against the couch cushions. "Rafe," she said calmly, "is addressing me as Charlotte because I asked him for months and months to address me as Charlotte. Charlie is a stupid, childhood name."

Nicole seemed to consider this for a few moments, and then shook her head. "No, that can't be it. Is he angry with you because you won't marry him?"

Charlotte was fairly certain that Nicole Daughtry could drive a saint to distraction. "Why would you think calling me Charlotte has anything to do with your brother being angry with me?"

"I don't know. Maybe it's the way he says *Charlie*. He could be saying *my darling*. He isn't, of course, he's saying *Charlie*. But…well, no, that's all—it's the way he says it. And don't tell me you haven't noticed, because I may be young, Charlotte, but I wasn't born only yesterday."

Charlotte didn't know what to say. She couldn't ask Nicole if she was teasing, or if the girl really had noticed something in Rafe's tone when he said *Charlie*. But just the thought that Nicole believed what she was saying was enough to start a small smile playing around the corners of Charlotte's mouth.

"Miss Seavers?"

Charlotte looked up, startled, as the imposing majordomo stood in the entrance to the drawing room. "Yes, Harris?"

"There is a Mr. Hugh Hobart without, madam, requesting permission to speak with you. Most adamantly,

Miss Seavers, on a matter of some importance, or so he says. I've put him in the small reception room on the ground floor."

Because Hugh Hobart doesn't quite look as if he belongs in the drawing room, Charlotte thought, but did not say the words aloud.

"He wishes to speak with me, Harris? Are you quite sure? I would think he'd want to speak with the duke."

"He most expressly asked for you, Miss Seavers," Harris said, bowing again. "Shall I refuse him?"

Charlotte sighed. She would very much like to refuse the man, but then she'd do nothing but wonder and fret about what he might have wanted, and regret her decision. "No, thank you, Harris. Please tell Mr. Hobart I'll be down in a moment, once you've summoned Mrs. Beasley to accompany me."

"Mrs. Buttram," Harris corrected. "You'll want Mrs. Buttram."

"No, Harris, I know who I asked for, thank you." Charlotte had no great desire for the paid chaperone to know any more Ashurst business. Mrs. Beasley, however, was deaf as a post to any conversation that took place more than five feet away from her, which made her the optimum companion.

"Who is Mr. Hugh Hobart, Charlotte?" Nicole asked, concern furrowing her brow. "You went rather pale when Harris first said the man's name."

Charlotte got to her feet, patting at her hair to be sure her pins were all in place. "Mr. Hobart was on your cousin George's yacht when it sank," she told her. "For some reason known only to Mr. Hobart, he believes this happpenstance should serve as some entry to your brother's company. A feeling your brother doesn't share, by the way. But I should at least listen to what he wants."

"Well, I don't see why. After all, if he was a friend to either Cousin George or Cousin Harold, he is probably both crude and unpleasant. Tell Harris to send him away with a flea in his ear. That's what I'd do."

"Yes, Queen Nicole, I know you would, if you didn't just order someone to lop off his head," Charlotte said, anxious to head for the hallway even as she dreaded seeing Hugh Hobart again, her stomach fluttering nervously. "But sometimes, Nicole, one can't simply avoid that which one doesn't like."

"Well, *I* can, and I will. It's all in not caring what anyone thinks of you but you, that's what I think. And I think I'd think very well of myself for turning away a person who made me feel as uncomfortable as you look right now, Charlotte."

Charlotte smiled at the girl. "You know, Nicole, sometimes I think that, for all you try to hide it, you're smarter than all of us put together. Please watch the kitten while I'm gone, so he doesn't wander."

Harris was waiting for her at the head of the staircase, and then preceded her and Mrs. Beasley down the winding stairs to the small reception room with the elephant's foot table.

Mrs. Beasley was about to curtsy to Hugh Hobart when she cocked her head to one side, looked him over again, and then only walked past him to settle herself in a small chair in the corner. A good judge of character, Mrs. Beasley.

"Miss Seavers, so good of you to see me," Hobart said, bowing with a flourish.

"Mr. Hobart," Charlotte said shortly as she sat down on a straight-back chair, pretending not to notice that he wore a much better-fitting if still faintly outlandish suit of clothes today than he had upon their first meeting. Clearly at least a part of the five thousand pounds Rafe had turned over to him had not spent too much time in the man's pockets.

"You're probably wondering why I have taken the liberty of once more broaching this lovely domicile," he said in his rather oily voice. "But I have news, Miss Seavers. News His Grace, by refusing to grant me an audience at the War Office only an hour past, I feel it necessary to impart instead to you forthwith."

Charlotte sighed at both the man's ridiculous speech and to learn that she was giving the man a toe in the door that Rafe had chosen not to offer. "Perhaps you should write to His Grace instead, Mr. Hobart? I can't fathom what assistance I can be to you."

"It's not your assistance I'm after," Hobart said quickly, rather harshly. He then smiled widely, as if to soften his words. "Your pardon, Miss Seavers, but it has been a harrowing morning. No, madam, I am here because I put it to myself to find out who had dared to attempt to injure His Grace and yourself the day we met in the Square."

She couldn't hide her interest. "Really, Mr. Hobart? I'm sure that wasn't necessary. Yet very kind of you."

"I could have been injured, as well, Miss Seavers, or worse. Indeed, who's to say it wasn't me that masonry was aimed at, hmm? In my line of work, if you'll pardon me, it is possible to acquire, if not enemies, precisely, people who might at the very least wish me ill. If you take my meaning."

"You're a cardsharp who collects IOUs from green-as-grass young gentlemen from the country and fleeces the foolish and the unwary. There could be people who owe you money and may decide it would be easier if they did not have to pay you. Is that the way of it, Mr. Hobart?"

He sat down all at once, grinning in a way that sent a shiver down her back. "All right, if you wish to be blunt, yes, Miss Seavers. For some, life would be easier if I were to stick my spoon in the wall."

She shouldn't be encouraging the man. "And is this what you learned, Mr. Hobart? You learned that His Grace and I only happened to be standing with you when one of your unfortunate debtors decided to cut his losses?"

He took in a deep breath and let it out slowly as he shook his head. "Sad to say, no. What I discovered, Miss Seavers, is that there is someone who wishes to put a period to the duke's existence."

Charlotte's blood ran cold, so cold that she gave an involuntary shiver. "Par…pardon me?"

"I've found, Miss Seavers, that a few shillings dropped into the right hands, a few words whispered in a few corners, and information a person would believe safe can become very much less so. In short, madam, I located a rough character who, with the introduction of those few shillings, admitted that he had been hired to station himself on that roof and then nudge the loose masonry if and when His Grace appeared below him on the flagway."

"Oh, my…"

"Yes, Miss Seavers. *Oh, my.* It took three days before you and His Grace ventured down the flagway, a delay that made my new acquaintance quite unhappy, as he felt he'd been grossly undercompensated for such a lengthy vigil."

"Where is this man? Do we know who hired him?"

Again, Hobart sighed and shook his head. "You do not hire a thug to do your bidding, Miss Seavers, and then gift him with your name and direction, or with your motives. My knowledge is limited to that of the man I spoke with at the tavern. Still, I thought it enough to come to His Grace, to warn him that his life may very well be in danger."

Charlotte got to her feet. "Yes, well, thank you, Mr. Hobart. I very much appreciate your concern, and will most certainly inform His Grace as to what you've told me. I cannot thank you enough."

Hobart glanced behind him, to where Mrs. Beasley sat looking dreamily out the ground-floor window, and then turned his narrowed eyes back to Charlotte. "Yes, about that. Being thanked, that is. It would appear I've had a plaguey run of luck at the tables this past fortnight or more. Lately those green-as-grass youths from the country you mentioned are neither so green nor so gullible as they should be, unfortunately, so that I've found myself rather strapped for the ready…"

"Five thousand pounds, Mr. Hobart. Are you daring to tell me that you have run through five thousand pounds in only a few weeks?"

"Madam, I ran through those five thousand pounds in less than one week. But my luck is bound to turn. It always does. All I need are a few thousand pounds to set up my own Faro bank in one of the smaller gaming hells and then—"

"And you want the Duke of Ashurst to—"

"Yoo-hoo! Excuse me!" Nicole trilled from the doorway, poking her head just inside the room, and then following it with the rest of her body. "I'm so embarrassed, and loath to interrupt you, Charlotte, but I fear we have a small emergency in the kitchens that needs your immediate attention. Not that it was a very *large* fire…but I'm sure this gentleman will excuse you now."

"Mr. Hugh Hobart, my lady. My lady, an honor, I'm sure," Hobart said, leaping to his feet even as he bent forward into a bow that had him uttering his unsolicited salutation to his boot tops.

Nicole rolled her eyes at Charlotte.

Charlotte shook her head at the girl, who held the black-and-white kitten next to her cheek; a heart-stoppingly beautiful portrait of innocence, and yet danger at the same time. "Thank you, Lady Nicole. I'll be there directly, but first I must finish speaking with Mr. Hobart here."

"No, you mustn't. Mr. Hobart understands that there are times domestic affairs trump all else. Don't you, Mr. Hobart? Mr. Hobart!"

Hugh Hobart was leering at Nicole in a way that made Charlotte itch to throw a blanket over the girl's head to hide her. "I… But of course. That is," he said, licking his lips, "I could return tomorrow, after you've spoken to His Grace.…"

As Hobart stumbled through this small speech, his

eyes never left Nicole's face, except to travel down and back up the length of her body. Charlotte was put suddenly and quite uncomfortably in mind of the way Harold Daughtry had looked at her that night in the stables, once he'd ripped her bodice.

Charlotte quickly stepped between them, blocking his view of the young girl. "Harris!" she called out, relieved when the man, who apparently had been hovering just outside the open door, immediately stepped into the reception room. "Mr. Hobart is leaving, Harris."

"Yes, Miss Seavers," Harris said, glaring at Hobart. "This way, sir."

Once they heard the door to the street close, Nicole and Charlotte exchanged looks before Nicole leaned against the doorjamb and began to giggle. "Well, I hope you've learned your lesson, Miss Seavers," she said in her best Mrs. Buttram voice. "Breeding will *out*, you know." And then she giggled again as the kitten nuzzled into her neck.

Charlotte attempted to appear amused. "Yes, thank you, Nicole," she said as they climbed the stairs to the drawing room once more. "I shouldn't have met with the man. That's obvious."

"And you wish to thank me for rescuing you," Nicole added. "You meant to say that, too, correct? In fact, you are so grateful to me that you're going to tell me what the man wanted in the first place."

"No, Nicole, I'm not," Charlotte told her firmly as Lydia joined them in the upstairs hallway. "Lydia, what's that you've got?"

The girl blushed prettily and kept walking toward the staircase. "Only another letter for Captain Fitzgerald,

Charlotte. I was hoping to get it into the pouch before the afternoon post. Although he may already be on his way home—that is to say, back to England."

Nicole watched her sister descend the stairs. "You and Rafe dancing about each other, oblivious to what is so very apparent to everyone else. Lydia dreaming of her captain, just as if anything will ever come of that. Charlotte, am I the only female in this household with any sense, do you think?"

But Charlotte wasn't listening. She was too busy thinking about everything the odious Hugh Hobart had said, and how she would tell Rafe.

CHAPTER FIFTEEN

FOR A MAN WHO was doing his best to convince the love of his life that he truly loved her, Rafe was doing a credible imitation of a man doing his worst to make the woman wish to throttle him.

If he listened to Charlotte, if he believed a word Hugh Hobart had said to her, then he would also perhaps be more concerned for his safety.

But as he had explained to Charlotte—patiently, and then repeated to her not quite as patiently—when a man offers information one moment and then, before taking so much as a breath, asks for money? Well, it was very difficult to take such a man seriously.

Hugh Hobart was what he was. Rafe had made inquiries, and learned that the man operated on the fringes of Society, plying his trade in a variety of gaming hells devoted to fleecing the unwary of their allowances and breaking bones in order to collect IOUs.

He was also known to have connections to a certain abbess just off Piccadilly, who always seemed to have a fresh supply of "virgins fresh from the country and free of disease."

Just the sort of fellow his cousins would have befriended, unfortunately.

Initially, Rafe had bitten his tongue so that he didn't rail at Charlotte for seeing the man in the first place, and then he had attempted to explain the difference between a true problem and one manufactured for one's own benefit.

He'd even at last, in desperation, gone so far as to give her the name of the abbess, believing that the appellation Lottie Lusty would convince her that Hobart was not a man to be trusted to give a person so much as the proper time of day.

Charlotte had not been impressed, and when he'd refused to take Phineas with him when he traveled to the War Office or elsewhere in the metropolis, and when he likewise declined her suggestion that he go everywhere in a closed coach…well, to say that the air had rather cooled between Charlotte and himself the past few days might be in the way of an understatement.

Rafe picked up the black-and-white kitten—now dubbed Mischief, and for good reason—and went nose-to-nose with the small creature.

"Females," he said as the kitten stuck out its pink tongue and licked his nose. "A word of warning, my friend. You will never understand them, never. They don't believe you when you're being completely honest, baring your soul, as it were. But let some lowlife scum fill the air with lies, and they'll take every calumny as gospel. Oh, hello, Charlotte, I didn't hear you come in."

"Yes, you did. I saw you peeking at me out of the corner of your eye as you spoke," she said, dragging herself to the facing couch and collapsing into it. "Oh, I'm exhausted. I had no idea how old and decrepit I am until I was faced with shepherding your sisters up and down Bond Street hour after hour in search of just the most *perfect* ribbons to change out their bonnets for the peace celebrations they're certain will occur."

"They'll occur without us," Rafe told her, longing to take her in his arms and let her rest her head against him. "I know you haven't had the Season I'd hoped for you, and I apologize for that, but now that Bonaparte is defeated, I want to get back to Ashurst Hall. I've had a letter this morning from John Cummings."

Charlotte sat up straight. "Is there something wrong?"

Rafe smiled. "That, I would suppose, depends upon your idea of *wrong*. At the end of a detailed listing of mundane things like broken plows and repairs to the buttery, our Mr. Cummings calmly mentioned that he attended a wedding last Tuesday, for which he felt justified in ordering the butchering of two pigs."

"A wedding? Well, that's nice."

"The marriage united my housekeeper, Mrs. Piggle… with my butler."

Rafe waited to see Charlotte's reaction.

"*Grayson?* But…but they *hate* each other!"

He thought of saying that the relationship might have taken a large leap forward the day Mrs. Piggle had seen Grayson without his drawers, but quickly reconsidered.

"Yes, Charlotte, one would think so, considering their many epic battles. But, then, there's no accounting for love, is there? Or so I've heard."

She looked up at him from beneath her lashes. "What is that supposed to mean?"

"I'm not sure," he said, replacing the kitten in its basket. "But it must mean something. There was another list in the newspaper today. A shorter one, thank

God," he then said, in aid of nothing except wishing to change the subject.

Charlotte's eyes widened. "I thought we were done with those horrible lists. Lydia has been beside herself these past ten days or more, searching for Fitz's name among the wounded. But there hasn't been another list for two days."

"Unfortunately, some of those previously listed as injured have succumbed to their wounds. Charles Canning, an aide-de-camp to Wellington. A good man. William de Lancey. Several others, all of them previously listed as wounded. As we move toward the heat of summer, I'm afraid there will be many more."

"I only wish we would have some word of Fitz."

"His name appeared on no lists, and he wasn't mentioned in any of the dispatches that were couriered to the War Office. He's fine, Charlotte. I expect to hear from him with each delivery of the post. Either that, or to hear his voice as he arrives here unannounced, to surprise us. Ah…hello there, sisters mine. I hear you've beggared me in Bond Street."

"Not quite, Rafe," Nicole said as she settled herself beside Charlotte on the couch. "In fact, Lydia spent more than I, didn't you, Lydia?"

Her twin blushed, and nodded. "There was a bolt of blue material I could not resist, a blue just the color of the sky at dawn. Captain Fitzgerald believes the shade flatters my eyes."

Rafe and Charlotte exchanged glances. Yes, when Fitz came home from Brussels there would be rejoicing all around. And perhaps a few problems, hopefully problems that would sort themselves out without too many complications. After all, there could be no better man in the world for his sister than his best friend.

"Ha! If Captain Fitzgerald said cutting off all your hair would flatter you, you'd knock me down running for the shears," Nicole said, sniffing. "Captain Fitzgerald, Captain Fitzgerald. Honestly, Lydia, there are times I believe you have no other conversation."

And then Nicole winked at Rafe, to show that she was only teasing her twin.

"Your pardon, Your Grace," Harris intoned from the doorway. "The Duke of Malvern has asked to be shown upstairs."

Rafe leaped to his feet. "Blake's here? Well, for God's sake, man, send him up!" And then, as fast as joy had flooded him, it disappeared. "Harris? Wait. The duke is alone?"

Harris lowered his eyes. The man had been a soldier. He knew what Rafe meant by his question. "Yes, Your Grace, he is alone."

God. Oh goddamn. No. No. "All right, Harris, thank you."

Rafe felt Charlotte reach up to slip her hand into his and squeezed it hard. "Lydia, Nicole? Go to your rooms, please," he said, his tone hopefully betraying nothing that he felt as he watched the doorway.

"No," Lydia said in unusual defiance, she who, as Nicole would tease, wouldn't say boo to a goose. "The duke may have word of Captain Fitzgerald."

"Lydia, for God's sake—" And then Rafe looked at his friend, and instantly knew for certain what he had only guessed. "Oh, sweet Jesus God…" he whispered, all the strength leaving his body.

Tanner Blake, Duke of Malvern, had entered the drawing room leaning heavily on a cane, his handsome face grave and wearing an unhealthy pallor, his uniform brushed, but obviously mended at one knee.

He looked at Rafe, and then at the three females who stood facing him.

"Rafe, I'm sorry. I came here as quickly as I could. I haven't even been home to Portland Square," he said quietly. "I know how you felt about Fitz. He was a good man, a good friend. I'm so, so sorry…"

"No! Don't say that!"

Rafe looked to his sister. "Lydia, sweetheart—"

"No! He can't say that. I won't let him say that!" Lydia advanced on Tanner Blake, her hands drawn up into tight fists. *"Get out! Leave!"*

"You're Lyddie?" Blake asked gently. "Yes, of course you are. Fitz spoke of you often. I'm so sorry, Lady Lydia, but please know that his last thoughts—"

"No! It's not true. He can't be dead. He *promised* me. You're lying. You're a terrible, evil man! *I hate you!*"

Lydia had now closed the space between the duke and herself, and she pounded her fists against his chest as she berated him.

"Lydia!" Rafe said, going to her, only to have Tanner Blake wave him away.

Blake dropped his cane and put his arms around Lydia, pulling her close against his chest even as she beat at him, holding her there until she stopped struggling and sagged against him, sobbing as if her heart would break.

Nobody else moved. Nobody said anything. There was nothing for anyone to say.

At last Nicole, tears streaming down her cheeks, went to her sister and put her arms around her, urging her to come upstairs.

"Blake, I'm sorry," Rafe said as Nicole led Lydia away. "She…Lydia's overset. Come sit down, and I'll get you a glass of wine."

Charlotte squeezed his hand and then let it go. "I should leave you two alone, go help Nicole."

"No, stay," Rafe said, perhaps too quickly. The last thing he wanted was to have Charlotte leave him here alone, to hear what Blake was going to tell him.

"All right," she said quietly. "I'll just ask Harris to have some food sent for His Grace, and I'll be right back."

"Thank you, ma'am, but I'm not hungry. If I might just sit down…"

Blake had bent to retrieve his cane and was already limping toward the spot Lydia had so recently vacated.

Rafe poured them each a glass of wine with shaking hands and then took up his own seat on the facing couch. Fitz was gone. Fitz was dead. He'd never see his friend again, joke with him, share the world with that splendid man. Rafe still couldn't seem to take it in.

"How?" he said, unable to say anything else.

"I don't know," Blake said, holding the glass but not drinking from it. "He was one of those at this crossroad called Quatre Bras, dispatched there under Picton when the battle was going badly. We'd last seen each other at the Duchess of Richmond's ball, and promised each other we'd meet at a certain tavern after the battle. We were going to then tear up the Wills we'd written and exchanged, and drink ourselves senseless. You know how it is, Rafe."

"I do," he said, and Charlotte slipped her hand into his once more. "We'd joke that all we'd be leaving to our families would be the lint in the bottom of our pockets. But we always wrote those Wills."

Blake nodded, and then finally took a sip of wine, as if his throat might otherwise be too dry to continue speaking. "When he didn't come, I went looking for him. I found him in a barn, his right leg shattered, his head half-hidden in bandages. I nearly passed him by without recognizing him."

Charlotte made a small sound, a stifled sob, and pressed her face against Rafe's sleeve.

"Forgive me, ma'am," Blake said, looking to Rafe, his eyes tortured. "All he could say to me was that I should take care of his Lyddie. He made me promise. And then he was gone. I think he'd only been holding on until I got there, until I'd promised. I…I wouldn't leave until I'd seen him properly buried in a small churchyard. So many poor bastards on both sides were still lying in the fields when I left. I only gave his name to headquarters for the casualty lists the same day I sailed from Ostend. I wanted to be the one who told you, Rafe. As his friend, as your friend, I felt I owed you both that. I only wish I could have done more."

He reached inside his uniform jacket and pulled out an oilskin packet and placed it on the table. "I know you'll take care of everything, Rafe." Putting one hand over the other on the top of the cane, he levered himself upright. "Ma'am," he said, inclining his head toward Charlotte.

Rafe, his eyes still on the packet he recognized so well, said, "I'll walk down with you," and got to his feet.

Blake paused in the hallway, to look up the curved

staircase before beginning a slow, careful descent to the ground floor. "Your sister. She was very precious to Fitz. Such a pretty young girl." He turned his gaze on Rafe. "She'll be all right?"

"Fitz was aware of her age, and promised me he'd wait until she was older to declare himself. But I think he knew that Lydia had already made up her mind."

"Too many tears, Rafe, too many heartbreaks. And all to cage a man we'd already caged. What now for you? I know I have to get back to Malvern."

"The same for me. There's no more reason to remain here, so we'll be heading to Ashurst Hall in the next few days. As Fitz told me last year, we seem to have run out of enemies to fight. This time, please God, let those words be true."

Blake and Rafe clasped hands, and then embraced for a moment before Harris personally opened the door and escorted the Duke of Malvern to his carriage.

Rafe stood stock-still in the foyer for a long time, staring at the closed door. Fitz would never again walk through that doorway. They'd never sit together again, in front of a campfire on the edge of a battlefield, before the fireplace in the study at Ashurst Hall, talking of matters both serious and silly. He'd never again hear the man's merry laugh....

"If I might offer my most sincere condolences, Your Grace. The captain was a fine man," Harris said quietly, shaking Rafe from his reverie.

"Yes. Yes, he was that, wasn't he? A fine man. Thank you, Harris," Rafe said, and then headed back up the stairs to the drawing room, wanting to see Charlotte. Needing to see Charlotte.

She was waiting in the doorway, and he put his arm around her as they walked back over to the couches, and the oilskin packet that sat on the table. The only thing he had left of his friend.

"You don't have to look at that now," she told him as they sat down.

He shook his head as he reached for the packet that had traveled with Swain Fitzgerald through six years of war, and more. "I already know what's in it, but I have to do this now, or I'll never do it."

He pulled one end of the cord and the bow untied, spilling the contents onto the table. There was pitifully little. Charlotte reached for the gold pocket watch, but then drew back her hand. The thing was crusted with dried blood. Fitz's blood.

There was nothing surprising contained in Fitz's Will. Everything he had, which, other than the watch, consisted of a small, run-down estate somewhere in County Cork in Ireland, was all Rafe's now, for him to hold in trust for Lydia until she reached her majority.

And then there was the letter, a single folded sheet of paper with *My darling Lyddie* written on the outside fold.

"Oh, Jesus," Rafe said as he picked up the letter. "Do I give this to her?"

Charlotte was wiping at her eyes with her handkerchief. "Do you really have any choice, Rafe? Fitz wanted her to have it."

"I wasn't there, Charlie. I wasn't with him. If I'd gone with him…"

"Don't do that, Rafe. Please. Fitz went where he was needed, and you did the same. You have to think about Lydia right now. She needs you."

He turned his stinging eyes on Charlotte. "What can I do? What can I say to her?"

Charlotte kissed him on the cheek. "You don't have to say anything, Rafe. Just go to her. Hold her. Let her grieve. The both of you need to grieve."

Rafe drew in a shuddering breath as he nodded his agreement. "I need you, too, Charlie. I can't even tell you how much…."

He tucked Fitz's letter inside his waistcoat and stood up, facing the stairs as he would the thirteen steps to the gallows. But he would do what he had to do, what his friend would want him to do.

He knocked on the door to Lydia's chamber and, moments later, Nicole opened it and stepped into the hallway, softly closing the door behind her. Her violet eyes were moist, and filled with a pain that hurt his heart.

What had Fitz said to him one time when they were deep in their cups after a bloody battle in which too many good soldiers had died? *Men fight, women and children mourn. It's always been that way, my friend, and always will be, until we all learn a better way.*

"Nicky? How is she?"

"She's in pieces, Rafe," Nicole said quietly. "I can't console her."

"Let me talk to her."

Nicole nodded, but then lifted her chin in a sort of wild defiance. "I will never let that happen to me. I will never let love do to me what it's doing to Lydia. I will never love any man. Not *ever.*"

Rafe said nothing, for there was nothing to say, but only watched as Nicole lifted her skirts and ran down the hallway. So young. She and Lydia were still so young.

But Lydia had just grown a lot older.

He knocked on the door once more, not expecting an answer. After a moment he depressed the latch, and stepped inside.

CHAPTER SIXTEEN

THE MANSION in Grosvenor Square, like so many residences in London and all over Great Britain and Ireland, was now a house of mourning.

When the bell had rung for the evening meal, no one appeared in the drawing room, and Charlotte had at last ordered that trays be made up and delivered to the chambers of the duke and his sisters.

She ate her own meal alone in the morning room, or at least pretended to do so, while Mrs. Buttram had attempted to make conversation, only to be met with little response. The woman had possessed the sense to quickly finish her meal and depart.

That left Charlotte to hug a pillow to her chest and stare blindly out through the large oriel window as dusk fell and the skies turned dark and became sprinkled with bright stars, a sight unusual over London.

Which star belonged to Fitz? she wondered.

The hallway clock was striking nine when she slowly hauled herself upstairs, feeling older than the world. Her maid, her own eyes red from weeping, immediately suggested a soothing bath, and Charlotte nodded silently, hoping she might then be able to sleep, and not dream.

Two hours later, she knew the bath hadn't helped. Not wishing to bother her maid, Charlotte threw back the covers, slid into her slippers and dressing gown, and headed downstairs to beg some warmed milk in the kitchens.

She got as far as the door to Rafe's bedchamber, and stopped.

He was in there, grieving.

She was out here, grieving.

And that was wrong.

Before she could change her mind, she lifted her closed hand and lightly knocked on the door.

There was no answer. She could walk away. She could knock again.

She could stop being so blockheaded and stupid and think of someone other than herself, something other than her own stupid fears.

He needed her. He'd said so.

She needed him, even if she didn't understand exactly what it was she needed from him, wanted to give him in return.

Charlotte depressed the latch and stepped into the dim bedchamber. The only light in the large room came from the moonlight throwing long shadows through the tall windows and the fire burning in the grate. But that was enough for her to see Rafe sprawled in one of the wingback chairs flanking the fireplace, his long legs thrust out in front of him.

"Rafe?" she ventured softly. "May I sit with you awhile? Please?"

His face in profile, he lifted his right arm slightly, the hand holding a snifter of brandy, and then let it fall again.

She decided that meant he didn't mind.

Instead of taking her seat on the other wing chair, she padded straight to his and went down beside him, laying her cheek on his knee.

For a long time the room was quiet, the two of them watching the dancing flames in the grate. After a bit, Rafe put his hand on her head and began stroking her hair. She closed her eyes and bit back a sob.

"Why?" Rafe asked her at last. "Why Fitz? Why such a good man?"

"I don't know, Rafe," Charlotte whispered, putting her hands on his knee and looking up into his face. His features seemed so sharp, etched with his grief.

"I understand war. God knows I've seen enough of it. There's never any reason, at least never a good one. I do understand that. Just not Fitz, you know? He was always…invincible."

"He was a good man," Charlotte said earnestly. "He loved you."

Rafe smiled sadly. "We were brothers in arms, and so much more. I only hope he knew I loved him."

Charlotte blinked back fresh tears. "I'm sure he did, Rafe. Just as I know I love you."

He smiled down at her. "Thank you, Charlie."

"No, Rafe. Don't thank me. Forgive me. I've…I've allowed stupid fears…and possibly pride to keep me from what you want from me. From what I want for both of us. Rafe, you are so much more important to me than my fears. It's you I should be holding on to, not what happened in the past."

"Charlie…"

"No, please. Please let me say this, Rafe. I've

allowed myself to be afraid of ghosts, which only kept them alive. I thought I had time, that we both had time…but Fitz and Lydia probably thought they had time, too. If…if I lost you…if I'd never come to you, if I'd never known what it was like to love you, really love you, completely and utterly…"

He put the snifter down on the table and took her hands, drawing her to her feet with him. "Do you know what you're saying, sweetheart?"

Her eyes searched his in the dimness. "Yes, I… No, no I don't know. I only know what I feel, Rafe. I feel the need to be with you. I want to hold you, comfort you, and I long for you to comfort me in turn. I'm not a child, Rafe. I'm a woman, and I want to be like other women. Loved…and loving in return. I want us to be able to reach out to each other, and find what we need. Tonight more than ever before. I think we need each other tonight."

He laid his hands on her shoulders. "If we're happy, to be happy together. If we're sad, to be sad together. To always know the other is there for us. The best of friends…and so much more."

She pressed her palms against his chest, feeling his heartbeat through the soft lawn of his shirt. She loved this man. Dear God, how she loved this man, had always loved this man. "You've wanted to help me heal, Rafe, and you have. Now let me help you…."

He scooped her up into his arms and carried her to his bed. He laid her down gently against the sheets, and followed after her, taking her into his arms and softly pressing his mouth against hers.

Tears stung her eyes as she melted into his embrace, a feeling of homecoming all but overwhelming her.

There was no fear, because she wasn't thinking about herself, not when Rafe was so much more important. Not when he needed her. In caring for him, in her desire to help him, her own feelings counted for nothing.

She wrapped her arms around him and returned his kiss, unwilling to lie passive in his arms or, worse, shrink from him.

She ran her spread hands over his back, felt his body shudder as she opened her mouth to him and he was able to plunge his tongue inside, a move that made her aware of a sudden, pleasurable tightening between her legs.

"Charlie…" he breathed into her mouth. "I need you so much…."

He began trailing kisses down the side of her throat, onto the modest expanse of skin above her dressing gown. She felt the slight tug as he slipped open the ties holding the dressing gown closed, eased the material off her shoulders.

Now he kissed her along the scoop neck of her thin lawn night rail, even as he slowly tugged the material down, exposing her left breast, inch by tantalizing inch. His mouth was warm against her revealed flesh, and she sighed and lifted herself slightly from the mattress as at last he closed around her nipple, his tongue rasping across its very tip.

Charlotte's breathing became ragged, shallow. As if she'd somehow forgotten how to do it without giving the exercise conscious thought.

Not knowing what to do, she did nothing other than hold on to him and revel in what Rafe was doing to her, what he was bringing to life inside her. She wouldn't stop him, would never stop him.

His teeth. His tongue. The light pulling, suckling, that turned the tightness between her thighs into a delicious burning that at the same time felt like an opening, a flowering, a blossoming of her body that would serve as some sort of welcome to this man who was so precious to her.

When he left her, Charlotte's eyes flew open in concern, but she needn't have worried.

She lay there, tremulously smiling up at him as he unbuttoned his shirt even as his hot gaze never left her face. In the near dark, he unbuttoned his breeches and let them fall open around his hips, his hands hesitating, as if he was asking her permission.

Charlotte looked down, saw the nesting of dark hair above the opening of his breeches.

"I'm not afraid, Rafe."

But, moments later, she most definitely was amazed.

When he reached for her night rail and began tugging it upward, she raised her hips, helping him.

He hesitated, the night rail exposing her up to her knees, both of them knowing he was about to remove the last barrier that lay between them. Nearly the last…

"Are you sure you're not afraid?"

"No…no."

"I love you so much…."

"I know." She reached out to touch his bare chest, the muscles that rippled convulsively as she drew her fingertips along his rib cage. "You're beautiful…."

His smile broke her heart at the same time as it sent it soaring.

Then her night rail was gone and Rafe was covering her with his upper body, his flesh hard against her softness.

He took her mouth again, coaxingly, daring her to

take the initiative, mirror his actions with her own, and when he sighed, she felt a ripple of triumph that she was certain was part of the joy of being a female. He was hers, and her pleasure was his pleasure.

How could she have ever thought fear, or ugliness, had anything to do with what she and Rafe were about to share?

When he slid his hand between their bodies, when she felt his fingers insinuate themselves lower, lower, until he was touching her so intimately, it was impossible not to smile, sigh her delight at his touch.

"Open for me, sweetheart," he whispered as he continued to kiss her ear, her hair, her mouth, as his fingers stroked her, sliding along her, spreading her, destroying any inhibitions with each new rush of sensation that had her spreading her thighs wider so that he might keep touching her, learning her, teaching her.

And then the feeling changed as he seemed to understand that he'd found what he had been seeking and her entire body stiffened, signaling without words that he'd located her very center.

"Rafe…?"

"I know, sweetheart. I know. Let it happen, just let it happen…."

His fingers moved faster, faster, never leaving her, and she held her breath, unable to believe the sensations building inside her, the magic he was bringing to her…the heaven…the sweet, hot, pulsing heaven….

"Rafe!"

Even as she was trying to take in what had just happened to her, he levered himself completely on top of her, coming to rest between her spread thighs.

His movement was swift, the pain fleeting, and then he was inside her and she was reaching up to him, her fingernails digging into the flesh of his back, her body straining against his, welcoming him, trying to give him what he had given her.

They were two halves making one wondrous, fated whole, and as he shuddered and emptied his seed into her the very last shadow left Charlotte Seavers's heart. There was no room in that heart for anything or anybody except Rafael Daughtry.

Her friend.

Her lover.

Her life.

As he lay spent on top of her, she held him, cradled him, showering kisses over him, their tears mingling, the salty taste of them in both their mouths.

And as they fell asleep in each other's arms, the last thing Charlotte saw before she closed her eyes were all the stars twinkling in the midnight sky above the rooftops just outside the window. Perhaps it was fanciful, wishful thinking, but one of them seemed to be particularly bright.

SHE CAME TO HIM EACH night, her arrival met with the only smiles she saw from him that long, sad week. As the weather turned too warm for them to sit in front of a fire, they often stood at an open window, looking out over the silent Square as the evening breeze washed over them, or she sat on his lap, cuddling into him as he told her stories about the years he and Fitz had been together.

Sad stories, almost hilariously funny stories of adventures they'd shared…healing stories.

Eventually, they would make love. Inevitably. Because the so-intimate union seemed to be a part of that healing, for both of them. Their coming together could almost be taken as a sign that they were both still alive, that the world did go on, and that they would move on with it.

Lydia kept to her rooms, Nicole refusing to leave her side, even sleeping beside her in her sister's bed, as if they were children once again.

The lists of names, which had faded to a trickle, began to grow longer again, just as Rafe had said they would, and church bells never seemed to stop ringing across London. Mrs. Buttram learned of the death of a beloved nephew and asked permission to travel to Kent to be with her sister. She departed a subdued woman, and only after giving genuine hugs to everyone.

The Duke of Malvern returned to Grosvenor Square twice, to closet himself with Rafe in his study, and to inquire about Lydia. He'd wondered if she might wish to speak with him, so that he could tell her more about Fitz's last weeks in Brussels, but Lydia declined each time. To her, Rafe thought, Tanner Blake was her own personal Angel of Death, the man who had taken her Captain Fitzgerald from her.

Charlotte had assured Rafe that Lydia needed time, reminded him that she was still so painfully young. She suggested they return to Ashurst Hall where, yes, Lydia would face more ghosts. But, at the same time, perhaps she could then begin to heal.

As he had begun to heal, thanks to Charlotte.

How had he existed all these years, without love in his life, without his beloved Charlie in his life?

"Let me do that," he told her softly as she sat on a low velvet bench, brushing her hair at the dressing table that had most probably belonged to his late aunt, and several duchesses of Ashurst before her. "After all, I think I'm the one who tangled it for you."

"Why, sir, I think you are at that." She smiled at him in the mirror and held up the pair of silver-backed brushes she'd been using. She looked so delicate, almost fragile, wearing his maroon silk banyan and nothing else, the sash wrapped twice around her waist, the overlong sleeves falling back to expose her arms to the elbow.

He bent and kissed the back of her hand and then took one of the brushes and began smoothing it over her warm brown hair, his hand following the direction of the brush, his palm and fingertips tingling at the gentle intimacy.

"That's nice, that's very nice."

She put down the other brush and sighed in contentment. She'd gone from a skittish girl who flinched from his touch to an aware, sensual woman who gloried in it. He was so proud of her, and so very grateful.

"Why do you females twist and torture and confine your hair, and fill it with pins, do you wonder?"

"To impress the gentlemen, I suppose," Charlotte answered, her gaze still meeting his in the mirror. "Putting up one's hair is the sign that a woman is grown up. Just as a spinster covers her hair with those horrid caps, to signal that she's on the shelf. I already have three of them, but haven't been able to bring myself to wear them. Ouch!"

"Sorry," Rafe said, leaning past her to lay the brush

on the dressing table. "It must be the thought of covering your hair that distracted me. You look so beautiful when it's down. I love to touch it."

To prove his point, he placed his hands at her temples and slowly drew his fingers through her hair, and then, as she closed her eyes and tipped her head, allowed its sleek length to fall over her right shoulder as he bent to kiss her nape. "Just as I love touching you."

"Rafe…"

He put his hands on her slim shoulders, gently kneading her muscles until she relaxed her head back against his lower belly. The action pulled the silk of his banyan tighter over her breasts, enticing his hands to wander.

He slid them down over the silk, lightly cupping her breasts, his thumbs finding her nipples, which had grown taut at his touch.

"That…that's nice," Charlotte purred.

He watched her in the mirror as her eyes opened, the pupils gone dark and almost indolent as she allowed him to do what he wished.

He hooked his thumbs inside the edges of the banyan and spread them, exposing her breasts, then took each nipple between thumb and forefinger and rolled them, tugged them lightly, felt them grow hard.

He watched, mesmerized, as Charlotte's chest rose and fell, her breathing becoming ragged, and then locked his gaze with hers in the mirror.

"Rafe, I…"

"Shh," he cautioned. "Don't say anything, Charlie. Just *feel*."

Her breath escaped on a sigh and her eyelids fluttered

closed, then shot open once more as he knelt behind her so that he could put his cheek next to hers. Still cupping her left breast, he used his free hand to tug open the sash, so that the dark silk slid away from her body.

"Rafe, no…"

"No, that's not what you wanted to say. You wanted to say, *Rafe, yes,*" he whispered, his hand sliding between her thighs. Despite her protest, she was ready for him, hot and moist, and instantly responsive.

He found her sweet center and exploited it, deliberately giving her what she wanted, and then taking it away each time he felt her nearing the brink.

She moaned low in her throat, moving her body against his hand.

"You keep closing your eyes. Open them, sweetheart. See what I see."

She did as he said, those eyes now smoldering and intense as she looked at her reflection.

"Yes, that's it," he whispered against her hair. "Now put your hands on mine. Help me love you."

He could see the new apprehension in her eyes, but after only a slight hesitation, again, she complied.

His entire body sang with pleasure as she not only did what he'd asked, but lifted her hips even as she pushed down on his hand, holding him where she wanted him, needed him.

Her mouth opened slightly, for she was breathing harder now, and he could no more deny her the pleasure she craved than he could stop loving her…his beautiful, fearless Charlie.

"Say yes," he whispered as he caught her rhythm, took her higher. "Say yes for me. Yes to loving me. Yes, to letting me love you, be with you. Yes to marrying me. My duchess, my wife, my life. Say yes, Charlie."

He watched the movement in her long throat as she swallowed convulsively and her entire body went tense and still except for the wild spasms between her legs. "Yes," she said quietly, almost fiercely. "Yes, Rafe. Yes…yes…*yes*…"

And then she turned on the bench, so swiftly and with such typical Charlotte determination that he couldn't react before she had him on his back on the floor. She fumbled at the buttons on his pantaloons, her gaze hot on him.

"Say yes for me, Rafe," she said as she knelt over him, even as she touched him intimately, closed her fingers around his hard length. "Say yes…"

CHAPTER SEVENTEEN

"GOOD MORNING, ALL."

Charlotte didn't quite meet Rafe's eyes before he picked up a plate and availed himself of a bit of everything that had been loaded onto the sideboard in the morning room. Three fried eggs, toast, two thick slices of ham fresh from the country and a rasher of bacon were all piled on the plate he held in one hand while he dipped some porridge into a bowl with the other one.

The man was going to eat as if he'd spent the entirety of the previous night running round and round the mansion in Grosvenor Square, so that his appetite was ravenous.

Although he certainly had been rather active last night, hadn't he?

Charlotte felt her cheeks burning as she dipped her head and pretended to concentrate on her own dish of coddled eggs and roasted tomatoes. For all their new intimacy, last night had been so intense, so very personal, that she was having some difficulty pretending that this particular breakfast was just the beginning of another ordinary, mundane day.

The day they would formally announce their betrothal. She hadn't known anyone could be so happy, feel as fulfilled as she did now. In the midst of sorrow, love could still make life worth the struggles and heartaches.

Nicole and Lydia had finally joined them for the meal after Nicole's now-daily short morning walk in the Square, and while Lydia was still mostly lost in her own world, nothing ever got past Nicole.

Obviously.

"Charlotte, why won't you look at Rafe? Don't tell me you two are at dagger points again. Don't I have enough on my plate, without worrying about you, too?"

Charlotte looked at the girl sharply, something in the tone of Nicole's voice indicating that the weight of the entire world was on her shoulders and, being Nicole, she wasn't very happy about it.

Lydia must have heard that veiled anger, too. "I'm sorry if I've been a trial to you, Nicole. I'll try to do better, really I will," she said quietly, the food on her plate growing cold and nearly untouched.

"Oh, no, sweetheart," Nicole apologized quickly, putting her hand on her sister's arm. "I didn't mean you. You're not a trial to me. But you know how I am. Saying silly things without thinking. Please forgive me."

Lydia's smile was so sad it nearly broke Charlotte's heart, and she heard Rafe's involuntary intake of breath that told her he, too, was still very worried about his sister's well-being.

"We'll be leaving for Ashurst Hall tomorrow," he said into the awkward silence that had followed Lydia's words. "And do you know what I'm thinking? I'm thinking that you ladies should indulge yourselves with one last foray into the shops. I imagine you'll wish to take home some small tokens for the servants, as well as leaving gifts here to show our appreciation for the staff. Perhaps some boxed candies for everyone? Charlie? What do you say about that?"

She wanted to throw herself on his neck and thank him for his brilliance, but she restrained herself, saying only, "I think, since the weather is fair, if cool, and none of us save Nicole has so much as put a foot outside in over a week, that an outing is more than overdue. Girls, what say you?"

Nicole's answer was just what Charlotte had expected, but Lydia surprised her by agreeing to the plan. So, with Rafe heading out to the War Office one last time, and then to meet the Duke of Malvern at their club for an hour or so, the three ladies struck out for Bond Street an hour before noon.

Before they'd left, Rafe had cornered Charlotte in the upstairs hallway and kissed her most thoroughly, banishing the last of her apprehension about her wanton behavior of the previous evening. She supposed that was just how her life would be from now on…circumspect and all that was proper while the sun shone, and then Rafe's, all his, once darkness fell and they could be alone.

Actually, she was already looking forward to dusk, and the moment they could be alone again. It was rather delicious, feeling decadent.

On the advice of their majordomo once Nicole had applied to him for his recommendation, the ladies did not order the coach to Bond Street, but instead were driven to a smaller street more out of the way, one that was home to a confectioner Harris had sworn produced the best candies in all of London. That the proprietor was Harris's sister, of course, had nothing to do with his opinion.

They wandered around the shop, picking out pretty tins and deciding just what should be put in each one, and who should be the recipient of sugared fruit, who should be given the tin of toffee—certainly not Mrs. Piggle, who seemed to lose another tooth every year—and would the cook, did Charlotte think, appreciate a half pound of jasmine tea?

"I'll just go load these into the carriage, all right? And I want to give the groom and the coachman theirs now so I can see their faces. I so adore giving people presents," Nicole told Charlotte, picking up a cloth bag filled with small, colored tins.

"No, I don't think so," Charlotte said. "I agree that this is a quiet street, but it's still London, not the country. We'll only be a few more minutes."

Nicole rolled her eyes. "Honestly, Charlotte. I'm not a baby in need of a nanny. Haven't I proved myself to be grown up by now, after what's been happening this past week? Just let me take these things out and then I'll be right back. Lydia is still dawdling over that jar of licorice, and I don't wish to disturb her. She looks better, doesn't she?" she ended almost desperately.

"Yes, Nicole, she does, with many thanks to you. She couldn't have a more loving sister." Charlotte looked through the glass at the front of the shop, to see the rear of the carriage visible. The groom and coachman were right there, and it was the middle of the day. "Oh, all right. But come straight back."

But Nicole didn't come straight back. Charlotte

glanced to the window several times as Harris's sister—
who so unfortunately resembled the red-faced man—
scooped small squares of licorice into a paper twist and
handed it to Lydia, with her compliments.

"Nicole's waiting in the carriage," she told Lydia,
and the two of them stepped outside onto the flagway,
to see the driver and groom both sitting up on the box,
their attention fully engaged by a fistfight taking place
in the middle of the narrow street. Neither of them
noticed her or Lydia, and neither of them was munching
sweets from a pretty tin box.

Worse, the carriage was empty. Worse still, the cloth
bag Nicole had been carrying now lay on the flagway,
its contents spilling out into the gutter.

Charlotte ran to the front of the carriage and called
up to the two men even as the ruffians who had been
busily knocking each other down turned and ran into a
nearby alleyway, smiling and laughing, looking over
their shoulders at Charlotte, their contretemps seemingly forgotten. One of them even waved to her.

And that was when Charlotte knew for certain that
Nicole was in very big trouble.

"Charlotte?" Lydia asked, looking up and down the
street. "Where's Nicole?"

"Ma'am?" the coachman asked, doffing his hat even
as the groom lightly leaped down to the flagway, ready
to open the carriage doors for them. "Quite the dustup
we were watching there for a bit. Two fools could barely
manage to hit each other."

"Never mind that. Where is His Grace?" she asked
the coachman, demanded of the coachman.

"Ma'am?"

"His Grace," Charlotte repeated, her heart pounding in her chest. "Wait…he said he was going to his club to see the Duke of Malvern." She looked at the coachman beseechingly. "His Grace's club, man. Do you know where it is?"

The coachman, obviously recognizing the urgency in Charlotte's voice, only nodded furiously.

"Then take us there. *At once!*"

"But, Charlotte," Lydia protested as Charlotte grabbed her by the elbow and steered her toward the now-open door to the carriage. "We can't leave without Nicole."

"Seeing as how she left without us, yes, we can." Charlotte lifted her skirts without a thought to propriety and climbed up into the carriage behind Lydia, pounding one gloved hand on the front side to give the coachman the office to move on almost before the groom could jump onto the back.

Charlotte didn't know what she would do when she arrived at Rafe's club, but as it turned out she wasn't forced to find out. An agonizingly slow quarter hour later, as the carriage pulled up in front of an imposing structure with a lovely bay window looking out over the street, it was to see Rafe standing outside, deep in conversation with the Duke of Malvern.

"Rafe!" she shouted, pushing open the door even before the carriage settled over its wheels. "Rafe, she's gone! He's taken Nicole!"

Charlotte ignored Lydia's sharp intake of breath and all but leaped into Rafe's arms, not waiting for the groom to put down the steps.

"Charlie! What are you talking about? What do you mean Nicole's gone? Who took her?"

She pressed her hands to her mouth for a moment, trying to calm herself, knowing what she would say next would sound ridiculous. "Mr. Hobart. Hugh Hobart, the man who was with your uncle and cousins that day."

"Yes, yes, I know who he is. But why would you—?"

"That day…that day you refused to see him at the War Office and he came to Grosvenor Square. Remember, Rafe? Nicole decided to rescue me from him. She came downstairs and…and the way he *looked at her*, Rafe! If you could have seen the way he looked at her!"

"Rafe? What's going on?" Tanner Blake asked, looking at Charlotte. "Miss Seavers, clearly you're upset. Can I be of any assistance?"

By this time Lydia had descended to the flagway, stopping some distance from everyone else, most probably because the hated Duke of Malvern was on the scene. But Charlotte couldn't care about Lydia's unreasonable sensibilities right now.

"Yes, Your Grace," she told Blake. "If you could please find yourself clear to escort Lady Lydia back to Grosvenor Square?"

"No!" Lydia ran up to Charlotte and put both her hands on her arm. "I won't go with him. Don't make me go with him."

"Lydia," Rafe said, an authority in his voice that even had Charlotte's head snapping up to look at him. "Do as Charlotte says. Do it now."

"But…but. Nicole. What about Nicole?"

"We'll find her," Rafe told his sister. "Tanner, thank you."

"No thanks are necessary," the Duke of Malvern

said. "I've got a brace of dueling pistols in my coach, Rafe, as I was on my way back to Malvern after saying my farewells to you here. Let me get them for you."

"Charlotte?" Lydia's huge blue eyes brimmed with tears. "Surely Rafe doesn't need pistols. Oh, please be careful. I would die if I were to lose Nicole, too. If I were to lose any of you…"

The Duke of Malvern had returned with a long, burled wood case and handed it to Rafe. "Do you know where you're going?"

Rafe shook his head.

"I do," Charlotte said. "I've had more time to think about this than you, Rafe. And I saw the look in Mr. Hobart's eyes when he saw Nicole. He looked so like George and Harold did that awful night that there could be no question what he was thinking. We need to go to Piccadilly. To this abbess you told me about."

"Sweet Jesus, are you certain? Never mind, of course you're certain." Rafe took her hand. "This is my fault. I wouldn't give him any more money," he said, and then swore under his breath. "With someone who looks like Nicole to use as barter, the man could make a fortune in the right circles. With men like my uncle, my cousins."

He turned to the duke. "Take them both to Grosvenor Square, Tanner. You know now where I'm headed."

"Absolutely not!" Charlotte said sharply. "I need to be there when you find Nicole. You can't let her face this alone the way I was forced to, Rafe, you can't. I won't let that happen to her. Not Nicole."

Rafe opened his mouth, most probably to protest, but

then merely nodded. "It's all right, Tanner. Charlie's coming with me."

"And I'll meet you there as soon as I can. Lottie Lusty's, correct? I've heard some of the stories. Nothing good happens there, Rafe. You'd better hurry."

RAFE HURRIED TO LOAD the brace of pistols as the carriage headed toward Piccadilly. But he needn't have rushed, for the streets were clogged at this hour of the day, making their progress maddeningly slow.

At least this gave him time to think, time for him and Charlotte to come up with some sort of plan.

They would approach quite openly, going directly up the stairs to the front door of the brothel. Charlotte would have the pistols in her cloak pockets—not well disguised, but he doubted their welcome if he were to show up on the doorstep brandishing a weapon in each hand.

They were to be brother and sister, chasing after their errant sibling who had run away from their home in West Sussex and been traced to a coach that stopped at the White Tavern here in London. The hoydenish Marianne Wilcox had been seen leaving the coaching inn yard two days earlier with a motherly woman—Rafe had heard that Lottie Lusty often took the tack of a sweet old lady hiring girls fresh from the country for her milliner's shop. More inquiries had given them this address, and they were here to thank the kind woman who took their Marianne in, and to haul the willful girl back to their frantic widowed mother in Lower Beeding.

Once inside the door, Rafe would take the pistols

from Charlotte, and the devil with pretense. They would demand that Nicole be brought to them at once.

"Put up the hood of your cloak to cover your face, Charlie," Rafe ordered as the carriage stopped around the corner from the brothel. It would do them no good if anyone peeking out through the curtains spied the ducal crest on the side doors. "And thank God again that it was still cool when you left Grosvenor Square, and you brought the cloak with you. I don't think we could have hidden the pistols in your bonnet."

Charlotte did as she was bade, her hand ice-cold as he helped her down from the carriage. He stared down passersby as they then walked along the filthy brick flagway and rounded the corner.

With his soldier's eye, Rafe scanned the dim, narrow street in front of him. The sun hadn't made it to the ground here, not with the tops of the tumbledown structures building out from every lower level, until the topmost stories nearly touched across the narrow street.

Once his eyes has adjusted to the lack of sunlight, Rafe spied out a rather tall, thin man dressed completely in black and attempting to lean nonchalantly against the drainpipe of a house across the street.

When the man saw Rafe, he pushed himself away from the drainpipe and hastened across the street, head down, and into the alleyway that ran beside the brothel.

"That's one," Rafe said quietly, passing his gaze over others on the flagway and dismissing them as irrelevant. "You saw two men fighting in the street, so there's one more. All right, Charlie, there he is, just slipping into that doorway. I can see the way of it. One to follow us in, one to come at us from the rear should we get inside.

And Hobart? I don't want to think about where he is, except that I know he won't touch her. She's worth too much to him."

"You really think he plans to sell her? I thought…I thought he wanted her for himself."

As if to answer Charlotte's question, a dark, unmarked traveling coach, its shades drawn over the windows, appeared behind them, then stopped just outside the doors to the brothel.

The door of the coach was swung open and a large man wearing a black domino, his hat pulled down over his eyes, stepped out onto the flagway and, without looking either way, took the stairs to the brothel two at a time, the door opening for him as he ran. "Where is she?" he bellowed loud enough for Rafe and Charlotte to hear. "And she'd damn well better still be intact!"

"Perverted son of a bitch. Charlie, stay here," Rafe ordered, but she was already running, her hands pressed against the pockets of her cloak to keep the pistols from banging against her legs.

The thug watching the doorway sprinted across the street, already swinging the stout club he had held concealed behind him. But Rafe hadn't forgotten him. Bracing one hand on the railing of the stairs to the brothel, he turned and kicked out with all his might, catching the henchman cleanly under the jaw with his Hessian.

"Here!" Charlotte had managed to free one pistol from her pocket and was holding it out to him even as she struggled to extract the second one. "Rafe! Behind you!"

Whoever had opened the door for the anxious purchaser, a very large man as it turned out, had come outside to see what was happening. He very nearly had his hands on Rafe's shoulders when, thanks to Charlotte's warning, Rafe ducked low, pivoting on his heels, so that he could come up hard with his head, straight into the large man's gut. At the same time he grabbed the man's thighs, lifting the bulky thug up and over him, so that he landed on his face on the bricks.

"My goodness," Charlotte said, her eyes wide. "That was...very tidy."

"Something I learned from Fitz," Rafe said, grabbing Charlotte's hand. "Come on, Charlie. Door's open, so we'll just walk in, all right? Give me the other pistol."

"Never mind that. I have it."

There was no time to argue. Rafe entered the small vestibule first, his pistol at the ready, and then Charlotte followed him.

There was a kindly looking gray-haired woman standing there, her modest gown giving her the appearance of a benevolent grandmother.

"Where is she?" Rafe demanded, consigning his plans to the devil as anger rocked him. "Where's the girl Hobart brought to you today? Answer me!"

"What's going on here?" the pockmarked man from the coach bellowed, shrinking against the wall, his bugged-out eyes concentrated on Rafe's pistol. "Who are you? I was here first, blast you! Came here straight from my club when I got his note. Damn that Hobart for a liar and a thief. You can't sell a virgin twice!"

"Is that so? And I hear you can only die once. Would you care to test that theory? I know I'm amenable. You pitiful excuse for a man, I'd be doing the world a service," Rafe said coldly, cocking his pistol and leveling it at the hopeful purchaser.

The man nearly knocked Charlotte down in his race to put distance between himself and an obvious madman.

"Charlie," Rafe said, turning the pistol on Lottie Lusty. "Lock the door, sweetheart. I don't think we need any more visitors."

The abbess raised her hands almost leisurely, seemingly neither impressed nor shocked by the events transpiring in her business establishment.

"He's upstairs with her now," she said, and then sighed. "I knowed this one was trouble the moment I put m' peepers on her. Dressed too good, you ken? Got to be careful what flowers yer pick, that's what Lottie says, I do. Never been more'n trouble fer me, my friend Hughie, and robbin' me blind into the bargain most times. Not enough to have me tossin' him, you understand. He does have his uses."

"I said, where is she?"

"Yes, yes, where is she. Where is Hughie, you mean. Third door on the left upstairs, Your Worship, best in the house. The bridal suite, I calls it. No pistol, but I wouldn't put it past him ta have a sticker. Nobody else up there. Too early in the day, yer ken? Just a few of m' girls, sleepin'."

Rafe lowered the pistol. "Charlie, once again—stay here."

"Yes, do that, dearie," Lottie encouraged. "And put down that pistol why don't you. We'll have us a dish o' tea in m' parlor while you waits here fer the gennulman. The gel's safe as houses. Hughie's a piece o' work, but he's not that stupid. Oh, a question iffen you don't mind. You the duke?"

Rafe already had one foot on the stairs. "I beg your pardon?"

"Not mine, Your Grace," Lottie Lusty said, shrugging. "It's Hughie's you should be beggin', at least that's how he sees it." She cocked her head to one side, looking Rafe up and down. "Nope, don't say as how I can see the resemblance...."

"Let me talk to her," Charlotte said, holding out the pistol to Rafe. "Here, take this."

"No, you keep it, Charlie. It's not as if you could hurt anyone with it, except by accident, but I'd rather you had it. Watch for Tanner and let him in, but I want him to stay downstairs with you. He should be here soon."

"Be careful," she warned him unnecessarily, because that was his plan, to be careful. His sister was upstairs with Hugh Hobart, and the man had most likely heard the commotion. He was probably holding a weapon to Nicole's head, hiding behind her, his back to the wall, ready to try to talk his way out of Rafe wringing his neck.

The man would be better served saving his breath for his last prayers.

Rafe counted down the doors, opening each one on either side of the hallway, not taking Lottie Lusty's word as gospel and unwilling to be surprised by anyone coming up from behind him.

The two rooms on the left were empty, but there were young girls in the three small rooms on the right, girls no older than Lydia and Nicole. He'd never seen such ancient, uninterested eyes.

"Stay where you are," he told each girl quietly. "Get beneath your bed, and don't come out."

At last he was left with only the one door, the third on the left.

Rafe took a breath, held the pistol level and gave the door a mighty kick with his booted foot, sending it swinging back sharply on its ancient hinges, to bang against the wall and swing closed once more.

But Rafe had already slipped inside the small room.

He stopped, blinked and then lowered the pistol, shaking his head. "Nicole, what in the devil...?"

Nicole sat on the edge of a large, hideously carved bed draped in threadbare red velvet draperies, her slippered feet crossed at the ankle and swinging back and forth as if she was entirely at her ease.

She looked almost *normal*. Except, that is, for the dangerous-looking fireplace poker she held clenched in her hands.

Hugh Hobart was sprawled faceup on the filthy carpet, a lump the size of a pigeon's egg on his right temple. He spied Rafe and moaned, tried to push himself up on his elbows.

"Don't do that, Mr. Hobart," Nicole warned sweetly. "You don't want me to hit you again, now do you? What little brains you have might come flying out of your ears. Really, you should have known me better than to think I wouldn't protect myself. Yes, there's a good fellow," she ended as Hobart closed his eyes and sank back onto the floor.

"She's right, Hobart. Stay where you are." Rafe looked at his sister, caught between wanting to hug her and boxing her ears, because he was beginning to think she might not be as innocent as the first flowers of May. "You want to tell me what happened here?"

Her bravado left her in a loud sigh. "I'd rather not, seeing as how it's all my fault. I believed him, you see, when he said he could help me find the person who has been trying to kill you."

Rafe was genuinely shocked. "What do you know about that?"

Nicole rolled her eyes. "Oh, please, Rafe. Do you really think anyone's secrets are safe from me? I was listening at the door the entire time he was speaking with Charlotte that day. In any event, Mr. Hobart and I have been meeting in the Square almost ever since I first saw him. Well, not meeting, not all the time. He leaves me notes tucked under one of the benches. I retrieve them when I take my morning walks, and then I leave him notes in return. It was all…rather exciting."

Rafe shot a look at the man sprawled on the floor. "You're a dead man, Hobart."

"Nothing happened, Rafe," Nicole protested quickly. "That is to say, not after he got me here and tied me up. Now I ask you, why would any sane person tie another person's hands in *front* of her body? Especially since I have very strong teeth. Oh, stop glaring at me, Rafe. I'm sorry. I thought I was helping and I wasn't. Captain Fitzgerald is gone. We couldn't lose you, too. Mr. Hobart here told me he knew who had tried to kill you. I felt I needed to speak with him directly. I sent him a note this morning once I knew where we were going today and— do I really have to go on? I'm horribly sorry, Rafe."

"Yes, I'm sure you are. But you seem to have rescued yourself. I'm feeling a tad superfluous."

"Oh, no, Rafe, I still need you. I was waiting for you. After all, I have no idea where I am, except that it's ugly and dirty and nothing in it smells very good. Is Lydia all right? She had to have been very frightened when she realized I was gone."

"Lydia's fine," Rafe assured her, deciding that having loving sisters might just be worse than having enemies. "Give me that," he then said, indicating the poker. "We don't want to kill him, you know."

"I do," Nicole said cheekily. "All I did was step outside the door of the shop to look for him, and this horrible, smelly sack came down over my head and pinned my arms to my sides. Then I smelled something terrible being pushed against my face and nose—so many smells, Rafe—and the next thing I knew I was lying on this hideous bed, my wrists and ankles tied. I thought about having strong hysterics, but then I told myself that wouldn't be in aid of anything, so I untied myself and took up the poker and waited behind the door for someone to dare to enter the room."

"And Hobart here accommodated you."

She nodded furiously. "It was very kind of him to put himself just where I could reach him from behind the door, and give him a good hard conk on the head. Because," Nicole ended, preening a little, "I'm not kind at all."

"No, I suppose you're not." Rafe gave her back the poker. "Here, keep this at the ready for a moment. I want to call down to Charlie, have her join us."

"Charlotte's here? Oh, that's just delicious! We're having a party."

"Cheeky bitch," Hobart said, closing his eyes as he

lay back on the carpet as if about to pass out from his injury.

"Cheeky indeed," Rafe said, and then he gave Nicole a quick, hard hug before summoning Charlotte upstairs.

It was Tanner's voice that answered his call, assuring Rafe that all was in hand down there, and then Charlotte raced up the stairs, to brush past Rafe and into the "bridal" chamber.

"Oh, Rafe, what did you do?" she asked worriedly. "Surely he isn't dead?"

"I couldn't swing hard enough," Nicole informed her, reluctantly passing the poker back to Rafe. "Now, if no one minds too much, would somebody please tell me why this horrible man lied to me? Why he kidnapped me."

Rafe looked to Charlotte in brotherly panic. She rolled her eyes, clearly not anxious to impart such a sensitive explanation that, knowing Nicole, would only raise another dozen questions. "I will, Nicole, once we've got you safely home. Rafe?"

"In a minute, sweetheart," he said, already in the process of hauling Hugh Hobart to his feet. He flung the man in the direction of the nearest chair. "As soon as Mr. Hobart here gives me the name of that piece of offal we encountered downstairs. I plan to pay him a small visit. He left here running. But that's only because he still has two intact knees, a temporary condition."

Hobart had dropped his head into his hands, then began rubbing at the back of his neck. "Oh, what does it matter now? I'll give you his name. I'll give you any number of names," he said, and then he moaned. "Just take her and go. Stupid bitch, she could have killed me."

"I still could, you horrid, wicked man!" Nicole warned, advancing toward him, obviously heady with triumph.

That's when Hobart, who had appeared so totally defeated, leaped up from the chair and pulled Nicole in front of him, a wicked stiletto he'd pulled from its hiding place held to her throat.

A cardsharp's trick, Rafe realized too late. Hobart had a leather sheath strapped to his back, for a card cheat never knew when he might need to defend himself.

"Let her go, Hobart," Rafe warned, keeping his body between Hobart and the door. "The Duke of Malvern and at least a half dozen of his most brawny servants are downstairs. You're going nowhere. Simply tell me what you want, and let my sister go."

"I'll go fetch him," Charlotte said quietly.

"No, don't. We don't want to upset Hobart," Rafe answered just as quietly, and then motioned to Hobart. "Come on now, do as I say. Let her go."

"You'll kill me if I let her go."

Rafe shrugged. "Possibly. However, if you harm her, that outcome rises to a certainty. I'd say your odds lie in releasing her. You understand playing the odds, don't you, Hobart?"

"I don't know. Nothing's gone right. Not since the beginning," Hobart said, and Rafe believed he could actually see tears in the man's eyes. "I thought I was good enough, but I'm not. I'm just Hugh Hobart, and nobody cares. I've had to scramble for everything I've ever gotten. But you wouldn't know how that is, would you, *Your Grace?*"

"I might," Rafe said as Charlotte put her hand on his

upper arm, probably in an effort to keep him calm. He appreciated the gesture. Mostly, he wished she'd go downstairs, but if she tried to leave, Hobart might injure Nicole, and he was sure they both knew that.

"It was going to be so easy, you know? For a patient man. Even when you made it home from Elba, I still had my chances." Hobart blinked back tears, the tip of the stiletto pressing more closely against Nicole's throat, until a small drop of blood appeared. "And I am a patient man. I've had to be a patient man. But there comes a time to see that what you want isn't going to happen, and you need to walk away. You've got the devil's own luck, Your Grace, and I'm the bumbler she always said I was. Not a nice thing for a mother to say, was it? But she was right. It was time for me to cut my losses and go. Too many debts, too many people wanting money I don't have to pay to them. America, I thought. Nobody cares who you are in America."

"Mrs. Lusty told me about this downstairs," Charlotte whispered. "I'll tell you later. He wanted the dukedom, thinks it belongs to him. Nicole's bleeding, Rafe. You have to do something now."

"Shh," Rafe warned her. "Elba, you said, Mr. Hobart? How did you know I was assigned to guard the emperor?"

Hobart's eyes shifted left and right, and then he stepped back toward the single window in the room, dragging Nicole with him. She had grabbed hold of his forearm with both hands, but she wasn't struggling. It was almost as if she was helping him hold on to her, but she was only attempting to protect herself. The stiletto was too sharp for her to struggle against it.

"How? Money greases palms. Everybody knows that. But I mangled that, too. Still, I kept trying, fool that I am. I should get something from you. After all my trouble. Ten thousand pounds. Ten thousand pounds! That's what she was going to sell for, you know, and cheap at twice the price. With more time, if I could have put her to the bid. Soon as I saw her, I knew her worth. Strip her down, stand her up, watch the fools beggar themselves to outbid each other to be the first to poke her. After that, they could all have her, as long as I got mine."

"Shut up, Hobart," Rafe warned him as Nicole began to cry silently, huge tears coursing down her cheeks.

"But it's true. I would have gotten three times that—five times that. Not the title, not what I deserve, but you should have died easier, and I wouldn't have been forced to do this. I would have kept her for myself then, and no one the wiser. But I should have known it wouldn't work. Nothing works, not for me."

"He's mad, Rafe," Charlotte whispered. "He thinks he should be the Duke of Ashurst. Mrs. Lusty says he has proof. Perhaps you should humor him?"

"How in bloody hell do you propose I do that?" Rafe asked her in frustration, his borrowed dueling pistol still hanging at his side. "Hobart? Was that you on Elba that night? Hobart! Stand still, damn it. And be careful with that knife."

"They were so much easier, you know? My *family*. They only tolerated me because I brought them the women. That's what made them easier. Drunk off their heads…otherwise *occupied*. Some drugged wine, the whores I provided for them. Shame, losing them, but needs must, so they say. Three of my best earners. Only one I had to shoot when the yacht was going down." He squeezed his eyes shut and then winced. "Didn't know females could swim…"

"Rafe," Nicole whispered hoarsely as a thin stream of bright red blood ran down the side of her throat.

"Be still, sweetheart," he told her, never taking his eyes off Hobart.

"This one would have to die, too, o' course. Pity, but she couldn't be left to talk, could she? Or maybe a brothel across the Channel? No," he muttered, shaking his head, "that wouldn't work. Besides, they mostly die that first night anyway…."

"I'm going to kill him, Charlie," Rafe whispered fiercely as Hobart continued his obscene ramblings. "I'll pass Nicole to you and you take her down to Tanner. But the bastard dies here, and I don't care if he's mad as a hatter. I don't care if he thinks he's the bloody Prince of Wales."

Again, Charlotte squeezed his arm in some sort of warning, as if she had a plan. "Mr. Hobart, it is time for this foolishness to end. You're injured. You need a surgeon to see to those injuries, and we really need to tell the duke who you are, that you're Hugh Hobart Daughtry. You know you want to tell him so that he'll understand. You want to let go of Lady Nicole now, and we'll help you. I promise."

Hobart smiled, once more backing toward the window. The open window. Rafe could hear the noise of the street coming up to them. "And *then* you'll have me served up to the hangman? It would have been better if my mother never told me. If I'd never known. She should…should have known I'd mess it up. Never done anything right in all these years…."

Rafe moved forward slowly, one step at a time.

Hobart saw him, and backed up two steps. He was now only a few feet from the open window…and the street, two stories below.

"Clearly you have a grievance against my family. You were speaking of my uncle and cousins, weren't you? I'm sorry I wasn't more accommodating, Hugh," Rafe said, forcing himself to remain calm. Charlotte knew something he did not know, and believed that knowledge could be used to their advantage. "You came to me, and I wasn't willing to listen to you. That's my fault, and I…I apologize."

"As well you should," Hobart said, actually smiling. "It was very unsporting of you not to die, Your Grace. They were easy, almost too easy. But not you."

"Yet you saved my life. Why did you do that, Hugh?"

"You still don't understand, do you? I wasn't trying to save your life. I thought I was pushing you *into* the path of the masonry, not out of it. More fool me, yes? I knew then I'd lost. I'd never be able to kill you. Then I saw this one, and decided to make the best of things, you understand?"

"No, I don't. Explain that to me," Rafe said, his gut turning over as another thin red line of blood followed the first down the side of Nicole's neck.

"It's simple. If I couldn't have the dukedom, I could at least profit from it, yes? Another hour and this pernicious little piece would have been on her way to quite a lively party of eager gentlemen in Hampshire, and me on my way to the docks and a new life."

Hobart backed up another two paces, and Nicole began to struggle in his grasp.

"Nicole, be still!" Rafe warned her tersely.

"Mr. Hobart," Charlotte said quietly. "You can still be on your way to the docks. Truly. Just let her go and we'll let you go. Rafe, tell him."

Hobart took a quick glance over his shoulder, and then pulled Nicole closer to him, so that she had to stay on her tiptoes or else the knife would only go deeper. "No. You might do it. But *he* won't. Look at him. He's going to kill me. It's over, and I've made a mess this time that nobody can fix. But if I can't leave alone, I will at least not lose alone. Not this time. So we'll be leaving together. Who knows, *Your Grace,* one of us might even survive the fall, although I don't like the odds."

"Don't do it," Rafe pleaded, beyond any consideration but wanting Nicole safe. "I'll give you anything. Safe passage. Money. Whatever you ask."

Hobart smiled. "Isn't that sweet, Your Grace. Tell me, do you love her?"

Nicole whimpered, and then grimaced as the tip of the stiletto prodded deeper.

"Yes. Yes, I love her."

"Good. Then I do win. Goodbye now…"

Rafe dived forward as Hobart threw himself backward, still holding on to Nicole. His sister screamed, letting go of Hobart's arm and pulling away from the point of the stiletto.

But Hobart still had a tight grip around her upper chest.

Rafe caught her by the calves, halting Hobart and

Nicole so that their bodies were caught half in and half out of the window. The stiletto fell to the floor. Now Hobart held Nicole with both arms tight around her.

Charlotte rushed past Rafe. He could see the dueling pistol still in her hand, watched as she raised it.

"You will release her now, Mr. Hobart," Charlotte ordered in a cold, measured voice Rafe had never before heard from her.

"Charlie!" God. The woman couldn't shoot worth a damn. If she fired, she could hit Nicole. Or the building across the street. Besides, she was a woman. She couldn't do it. She wouldn't shoot a man. And Hobart had to know that, believe himself the winner here. He wouldn't let Nicole go, not when he liked the odds.

Then Charlotte spoke again.

"You're worse than they were. They were animals, but you fed them. Them, and others like them. I am holding a pistol to your head, Mr. Hobart, and I will fire it, I promise you I will. Let…her…go."

Nicole was crying in earnest now, knowing she was inches from certain death, nearly half of her body projecting outside the building. Even worse, the window frame was beginning to give way; Rafe could hear the crack of the dried and rotted wood.

Rafe, who'd thrown himself full length onto the floor, was losing his grip on his sister, her skirts and petticoats keeping him from gaining a strong hold on her, Hobart and simple gravity combining to pull her away from him. But if he tried to get to his feet, he might lose her entirely. "Charlie, never mind him…grab on to Nicole! Charlie—I'm losing her!"

He flinched as the report of a pistol reverberated in

the room, and suddenly he and Nicole were tumbled together on the floor. She was safe. He pulled her into his arms and held her tightly, pushing her head into his chest as he looked toward the now-empty window frame. And Charlotte.

She still held the dueling pistol, blue smoke curling from its barrel. Hugh Hobart was gone.

"Charlie…" he said quietly as she turned to him, dropping the pistol to the floor even as Rafe heard footsteps pounding on the stairs. Tanner Blake burst into the room, his regimental saber in his hand.

"What happened!" he called out, standing over Rafe.

"Mr. Hobart made a choice, Your Grace," Charlotte said quietly, her voice as steady as if she'd just said *Mr. Hobart would like tea.* "This time, however, I had a choice, as well."

EPILOGUE

THE TWINS WERE INSEPARABLE, spending their days walking hand in hand in the gardens, or with their heads—one so dark, the other so fair—bent close over a shared puzzle or collection of leaves they were sorting before pressing them into a book they were preparing for their aunt Emmaline.

The summer days were long, and quiet, and healing. Charlotte had no fears anymore for either twin. They might be seventeen, but events in their lives had matured them both beyond their years, so that when they passed their eighteenth birthday in December, and traveled back to Mayfair in late March, there would be no question that each was ready for her Season.

Charlotte would be proud to present them, even if she sometimes worried that Lydia wouldn't put herself forward enough, and Nicole might make good on her promise to break at least a dozen hearts.

She and Rafe, as the Duke and Duchess of Ashurst, would host balls and breakfasts, and behave most responsibly, as proper guardians should…and then they would retire to their rooms and be Rafe and Charlie—friends, lovers, husband and wife.

She could only hope the same for Lydia and Nicole,

when they found the friends and lovers they each deserved.

Charlotte thanked the footman who brought the mail pouch to her as she sat dreaming in the morning room, and she lazily sifted through the letters until she sat up straight, holding a letter addressed in Emmaline's distinctive hand and franked by the Duke of Warrington.

Getting to her feet, she went in search of her husband, running him to ground in his study, where he was frowning over a paper he held in one hand in front of him, a drying pen in his other hand.

"Charlie, good," he said without looking up, as if he could recognize her footfalls, which he probably could. "Quickly, what would be another word for scoundrel? I think I've called Bonaparte every name I can conjure up writing this blasted book. If Fitz were here, he'd be laughing at me, the way he laughed when I told him I planned to write the book in the first place."

"Fitz would be nothing less than proud of you. Rafe, put that aside for now. I've a letter here from Emmaline."

"Really? Then the babe has arrived?"

"I don't know yet. I wanted to wait so that we could read the letter together." She slid her fingertip beneath the seal and unfolded the single sheet. "Ah," she said moments later. "It would appear the duke will have to try again for an heir, not that I imagine he or Emmaline will consider that a hardship."

Rafe grinned as he read the letter over her shoulder. "Hardly. Is there a name?"

"Yes, right here. Lady Anne Emmaline Lucas was born three days ago. She's beautiful, by the way. Emmaline swears it." She lowered the letter to her lap and turned about to face her husband. "Can we travel to Warrington Manor soon, do you think? John Cummings is more than capable to oversee things here, and I'm sure the twins would adore seeing their new cousin."

"If I say no, will you promise me anything to convince me?"

"No. But you can say yes, and then I can promise you anything to thank you," Charlotte said as Rafe walked across the room to where the family Bible rested on its own podium. "Are you going to write in Anne's name?"

Rafe picked up the large Bible and carried it to the desk. "Yes, and I promise to be thorough." He dipped his pen and wrote *Anne Emmaline Lucas, female.* "There, we'll add the particulars later."

Charlotte frowned, turning to the previous page and the list of Daughtrys written there in many different hands. "Marion Daughtry," she said, running a fingertip along one faded line. "Even Emmaline thought he was a female child. I remember seeing the name when we were attempting to contact your relatives when the late duke died, and again when Nicole was searching out names for prospective chaperones so that she could go to London. We none of us realized our mistake."

"Marion Daughtry, the obligatory black sheep," Rafe said, closing the Bible. "Disowned, disinherited, banished under a cloud, the girl bought off and married to our own Grayson's brother once she'd healed, or else we'd never have understood what happened. Come on," he said, sliding an arm around Charlotte's waist. "Let's go tell the twins the good news."

"Rafe, wait," Charlotte said, holding her ground. "I know he's dead—I should know better than anyone—

but if the Daughtry family tree is to be complete, Hugh Hobart Daughtry should be listed. We saw the marriage lines he kept in his room at Lottie Lusty's…establishment. Turned off by his family or not, Marion did marry Hugh's mother. If you…if you had died in the war, Hugh *was* next in line to be the Duke of Ashurst."

"And I wouldn't be the Duke of Ashurst if he hadn't murdered my uncle and cousins. Although I'm afraid it must be said—Hugh certainly resembled my uncle and cousins in many ways. Charlie, if Hugh's name were in the Bible, it would be my duty as head of the family to expunge it. And if this has to do with any feelings of guilt you might have over—"

Charlotte shook her head vigorously. "I don't. Really, Rafe, even though it frightens me sometimes to feel so cold about what I did, I have no regrets. I'd do it again."

Rafe bent and kissed her cheek. "You know, I believe you. You're the bravest woman I know. Fitz would have raised you up onto his shoulders and carried you around the barracks, had you been one of his men. As it was, I had to take the credit for ridding the world of my miserable cur of a cousin, to protect you and Nicole, when I'd rather have openly called you both heroines."

"Nicole might have liked that," Charlotte said as, arm in arm, they headed into the hallway. "I think they're in the west garden. Lydia was going to beg some more flowers from Higbee, to plant for Fitz."

The memorial Rafe had commissioned for the west garden in memory of his good friend—an impressive obelisk with *Captain Swain McNulty Fitzgerald, Soldier, Friend and Brother* carved into the ebony marble—had lost much of its stark formality when

Lydia had planted a garden all around it. But Fitz probably would have liked that, too.

"Rafe? It would be much quicker to go through the morning room," Charlotte said as he steered her toward the foyer.

"I know," he said, bending low to whisper the words in her ear. "But I thought we might delay the news for a little while. Little Anne's birth has reminded me that it is my duty as duke to ensure my own line. Who knows how many little Annes *we* might get before you produce my heir, hmm? I mean, I do have a responsibility. I thought we should perhaps get in a little practice."

He turned her toward the stairs, and then gave her a playful smack on the rump that had the young footman giggling into his fist.

"Rafael Daughtry, you should be ashamed of yourself!" Charlotte scolded. But then she saw the look in his eyes, the smile that curved his lips, and gave a small yelp, lifted her skirts and ran up the stairs.

Rafe winked at the footman, and followed after her at his leisure….

* * * * *

If you enjoyed
HOW TO TEMPT A DUKE,
don't miss Nicole Daughtry's story,
HOW TO TAME A LADY,
coming in October 2009
from Kasey Michaels
And HQN Books!

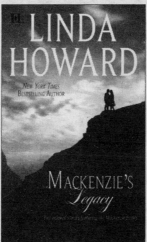

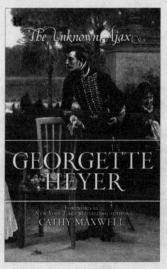

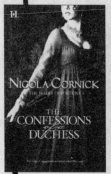

REQUEST YOUR FREE BOOKS!

2 FREE NOVELS
FROM THE ROMANCE/SUSPENSE
COLLECTION PLUS 2 FREE GIFTS!

YES! Please send me 2 FREE novels from the Romance/Suspense Collection and my 2 FREE gifts (gifts are worth about $10). After receiving them, if I don't wish to receive any more books, I can return the shipping statement marked "cancel." If I don't cancel, I will receive 4 brand-new novels every month and be billed just $5.74 per book in the U.S. or $6.24 per book in Canada. That's a savings of at least 28% off the cover price. It's quite a bargain! Shipping and handling is just 50¢ per book.* I understand that accepting the 2 free books and gifts places me under no obligation to buy anything. I can always return a shipment and cancel at any time. Even if I never buy another book from the Reader Service, the two free books and gifts are mine to keep forever.   185 MDN EYNQ 385 MDN EYN2

Name _____ (PLEASE PRINT) _____

Address _____ Apt. # _____

City _____ State/Prov. _____ Zip/Postal Code _____

Signature (if under 18, a parent or guardian must sign) _____

Mail to **The Reader Service:**
IN U.S.A.: P.O. Box 1867, Buffalo, NY 14240-1867
IN CANADA: P.O. Box 609, Fort Erie, Ontario L2A 5X3

Not valid to current subscribers of the Romance Collection,
the Suspense Collection or the Romance/Suspense Collection.

Want to try two free books from another line?
Call 1-800-873-8635 or visit www.morefreebooks.com.

* Terms and prices subject to change without notice. Prices do not include applicable taxes. Sales tax applicable in N.Y. Canadian residents will be charged applicable provincial taxes and GST. Offer not valid in Quebec. This offer is limited to one order per household. All orders subject to approval. Credit or debit balances in a customer's account(s) may be offset by any other outstanding balance owed by or to the customer. Please allow 4 to 6 weeks for delivery. Offer available while quantities last.

Your Privacy: Harlequin is committed to protecting your privacy. Our Privacy Policy is available online at www.eHarlequin.com or upon request from the Reader Service. From time to time we make our lists of customers available to reputable third parties who may have a product or service of interest to you. If you would prefer we not share your name and address, please check here. ☐

BOB09

Carole Mortimer's
debut Harlequin® Historical novel

THE DUKE'S CINDERELLA BRIDE

The Duke of Stourbridge thought Jane Smith a servant girl, so when Miss Jane is wrongly turned out of her home for inappropriate behavior after their encounter, the duke takes her in as his ward. Jane knows she cannot fall for his devastating charm. Their marriage would be forbidden—especially if he were to discover her shameful secret....

The Notorious St. Claires—
From plain Jane to society bride!

Available September
wherever you buy books.

HH29560